"The search for family and belonging in the midst of the dangerous bootlegging industry."

"Edith must determine what the people in her life, Leroy included, mean to her and what she would sacrifice for them. Storm Surge raises questions around motherhood and the anxieties that face many women as they care for the children in their lives. Edith's struggle against conservative gender roles began in A Gathering Storm *and was continued throughout* Storm Surge, *in particular relating to her maternal capabilities.*

Storm Surge *introduces us to a new Edith Duffy that is beginning to allow herself to form emotional attachments and becomes vulnerable once more. It is that vulnerability that shows her progress and recovery following the events of* A Gathering Storm, *beyond just the development of the bootlegging business itself.*

The desire for family is the heart of Storm Surge.*"*

Independent Books Review

The turbulent times of Prohibition and the Roaring Twenties have been an inspiration for me. If you enjoyed this book, I invite you to check out the other books and series I've written. There is plenty of overlap with characters and references to other books. Writers call them Easter eggs- hidden treasures to discover ~ SD

MOONSHINER MYSTERIES SERIES

(the main characters in this Montana-based series are Delores Bailey, Lucie Santoro, Sheriff Sam Brown, Charlie Chaplin, and Lash)

Big Sky Murder
Stamp Mill Murder
Soiled Dove Murder
Whiskey Wars

RUM RUNNERS' CHRONICLES SERIES

(the main characters in this Florida-based series are Edith Duffy, Cleo Lythgoe, soothsayer Cassie and her ward Leroy, and Darwin)

Gathering Storm (Book 1)
Storm Surge (Book 2)
Eye of the Storm (Book 3)

BOOTLEGGERS' CHRONICLES SERIES

(the main characters in this Philadelphia-based series are Maggie Barnes, Frank Geyer, Edith and Mickey Duffy, the Bailey family)

Innocence Lost (Book 1)
Tasting the Apple (Book 2)
Best Served Cold (Book 3)
Watch Your Back (Book 4)

Come at the King (Book 5)

THE PROMISE TRILOGY

(the main character in this New York-based series is Lucie Santoro. The three novels in The Promise Trilogy are due out in the Spring of 2026.)

SHERILYN DECTER

STORM SURGE

BOOK 2 OF THE RUM RUNNERS' CHRONICLES

Sherilyn Decter

Storm Surge is a work of historical fiction in which the author has occasionally taken artistic liberties for the sake of the narrative and to provide a sense of authenticity. Names, characters, organizations, places, events, dialogue, and incidents are either products of the author's imagination or are used fictitiously.

Print ISBN: 978-1-7771277-2-5

EPub ISBN: 978-1-7771277-3-2

Edited by: Marie Beswick-Arthur www.mariebeswickarthur.com

Developmental Edit by: Independent Book Review

Cover Design by: JDSmith Designs www.jdsmith-design.com

CHAPTER 1

Florida weather: seven months of summer and five months of hell. August was one of the hell months. The thermometer hadn't dipped below eighty degrees for weeks and the humidity was suffocating. Huge anvil clouds gathered offshore, and Edith was keeping a close eye on them as she drove her 1931 Ford truck that she'd recently bought back from Miami.

Everybody figured Florida was the Sunshine State, but nobody ever talked about the daily rainstorms in the summer. They're not gentle, but torrents of water pouring from the heavens and then, poof, they're over, leaving everything pounded and drenched. It should feel cooler after the rain, but it didn't. The temperature dropped but the humidity rose. August in Florida: hell month.

Edith wiped the back of her neck with a small, lace-trimmed hankie. It came away black. Dust from the open truck windows billowed in; if she rolled them up the heat was worse. A puddle of sweat; mix in the dust and she felt like she was baked in mud.

She fiddled with the dial on the radio. *New-fangled thing.* The first two stations crackled, and she tried to find another that would come in better.

> *"The economy continues to deteriorate with President Hoover in his re-election speech claiming his anti-Depression measures were preventing the total collapse of the economy. President Hoover warns that Roosevelt's New Deal would support an activist federal government whose centralized and coercive powers would endanger traditional notions of individual liberty.*
>
> *"In other news, there were no new led in the tragic Lindbergh kidnapping.*
>
> *"Now to sports. Babe Didrikson has won another medal at the Summer Olympic Games in Los*

Angeles. Joe Williams, sportswriter for the New York Telegram, said in his column today that 'It would be much better if she and her ilk stayed at home, got themselves prettied up, and waited for the phone to ring'."

Edith scowled and turned off the radio. *Better silence than listen to that. What a day. Busy but productive. If God put me on this earth to accomplish a certain number of things, I'm so far behind I don't need to worry about dying anytime soon.*

She pulled into the parking werea at the top of the hill and looked at the building below. Major construction had just finished on the exterior. Sawhorses and scrap lumber still litter the ground. Only six months ago, the site was a burned-out scar of hopes and dreams. Hard work and grit had cleared the burned carcass of 'Gator Joe's and raised a magnificent new vision, Mickey's Goodtimes Saloon. Hard work, grit, and Edith's healthy bank balance. *Thank goodness the house in Philly sold.*

Earlier that morning, at a salon in Miami, she'd had her chestnut hair styled in a fashionable Marcel wave. Businesswoman extraordinaire, she was every bit the looker; her curves had gotten more than one fella in trouble with his dame. When she saw what she'd been able to pull off, she got tingly. *I did this. Me. You take one look at it and think success.* Although, today, that euphoric feeling was tempered by damp sweat.

I hope Darwin got the bathroom finished. I could really use a long, hot soak in that big tub.

Edith walked from the carpark, passed the large couldvas tent used as a temporary kitchen, and crossed Goodtimes' broad veranda. She still wasn't used to the brass hurricane lanterns, installed yesterday. They flanked the ornate wood-paneled front door. There were so many changes from 'Gator Joe's rustic charm. Goodtimes was all about class, from the top of its Spanish-tiled roof to the sweep of the wraparound veranda and second story balcony. More than she ever did at 'Gator's, Edith felt like she was coming home when she

8

saw Goodtimes. *And if it was this perfect now, imagine what it will be like when all the work is done.*

She stepped into the barroom, the first part of the building completed. it was a cavernous space. New tables and chairs, some still wrapped in burlap, were pushed against the wall. No second-hand furnishings here; this furniture was the best that money could buy. She headed to the bar where a bottle of champagne cooled in a bucket of icy water.

Leroy, a small, barefoot boy of eleven, barreled across the room, wrapping himself around her. She looked over his head to a pair of somber men who were sitting at a table covered with plates and food.

Edith peeled off his arms so she could pour herself a glass of bubbles. "How did you know?" she asked them, waving the bottle.

"Know what?" Leroy asked.

"About the new refrigerator. I left it in the back of the truck. Isn't that what we're celebrating?"

Leroy beamed up at Edith. "The champagne's for you on account of my birthday. Darwin went out to Rum Row and got it special as a surprise."

Edith's heart sank. *Leroy's birthday? Darn, I was sure that was next week. I could have brought him something back from Miami.*

Darwin shrugged. "It's sort of an unofficial christening of the barroom. Leroy's birthday is our first official event in it."

"That's right. It is your birthday," she said brightly, hoping to disguise her gaffe.

Leroy tugged her toward the table where the others were waiting. "Hang on a sec, Leroy. I have something for you." Edith went back to the counter and pulled out her wallet. "I seem to have misplaced your card." She handed him a dollar.

"Wow, this is great, Miz Edith. Thanks a bunch. I don't need a card. I can buy a whole bunch of comic books with a whole dollar."

Edith's smile was triumphant as she looked over at Darwin. "Or maybe a baseball glove. You can spend it on whatever you want."

Leroy grabbed held of her hand again, dragging her to the table. "Lucky made me a cake and put my name on it in the icing. See?"

The remains of a cake sat in the center of the table.

"That's swell, Leroy." Edith put the champagne bottle on the table in front of her and took another gulp from her glass. *I'll get him something next time.* "You'll love the new refrigerator, Lucky. it was the biggest one I could find," she said to the small, middle-aged Asian man who was sitting quietly.

Lucky nodded, but didn't meet her eyes.

"We saved the best piece for you. It was the one that had an 'L' on it. For Leroy," the boy said, sliding a big slice of cake over to her.

"Looks tasty." Edith pushed the cake to one side. "Wait 'til you see the fridge. And I got the best deal. The fella in the store was going to charge me full price, but I talked him down. With a bit of charm and fluttering eyelashes, I picked up a sweetheart deal. I've still got what it takes." She winked at Darwin, a well-muscled fellow whose battered Panama hat, with 'gator teeth forming a hatband.

Darwin frowned. "Where were you? You were supposed to be home hours ago."

Edith could feel the disapproval radiating off him.

"Oh, sorry about that. I wanted to get my hair done." She patted at her hair. "Whaddya think?"

Stony silence met her excuse. Leroy stared at the floor. Edith shrugged and poured herself more champagne. "And then I met up with Mae Capone for lunch, and you know how that is. Girl talk over martinis. I lost track of time." She toasted them with her glass.

"Although, if I'd known we were having champagne, I would had hurried home."

Leroy slumped into his chair, his head low.

Edith glanced at him, the smallest twinge of guilt flickering behind her hazel eyes, and then turned to Darwin. "I also stopped by the lumberyard and ordered—"

"It was Leroy's birthday, Edith" Darwin said, still frowning. The words echoed in the silence of the room.

"I said I was sorry."

Darwin shook his head. "No. You didn't."

"Well, maybe I didn't say it out loud, but that's what I meant. Gave me a break, here. I'm working hard for this family. I think you all should appreciate that more."

"It's Leroy's birthday," Darwin said. "He's eleven."

"That's okay, Darwin. I don't mind. Not much, anyway." Leroy straightened from his slump. "The cake was real good, Lucky."

Edith shared a look with Darwin and turned to Leroy. "I'm sorry, sweetie. I really am. You deserve a wonderful gift, a huge celebration. I've been so caught up in work that I truly thought your birthday was next week. How about I make it up to you, and we go into Coconut Grove and buy a radio to replace the one lost in the fire?"

Leroy bounced, his eyes shining. "That would be great. The Shadow is on tomorrow night."

"Held your horses. I can't do it that quick. I've got too much paperwork on my desk. Tomorrow won't work, but we could try the day after that."

"But The Shadow is on tomorrow," Leroy said, pouting.

"Don't be difficult, Leroy. You've missed so many episodes, one more won't hurt. When we get the kitchen finished, we can put the radio in there."

"In the kitchen? You said it was going to be my birthday present. That means it's just for me."

"I don't need radio, Miz Edith. Let Leroy keep. He can listen to his stories in his room," Lucky said, nodding and smiling at Leroy.

"And baseball games." Leroy looked at Edith, a hopeful smile on his face.

Outside, the thunder rumbled.

"Don't be selfish, Leroy. Everyone should be able to enjoy it. Not just you. Now, let's get that refrigerator unloaded before the rain comes. We can plug it into the generator and put it in the kitchen tent until the real kitchen is ready."

They're all getting too soft. Someone has to be the boss. Someone has to rule this roost. Leroy is getting spoiled. And Cassie would agree. And he's got way more than he had when he was living with her in the 'Glades.

Edith rose, tossed back her curls, and headed outside. Three pairs of eyes followed her: one set confused, another angry, and the final pair resigned. Her plate of cake with the 'L' on it was left untouched.

CHAPTER 2

Everything in the sea seemed to wash up on shore sooner or later. One of Leroy's chores at Goodtimes was to keep the beach clean; a storm like the one last night delivered all kinds of wreckage. He drifted from bright, shiny objects to things squishy and disgusting. Among the treasures, he picked up broken palm leaves and other storm debris.

Included in the dregs and dross on the beach were a few bottles of liquor. It was common practice among rum runners on Biscayne Bay to dump contraband booze overboard when they were being pursued, a hasty ditching of the evidence. Swallowing the bottles, the rolling sea rewarded beachcombers. Leroy carefully examined the bottles to make sure they held liquor, not seawater, and then stacked them to the side.

"Leroy?" Edith was on the veranda, shouting down the path that led to the beach.

Leroy waved. "Here, Miz Edith. Trying to clean up the mess the storm left behind."

"Lunch in half an hour. Lucky's got some of your opossum stew on the go."

Even with the steady sounds of hammer and saw, and the bustle of activity around the construction site, the past six months had almost seemed like a holiday for Leroy. There were no tables to clear, no crates of beer and empties to haul back and forth from the shed. He got to spend sunny days out on the water fishing with Darwin, and cloudy days exploring the thickets, creeks, and swamps around Goodtimes, slingshot in his back pocket. On stormy days he curled up with a good book. it was a swell life for a boy like Leroy. Except for the chore of cleaning up the beach and sometimes giving Darwin and Lucky a hand, his days were his own.

Leroy picked his way through the storm's deliveries, then turned to the hum of a motor out on the water. It was a small dory,

13

the type of tender the bigger ships on Rum Row used to come into shore. Cleo Lythgoe had her hand on the tiller and the other was signaling. Leroy ran onto the dock to help tie up the little boat.

"Hiya, Miz Cleo, some storm last night. What was it like out on the water? Were you scared? It would scare me. Yesterday was my birthday. We had a cake with my name on it. But it's all gone, now."

"Hiya, yourself, lad. Yes, I was aboard the *Arethusa* and the weather was 'a mite dirty' as the sailors say. Is Miss Edith at home? I have her order and thought I'd bring it by myself."

Leroy began to take the hams of liquor—six bottles padded then stacked in a pyramid and wrapped in burlap resembling the shape of a ham—from the tall, muscular, nut-brown woman. He sat them on the dock.

"She's getting lunch ready. Well, Lucky is. I caught an opossum yesterday and we're having stew today. Can you stay for lunch? Lucky makes great opossum stew."

"I don't think I've sampled opossum. It isn't something you'd find on the menu in London's cafes." Leroy piled the hams on the dock, then they gathered them and trudged up the path from the dock to the building.

Turtles, sunning themselves on fellen logs, craned their long necks to look at the invaders to their private beach. Leroy pointed out a poisonous copperhead snake whose body was as big as a man's thigh. Cleo gasped and stepped back, not taking her eyes off it until the snake moved with lethargic ease deeper into the Everglades.

The screen door on the veranda banged open and Edith stepped out. "Cleo, welcome. Did you bring me my Gordon's? I haven't been able to make a martini in weeks."

"Hello, ducks. Yes, I've got the gin. Although, from the look of this place, you'll be placing orders for the barroom soon. You've been busy since I was here last."

"We're almost ready to open. Working around the mess. I'll gave you the grand tour." Edith looked over her shoulder. "Darwin, Cleo's here. Could you help with the hams?"

Darwin appeared from inside Goodtimes and relieved Cleo of her bundles, leaving Leroy to manage his own. "Good to see you, Cleo."

Goodtimes, an impressive two-story building in French Colonial style, had a wraparound veranda, and a balcony off the second floor. The main entrance was a Palladian doorway. The ornate screen door was flanked on either side by long, narrow windows, and the entire unit was capped by a graceful, curved window. A dozen floor to ceiling arched glass doors with heavy storm shutters opened onto the veranda. Lacy wrought iron columns along the front supported the balcony on the second floor. The balcony and the second-floor French doors had magnificent views of the water. The exterior walls were a pastel shade of tangerine with dark green shutters, pillars, and trim. The whole effect gave Goodtimes a luxurious tropical air.

Cleo admired the new wicker tables and chairs along the veranda, the potted palms in large jardinières, a pair of brass lanterns on either side of the front door.

"It's looking good, Edith. You've done an incredible job. It's miraculous to see how quickly you've managed to rebuild."

Edith rolled her eyes. "Miracles are only half the story. A bit of divine intervention with the weather has helped some, but the rest is a liberal application of cold, hard cash to Miami's contractors."

Cleo chuckled. "How'd you do through last night's storm?"

"Closed the shutters and pushed everything not nailed down against the wall. Goodtimes came through with flying colors."

"I see you already got a name for it. Not calling it 'Gator Joe's like the old place?"

"That was then, this was now. Its full name is Mickey's Goodtimes Saloon, after my late husband. I think he would had gotten a kick out of that. I told you he was King of the Bootleggers back in Philadelphia, didn't I?"

Cleo laughed. "The name Goodtimes? That might be a bit gregarious for such a gracious building, but you know your market. 'Gator's was a blind-tiger. This looked like a mansion you'd find in the French Quarter in New Orleans, although the color reminds me more of the Bahamas."

Edith beamed. "I wanted something more top-shelf than before. You'll remember there wasn't much leftstooding after the fire. I didn't want to build my dreams on cold ashes, so we knocked down what was left and started again."

"I can't believe you've been living in the barn all these months. It must seem like heaven to have finally moved into the big house."

"Oh, it is. Having privacy again. Fortunately, we'd fixed up the barn for Leroy and the weekend bands, sort of like a bunkhouse, before the fire. But having Lucky, Leroy, and I all under one roof meant for close quarters. Especially when it rained, which it does a lot in the summer."

"So I've noticed. These storms are never fun at sea."

"How did you make out last night? Was it rough out there?"

"The *Arethusa* has a great crew, so we were fine. Like babes being rocked in their mothers' arms," Cleo said. "Even if some of the rocking arms were a bit more muscular than a mother's." A small giggle escapes.

One of Edith's eyebrows climbs. "Really? Do tell."

Cleo, with a small smile, blushed. "Too soon to say, but a girl can hope. 'Cupid was a knavish lad, thus to make females mad.' "

Edith adopted a mock scowl. "Oh, you Brits and your Shakespeare. Give me a good Hemingway any day."

16

Laughing, Cleo took another look at the front of Goodtimes. "What improvements did you make to the original design? The building itself looks so much bigger."

"I wanted to build it not just for the business we have now—the blind-tiger and maybe some gambling, but for what will come after Prohibition. Florida will be a tourist mecca and I want to be part of that wave."

Cleo chuckled. "Atta girl. Always thinking one step ahead."

Edith linked arms with Cleo. "Come and let me show you what the magic of money can do."

CHAPTER 3

Arm in arm, Edith and Cleo toured the new Goodtimes. They started at the back in the kitchen, still under construction.

"As you see, there's still lots of work to do back here. Lucky's working out of a tent right now. The priority has been to get the barroom open and start bringing in money. Then the next priority has to be finishing the living space upstairs. It was probably premature to move in but, like I said before, I was reaching the end of my rope living cheek and jowl with Lucky and Leroy in the barn."

"Darwin's still sleeping on the boat?"

"Oh yes. It'll take a better woman than me to coax him onto land."

"I always thought there might be something between you two."

"Darwin? And me?" A loud guffaw erupted. "Don't be ridiculous, doll. Darwin's—well, just Darwin. I was married to Mickey Duffy. I'm looking for another king, not someone like Darwin."

"He's a nice man, Edith. And reliable. You could do worse."

"Now I know you've got it bad. This new romance of yours has your head in the clouds and has given you a compulsion to match-make. I would rather be alone than with a 'you could do worse' fella. Really, Cleo."

Cleo shrugged. "I've been rethinking the alone part. I don't know whether I want to grow old alone."

Edith softened and held Cleo's hands in hers. "You'll not need to worry about that, Cleo. I'm sure this new fella will work out. You're one exceptional gal and he'd be stupid not to see that." She squeezed again, then cleared her throat. "Now, if you want to talk about *my* future, let me tell you about the plans I've got for a real restaurant kitchen."

They moved down the hallway, past the stairs to the second floor, and back into the barroom where Leroy had unwrapped the gin and was setting up the bottles on the counter behind the bar.

"It'll gave us more opportunities to expand the menu and add a full supper service. I picked up a huge, new refrigerator yesterday so I could offer you a cold drink."

Cleo chuckled. "That sounds lovely. Does Lucky have any lemonade?"

"Always. Leroy, could you run and fetch us a pitcher and some glasses? Miss Cleo and I are parched and would like some lemonade."

"Sure thing, Miz Edith," he said. He dashed off toward the rear of the building. Edith and Cleo heard the back door slam behind him.

Cleo chuckled. "So much energy."

"I know. It's hard to keep up with him. You have your mystery man, I have Leroy. Although, I never expected to be responsible for an eleven-year-old bundle of mischief."

"Boys can be a handful. Or so I've been told. Sadly, I've never had one of my own."

"Beware what you wish for. Leroy's always talking, full of questions. He never does what he's told without kicking up a ruckus. And his appetite, Cleo—like a horse."

"Sounds like you have it as bad as I do. You're crazy about the kid, aren't you?"

Edith chuckled. "That obvious, eh? He's saved my life in more ways than one." She sighed, giving her head a small shake. "Back to the tour. As you can see, the barroom is on the main floor just like before, only we've added indoor plumbing so customers don't have to go outside. I also added an office behind the bar so I can keep an eye on things without being on the floor." Edith pointed to a frosted glass door behind the bar.

"And over there is a private party room that will eventually be where we put the slots. Right now it's unfinished." She gestured to another frosted glass door on the far side of the barroom.

"Oh, this was gorgeous," Cleo said, running her hand along the unusual wood paneling on the front of the bar.

"It's pecky cypress. I commissioned it before we'd even started construction on the main building. I wanted something that would really set the tone for the place."

"I love these holes in the grain in the wood. It looks like it was built from a giant sponge."

"Thank you. They finished it last week. Darwin's been able to take out the *Marianne* and do a bit of rum running during the construction. That, and some extra money from Philly, had given us the cash to make Goodtimes really special."

"You can easily see that, Edith. It's fantastic, and a huge change from 'Gator Joe's."

"The biggest improvement since the last time you were here is upstairs. I have—or will have—a nice little suite with a bedroom and sitting room. Even unfinished, it's like a little treasure box up there. Wait 'til you see it. And, as a special luxury, I had them put in a real bathroom off the bedroom, just for me. It has a big, claw-foot tub. Darwin finished the plumbing on it yesterday. There's a small guest room up there, too, if you're ever tempted to stay over."

"No more trips to the outhouse," Cleo laughed.

Leroy came back through the barroom carrying a tray with glasses and a sweating pitcher. "I have my own room, too. Next to the kitchen. Lucky's in the room beside mine. I don't have to sleep in the barn anymore. Wanna see?"

While Edith pours, Cleo gives Leroy's head a pat. "You bet, champ. But let me chat with Miss Edith a bit, first." She took a glass of lemonade off the tray and had a long drink. "Delicious." Cleo nodded to Edith's waist. "I see you're still wearing your sidearm."

Edith gave a grim laugh. "It's come in handy a couple of times to shoot at snakes, both the slithering kind and the two-legged kind."

Cleo took in the circles under Edith's eyes and the rumpled, less-than-fresh housedress that looked like it had been slept in. "It's been ages, Edith. How are you?"

Edith shrugged and moved away from the lemonade, putting a few gin bottles on the empty shelves.

Cleo stepped forward and reached out, putting her hand on Edith's arm. "Really, how are you?"

"You know how it is. I'm still not sleeping well because of the fire—more than a few nightmares and flashbacks. I'm working myself to the bone, living in the middle of constant noise and chaos, and I'm anxious about the future. I won't rest easy until I know for sure this is the best idea I've ever had and not some colossal mistake."

Cleo gave her a warm smile. "It will get better, ducks. Looks as if you're in the home stretch."

Edith heaved a deep sigh. "On top of it all, I'm still having issues with the townsfolk. Nothing I need is ever in. Just like last time. It doesn't matter if it's supplies for the kitchen or behind the bar, building materials for the buildings, or repairs to the equipment. It gets tiresome and expensive to always be bringing it in from Miami."

"They won't sell to a woman?"

"No one has said that directly. I've mentioned how much I'm spending—they're businessmen after all—but it doesn't seem to matter. And a couple of them had women behind the counter. I thought that might make a difference, but no."

"Maybe it's running the bar? It is Prohibition, you know. You are technically breaking the law."

Edith snorted. "In this town? Come on, Cleo. One of the things about living isolated on the coast of Florida is everybody seems to be an outlaw or a recluse of some kind or other. I mean, why else are they here? Out in the middle of nowhere, thumbing their noses at the rest of society? The blue ocean on one side and a sea of green swamp on the other." *Smack.* "And I hate these mosquitoes."

"Better than snakes. Leroy and I saw a gigantic one on the way up the path."

"Oh, yes." She shuddered. "I hate snakes. At least the rats are gone."

"Rats?"

"You remember, I was having quite a problem with rats, dead ones showing up in strange places—like on my pillow—but I have't seen one now for almost five months."

"Maybe the alligators got them?"

"Yes, or maybe they moved to Tampa."

Cleo raised an eyebrow.

"You remember those two lay-abouts I had working for me? Once Ottis and Zeke skedaddled to Tampa, the rat problem disappeared."

Edith drained her glass of lemonade then grabbed a key from inside the cash drawer in the bar. "Let's go put the rest of these bottles away, Leroy. We can show Miss Cleo where we're storing the liquor."

The trio headed through the unfinished kitchen to the back porch. Next to the tent-kitchen was a large, new shed.

"You know, besides the rats and snakes, the other thing I hate is always being damp," Edith said. "Philly was humid sometimes, but never like this." She sniffed herself and grimaced. "Clothes stick and there are more days I need a bath than I have time for."

"Sometimes my Aunt Cassie calls me Koone. Koone is Miccosukee Seminole for skunk. But I ain't no skunk. Am I, Miz Edith?"

22

"Oh, no. I'm sure she meant it as a term of endearment, Leroy," Edith said with a wink at Cleo.

"Living on a ship is like that, too. The crew all strip down andstood naked in the rain to get clean," Cleo whispered so that Leroy couldn't overhear. The gals giggled.

"Really? What do you do?" Edith asked, unlocking the shed door. "Here we are."

Like Goodtimes itself, the shed was bigger than the previous one. They went inside where it was dark, and the air was stuffy with heat.

"Wipe that leer off your face, Edith Duffy. I go below and wait in my cabin, like any proper English woman would do. But it also means I only get a bird bath now and then. Water's in short supply on long voyages, too precious for a full bath."

"Feel free to have a bath in my new tub anytime," Edith said and then looked wistful. "I miss spending a couple of hours getting all dolled up to go out: bath, makeup, hair, a special dress, the whole nine yards. Oh, and heels. I do miss high heels. You can't wear heels with all this beach sand."

"You could be somewhere more populated, Edith. Running a club in Miami sounds more your style, even though the new place certainly makes an impressive statement. It wouldn't be out of place in Palm Beach or Key West. You've got an eye for design and class."

Edith showed Cleo inside the shed, and the inventory she'd built up so far. They blinked as they left the shed and returned to sunlight.

"And you should think about somewhere else to store your liquor, Edith. My professional advice is somewhere cool and dry. Not a hot shed," Cleo said while Edith re-locked the door.

Edith threw back her head and cackled. "Cool and dry? In Florida? In the summer? That ain't going to happen, Cleo."

Passing the large canvas kitchen tent, they could hear Lucky curseing a blue streak in Cantonese.

Edith raised her shoulders and rolled her eyes.

Back inside the barroom, another glass of lemonade hit the spot.

Cleo wiped her forehead with her sleeve. "Seriously, Edith, I don't understand. You had the chance to move anywhere after the fire. What kept you here and not establishing yourself somewhere else? A bit more civilized?"

"I've lived in a big city, and I'll never live in a place like Philadelphia again. Miami was built to reflect that northern big-city feel, only with palm trees and beaches. And the people in Miami are mostly displaced northerners. Despite the complaining, I like being out here. When Mickey died, I needed the space to breathe and be on my own. I thought 'Gator Joe's was perfect, but Goodtimes is even better." Edith pulled the shed key out of her pocket and two tarot cards fell out.

"Hello?" Cleo picked up the cards. "I never took you for a tarot follower."

"I don't follow the cards. They seem to follow me. I find them in the strangest places: tucked into a pocket or behind a bottle or under my pillow. They just show up out of nowhere. Leroy is good with cards and will tell me what they mean. His aunt believes she can see the future in the cards, but I still hadn't had her read my cards."

"You don't know what you're missing. I look forward to getting mine done when I'm on land and always have a deck in my kit bag. There's usually a sailor or two on every ship that likes to read them, as well. Sailors are a superstitious lot. Living at the mercy of the sea gives you an inclination to check in on fate and your future a bit more, I guess."

One in each hand, Cleo held the cards toward Edith. "These two cards are from the wand suit. These sticks are called 'wands' in tarot.

24

Wands represent what was important to the core of your being and deal with feelings, ideas, and thoughts."

She waves the card in her right hand. "This is the Ten of Wands. See the man carrying a large bundle of sticks? His back is bent, and he appears to be weighed down by the pack on his back. He's going toward a small town and knows he will soon be able to release the heavy weight he is bearing."

"I know why I got that card. I've been feeling exhausted and burned out with all the construction. Although I don't think I'll be setting down my burden any time soon. There's still too much to do."

Cleo frowned at Edith's obvious fatigue. "You definitely need a holiday, my friend."

She held up the other card: the Five of Wands. "The five men are fighting each other with staves or wands, and it means that there are disagreements or competition." Cleo waved it at Edith. "Fives typically represent conflict and change; Five of Wands is no exception. It shows you are in the middle of a battle. Maybe there is tension and competition with others? Whatever it is, it is impacting your ability to move forward with your goals. Who are you fighting with, Edith?"

Edith shrugged. "I wish I knew. It would make it easier to either attack, or stay out of his way."

Cleo waited for Edith to explain more.

"I had all that trouble with the Wharf Rats. They burned down 'Gator's and Darwin always has to keep an eye out for them when he's on Rum Row."

"I know them well. Pirates are a wicked bunch. They prey on the small boats that come out to the schooners on Rum Row."

"I wish I knew who's leading them. Mickey always said a double tap to the head is the best way to put somebody down so they stay down."

Cleo looked aghast.

Edith leans over and patted Cleo on the arm. "I meant I need to deal with the head of the organization. I don't intend on shooting him in the head. Although, I've been tempted. We've had lots of job-site mischief during the construction: tools going missing, materials stolen kind of thing. The Miami contractor put a guard on the site and that has helped. But I can feel them out there, lurking."

"And you want to talk with them?" Cleo asked.

"I do. I thought I'd met with the boss just after I came out here, but it wasn't the top guy. Nothing got resolved. Mae Capone and I carried out a midnight caper in retaliation for some attacks when it was still 'Gator Joe's. I figure that's when they decided to burn the old place down."

Edith gave a wry chuckle. "A friend of mine said, 'tit for tat leads to rat-a-tat-tat.' I'm not making the same mistake twice and want to nip all this harassment in the bud. But it's been a real problem not knowing who's in charge of the Wharf Rats. I don't want to spend time chasing after a nobody. I'd rather talk to the leader, the boss-man."

Cleo nodded and held out the Ten of Wands again. "And what about this Ten? You've been pushing yourself to your limits and working very hard, Edith. I meant it before. You should take a break.

"And like I said before. Where would I find the time for that, Cleo? Be realistic. The place would fall apart if I wasn't here."

"Well, the Ten of Wands card also mean that at least you're taking those final steps on the path to realizing your dreams. Even though you might collapse in a heap of exhaustion when you get there, it'll have all been worth it, and well earned.'"

Edith chuckled and hugged her friend. "You put that last bit in there so I wouldn't give up, didn't you?"

"You always need hope, Edith."

There was a knock at the front screen door. A paunchy man who looked like a giant leprechaun stepped in. "Hello, Miz Edith."

CHAPTER 4

Tucker Wilson operated another speakeasy, known locally as a blind-tiger, in Cutler, a village just down the highway from Coconut Grove. When Edith had opened 'Gator Joes, he'd offered to purchase it with funds from a mysterious backer.

"Tucker, what a pleasant surprise. What brings you here today? You haven't got another offer in your pocket to buy my blind-tiger, do you?"

Tucker blushed. "Nah, that arrangement's fallen apart, Miz Edith. Although I am here to offer you some business. You got a place where we could talk private?"

Cleo picked up the empty lemonade jug. "I'll get Lucky to refill this and bring back an extra glass."

Tucker waited until she was out of earshot. "I expect you know that Darwin's been doing a bit of rum running for me?"

Edith nodded. "So I've heard. On a casual basis while we're waiting to get Goodtimes opened."

"I'd like to talk to you about making it more permanent before you get busy with your own rum running. And from the looks of it, that's going to be pretty darn soon, too." Tucker looked around the barroom, taking in the size and the level of finish. He whistled. "This was going to be a whole different crowd than mine, Miz Edith. Puts my little blind-tiger to shame."

"You've got a great little place, Tucker. Different kinds of customers. I'm planning on more of a Miami crowd."

"I can see why they'd drive out."

Edith watched him mentally count the stacked chairs and smiled. "You want to formalize the rum running we've been doing for you?"

Tucker focused on Edith. "I've had to cut back on what I could bring in and well, you know, a dry bar is an empty bar."

Edith knows. "Pirates?"

"They're terrible right now, Miz Edith. I used to be able to pay a bit of protection money and they'd leave me alone. But those days are long gone. My missus is worried about me." Tucker's face grew grim. "I've been running my place since before Prohibition and it was never supposed to be a life or death decision. You know what I mean?"

"I look at it differently, Tucker. Pirates and hijackings are just part of the business we're in. They've always been part of the speakeasy scene—when I was in Philly, and now here. It's the reason we get to charge so much for a cheap glass of whiskey."

"I'd rather pay somebody else to carry that problem. I'd ask young Harley Andrews, but his boat is too small. I figure with the *Marianne*, Darwin will have enough room onboard to keep you supplied as well as me."

The wheels in Edith's mind began to churn. *Bootlegging for other speakeasies. I'm sure we could handle Tucker, but I wonder what else is out there. And what would be the profit on that? How big a business could it be?*

Tucker, anxious about the silence, coughed. "Maybe you don't want to take it on, Miz Edith. It is doubling your risk. I just figured you're out there anyway and Darwin's good at it. I hope you consider it."

Edith realized that Tucker had misinterpreted her silence, and smiled to reassure him. "Supplying another saloon is an interesting idea, Tucker. It hasn't been a problem to do a bit of rum running casually while my new saloon's been under construction, but a formal arrangement now that Goodtimes is almost ready to open is something else. I'm not sure we can do both. I'll talk it over with Darwin and see what he thinks. He's heading out later tonight, but how about I send him round to speak to you tomorrow?"

"That'd be swell, Miz Edith. I'm sure we could can to some kind of understanding where we're both winners."

As she watched him, an electric current ran from the tips of her toes to the top of her ears, leaving her body tingling. *Bootlegging on a grand scale. Just like Mickey did. Could I pull something like that off?*

Edith went in search of Cleo, finding her in the kitchen tent with Lucky and Leroy.

Cleo turned, the full jug of lemonade in her hand. "I was just bringing this in."

"Not to worry. Tucker just left. Say Cleo, come with me and I'll show you the second floor." Edith explained Tucker's offer while they werestooding on the balcony off her bedroom, looking out at the sea. "What do you think?"

"Edith, I'm in the wholesale liquor business. I see a wonderful opportunity for you to increase my sales. But you're the one with the extra risk and hassles. The important question is what do you think? And Darwin? Can you take on one more project given everything else on your plate?"

"You're right. It would be something else to worry about, one more bit of risk. But I could make a lot of money. Think of it, Cleo, I could supply the speakeasies and casinos all along the coast of Florida. Right now, everybody's running out to Rum Row on their own: a fleet of small-time smugglers. I could contract with them and corner the market."

"Whoa, not so fast. Maybe you should talk to Darwin first? See if you can handle Goodtimes and this Tucker fellow before you start building an empire?"

Edith's eyes were shining. "And after Prohibition, all these places and the ones that come next are going to need some kind of distribution. I'd be the middle-man between the suppliers like you and the bars and casinos."

"Casinos are Lansky's turf, Edith. Don't go stepping on any toes. Like I said, test the waters—no pun intended—and see if this is something you can handle. You don't want to be jeopardizing Goodtimes with a second business."

Edith breathed deeply, staring out over the horizon. "I bet I could be a great bootlegger, Cleo. I have the chance to build something even bigger than Mickey did. The East Coast was already crowded with competition by the time he got into the game. It's wide open down here in Florida."

Cleo frowned and put a gentle hand on Edith's arm. "There's competition here, ducks. And they are the same players as up north. Be careful."

"Risky business is rewarding business. Are you trying to talk me out of a sale, Cleo? You're as ambitious as I am when it comes to business." Edith grinned at her friend.

"That's true, just know your limitations. If you focus on the small-time operators like that chap that was here earlier, you won't have any trouble. And you're right about the mark-up and potential profit. For example, that case of gin I brought you sells for $11 in Scotland and you paid $50 for it."

"Oh Cleo, that's outrageous."

Cleo shrugged. "I'm a businesswoman and it's a fair price. If you find the same quality cheaper, I'll match it. But I'm fairly confident saying it won't happen. And if you decide to get into smuggling on a bigger scale, let me know. I could get you anything you need. I'm the agent for White Horse whiskey, Canadian Club, Martell cognac, Gordon's dry gin, and John Haig scotch whiskey, but I can get you anything."

"You never miss an opportunity, do you?" Edith said, smiling.

"You told me yourself, if opportunity knocks, don't complain about the racket."

"Ha, ha."

Side by side, the two women leaned against the railing, lost in the view of the vast ocean.

"A lot of this would fall on Darwin's shoulders," Cleo said. "Have you thought about that?"

Edith nodded. "I'm going to talk to him before I make any decisions."

"You're building a nice little partnership there, Edith."

"He's not the easiest fella to work with, but I can trust him."

"I also think it's interesting that a big fellow like that Tucker Wilson is asking you to do something he's afraid to do. You're building a reputation, Edith Duffy. Not backing down or giving way. And being smart about it."

"Oh, pooh. Don't flatter me or it will go to my head. Are you staying for some of Lucky's stew?"

"I wouldn't miss it. I hear that a famous woodsman hunted down the ferocious opossum himself to grace the stew pot."

* * * *

After lunch, Edith saw Cleo off at the dock and went to help Darwin move the tables and chairs into place in the barroom. It was exciting to watch the empty space slowly transform itself into the club of her imagination. All it needed was customers.

While they worked, Edith brought Darwin up to speed on Tucker's offer. "So what do you think?" Edith asked as she picked up the broom to give the floor a sweep.

"I'd prefer to get Goodtimes open and running before we take on something new. One thing at a time."

"But Tucker's offer is on the table now. He'll find somebody else if we say no. It could be the start of something big."

Pushing his hat back, Darwin took a long look at Edith. "The start of something big? Isn't Goodtimes big enough? We're sitting pretty at the moment. And should do well out of this place once it's open."

"Money's only part of it, Darwin, and not even the most important part. We have to keep growing. This could open a lot of doors after Prohibition if we play our cards right. The start of something amazing."

"Goodtimes is amazing enough for me. I don't see the need to take on something else. Besides, if we do more smuggling runs, when would I get my fishing in?"

"Fishing? You're prepared to give up the chance to own Florida's liquor smuggling racket—for fishing?"

Darwin winked. "A man's gotta had priorities, Edith."

Edith shook her head and smiled. "I thought you were serious for a minute there. I told Tucker you'd talk to him about it tomorrow."

"All right, I'll give it some thought. Picking up booze for two places means I'd have to go out more, which increases our risk and our exposure to pirates and the Coast Guard."

"But *Marianne*'s Liberty engines are powerful enough to outrun most," Edith said, grinning up at Darwin.

"She's fast, I'll gave you that. But I don't go looking for trouble, Edith. Dosen't matter whether you're talking Coast Guard or Wharf Rats, I've got a good sense of the way they both operate and I try to avoid them. If I can't, I've got a fast boat to outrun them. Worst case is, I know that I'm prepared to give up the cargo and live to fight another day."

"And I suppose there's the weather. This summer's been wild with storms. We'd need to put a radio on board in case of trouble. What do you think about mark-up?"

"Ha. What was that? A quick token concern for my well-being so we can put it aside and talk money?" Darwin grinned, an eyebrow raised.

Edith swatted at Darwin's legs with the broom. "The concern is real. But we can't talk risk without understanding the size of the reward."

"True enough. I've got to head out to Rum Row tonight, and on the way out I'll mull over some numbers and see if I can get them to work. It's just Tucker, right?"

Edith looked around Goodtimes: all the warm wood shining from the sun's rays, stacks of tables and chairs just waiting for thirsty customers, the pecky cypress bar and the mirrored shelves aching to be filled with bottles of premium liquor, the frosted glass doors on her office anticipating it's manager, and the room that will eventually hold the slot machines gives off an air of impatience. And then she looked out the French doors to the blue ocean beyond.

She nodded, her fingers crossed behind her back. "Of course. One step at a time."

CHAPTER 5

The small town of Coconut Grove hugged the coast of Florida—sometimes clinging to it. It appeared the typical charming place: clapboard houses sheltered by palm trees, neat gardens behind freshly painted fences, shops with polished windows shining in the tropical sun. Looks could be deceiving.

In 1927, Miami grabbed the sleepy hamlet to adjust for the massive expansion that happened during the land boom. Powerless to protect their town from the annex, townspeople held their breath waiting for change... that didn't happen. Seemingly over before it started, the building boom was swallowed by fate—the roots of the Great Depression and a hurricane that smashed the boom to smithereens. Residents celebrated, grateful for the divine intervention that drove away speculators and developers. The people of Coconut Grove were left in relative peace. God does work in mysterious ways.

While Coconut Grove may officially be part of the big city of Miami, on a Sunday the streets were quiet. The only sign of activity was at a simple, white, wooden church boasting a steeple above the front door and a row of gothic arched windows running along each side of the building. Behind the church was a weathered barn next to a wooden, single-story house for the preacher. Parked cars were in the church's lot, and on nearby streets.

Inside the church, the choir in their purple robes were just finishing a rousing chorus of 'How Great Thou Art'. They were a loud and enthusiastic group of middle-aged women, and terribly off-key.

The preacher, a tall, thin man dressed in black clothes, over which he'd put on a black flowing robe and draped it with a purple stole, strode to the pulpit. He tightly gripped both sides with slender hands, his eyes narrow as they slid around the room, spotting transgressors, nappers, and matching absentees to empty spots in the pews.

The congregation shifted under his judgemental gaze; fans were flapped, collars were tugged, small children were hushed. Everyone settled and waited.

"Today is Sunday, the day you give to the Lord, but what were you up to yesterday? Saturday nights when the worshipers of sin go to carouse in their temples: the blind-tigers and saloons. There they drink forbidden liquor and fornicate with wickedness. Have they forgotten the wisdom in Proverbs? 'This was the way of an adulteress: she eats and wipes her mouth and says, *I have done no wrong.*' And in John 3:8 'Whoever makes a practice of sinning is of the Devil, for the Devil has been sinning from the beginning. The reason the Son of God appeared was to destroy the works of the Devil.' The Devil and his spawn walk among us, brothers and sisters, and we need to be wise to their evil, tempting ways."

Mavis Saunders, sitting attentive in her usual spot in the third row, nodded along. "Hallelujah." She nudged her husband, Lt. Commander John Saunders of the Coast Guard. He was just back from his two-week tour aboard a six-bitter cutter and his gentle snores rumbled beside her.

Brother Silas took a breath and leaned into the pulpit. "These vice-filled establishments only appear to offer comfort. But beware," he shouted, wagging his finger at the congregation. "They are false facades, pits of temptation, waiting to lead you astray. But you must not just resist the allure, you must fight it. Be the champion of goodness and light."

As if to underline his point, Brother Silas rubbed his left eye while he glanced down at his sermon. He grabbed hold of the pulpit again and cast a baleful glare at the members of his congregation. "If thy right eye offends thee, pluck it out, and cast it from thee: for it is profitable for thee that one of thy members should perish and not that thy whole body should be cast into hell."

Praise for the Lord who works in mysterious ways.

* * * *

In the front row, Miss Mildred White, a plump, perspiring woman in a stiff but well-worn Sunday-best dress gazed up at Brother Silas in rapt adoration. She was open-mouthed as he continued his sermon on the evils of temptation. Somewhere, behind the row of pearl buttons that marched regimentally down the front of the starched linen bodice, beat the heart of a schoolgirl.

On the pew, crowded beside her, were a gaggle of small, restless children. Their legs were swinging, their behinds were twitching, thighs were pinched, giggles suppressed behind sticky hands. They remembered the rule—silence was golden—but, oh, there were so many ways mischievous energy could find release. A prayer book, balancing on the edge of the pew, crashed to the floor.

As the director of the local Florida Children's Home, the children were Mildred's charges. Her fists clenched at the distraction; she glanced warily at Brother Silas who had stopped his preaching.

"Ezra," she hissed. "Gave me that." She snatched at the book, stuffing it between herself and the startled child beside her. "Behave. Or else."

Brother Silas nodded and continued.

Oh Lord, forgave me for interrupting. The children are so unruly today. It must be the weather. The church is hotter than... well, it's warm for sure. And I can feel the daggers Mavis Saunders is digging into my back. What does she know about keeping one child obedient, let alone a half-dozen?

Mildred itched to turn but kept her eyes forward. *I'll meet up with her and the rest of the Homemakers' Guild after the service. The children will be outside and better behaved. Hopefully, the ladies will invite me to be part of another funding drive for some of the poor fruit-pickers traveling through town on their way to work in the orchards.*

She settled further into the pew and smoothed her skirt, peeking up at Brother Silas. *I thought the last drive went very well. Brother Silas was very complimentary and so helpful, carrying the boxes of used clothing and food to the hall.*

Mildred risked a sliver of a smile and directed it to Brother Silas, but he was caught up in his sermon.

His faith is so powerful. And his voice. And those eyes. What would it be like tostood beside him, the town looking up to us? The Guild was always fluttering around him.

Feeling the child next to her squirm, her hand came down on the soft leg in a firm grip. "Last chance, Ezra," she whispered harshly. Ezra froze, and Brother Silas continues to preach.

* * * *

Brother Silas stood outside the door on the church's front steps and shook hands as the congregation filed out; a personal word or two his gift for each member, always remembering to ask after sick family members or absent friends.

Inside the church, the scorching August heat had given the congregation a taste of the perils of sin. Mavis and John moved along up the aisle toward the front door and the welcome outdoor breeze.

Brother Silas greeted the next parishioner in line—a large, round man with perspiration stains on his tan uniform. "Deputy Purvis. I hope you enjoyed the service?"

"Always enlightening, Brother Silas."

"I had hoped you'd be inspired."

Behind the deputy, Mavis cleared her throat. Brother Silas glanced at her and then turned back to the deputy again. "May I have a word with you after I've said goodbye to the good people behind you? I'd like to get your opinion on an issue arising from the sermon."

Deputy Roy Purvis took out a large hanky and wiped at his forehead then puts his hat on his head. "Of course, Brother Silas. I'm at your service."

When the Saunders reached the preacher, Brother Silas wrapped Mavis' warm damp hands in his cool ones. "Thank you for coming, Sister Mavis. Commander."

"A lovely service, Brother Silas. We do live in threatening times," she said. "As leaders in the community we have a duty to set an example and show people the error of their ways."

"Indeed, Sister Mavis. I'm grateful that you can see the perils and hope you have the strength to challenge them. And you as well, Commander Saunders. Your very life given over to keeping evil from our shores. We are grateful for your service, sir. "

"*Ahem*, yes. Thank you. Come along, Mavis, don't keep the good folk behind us waiting."

Mavis shrugged off the commander's hand on her arm.

"How is your stamp collection coming along, Brother Silas? We haven't heard from John's brother, you remember he's in the navy, for a few weeks now but, as soon as we do, I'll bring the envelope's stamp with me to choir practice."

The pale face relaxed into a genuine smile. "Why thank you, Sister. You are so good to me, and I thank the Lord every day for your kindnesses."

Mavis beamed under his attention.

Brother Silas, his eyes alight, two bright red spots on his cheeks in an otherwise pale face, leaned in. "I completed the sections on the previous century's American presidents this week when I came across a purple three cent James Monroe from 1904 commemorating the

Louisiana Purchase. It was a difficult pursuit as there were no stamps of definitive issue honoring him."

"How exciting. Wherever did you find it?"

"A fellow collector was persuaded to part with it."

"And are you still looking for foreign stamps?"

"Always. They are the backbone of my collection. I have a few now from Canada marked Dominion of Canada rather than Dominion of the British Empire. Our northern neighbor has such an interesting colonial history."

"A fascinating hobby, Brother Silas, and now we really must be going, Mavis." John tugged on her arm and they descend the steps to the lawn where other members of the congregation were visiting.

Gathered on the lawn were the good parishioners of Coconut Grove. The adults stood quietly in groups, visiting with friends and neighbors. Children ran, reveling in their release.

"More storm clouds." "Hot, ain't it?" "Hot enough to fry eggs on the sidewalk." "You wish it were just that hot. It's so hot, my hens are laying hard-boiled eggs." "Supposed to be a whopper coming." "Not like '26. Now that hurricane was a doozy."

Moving along the walkway, John Saunders whispered in his wife's ear. "I know you hold him in high regard, Mavis dear, but Brother Silas seems overly fascinated by the vice in Coconut Grove. The last few sermons have been very focused on the subject. I'm not sure it is seemly."

"When they're not out on the water, all those smugglers you're chasing on the sea are here in Coconut Grove, John. Brother Silas is just doing God's work on land, as you do on the water," Mavis said, scanning the crowd for her fellow Guild members.

Mavis missed neither glance, word, or indiscretion. Knowledge was power and, in Coconut Grove, Mavis Saunders knows it all. As she stood next to John, fanning herself, Agnes Matheson joined her. "Did you hear about Elizabeth? Her man's run off—she said to look for work, but that fast Pruit girl is gone too."

John cleared his throat. "I see someone I need to talk to, dear. I'll be just a moment."

"Agnes, I saw it coming for months. That girl is such a brazen hussy. And poor Elizabeth. We should go and comfort her."

Several more Guild members drifted over, flies to honey.

"Oh yes, I'd love to hear the real story." "She always was trouble. I don't know what that boy ever saw in her." Elizabeth's reputation was shredded in a matter of moments.

"Good afternoon, ladies. An inspiring sermon, was it not?" Mildred White, handbag clutched as a shield, arrived.

"Miss White. How nice to see you out. And with all your charges. How many is it today?" The Homemaker's Guild members turned to watch a dozen children chasing each other, whooping and hollering.

"Six of them are mine. The Children's Home is very busy these days. We've got them stacked like cordwood, waiting for placement."

"Such a noble calling you have, Sister Mildred. 'Let us not love with word and speech but with actions and in truth'." Brother Silas had joined them, keeping one eye on the children.

"Brother Silas. Thank you for your sermon today. There is entirely too much laxity about the drinking issue in Coconut Grove. Drink is one of the reasons we had so many children under our care. Even in these tough times, there seems to be money for alcohol. It is an evil drowning local families in grief." Mildred White plucked at Brother Silas' sleeve as she spoke.

He patted her hand and gently put it aside. "Excuse me, but I must talk with Deputy Purvis before he leaves."

"But Brother Silas, I was hoping we could talk about the hardships endured by the fruit-pickers?" Mildred's hand stretched out after the preacher.

"Of course, Sister Mildred. Why don't you and Sister Mavis arrange something and let me know how the church could assist." His robes fluttered behind him as he strode off.

Each of the women in the group, each with her own thoughts, watched him move through the crowd. He gave a nod here, offered a word there, until he reached Deputy Purvis. The two men leaned toward each other, heads almost touching, quickly deep in conversation.

"I must get back to the Home. I hope we can get together soon, Mrs. Saunders." Mildred waited anxiously for any sign of agreement.

Eventually, Mavis tipped her head ever so slightly and gave a small smile of benediction. "Of course, Miss White. Someone from the Guild will be in touch."

Mildred bobbed her head. "Thank you, Mavis, I mean Mrs. Saunders." She turned, clapping her hands. "Children, it's time to go. Line up please. Now, children." Like a sheepdog, she moved through the flock, separating her charges from the other children.

Agnes and Mavis sniffed in disapproval. "She claims to be a mother to them, but there's more to motherhood than just caretaking," Agnes said, frowning.

The other women dove in, eager to add their own two cents. "It's not natural, being paid to mother other people's children." "I've heard there were some mothers who want their children home and she won't gave them up." "Tsk. Who does she think she's fooling?"

"These urchins are causing an outbreak of petty theft. Mr. Peacock down at the S&P Mercantile said he's never seen anything like it. Nimble fingers have goods flying off the shelves," Mavis said, clutching her purse closer.

"Are we going to do another drive? Doesn't it just encourage these fruit-pickers to linger in Coconut Grove?" Agnes said, watching for Mavis to make the final decision. The rest of the group awaited orders.

"If Brother Silas is concerned about their well-being, then we must be as well. Perhaps you can arrange something, Agnes dear. And if you need an extra pair of hands," Mavis said, rolling her eyes, "I'm sure Miss White will be most willing."

Lt. Commander Saunders rejoined his wife as a rumble of thunder interrupted the conversation. "Come along, Mavis. We don't want to get caught in the rain."

The group looked to the threatening sky. A large fat raindrop fell on Mavis' upturned face.

CHAPTER 6

It was pitch black on the sea. The angry water was turbulent and unforgiving. Monstrous waves slammed against the ship like fists. Gale force squalls tore at the sails as the crew struggled to pull them down and tie them off. The howling wind, screaming under serious clouds, drove shards of rain into their faces as they battled on the slippery deck.

"Ship's hove to and battened down, skipper," the first-mate, Mr. Barney, yelled to the captain, Bill McCoy. Strong gusts snatched away his words. A large wave broke over the bow of the ship, washing the deck with seawater. Even though sails were trimmed, the booms swung wildly against the sheets.

Bill leaned into the wind. Seawater sloshed around his feet as he stared into the face of the storm. Six foot two with shoulders like a cargo hatch, he had the rugged handsomeness that young girls' pirate dreams were spun from.

"Fine, Mr. Barney. Tell the men not at their posts to head below." He turned to the man gripping the wheel of the ship, guiding it through the storm. "I'll bring you up a mug of whiskey, Tobias."

Tobias nodded his thanks, his face lashed with salt and storm.

Bill turned to the woman waiting at the mainmast. "Come on, Cleo. There'll be no more contact boats tonight. Let's get below and ride it out." Even with his height and solid build, Bill needed to pull himself against the wind to reach Cleo.

Cloe Lythgoe was soaked to the skin. She let go of the mast and reached for Bill.

He grabbed her hand and pulled her against him. "This storm is brutal. It's madness to be out in this for the sake of a few bottles of rum."

Cleo looked up into his sea-blue eyes and laughed. "Ha, a few bottles of rum to you but liquid gold to me."

Laughter rumbled from deep within his chest. "What am I going to do with you, woman? Come on, down the hatch with you." She trembled against him as he held her close.

Cleo looked up at him, lips parted. "I'm half frozen. Maybe an evening down below decks wouldn't be such a bad idea."

Bill chuckled again and pulled open the hatch.

High on the mainmast, a lookout shouted down. "Boat coming, sir."

Bill's head snapped up to stare at the crow's nest and then out on the roiling water. There, a tiny speck on an angry sea, a small sea skiff was beating its way to the *Arethusa*. Riding the waves up and down, it was being tossed about like a cork.

Bill, Cleo, and Mr. Barney rushed to the side of the schooner to watch the sea skiff come alongside. It was being driven by a stalwart young man with a heavy, dark beard and a grin as wide as the ocean.

The sea burst into foam about him, the wind tore at his clothes. There was a foot of water slopping about in the skiff's bottom. He had one hand on the motor's tiller and the other frantically working the pump to bail the water from the boat.

"Yer mad, boy. Whatchya doing out in this?" Mr. Barney yelled over the roar of the storm.

Cleo squinted against the sea spray. "Harley?" The name was snatched by the wind.

"Fifty cases," the young man shouted.

"Where's yer money?" Mr. Barney shouted back.

Harley was almost tossed overboard as he waved a tight roll of money over his head.

Mr. Barney grabbed a long pole with a net on the end that came in handy for fishing, and extended it toward the small skiff. At that same moment, the waves raised the skiff like an elevator until the crew of the tall-masted schooner had come eye to eye with the fool-hardy customer.

Bill gripped the gunnels of his ship as waves crash over, the deck awash. "Son, you don't want to haul more than twenty-five cases in that boat of yours. If you had any sense, you'd be ashore, anyhow."

Cleo reached back to grab the shroud netting attached to the mast and hung on.

"Fifty cases. I know my boat." Harley, wind tearing at his coat, stood firm in his small craft. He placed the roll of money in the net and grinned while the crew onboard cussed him plenty, but admired his nerve.

"It's Harley Andrews from 'Gator Joe's," she yelled, swinging with the roll of the ship.

Bill scooped the money out of the net. He passed it to Cleo, then looked from her, to Harley, and back again, shaking his head. "You're both mad."

The small boat dropped from sight as a rolling wave carried the *Arethusa* high. Bill called to his first mate. "He made it out here, let's get him loaded."

"Aye, skipper."

Holding the small skiff with oars and boathooks so it didn't smash against the *Arethusa*, the crew slid burlap-wrapped bags of liquor across the slippery deck from the cargo held. They worked with the timing of the waves as they passed them over to Harley, the small boat rising as the schooner sank on a trough as though they were on alternating elevators.

A next towering swell lifted the *Arethusa* high. As she was lowered on the back side of the wave, the same roller heaved the sea skiff aloft and literally floated it onto the schooner's deck. Cleo gasped. Clutching the mast and hanging on so she wasn't swept overboard, she watched as the crew, waist deep in water, struggled to get the skiff clear before the schooner rose again.

As they pushed the small craft clear, Bill and Harley threw back their heads and laughed with the sheer joy of the moment. The wind whipped the hat off Bill's head, tossing it into the crashing waves.

"Tie her down, boys. There's another roller coming." Bill shouted, his words whipped away in the wind.

With the small craft lashed to the *Arethusa*, the last of the liquor was loaded. Bill tossed a ham to Harley and, in a moment of relative calm, shouted over. "What drags you out in this? Can't be greed," Bill asked.

"My girl, sir. We're getting hitched. Deserves the best of everything. She's worth taking risks for. Three thousand a trip."

"Son, I'm buying you a whiskey next time I'm ashore. See you at this 'Gator Joe's place."

"'Gator's burned, Captain McCoy, sir. New place opens soon. Miz Cleo knows where to find it."

Mr. Barney untied the lines securing Harley's skiff and gave it a shove. Hands on either side of his mouth, he bellowed across the water. "Yer loaded, lad. God speed."

The *Arethusa* rose again and, for a moment, they lost sight of Harley. With the returning wave, he took a hand off the side of his skiff to wave to Cleo and give Bill a sharp salute.

Hand over hand, Cleo pulled herself along the side railing to stand at the edge of the ship and shout into the wind. "You take care out there, Harley Andrews."

Wrapping an arm around Cleo and holding her tight, Bill followed suit, "Fair winds and following seas, Andrews."

And, for a few more minutes, the fair winds prevailed. The lookout in the crow's nest hollered down. "Pirates off the port bow."

"Does no one have the sense to stay ashore?" Bill strained, looking out over the water but could see nothing. Closer, though, he knows Harley was still right beside the ship. Yelling his name to get his attention, Bill picked up a sawed-off shotgun with six loads of buckshot in the magazine and tossed it over the side of his ship to Harley. "Burn them up if you need to. Always open season on pirates."

Harley picked it up from the bottom of his boat where it had fallen. "Appreciated, sir. I'll return it when you buy me that whiskey," Harley shouted as the storm once again began to gather force. He gripped the tiller and turned his skiff to home. Somewhere across the inky blackness was the coast of Florida and safe harbor.

Bill McCoy stood beside the forward Colt-Browning machine gun and watched Harley bear off. He wiped the salt from his eyes, straining to see into the darkness.

"There, skipper," Mr. Barney said, pointing to an approaching boat on the far side of Rum Row. Hijackers, in a large speedboat, come around the *Arethusa* and spotted Harley. There was a shout as they gave chase. Bill could see neither the pirates' boat nor the men, only a white blur of water thrown up by her bow as the pirates jam the throttle up to pursue the skiff.

"I see 'em." Training the Colt-Browning on the pirates, Bill gave a burst of cover fire for Harley to build up a lead. He grinned as he imagined the cursing and yelling from the pirate boat as they sheered away. Bill gave another burst of firepower. "That'll teach 'em. Bastards."

Both boats were swallowed by the night and the raging storm.

"I hope he makes it," Cleo said, her body rocking against Bill's hard frame.

Bill grabbed held of her waist and pulled her closer. "Oh, he will. He's got saltwater in his veins and an eager gal on shore waiting for him."

CHAPTER 7

The storm blew itself out overnight. By morning, the sky was clear, and steam rose from the ground as the heat began to build.

Deep in the Everglades, the damp air was thick enough you could slice it like bread. Against this heat, a tall woman, raven hair pulled into a crown on her head, moved quietly around a small campsite. Cassandra was Miccosukee Seminole, one of the original people of Florida—one of a long line of wise women who looked inward to see the other side of the horizon.

The past six months, since she showed up at the end of Edith's dock, bringing water and other supplies right after the fire, had been months of adjustment for Cassie. It no longer hurt to breathe when she thought of her ward and nephew Leroy's absence. Causing more pain was his happiness at living with Edith. Since the fire, the boy had wound up visiting every few weeks for a few hours or days, and the camp would ring with laughter again. The pain around her heart didn't restart until he disappeared into the Everglades to head back to his new home.

It was the hardest thing she'd ever done, watching the boy go. She may have been the one that had sent him away, but it didn't make the hurt any less. He had been ten at the time—and growing up fast. She knew in her head that it was for the best. An isolated camp in the Everglades was no place for a curious, adventurous boy. His frustration at being kept away from town was rubbing a blister on their lives together and so he had to go if they were going to keep any kind of closeness. It was time for him to make his own way, but Lord, it pained her heart.

When Leroy had initially gone to Edith's, Cassie had debated about moving back into town to be closer to him. It was lonesome living way out in the swamp, and the risk of running into Brother Silas was less without the boy. But after seeing the violence and destruction that had rained down on 'Gator Joe's and Edith, she'd panicked. The town was no place for her on a long-term basis. No, she'd slip in and out to do her tarot readings and to pick up supplies, but she'd stay put in the Everglades, hidden and secure. Edith had the strength to look after the boy and keep him safe.

To fill the emptiness of the camp, all she had for diversion was watching the people and happenings in Coconut Grove through her tarot cards. The readings also served as her early warning system, keeping her inner eye on Leroy and hopefully preventing him from getting into trouble.

Sitting at a rough table in her chickee, an open-air gazebo-like structure topped with a thatch of palm leaves, Cassie drew a card from the deck and studied it.

The King of Wands held a blossoming staff in his hand, a symbol of life and creativity. The throne he was sitting on and the cape he wore were decorated with lions and salamanders, both symbols of fire and strength. The salamanders, biting their own tails, represented infinity and the ongoing drive to move forward against all obstacles.

"Well, hello handsome. What brings you to this part of the 'glades? I love the King of Wands— he's pure fire energy. I wonder how you fit into the stories today?"

Cassie addressed an empty chair across the table from her. Talking about the cards showed her was a habit from her customer readings. Her voice slipped into the sing-song patter of the Fortune Teller. "You had a clear vision of where you want to go. Others gravitate toward you because you are charismatic, focused, and determined."

She chuckled and put the card down. "I know I'm spending too much time alone when a man on a card gets my pulse racing." She patted the loose tendrils of hair back into place. "I can't help it, tho'. I love that direct, robust man-of-action approach of yours, your Majesty." She kissed the card and set it aside. "Ha, I hope you're a real man, and not just some kind of symbol."

Gazing unfocused into the dark forest that surrounded her, she stroked the card she'd left lying on the table. She laughed. "I know, I bet that Edith is about to have a romantic adventure. Oh, isn't she the lucky girl? A powerful man like you doesn't come around too often."

Cassie sighed deeply. "I miss romance. It wasn't like I had parties and picnics to go to when I lived in Coconut Grove, but it was nice to be with people: church on Sunday, working with the gals at the fish market. Oh, the stories they'd tell. I was just a slip of a thing then and ears too big for my age. These days, they talk about how times are changing with flappers and the 'new woman' and all, but they never heard those gals' stories. The more things change, the more they stay the same."

Cassie's aching heart lurched as her laughter echoed around the camp and died away. She took in the empty campsite and the edges of the dark forest. The only sounds were the wind, the birds, and the bugs.

Leroy. My Koone.

Cassie sighed again, gathered the cards, then shuffled. She closed her eyes and focused deep within. "Let's see, what else was going on in Coconut Grove."

She fanned them face down in front of her. Her hand hovered along the arc until she felt the familiar tug of a card wanting to be seen.

She turned it over and looked at a young boy wearing a blue tunic with a floral print and a beret on his head. He stood on the shore, the wavy sea behind him, holding a cup in his right hand. Surprisingly, a fish had popped its head out of the cup and was looking at the young man.

Cassie raised her head and spoke to the phantom in the extra chair. "Pages are often the messenger cards in the deck. The fish and the sea represent the element of water and all things to do with creativity, intuition, feelings, and emotions. And the surprise appearance of the fish means that creative inspiration often comes out of the blue and only when you are open to it." Cassie giggled. "Put the Page together with the King and you have nookie. Lucky Edith gets it all. A normal life near town, then Leroy, and now this king. Sweet romance, or maybe not so sweet? More like spicy, naughty romance. The best kind for a gal like Edith."

Cassie scooped up the cards and wrapped them in silk. *Enough of this. Time to get some water on to boil for supper.* She laughed to herself as she went down the chickee's steps and over to the campfire.

"You're a lucky girl, Edith Duffy. The Page of Cups is a sure sign that romance is in the air. There's a bit of magic headed your way, *ah-ma-chamee*. I wish it was me. I hope you can open your heart to it."

Chapter 8

When Edith had first seen 'Gator Joe's, she was certain she'd arrived at her destiny. And she ran with it: putting blood, sweat, and tears into reviving it and creating a lively blind-tiger. But that dream was destroyed in the fire which almost killed her. Undaunted, Edith made the decision to rebuild while she was still injured and lying in the ashes. Soon after, she reshaped her ambitions. Rather than rebuild to mimic the original 'Gator's, she seized the opportunity to build a saloon to match the vision in her heart.

Edith didn't want the new place to feel like a backwoods hangout where folks snuck off to drink illegal liquor. Instead, she wanted Mickey's Goodtimes Saloon to be a secret, private club, tucked out of the way. Isolation would be part of the mystique. A place where her patrons would have a sense of discovery and occasion when they arrived.

The structure of the building and the finishes inside lent an air of permanence and stability to Goodtimes. Edith built it with the intention that Goodtimes would remain after Prohibition was over—everyone said the end was coming. She was committed to ensuring Goodtimes would be a central part of the Florida tourism boom she was sure would follow.

To retain the sense of isolation and discovery that arriving patrons would feel, Edith knew she'd need to buy the land around Goodtimes to protect it from future development, and had factored that expense into the cost of rebuilding. She was relentless in her ambition.

Building off her success with the Miami Music nights during the short time she operated as 'Gator Joe's, Edith planed to incorporate other big-city touches to the lineup as soon as she could. Gambling, more entertainment, and the latest fad: mixed cocktails that were all the rage in the resorts and casinos in the city.

It had been a frantic six months, clearing away the old to make way for the new. Keeping an eye on the large crews of contractors from Miami, overseeing Darwin who was managing the rum running business on the side to augment her personal funds, sitting up late into the night to discuss plans, and rising at dawn to turn them into reality. Edith was in her element with the intensive activity and the challenge; a comfort zone was a great place to rest in but nothing ever grew there. At heart she was a risk-taker, thriving on the edge.

Helping her was a willing band of loyalists. Their belief in her was her life's breath through the long dark days. Darwin was her right hand. Cleo and her friend Mae Capone had an intuitive sense of what she was trying to create. There wasn't a task that Leroy and Lucky wouldn't gladly take on. As the walls had risen during the rebuilding, so had their friendship and commitment.

It had taken a few weeks longer than she'd expected but, with the finishing touches in place in the barroom and Cleo's delivery of premium liquor, Edith let it be known around town and at the Dinner Key Coast Guard Station that Goodtimes was open for business. It wasn't a grand opening, but rather a test run to make sure everything in the new establishment would work smoothly.

Edith threw open the front doors, inviting the public into Goodtimes. As she stood in the doorway, she inhaled deeply. To her, the night smells were alive with possibilities, whether from the cool, damp air left behind by the day's light rain, or the lingering scent of fresh paint and plaster. It mattered naught to Edith, and memories of 'Gator Joe's dissipate much like the day's earlier squall.

The word-of-mouth campaign produced a few early patrons.

"Welcome to Goodtimes. How'd you hear about us?" Edith asked a group of men who'd settled at a table.

"We were at a casino in Miami. Meyer Lansky said we should check this place out. Said he knows the owner."

"Does he now? Well, now you do, too. I'm Edith Duffy and I own Goodtimes. What can I get you?"

One of the men leaned back, looking up at her and whistled. "A dame owning a joint like this? He didn't mention that part." He winked at his companions.

"Well, she does. Now, what can I get you folks?"

There was a confident swagger to her hips as Edith headed back to the bar to pull together the order. Goodtimes wasn't just a lovely place to live and work, it had to make money, too. Having folks drive up from Miami, even before the hoopla of a Grand Opening, was a positive sign Goodtimes would be as successful as she believed it could be. If Edith had anything to say about it, customers would be lining up out the door.

Edith was mixing cocktails at the bar when another group walked in. Her face lit up at the sight of her favorite regulars. "Harley. Billy. Good to see you. Are you folks ready for a good time tonight?" She'd been working on the new slogan.

"Ha. Good times at Goodtimes." Harley Andrews grinned, slapping Billy Shaw on the back. "I get it."

Nancy, tucked under Harley's arm, grinned up at him. "Let the good times roll?"

"Oh, Nancy. That's even better," Edith said. "You get a free drink on the house for that. What'll it be, folks?"

"Black Jack Rootshines for Billy and me. Nancy'll have a cola."

"That was a great turn of phrase you had, Nancy. How about I make you something special to celebrate? I won't put any booze in it. Maybe something with pineapple juice?"

Nancy giggled. "Thanks, Miz Edith. That would be swell."

"Okay, go grab a spot and I'll bring these drinks over. Did you want anything to eat? Lucky's made up some gumbo that smells delicious."

"Just the drinks tonight. Next time we'll come earlier and have supper. What'd you say, Nance?"

Nancy nodded, and the trio head off to a table near the stage.

"You going to start bringing in bands from Miami again, Miz Edith?" Billy asked. "Those sure were some great nights." Billy Shaw worked as a senior mechanical engineer at the Coast Guard's Dinner Key station. He'd been one of Edith's regulars since 'Gator Joe days and was responsible for the large crowd of guardsmen that called 'Gator Joe's 'their' saloon, and hopefully would do the same for Goodtimes.

Edith set their drinks down.

"Of course. And we have a few other entertainment ideas up our sleeves. Gave us a few weeks to get things booked. I wasn't sure when we'd actually be open."

"Well, we're real glad you are. Aren't we, Nancy?" Harley said. "This place is something, Miz Edith."

Lowering her head, Nancy smiled into her frothy piña colada sans rum. "Yummy, this is delicious."

"We'll call it Nancy's Nectar. Just for you."

Nancy giggled and Harley beamed with pride.

The tables filled and drinks were poured. Lucky's gumbo disappeared, and Leroy was kept busy bussing tables and washing dishes.

Darwin brought in few more bottles of Chivas and Gordon's gin from the shed. "Deputy Roy is at the kitchen door, Edith. Said he needs to talk to you."

"Thanks, Darwin. Can you watch the bar?"

Edith walked through the dark, unfinished kitchen. A shadowy figure lurked at the screen door. He was a silhouette against the kerosene lamps burning in the kitchen tent behind him, the sides rolled up to catch the breeze. There, she could see Leroy standing at the washtub, up to his elbows in sudsy water.

She pushed open the screen door where Deputy Roy Purvis was waiting, hat in hand.

"Roy? What were you doing out here? What's up?" Edith asked, stepping outside to join him.

"Evening, Miz Edith. I didn't want to disturb you in the bar, but we need to talk a bit of business."

"Oh? was there a problem with our regular eye-doctor contribution? I thought we were up to date on the look-away money."

"I'm going to have to double the size of your contribution, Miz Edith. Expenses are going up and with the bigger place you got now... well, you understand."

"No, I don't understand, Roy. We're just getting our feet back under us. I was expecting an increase, but double? That seems steep."

"Ah, Miz Edith. There's some included in there for the extra trouble I have to deal with, now you've reopened. You wouldn't believe the fuss you've stirred up at the church. You're all they talk about at choir practice. My wife, Bernice? She's in the choir, and they are so riled up and contrary about Goodtimes they float upstream instead of down. Every day she tells me to close you down."

"And what about the other blind-tigers around? Is she as upset about them?"

"Of course, she's against them all, but whoo-whee, she does have a special thing about you and Goodtimes." Deputy Roy lifted his hat to rub the back of his neck. "Bottom line is that the contribution is going to double, Miz Edith. And that's that."

"For the record, I don't think it's fair. I should be treated like everybody else."

"Ain't that the truth? Although you sure ain't like everybody else, are ya?"

"It is what it is, I suppose. I'll bring it by the sheriff's office tomorrow."

"Much appreciated, Miz Edith. I'll get off your porch and let you get back to your guests. When are you planning the grand opening for? Folks in town will want to know."

"I'm thinking in a couple of weeks. We'll be bringing a band out from Miami, and Lucky plans to roast a whole pig on the beach."

"I sure do love a pig roast." Deputy Roy tipped his hat and left her, stopping at the kitchen tent to say hi to Lucky and Leroy.

"Everything okay?" Darwin asked when she got back to the bar.

"Sure. It was an expensive trip though."

Edith explained the increase in look-away rates. "I was struck by the attitudinal adjustment Deputy Roy's undergone. Last year he was happy to waltz through the front door and tonight he's hat in hand at the kitchen door."

"New place, new approach. Goodtimes says something about who you are in this town, and that you mean to stay."

Edith grinned. "Whatever is causing it, I like it. Let's hope I can afford it."

Edith and Darwin looked out at the Monday night crowd. Almost all the tables were full of people drinking and laughing and having a good time.

"It looks like you'll be able to keep poverty from the door," Darwin said dryly.

Edith chuckled and flicked her bar towel at him.

CHAPTER 9

Only the first evening, and a test trial at that—without official Miami invites or a booked band— and customers kept coming in the door. Even though she was scrambling, Edith loved every minute of it. Everything she'd dreamed about with Goodtimes was taking shape. The room buzzed with happy customers, Darwin and Leroy were hauling empty bottles out and full bottles in and, late as it was, Lucky was still serving up gumbo to lip-smacking diners.

Edith leaned against the wall, overwhelmed with relief and overcharged with anticipation. Suddenly, she went weak-kneed. A stranger had appeared in the doorway. Her heart stopped and time stood frozen. He was a towering man, slim-waisted and long-limbed. His steady eyes survey the grand room. There was a regal thrust to his jaw, and his authority and command of the room was like a mantel draped casually around broad shoulders.

Edith shivered as the large barroom suddenly seemed dwarfed, almost claustrophobic. Then her heart leapt, time restarted, and the usual noises of a busy saloon rush in.

The powerhouse at the door opened his mouth. "Harley? Is that you? Dang, it's good to see you still alive, son." His voice boomed like a foghorn.

"Captain McCoy. Come sit with us, sir."

Bill McCoy joined the table with Billy and Nancy and a few other Coast Guard members.

"This your special gal? Hope you know how lucky you are. This young man thinks the world of you." He and Harley spun the tall tale of Harley landing the boat on the deck of Bill's ship and outrunning the Wharf Rats. Folks around the table roared with laughter as Bill slapped Harley on the back.

Edith smiled, picked up her tray, and sashayed over.

"Welcome to Goodtimes." Her tummy flipped as he smiled up at her.

"Let the good times roll," Harley said, raising his glass in a toast and winking at Nancy.

"That's what they say in New Orleans: *laissez le bon temps rouler*." Bill's easy grin widened to a smile as his gaze traveled up and down Edith.

Mute and breathless, Edith was lost.

"Miz Edith, this here's the best rum runner on the Row: Captain Bill McCoy," Harley said.

Snapping out of her daze, Edith blushed. "A pleasure, Captain McCoy."

"That accent. I'd know it anywhere. You're from Philly. I grew up there nosing about the wharves along the Delaware like a bird dog ranges a stubble field."

"You're right. How wonderful you noticed. I haven't been back since I moved here to Florida. But I used to live in Overbrook. You must know it. A small place along the Main Line." Edith babbled, then gulped to stop it.

"I know a few folks out that way. But we have a mutual friend closer to home. Cleo Lythgoe is traveling with me on the *Arethusa*."

"Cleo? How wonderful. She's been here almost every week with orders helping get our shelves stocked for our opening. Please tell her I said hi."

"Will do. That gal's my good luck charm. Word spreads up and down the Row that the Queen of the Bahamas is on board and soon buyers in their contact boats are coming out in droves."

Throughout the night, Edith kept her eye on Bill. She warmed and smiled as the surf boomed through his words and the crowd hung on to his every word.

Such an interesting man. And obviously famous. Harley claims he's where the phrase 'the real McCoy' comes from.

Even as she pulled cold beer from the cooler, she was drawn to check on him. *Cleo never mentioned she was on his ship. Or what a handsome man he is. And the captain of a rum running schooner.*

It was the same when she was wiping tables; she couldn't keep her eyes from straying. *I should talk to Cleo about him. I bet she has some interesting stories.*

Finally, back behind the bar, Edith sipped a martini she'd poured for herself. *I wonder if Cleo might turn her hand to a bit of matchmaking? I'd love to get to know Captain McCoy better.*

As Darwin approached, Edith kicked at where she thought a wooden crate of empty bottles was, eventually connecting to rattle it. "Can you take these empties to the shed? Oh, and bring back some oranges for the cocktails."

Darwin followed her gaze to the captain, then rolled his eyes. "Sure thing. I'll get right on it, Edith."

The McCoy table was the last to leave. Edith was amused by the strange alliance of a notorious rum runner and Coast Guard Ensign Billy Shaw. Both he and Harley were enthralled by the captain.

Tray in hand, she moved in to clear their table. "I'm glad you could make it in tonight, Captain McCoy. I understood from Cleo that night-time was your work-time on Rum Row."

"That is the truth, but I had to bring a delivery to Miami myself—thought while I was away from the ship I'd check out your place. Cleo's been raving about the plans—and about you, and I can see why." He leaned over and slapped Harley on the back. "And I owed this young fella a whiskey. It's a calm night and a good one to slip away and leave things in the hands of my first mate."

Relaxed and in full command, he gave Edith a wink. "Although, I've learned to dread the periods when everything looks rosiest. Experience has taught me it's calm times like now when something will blow up in my face. You can say at least one thing about the rum running racket: it's never boring." There might as well have been a lion in front of her; his roaring laughter completely enveloped her.

"Trouble doubled and redoubled," said Ensign Billy Shaw.

"Ah, the exotic life of the rum runner, sailing the high seas. But it's time to call it a night, folks," said Edith. She nodded to Leroy, who, while stacking chairs, hovered as close to Bill McCoy's table as he could. The king had easily won over a faithful page.

"You know, I bet I'd be a good rum runner, Captain McCoy. Maybe sometime you'll take me to sea, sir?" Leroy said.

"From the look on Miss Edith's face, I wouldn't count on it, lad. I bet you're too valuable for her here on shore, working at Goodtimes."

"Leroy can have all the dreams he wants as long as he kept stacking chairs." She redirected Leroy with a warning look.

Folks at the table pushed back their chairs and stood. Bill threw his arm around Harley. "Come on, then. Let's clear out and let the lady close up." Turning to Edith, he dropped the arm and took her hand in both his paws. "Thank you for a wonderful evening, Miss Edith. I'm glad I came."

Edith's pulse raced. "You're too kind, Captain McCoy. Please remember to say hi to Cleo. Tell her I look forward to her next visit."

"Say, I have an idea. Why don't I come back Wednesday morning and run you out to the *Arethusa*? You gals can visit. I'll get Cookie to serve up some lunch, and you'll be home by the late afternoon. Plenty of time to get ready for your supper crowd."

"Why thank you. I'd love to."

"Can I come, too?" Leroy was hopping from one foot to the other.

"If it's okay with Captain McCoy, it's fine with me. But you must come back with me, too. No running off to sea with you, young man."

CHAPTER 10

With Goodtimes open, the days had settled into a routine. The sun came up. It rained. The sun went down. People arrived at Goodtimes thirsty, and left happy. Darwin made perilous journeys back and forth to Rum Row, bringing back boatloads of contraband liquor for Goodtimes' shelves, and for Tucker's place in Cutler. So far it hadn't been too much of an imposition, and Edith was intrigued with what Tucker's order said about his blind-tiger and its customers. No competition for Goodtimes there. In either quality or quantity.

The latest storm had left a few treasures on the beach. Leroy squatted and stared at his cache of liquor bottles buried in the sand. A few months ago, he'd finished reading the book Tom Sawyer. When he had taken it back, the librarian told him that 'there came a time in every boy's life when he had a raging desire to go dig for hidden treasure'.

And mine just floats onto the beach. "Neat."

After every tropical storm and heavy wind, Edith always sent him to clean up the beach. A while back, he'd discovered that sometimes luck shone on him, depositing a reward for his hard work: bottles of liquor thrown overboard by smugglers being chased, or bottles from part of an underwater retrieval system, or bottles simply washed away from wrecks or having been swept off a boat's deck during a storm. Regardless of how they got there, they were his now. Part of the salvage laws, according to Darwin.

Leroy sat on a log next to a covered hole. He'd buried fifteen bottles: gin, rum, whiskey, and brandy in there. *What the heck can I do with them? I could gave them to Darwin to sell with the other smuggled bottles. Nah, then I'd have to give him a cut.*

I could give them to Miz Edith to serve in Goodtimes. Nah, that won't work either. She only sells good stuff and these aren't good. Even I know that.

He shrugged. *I could drink them, I suppose. He wrinkled his nose. Nope. I'm not trying that again. Those couple of sips I took from a half-finished drink after clearing the table in Goodtimes were so disgusting I almost had to puke.*

"Leroy."

Leroy kicked more sand over his cache and ran to the front veranda. "Yes, Miz Edith?"

"Can I get you to walk into town for me? Lucky needs flour. I'd go in the truck, but I'm waiting on telephone calls—bands for next month's entertainment line-up."

"Sure, Miz Edith."

"Can you manage to carry it all the way from town?"

Leroy grinned, striking a muscleman pose. Minutes later he was kicking a rock down the road, some earnings tucked in his pocket along with the extra dime Edith had given him for the errand.

That Tom Sawyer fella sure had it figured out. He got all those kids to paint his fence for him. I'll swing past the library to see if they have anything new in. And I'll stop by the S&P and grab an ice cream for the walk home.

Leroy ambled down the Ingraham Highway. Aunt Cassie called it the Cutler Road. Folks in town say the Main Highway. Leroy didn't bother much for which name people used. On days when he didn't have an errand or jobs at Goodtimes, he'd follow Snapper Creek, which crossed it, back along until he got to Cassie's. The highway was his road to town and his branching off point to the camp in the Everglades.

If I had more money, I could buy Cassie something nice. Maybe a fancy hat like Miz Edith wears? I wonder what Cassie's doing right now?

The road was closely bordered with banyan trees and palmetto palms. Gray Spanish moss dripped down, floating in the breeze. Leroy couldn't see the birds but, oh, the racket they made.

Darwin makes lots of dough being a rum runner. If I sold my gin and whiskey, I could get a Panama hat like he has and make a snakeskin band to go around it. That would be swell. Everybody who saw us would think he was my pa.

As Leroy neared Coconut Grove, the trees thinned out and paving made Ingraham easier to walk on. Leroy usually stepped quickly along it, bare feet on the hot asphalt, but this early in the morning it wasn't too bad. Pretty houses began to line the road.

I wonder which house Cassie grew up in?

Ahead, a paperboy pulled a wagon door to door. Smaller than Leroy, the boy had quite a task; the wagon was full of Miami Heralds from the look of it.

That looks awful heavy to be hauling around in this heat.

The small boy trudged up a sidewalk, knocked at a door, handed over a newspaper and got some money in return. A seed of an idea fluttered to life inside Leroy.

Leroy passed a corner store, went in and bought two bottles of cold pop, then took a seat on the curb in front. A few minutes later the small boy came by on his route.

"You look thirsty," Leroy said. He guzzled down some pop.

The boy's suspicious eyes thirstily followed the drops of condensation that slowly traced down the side of the bottle.

"A friend of mine said he'd meet me here but never showed. I'll sell it to you for two cents." Leroy held the wet bottle toward the boy who was already jiggling coins in his pocket.

"Sure," the boy said, holding out his hand for the bottle.

Leroy waited until the two pennies were in his own hand before he handed it over. He clinked his bottle against the boy's. "Cheers. My name's Leroy. What's yours?"

"Jay." He sat on the curb next to Leroy and took a deep swig from the bottle, then burped. The boys laughed.

"Whatchya doing?" Leroy asked.

Jay turned and nodded to the wagon of newspapers behind him. "Collection day."

"Oh. So you're selling them newspapers?"

Jay looked at Leroy sideways. "Not exactly. Folks buy a subscription from the newspaper office. I deliver them to their houses and then go around every Monday and collect what they owe."

The pop slipped down nicely.

"You ever read Tom Sawyer, Jay?"

"Sure. It's one of my favorites. Why?"

"What do you think of Huck Finn?"

"I'd love to skip town and have adventures along the Mississippi like he does."

"You should come out to where I live. We got 'gators out there."

Jay shrugged. "Sure. Where do you live?"

"Outside of town. I work for a lady who runs a blind-tiger. You know what that is?"

Jay made a face. "Of course I do. It's a saloon where they sell illegal liquor, and there are pirates there, and the men are all drunk."

Leroy looked askance at Jay. Town kids weren't the smartest. "Yup. That's about the size of it. It can get a little wild and woolly when I'm working out there."

Both took another long swig of soda pop.

"How about Saturday?" Leroy asked.

"Saturdays are bad. I gotta help my pa at the shop. He looks after people's boats, and I help him on Saturdays. How about Sunday? It would have to be after church and I'd need to be home for supper."

"The next couple of weeks are crazy busy. I'm going to go out to Rum Row on Wednesday."

Jay's eyes go big. "Wow"

Leroy gives him a small grin and then shrugged. "No big deal. And then we got this big party happening out at Goodtimes. I'm going to help Lucky roast a whole pig on the beach. How about the Sunday after that?"

"How far is it?"

"Not too far. I can walk it in half an hour. It might be longer for you," Leroy said, giving Jay a gentle nudge. "Just kidding."

"Gee, I'm going to a blind-tiger to see 'gators. How neat is that?"

"How about I meet you here in two weeks? That Sunday after lunch? We can walk out together."

"Swell." Jay picked up the handle of the wagon and handed the empty bottle back to Leroy. "For the deposit."

* * * *

"Who's that sitting with the Carmichael boy?" The Boss was staring out the Sheriff's Office window, hands clenched behind him.

"Who?" Deputy Roy Purvis came over to get a better look. "Oh, that's the kid out at Edith Duffy's place."

The Boss continued to stare out the window at the boy, hands rhythmically clenching. Deputy Roy watched them, mesmerized.

"Really? I thought I knew him from somewhere else. Her son?"

"No, I don't think so. The chatter amongst the ladies is that he just showed up there one day."

The Boss smirked. "Trust them to know. It doesn't surprise me though. A Jezebel like that must have a lot of dirty little secrets."

Deputy Roy checked out the window to see if he'd missed something. "Just a couple of kids," he said. He struggled to understand the Boss' ongoing fascination with Mrs. Duffy. *Sure, the dame is a looker, but the way he's always harping on how evil she is... It gives me the creeps.*

"I imagine she's fond of the boy," the Boss said, eyes focused on the two boys.

The officer grew restless waiting for the Boss. He silently reread the notices posted on the bulletin board by the front door.

The Boss tilted his head to one side. "He remind you of anyone?"

Deputy Roy returned to the window. "There's some Seminole in there from the look of it," said the deputy, taking a closer look at Leroy.

"Did you increase the collection from her like I told you to?"

Back and forth between the boy and the woman. Them two are surely stuck deep in his craw. "Yes, Boss. She wasn't too happy about it, but she paid."

The Boss broke off his study of the two boys and turned to the Deputy.

A small bead of sweat rolled down Roy's forehead. He wiped it with the back of his hand. "Oh, right. Sorry, Boss. The money from the Duffy woman. I was just getting to it."

After he'd turned over the take, the Boss returned a few dollar bills to the collection agent cum Deputy.

"This is less than I usually get."

"A penalty for tardiness," the Boss said with a sneer.

"But—"

"You have a problem with that?" The Boss appeared to loom larger, the sun disappearing behind the clouds, casting deep shadows in the room.

"Seeing as she's got a bigger place and making more money, I just thought—"

"Thinking. Your first mistake, Deputy. Make it your last one."

Roy stared down at the counter and swallowed.

The Boss returned to his surveillance, but the boys had gone. "There could be a small bonus for you at some point, but you'll have to earn it."

"What do I have to do?"

"I want you to raid that Jezebel's new place."

"Oh, Boss. That will be tricky. You see, the sheriff in Miami— he's the head honcho in charge of the law out here—has some kind of deal with Mr. Lansky. We're to lay off her except for protection money. I go and raid the place I'll be in trouble. I work for him, too, you know."

The Boss gave up his vigil. His eye contact drained the blood from Roy's face. "Then I guess it's a question of whom do you fear more, Deputy: the sheriff and Mr. Lansky in Miami, or me here in Coconut Grove? And remember, you have used up your chances for making the wrong decision."

CHAPTER 11

Edith parked the truck in front of the post office and glanced up and down the street. Coconut Grove was such a pretty little town; she'd enjoy spending more time there if the people were friendlier. From the moment she bought 'Gator Joe's, the town had seemed against her.

Should I get something new to wear out to the ship tomorrow? Maybe pick up some fresh fruit for Captain Bill and his crew? I'll stop by the green-grocer before I head home and see what they have. A bag of oranges might go over well.

"Morning, Miz Edith. You sure look happy. Things going well with the new building?" Jasper asked from behind the wicket at the post office.

"Morning, Jasper. I have a few posters and some flyers to hand out. We've got Goodtimes' Grand Opening coming up in two weeks. A pig roast on the beach, live music coming out from Miami."

"I'll look after this. I surely do miss them bands of yours, Miz Edith. Nothing against the local fellas mind, but it's always nice to get entertainment from the city. Know what I mean?" He took the posters and exchanged them for her mail. "You've got a letter from that friend of yours from Philly. Did they have a nice honeymoon? I'd love to go to Italy."

Edith checked the return address on one of the envelopes. "This is from a different friend. Not the one that went to Italy."

It had taken her some time to get used to the fact that the postmaster knew everything in town. She has used it to her advantage promoting 'Gator Joe's and now she relied on him to talk-up Goodtimes.

It's like he's some all-knowing being like that wizard in the book Leroy was reading about the girl who got carried away by a tornado. You're not in Kansas anymore, Edith.

She smiled and tucked the envelopes into her handbag.

On her way out, Edith glanced at the notices on the bulletin board. Frowning, she saw that someone had tacked up a notice covering her earlier 'Coming Soon' announcement promising more entertainment at Goodtimes.

Typical, although maybe this kind of petty stuff is better than outright hostility.

Edith uncovered her original poster, removing the offender: the Homemakers' Guild, inviting people to listen to a man from the Florida Children's Home talk about new child labor laws. She smirked.

Too bad it's for today. Although something like that won't draw a crowd.

Edith pinned it lower down, then stood back to admire her own poster. it was *discrete. If anyone doesn't know where or what Goodtimes is, Jasper, our local Wizard of the Post Office, will fill them in.*

At Stella's Café, across the street, Edith settled in with the letter from Sadie. Sadie was the wife of Henry Mercer, her late-husband Mickey's business partner and lifelong friend, Henry Mercer. He'd asked his cousin Darwin to give her a hand out at 'Gator Joe's almost a year ago.

The envelope held treasures: pictures of Henry and Sadie's baby, Harry, Jr. *Although not so much a baby anymore. I wonder if he's walking yet?*

Edith and her friend Maggie were Harry's unofficial aunties. *Perhaps, when the baby's older, Henry and Sadie would bring Harry for a visit. He could play in the sunshine on the beach. It would be good to sit down with Henry over a drink and talk about business. I'd love the chance to tap into his bootlegging experience. And he knows his way around a successful club as well.*

I should write him and ask about delivery systems. Between the breweries he runs and the bootlegging, he'll have some good ideas about how I could set things up. If we do go big, all those runs up and down the Dixie highway will be time consuming and dangerous. The Prohibition agents are always on patrol.

Edith looked up as the waitress put her cup of coffee in front of her. *If we had a local person down near Homestead, Darwin could drop off the liquor closer to the delivery points. A spot on the other side of Key Largo would be handy.*

Of course, if we did that, we'd need to arrange for some kind of storage building. And I'd need to pay off the local sheriff's department. Despite all the extra details, it's an idea worth pursuing.

Edith sips her coffee and read Sadie's letter. News from home always mades her nostalgic. *I could take Leroy to Philly for a visit. Maybe at Christmas? He'd love the snow. We could go sledding. Maybe I could find some ice skates for him to borrow. Wouldn't that be something. Of course, he'd have to wear shoes for the trip.*

She picked up the photograph of Harry. *What a sweetie. He almost didn't have a daddy.* Edith remembers a very pregnant Sadie arriving on Henry's doorstep, her parents having ordered her to leave. Then all the hoops Henry had to jump through, including conversion to the Jewish faith, before they could marry. *They had a lot of hurdles to get over because of Sadie's religion. But their love for each other and Harry was strong enough to pull them through.*

Edith stirred her coffee while taking in the photograph of Harry. *I wonder who Leroy's father is? How could he leave such a great kid? Poor Leroy, all alone. I really need to make it up to Leroy for missing his birthday. I'll pick up that radio he's been after me to get so he can listen to his shows. Maybe I'll get two. I can afford it. One for the kitchen, one just for Leroy. Does he ever have anything else? Maybe his father left him something? Maybe Cassie would tell me who his daddy is, if I promised not to let Leroy know. There's something going on there. She was so spooked when she mentioned the father.*

Edith tucked the letter into her handbag and finished her coffee. *A lady of leisure I'm not. One quick stop at the green-grocer to fill Lucky's list and grab some fresh fruit, pick up the radio—or two— and then home.*

In the store, the freshness was instantly overpowering, and Lucky's list contained some things Edith didn't recognize. *Onions, carrots, yep. Bok choy. I wonder what that is and what he wants it for? I love his hot pots but I definitely don't want to know what's in them.*

The silence got her attention. The shoppers had stopped conversing with each other. *Probably gossiping about me. Kill them with kindness, as Mae always said.* Edith gave them a large saccharine smile which was returned by huffing and turned backs.

Edith was all graciousness as she stepped up to the counter to place her order. When the clerk had everything bagged, except the bok choy, which didn't seem to exist as a food item in Florida, Edith reached for a few candy sticks for Leroy. *And Darwin, too. He's the biggest little boy of the bunch.*

She stiffened at the sniggering behind her. *Old biddies.* One of the women behind her bumped past to put her items on the counter, knocking Edith in the process. The candy in Edith's hand fell to the floor.

"Excuse me." The woman's voice dripped sarcasm.

Leaving the candy on the floor, Edith grabbed her bag and marched out of the store. She slams the truck door, and guns it out of town. Halfway home she bangged her hand against the steering wheel.

"Dang. Stupid women. They made me forget the radio." She began to slow, preparing to turn, then puts her foot back down on the gas. "Oh, well. I'll get it for him next time."

* * * *

Down the street and around the corner, a chattering flock of women file into the Coconut Grove Playhouse. There were frequent 'you-hoos' and air kisses exchanged as gatekeeper, Guild chairwoman Mavis Saunders, greeted attendees at the auditorium entrance.

A younger woman arrived and whispers in Mavis' ear. "It's time to go in, Mrs. Saunders. Daddy Fagg is ready to start. I'll show you how to get backstage."

Watching the audience from the stage wings, Mavis patted her hair and peeked out. *The crowd isn't as large as I'd hoped. I hope Daddy Fagg isn't disappointed.*

At her cue, Mavis walked to the podium, took in a deep breath, and inhaled the crowd's attention. All eyes were on her and she thrilled to the moment.

"Ladies, thank you so much for coming today. Caring for the children of Coconut Grove is a serious calling we are all dedicated to. Remember that it is easier to care for small children than it is to repair broken men." Mavis had handwritten 'smile' in the margin. She looked up from her notes and delivered it.

"I know you're all familiar with the important work that the Children's Home Society of Florida is doing to protect abandoned, abused, and neglected children. These are challenging times for struggling families and we must all work together to keep the little ones safe from harm.

"Today we are honored to had State Superintendent Marcus, who we all know as Daddy, Daddy Fagg, with us to explain what he has been doing up in Tallahassee with his recent success at getting the child labor laws passed. I know, I know, we don't have the oyster canneries or mills like they have in other places. Coconut Grove is a haven from that kind of evil exploitation. But it was important passing that legislation because women's groups across the state spoke with one voice. We were part of the effort that helped push through this important act."

Scattered applause caused her to momentarily lose her place.

74

"We ladies of Coconut Grove took up that cause with our sisters in clubs across the state. We wrote letters and circulated petitions to legislators and the governor. I know that there was backlash, harsh words spoken about whether it was appropriate work for women to undertake. Thanks be that there were enough women with spinal cords starched stiff—women who raised their undaunted eyebrows and said, 'Ah, indeed!' to this masculine mandate—and then went forth and did as they saw fit."

The applause was louder this time.

"This important legislation would not have been passed without a broad coalition and no one knows better than we do how loudly a mother can speak when it comes to looking after the welfare of a child. 'To save a child is to save the world'."

Mavis checked the paper and followed the instructions. 'Smile. Breathe.'

"But you've heard me speak on this before during our meetings, so I won't go on about it. Instead, I know you'll want to listen to someone who is on the front lines. He's a champion of the recent Child Labor Law, is currently working on a Compulsory Education Law and a Wife Desertion Law. A compassionate man. A great leader. Ladies, please join me in welcoming 'Daddy' Fagg."

There was enthusiastic applause as an older, bespectacled gentleman in a white suit made his way to the podium.

Mavis left the stage to watch from the wings.

"Thank you, Mrs. Saunders for that kind introduction. Child labor is a particular evil because it forces children into the harsh world of adult-reality far ahead of schedule, introducing them to vice, fostering illiteracy and ignorance. There are factories, mills, canneries, and mines which prey upon our young ones and turn them into little machines for private gain. Thanks to you ladies and your compassionate hearts, you had vision enough to see that if the child was given a chance for mental, physical, and moral development in its tender years, they would become a much better citizen."

75

Daddy Fagg beamed at his audience and they loved him back.

"We have been fighting for legislation to protect these young innocents for thirty years. And ladies, I am pleased to say that, thanks to your efforts, we have finally accomplished our goal. Legislation has been passed. Florida has its first comprehensive child labor law establishing a twelve-year age requirement for young workers in factories, canneries, workshops, bowling alleys, barrooms, beer gardens, mines, quarries, and places of amusement where liquor is sold. Illegal liquor at the moment, but this legislation will protect them beyond the existence of the Volstead Act.

"However." Daddy Fagg took a dramatic pause before continuing. "While we have won the battle, we have not won the war. And it is a war we will not win without the penalties of enforcement. You have worked tirelessly to pass this legislation and, if the law was worth passing, it is worth enforcing. Sadly, local sheriffs' departments do not take this law seriously. I need your help again to convince them to uphold this law."

Daddy Fagg reached out both arms to embrace his audience.

"Ladies, the soft velvety hands of God's little children are at this moment outstretched in a supplication that comes straight from their precious hearts, praying for relief from their present bondage. Will you and the people of Florida hear their prayers? Will you suffer this intolerable condition of affairs to remain as a blot upon the fair name of the Peninsula State? Our only motive has been to protect the children of Florida... its future citizens. We want them to grow up to be strong physically, intelligent mentally, and right morally."

Thunderous applause rewarded his remarks. While the crowd may have been thin, they made up for it in commitment and zeal for the cause.

In the lobby, the ladies gathered around Daddy Fagg, congratulating him on the legislation and urging him to continue the fight.

"What can we do to help with this enforcement issue, Daddy Fagg?" Mildred White asked.

Mavis sniffed, strategically shouldering Mildred to the back of the group. "Yes, Daddy Fagg, what can the Guild do to help?"

"We don't have any oyster or shrimp canneries here. There are orchards and other farms, but surely it's all right for children to help out on the family farm. Or in family-run businesses? My husband owns a marine engine repair shop down at the pier and our boys sometimes help out," said Mary Carmichael. "I'd hate to think I was contributing to such evil as the exploitation of children."

"Not to worry, dear ladies. Outdoor labor such as farm work is a positive experience that builds character and improves health. And we all understand that parents know what was best for their own children when it comes to working in the family business. What we're talking about is something very different. Children, babies really, as young as five or six standing long hours barefoot on cold cement, in slime and filth, sorting and plucking in places like the canning factories. Their tender young hands are scarred from the knives. They are cold and hungry. At the end of a twelve-hour shift, their crippled bodies can barely carry them home. That is the evil we must fight against."

Mary Carmichael and Mavis Saunders both raise hands to their hearts, overcome with the image. The remaining women turn to each other with shocked expressions. "Oh, my goodness. I wish we had a factory like that here so we could close it down," Mildred said in a passionate voice.

"My goodness, there must be something we can do," Agnes said. "Mavis, how can the Guild fight against this evil practice?"

"The Florida Children's Home, which was founded by Daddy Fagg, has been very active safeguarding the youth in our communities, including here at Coconut Grove," Mildred White said, stepping forward to stand near Daddy Fagg.

"As director of fair town's local Children's Home, Miss White will undoubtedly play an important role in your efforts. She has experience and, of course, my ear, should a situation arise."

Mildred blushed and stammered her thanks. "Of course, Daddy Fagg. I'd be honored to help. The Homemakers' Guild and the Children's Home often work together in the interests of the community."

Mavis regarded her with narrow eyes.

Daddy Fagg tucked his fingertips into his vest pockets, rocking back on his heels. "Coconut Grove is indeed a blessed place to be spared the evils of the cannery or the mill. But there may be hidden pockets of evil amongst you. The young children of Ybor City who had been spending long days rolling cigars are an example. Or the newsies on the street corners of Miami, up at dawn and fighting over pennies. Or the telegram messengers working all hours."

"My son Jay delivers newspapers to people's homes. Do you think he might be being exploited?" Mrs. Carmichael's brow wrinkled with concern.

"Street corner newspaper delivery in the big cities like Miami is a different beast entirely, good woman. I'm talking about orphans fighting for territory. I'm confident the Miami Herald has an adequate arrangement for their home delivery out here in Coconut Grove." Daddy Fagg smiled kindly at Mary, who look relieved.

Mildred turned to the other women in the group. "Ladies, it's come to my attention that there is a very young boy working in a blind-tiger just outside of Coconut Grove. I shudder to think of his circumstances." The women leaned close to listen. "He's not yet twelve. Imagine the vice and wickedness he's seen with his tender eyes."

Agnes, who had been standing beside Mavis, took hdld of Daddy Fagg's arm. "And I've heard that he's not her son, so it's not a family business. The only trade he's learning out there is criminal."

Mildred took a step closer to Daddy Fagg. "Is this the enforcement you spoke of, Daddy Fagg? Our way of contributing to the cause. Of being able to root out the hidden pockets of evil here at home?"

"Exactly, my good woman. Be resourceful. Evil can be found even in paradises like Coconut Grove."

Mavis squared her shoulders. "This may be the very thing for our Homemakers' Guild members can take on as their next project. Coconut Grove has come to expect our leadership, ladies. We need to do something about that woman running the blind-tiger, leading our men astray. Remember what Brother Silas preaches."

"She's absolutely shameless. The way she looks. And all that liquor," Agnes said, glancing at a nodding Mavis.

"Don't forget we want to help the young boy," Mary Carmichael added.

Mildred, glancing at Mavis and then Daddy Fagg, stepped forward. "The Children's Home would work closely with the Homemakers' Guild, of course. With the Children's Home taking a lead role in the investigation and apprehension of the boy. What do you think, ladies? Is this a cause we can take on—together?"

The women surrounding Daddy Fagg nodded and smiles with excited murmuring about shutting down the blind-tiger.

Mavis smirked at Mildred and stepped forward, forcing Daddy Fagg to step back. "Working with local authorities to represent the best interests of the community is the role of the Homemakers' Guild. The very existence of Goodtimes is a stain on Coconut Grove and our good influence."

From the edge of the group, Mary Carmichael put her hand up to get everyone's attention. "closing the blind-tiger is one thing, but we keep forgetting about saving the boy. The reason for our concern. Daddy Fagg, you spoke about those tender hands reaching for help. Do you think we should become involved in answering his plea?"

The women stare at Daddy Fagg with a fierce intensity that made him step back even further. "Gentle women of Coconut Grove. You know best what you need to do to keep your little lambs safe from harm."

CHAPTER 12

The number of hours in each day doubled as Edith waited for Wednesday to arrive. She ran through the brief conversations she had shared with Bill McCoy, sifting through his words for hidden meanings. When she closed her eyes, she saw him, and in her dreams... well, her nights were mighty restless.

As promised, on Wednesday morning, Captain McCoy guided the *Arethusa's* small runabout dory to Goodtimes. Edith and Leroy formed an enthusiastic welcoming committee at the end of the dock.

"This is swell, Captain McCoy. I've never seen a big ship up close. Is it like a pirate ship? When we get there can I go up to the crow's nest? I'm a really good climber."

"Whoa, there, lad. How about we get out there first, get you two safely aboard the *Arethusa,* then you can go exploring with one of the crew."

During the trip out to his schooner, Bill and Edith used their Philly connection to fall easily into conversations about childhoods, hopes, and dreams. For the younger audience member, Bill wove in adventure stories from his time at sea. Leroy was spellbound, and Edith was constantly reminded of Mickey: both men were rulers of their kingdoms with crews of loyal vassals, and there was that sense of power and control that radiated with every word and deed. *Does Bill have Mickey's selfishness?*

The forty-five minute trip to the *Arethusa* seemed to be over in a heartbeat. Before they knew it, the mighty ship came into view. At one hundred and thirty feet, the two-masted Gloucester schooner was truly magnificent. For once, Leroy was speechless.

"Oh, Bill. It's a beautiful ship. Can I call her graceful?" Edith said.

"Aye, that's the perfect word for her. I've got several ships working Rum Row, but the *Arethusa* is my favorite. See there? Her long, low hull speaks of speed and style. As you say: grace. Her main boom is seventy feet. That there, along the top of her mainsail, is the gaff with a sixty-foot hoist. The first time I saw her she reminded me of a great lady entering a ballroom: elegant and majestic. I think, though, that I'll have to add graceful to the description."

They pulled alongside the ship and Bill's first-mate, Mr. Barney, helped them board.

"Edith. Ducks. You're here," Cleo wrapped Edith in a hug; laughter and kisses all around. "And Leroy, too. Welcome aboard, lad."

Bill introduced Edith to his senior crew. they were all big, two-fisted men. "Ideal when there is dangerous work to do, but hell raisers if you let them idle," Bill explained, chuckling.

"They're certainly... hairy," Edith said, causing much laughter and back slapping.

"Aye, they are that. But there's a purpose to it. Their beards are to avoid recognition when their rum running is behind them. And, what's more, the schooner has been out a long time and fresh water is scarce, so they rarely wash," Bill said.

"They look like Airedales and smell like camels," Cleo said with a twinkle in her eye.

"Captain McCoy, can I go explore the ship?" Leroy said, tugging at Bill's sleeve.

With a warning about falling overboard, Bill assigned the cabin boy to show Leroy around. In a blink, Leroy was scrambling up the shrouds, a climbing net made of heavy rope connecting the side of the ship to the masts. When he reached the platform known as the lubber's hole on the main mast, he leaned over and waved.

"Is he safe up there?" Edith said, shading her eyes to watch him.

"It's Bill's cabin boy I'm worried about. Leroy climbs like a monkey. He's a natural sailor," Cleo said, her eyes tracing Leroy's nimble movements.

Edith returned the wave, then faced Bill. "Tell me more about this beautiful ship."

"It was the best day of my life, Edith. I was standing on a Gloucester pier-head when I first saw her. It was toward sunset and the air was light, so she seemed a ghost as she came into the harbor's mouth under full sail. She was an aristocrat, a thoroughbred from her keel to the trucks at the top of her masts."

Edith sighs. "I can just see it. What a magical moment."

"Every man remembers his one true love and *Arethusa* is mine. The late sun turned her spread of canvas golden. She sailed in through the harbor that night and straight into my heart."

Cleo and Edith were amused when Mr. Barney, a grizzled Down-Easterner and born seaman, chuckled and rolls his eyes.

"Laugh all you want. There's strength beneath her beautiful lines. She was to be a high-liner fishing schooner," said Bill. "Landlubbers like you could never understand how much a Yankee-built schooner like the *Arethusa* can withstand. There are no better ships in the world than American fishing schooners, and I've proved it."

"When Darwin bought the *Marianne*, he had to retrofit her for rum running. Did you had to make many modifications?"

Bills nodded. "We added a larger auxiliary motor, of course, and I had to change out her fish pens for more cargo space. That gave us room for eight thousand cases of liquor."

"Which is worth $50,000 net a trip. Not a bad haul for a fishing boat," said Cleo.

Edith glanced between Cleo and Bill, noticing the smile they shared.

"And that's where you come into it?" Edith asked Cleo.

"Remember when I was at your place, I told you my position was called a supercargo?"

"Refresh my memory."

"A lot of the rum running customers ask for me by name. I supply the liquor that Bill or other rum runners take to the edge of international waters off America."

"Right. Rum Row. And what's in it for you? Do you get a slice of the profit from all the booze on board?"

"On mine. Right now, there're only a few bottles of my stock left in this cargo, but Bill also has cargo from a few of the other wholesalers working in Nassau that he's bought outright. His mark-up will be his profit while I sell mine on consignment."

"Do you travel as Bills supercargo often?" Edith asked. *What's going on between these two? Is it just business? Why did Bill ask me out here? To visit Cleo?*

"As much as I can. The *Arethusa's* got great cargo capacity and Bill and his crew are excellent seamen," Cleo said with another smile for Bill.

There's a whole lot of smiling going on here. Edith turned, taking in the details of the schooner. "I see you've also armed the ship," she said, noticing two Colt-Browning machine guns mounted on the deck. Partially hidden in the furled sails were several Thompson sub-machine guns, a half dozen Winchesters, and sawed-off shotguns. Colt forty-fives were strapped to the waists of many of the crew.

"Pirates and the local Wharf Rats make this part of Rum Row dangerous," said Bill, running his hand along the barrel of the aft Colt-Browning.

"Maybe you could give me some advice about pirates and how to deal with them. There's a very good chance we're going to be expanding our rum running business, which means we'll be expanding the danger as well. But first," Edith said, her arm sweeping the horizon, "I want to hear all about this famous Rum Row."

The sweep of her arm took in the long line of vessels that bow to the ocean's surges, swinging with the tide and wind.

"As far as the eye can see, you've got your schooners and yachts, wind-jamming square-riggers from Scandinavia, traps from England and Germany, converted tugs and submarine chasers, and anything else that has a bottom that will float, and a hold that can be filled with booze," Bill said.

"It's like you have your own little neighborhood out here."

"That's exactly right. Rum Row is a roaring, boisterous, 'sinful-and-glad-of-it' marine Main Street. You're looking at about a hundred boats and, come evening, there will be tourists and rubberneckers, boats with jazz bands, and hundreds of contact boats picking up cargo."

"And on the Row, Bill McCoy is the undisputed king," Cleo said as she gazed up at Bill with stars in her eyes.

Okay, maybe something more than a business partnership.

CHAPTER 13

Leroy was in heaven, exploring the *Arethusa*—from being pulled off the spike of the bowsprit at the front of the schooner to pestering the helmsman at the wheel in the stern; from the heights of the lubber's hole on the mainmast to the depths of the cargo held and everything in between.

Edith glanced quickly to the main mast, gasping as she saw Leroy lean over the lubber's hole to watch the gaff pull the sails up the mast.

"He'll be fine, ducks," Cleo said, following Edith's gaze. "I'll watch after him and make sure he doesn't go overboard." At Cleo's urging, Leroy and the cabin boy scrambled down the shrouds and they all went off to explore below decks. She seemed to be enjoying the novelty of having a small boy on board, answering a million questions and seeing the ship through new eyes.

With Cleo firmly focused on Leroy, Edith reveled in Bill's undivided attention. Bill McCoy was an enthusiastic tutor to the intricacies of smuggling liquor on Rum Row, and she was a willing pupil. Not only was this an important part of her business that she needed to understand better, but the lessons were being delivered by a captivating instructor. Her own attention was divided between the nuggets of wisdom he was sharing and watching the wind play with his hair, and those sea-blue eyes of his that were constantly roaming over the water, the ship, the crew, her.

"I've got an understanding with my customers that if the boat is flying the British ensign, they should stay away, but if she has no flag flying, then we're open for business." Bill pointed to an electric light high up in *Arethusa's* rigging. "That light guides contact boats to us and the bucket under the light keeps the deck in darkness as business is conducted."

Edith had been to Rum Row on a nighttime run once with Harley, so it didn't take much for her to picture herself bobbing alongside the ship, the waves, the tension.

"But it's not all glamor and excitement. Our days are spent in dull boredom waiting for the strenuous activity that will began as soon as night falls," Bill said. "Daytime aboard a ship on Rum Row can be tedious."

"So where to, skipper?" Mr. Barney asked.

"Let's hoist the sails and make Bimini for lunch." Bill turned to Edith. "Have you been there?"

"No, but I've heard about it, of course. It's in the Caribbean, right?"

"Aye. You'll get a chance to see how the *Arethusa* handles herself on open water, and then we'll drop anchor offshore Bimini and enjoy the view. Always nice to have a destination."

"Bimini is part of the Bahamas. I'm based out of Nassau, which is also part of the Bahamas," Cleo said, coming up behind Edith. With the crew busy unfurling the sails and hoisting the gaff rigging, Leroy was firmly tucked under one arm.

"From here, we're less than thirty miles away. It will take the *Arethusa* longer because we're under sail, but a fast motor launch could make it in under an hour, two hours from the coast," Bills said, watching his men hoist the main and foresails. The ship lurched as the wind filled the giant sheets.

"While it has gorgeous beaches, Bimini's most attractive quality is the liquor is legal because it's part of the Bahamas."

"I had no idea it was so close."

"The newspapers are always writing stories about the British installing batteries on the island and using it as a base to attack the US, but popping champagne corks are more likely to be heard than artillery shells," said Cleo.

"There were pirates there. I heard about it from my auntie," Leroy said.

"Bimini was the haunt of pirates during the 1600s and 1700s. Its location on the edge of the Gulf Stream made it a perfect place to engage Spanish galleons laden with treasure on their return route to Spain. Sir Francis Drake, Sir Henry Morgan, and Blackbeard all knew Bimini well. Now its proximity to the United States makes it a haven for a different kind of pirate, the rum runners," Cleo said.

"*Argh*," Bill growled in his best pirate voice. Cleo and Leroy giggle.

Throughout the voyage, Edith watched the dynamic between Cleo and Bill. *Was there something between them? It's been ages since I've had a man look at me like that.* She watched as Cleo turned, laughing at something Bill had said. Edith thought back to the way his gaze had traveled over her the night they met.

He was such a flirt at Goodtimes. But maybe he didn't mean anything special by it? Maybe he flirts with all the girls? Too bad for Cleo if he's looking for more. Just like a lot of the like other seamen I've known: a girl in every port. Although, maybe Cleo's not wanting anything more, either? A captain on every ship?

Edith studied him, trying to see behind his general good nature and that crazy bad-boy grin. *I can't understand how Cleo can settle for not being the only one. I have more pride.*

The truth wormed its way through. *Okay, I did it for years with Mickey, but that was different. I found out after we were married.*

Cleo put her hand on Bill's chest and he covered it with his own large paw, smiling down at her. *Cleo's confident and sure of herself. I've never met a woman so comfortable in her own abilities. But surely she wants to get married and find the man of her dreams? And that Bill McCoy is dreamy, alright.*

"Are you enjoying yourself?" Bill joined Edith as she sat on the cockpit roof looking at the water. Her heart pounded as the surf splashed over the bow as the *Arethusa* cuts through the waves. She scanned the deck, searching for Cleo; spied her with Leroy who was working at knots under the guidance of some of the crew.

"Very much." Edith's leg brushed Bill's. She smiled when he didn't pull away.

"You were saying you had a problem with pirates?" he asked.

"This new business expansion is going to put Darwin in harm's way more often. Don't get me wrong, I have a healthy respect for the danger bootlegging both to the business and to Darwin. It's just that its all part of the package. Routine." Edith nodded to the machine guns on the deck. "I'm used to the idea of hijackers. It was part of the business when my late-husband Mickey was bootlegging. There's always violence and guns."

"You're right. It is part of the business. From what I've seen when he's picking up cargo from us, your man Darwin seems capable. When he's out here, he's watching and aware. And he doesn't seem like the type to take foolish chances. He's got a fast boat and, much like when you're being chased by a bear, you only had to be faster than the other fella."

Edith laughed. "I'll keep that in mind."

"I shouldn't make light of it. The Wharf Rats are a nasty bunch, Edith. Hijackers come in all different flavors. Some are greedy, for others it's just a job. From what I've seen of the Wharf Rats, they enjoy the work too much, if you know what I mean. Take things too far. Too quick to shoot."

"I've had first-hand experience. What do you know of the boss?"

"Buford? Keeps his men in check. The most business-like of the bunch. The red-headed fella is the one you have to watch out for. Never turn your back on him."

The sight of Bimini's shoreline was the signal for Cookie to pop his head out of the hatch. "Lunchtime. Time to mug up."

Arm in arm, Cleo and Leroy joined the group. The crew settled in. Frenchie dragged out his violin and Slim grabbed an accordion. The men sang sea shanties, cleaning up the lyrics for Edith's and Leroy's delicate ears.

Bill laughed when he heard the revised lyrics. "It's like we're on a Sunday school picnic and not with a gang of hardened rum runners."

After a chowder lunch, Edith and Cleo sat on the deck and leaned against the masts. The warm sun and the gentle rocking of the ship had Edith more relaxed than she'd been in months. There was a buzz of activity around her that she had no part in; she didn't understand it, was unable to direct it, or to help. She was passive, and it felt good. "I don't think I even care whether we're back in time to open. Darwin can take over that job for once."

"Not to worry. There's no way that Bill would arrive late to Rum Row. You'll be home in time to greet the first customers."

Edith gave a contented sigh. "I can see why you love it out here.

Cleo grinned. "There are days when it's the most wonderful place in the world, and then there are other days when I go balmy, cooped up with all these men."

"Why don't you come stay with me for a few days? We can talk about your new romance." Edith held her breath, waiting to hear how Cleo would respond.

Both women's gaze turned to Bill who was explaining something about the lines and sails to Leroy. "I'd rather talk about Tucker Wilson's opportunity. It sounds like you took him up on his offer."

"I did. We're looking after Tucker's speakeasy, but I'm thinking there's a huge opportunity there beyond just Cutler. My late husband, Mickey, supplied booze to clubs and speakeasies from Philly to Atlantic City. There's no reason why I can't build something like that down here."

Bill wandered over and sat down beside them. Leroy flops down and rested his head on Edith's lap. His eyes closed as Edith stroked his hair.

90

"Will you be staying on Rum Row long?" Edith asked.

"I'm planning to go north to Montauk and Cape May day after tomorrow," Bill said. He glanced at the sun's position. "Let's head back to the Row and I'll take you in with the dory. It will be dark soon and time for us to get to work."

Cleo shook her head and gave a mock shudder. "Sorry, Bill, but the cold Atlantic around Cape May doesn't hold much appeal for me. I'm down to the last few bottles of my own liquor cargo. I trust you to finish the lot up for me. You could pick me up on your way back to Nassau."

She put a hand on Bill's knee. "You know, Bill. I think I'll spend some time ashore visiting with Edith."

Edith beamed. "You could be my first guest in the spare bedroom."

"Go north without my lucky charm? You'll be there at least a week until I can get back." Unlike Edith, Bill looked crestfallen. "Although I've learned you can't argue with Cleo when she's made up her mind, can I darlin'?" He pulled Cleo over to him and she snuggled in his lap.

Edith stiffened, looking away. A small, green claw rakes her heart.

Cleo smiled at Bill. "It's definitely made up. A week with Edith, girl talk, a real bed, and don't forget... she has a bathtub. Heaven."

Approaching the edge of international waters which formed the border for Rum Row, *Arethusa's* crew trimmed the sails, and the ship came about. A welcoming committee of sorts waited just over the invisible twelve-mile line.

The Coast Guard cutter *Mojave* patrolled by. Bill took two bottles of champagne from crates on deck and shook them until corks exploded.

Cleo laughed, turning to Edith. "It's the rum runners salute."

Grinning, Edith put her arm around Leroy and the pair waved to the *Mojave's* guardsmen who were shaking their fists at the impudence of those aboard the schooner.

Bill loaded Cleo, Edith, and Leroy into the skiff and they headed off on the return trip to Goodtimes. Bouncing on top of the waves, the sun overhead, and salt spray in her face; Edith grinned with joy.

Goodbyes were shared at the dock. Before Edith knew it, Bill and his boat had disappeared over the horizon. She, Leroy, and Cleo turned away from the sea.

Leroy, his eyes shining, wrapped Edith in a mighty hug. "That was the best day ever, Miz Edith. Thanks so much for letting me go. I can hardly wait to tell my friend Jay all about it."

Edith gave him a quick squeeze back and mussed his hair. "That ship was something, all right." She unwrapped herself and turned. "Well, let's get you settled in the guest bedroom, Cleo. You're my first visitor."

Leroy grabbed Cleo's bag. "Are you going to marry Captain McCoy?" He smiled shyly up at Cleo.

Edith rolled her eyes. "Sorry about that, Cleo. Leroy's mouth sometimes runs faster than his brain."

Cleo laughed, putting her arm around the boy. "Doubt thou the stars are fire; Doubt that the sun doth move; Doubt truth to be a liar; But never doubt I love."

"Huh?" Leroy's face was scrunched as he wrestled with the unfamiliar words.

What does she mean by that? Definitely more than a business partner. But how much more?

"Hamlet, dear boy. Now, do you had any of that gin left, Edith? I'm dying for one of your famous martinis."

CHAPTER 14

It's often said that money makes the world go round, and never more so than for pirates, smugglers, or rum runners. It's a cash business— where the size of your purse on any given night spells success or failure.

And in this Prohibition world, you might as well reach into that purse and toss a coin to try and tell the good guys from the bad guys. Were the Coast Guard on the side of the law or working with the crooks? Were the smugglers heroes or villains? Flip the coin and, while it's in the air, pick a side you can rooting for, depending on your thirst.

The main pier at Coconut Grove was like one of those two-sided coins, thanks to the Volstead Act and all that followed.

Pleasure-crafts for tourists, the dories of hard-working fishermen, and decadently outfitted yachts. All were tied up on one end of the marina. During the day, tourists—arm in arm and eating ice-cream—strolled along the wooden docks, smiling at the amusing boat names. Bobbing next to the Alice and Marie were Lickety Split, Knot Shore, Vitamin Sea, Aboat Time, Greased Lightning, Blew By Ya, Breaking Waves, Seas the Day, and the Wake-Up Call.

The other side of the coin and the other side of the docks were not so safe. Tourists don't venture to this part of the pier; there were no maritime postcard-like scenes of fishermen perched on crates or coils of rope, while they smoked pipes and repair nets, in this part of the marina. Well past the dories and yachts was a line of large but sleek speedboats. They created a feeling of menace with their hulls painted black. Each craft was equipped with two, or sometimes three, massive motors, usually Liberty airplane engines. Scrawled across the bow and stern were less lighthearted names: Sweet Revenge, Tyranny, Rebel, Devil's Hammer.

In daylight, this part of the dock was mostly deserted except for a lone watchman. Come nighttime, it was a different story—

The other side of the coin.

* * * *

What of the jobs–rare, well-paid jobs—that were a result of Prohibition? Toss that coin. Heads were the pirates. Good or bad? It all depended on how you looked at it.

Locally, Coconut Grove was the home base of Biscayne Bay's Wharf Rat pirates—a collection of men capable of doing whatever it took to grab what was someone else's and make it their own. While some Rats were local, others had drifted from shores afar, pulled in by a riptide of malevolence and greed.

The head of this crew of desperadoes was a mysterious figure known as the Boss. He lurked in the background. His right-hand man, Buford, a corpulent version of evil, was the public face of the Wharf Rats.

The Wharf Rats headquarters was in a barn in Coconut Grove. There they could share reconnaissance intelligence, and receive their orders for the night. The meetings also provided the opportunity for the Boss to dispense wicked wisdom. Lately, he was obsessing about the goings-on at Goodtimes, and the dent the blind-tiger was creating in his protection racket payoffs.

For reasons beyond the understanding of the Wharf Rats, the Boss had adopted an approach of harassment and abuse, initially toward 'Gator Joe's and now against its successor, Goodtimes, with the aim of driving the Duffy dame out of town. They accepted their leader must have a deeper purpose than making money off her business. Few questioned his rationale, happy to follow orders unquestioningly, and profit generously.

At tonight's meeting, there had been a great deal of interest in the *Arethusa* and the numerous smugglers' boats that would be pulling alongside her. Now, on the pier, the Wharf Rats were eager to get out on the water.

The setting sun cast long shadows as honest, hard-working fishermen headed home at the end of a long day, anticipating supper and rest. Shouldering past them, the Wharf Rats went to the other side of the pier where their speedboats were moored.

Weapons were checked, plans and strategies hatched, as the pirates settled into their stations. They shared a look of wary alertness for the night ahead, sparing a glance outward to the sea and the sky, evaluating fickle coastal weather.

"Should be easy pickings tonight, Jackson," said a man blessed with a thick mess of rusty red hair.

"It's a calm sea, Everett. Money in our pockets and booze in the boat by dawn," said Jackson, a large man with a boxer's cauliflower ear and broken nose.

Buford climbed aboard the *Sweet Revenge*. He shouted over to his Wharf Rats compatriots who were checking their weapons and milling about the pier. "The Boss has a taste for the finer stuff, so keep a look out for black ships flying the banners of single-malt scotch and premium gin. Bill McCoy's *Arethusa* especially. We'll hit the contact boats coming back from McCoy's ship first."

"What about French brandy?"

"Sure. Just no champagne. The Boss never acquired a taste for the bubbles, and his rich customers don't seem to care much for it either."

On the pier, a pale man with watery blue eyes and a shock of white hair took a pair of tommy guns from Everett. "Whaddya think about the Boss's 'eye for an eye' threat at the meeting tonight? The part when he was jabbering on about that Goodtimes dame?"

Everett paused in the act of passing over the ammunition to Whitey. "When you believe in an eye for an eye, eventually everybody's blind."

Whitey climbed aboard the *Sweet Revenge*. "Ha, everybody blind. That's a good one. Hey, was that why the saloon that the Duffy dame runs is called a blind-tiger?"

Buford sneered at Whitey as he took his place in the stern. "Time to go to work, you lazy louts. There's money to be made and you won't be doing it sitting on the dock gossiping like old women." He waited for Everett and Jackson. When they climbed aboard, their weapons clutched in their hands, he fired up the boat's three large Liberty engines.

The speedboats roared away in a plume of water.

The objective for this night's work was much the same as every night: plunder and greed. To take as much as they could from the prey they stalked on Biscayne Bay, the law and decency be damned.

* * * *

However, there's that tossed coin… Remember? Another job opportunity created by Prohibition and on the tails side of the coin were the US Coast Guard. They were heroes allegedly keeping the 'demon rum' from American shores. Or perhaps they were they soldiers of fortune trying to keep a hard working rum running man from earning a decent dollar to feed his family? It depended on how you looked at it.

Lt. Commander Saunders delivered the evening's assignments to his crew at the Dinner Key Coast Guard Station about the same time the Wharf Rats had gathered in the barn in Coconut Grove to receive their orders.

Tonight, the Coast Guard would also be targeting the *Arethusa* and her circling contact boats, aware of her captain's outstanding warrants for arrest.

Saunders had received word that there were six new black ships out on Rum Row and he was eager to see what kind of business they'd be generating. The shift's mission: focusing on upholding the law, and enhancing the safety and security of mariners on Biscayne Bay—danger and risk be damned.

96

At Dinner Key Station, Lt. Commander Saunders and his crew board the six-bitter cutter, the *Mojave*. Echoing the boarding procedure of the pirates, the Coast Guard checked their weapons, debated the night's strategies, and turned a watchful eye to sea and sky—evaluating their color, predicting the weather for the evening's work.

* * * *

As one, the adversaries roared out to Rum Row, a bobbing line of ships just outside an invisible thin blue line known as the twelve-mile limit. On the near side was the coastline of the United States of America. On the far side, the high seas were known as international waters. On the American side of the line, the US Coast Guard enforced the Volstead Act that mades it illegal to sell or smuggle liquor in American territory. On the other side of the invisible line was the rest of the world. There, America's rules were unenforceable and the infamous Rum Row of ships carrying liquor were beyond American jurisdiction.

Standing on the *Mojave's* bridge, Lt. Commander John Saunders peered out through binoculars at the rapidly approaching twelve-mile line. He spotted the six new black ships they'd been alerted to. They were flying coded banners advertising the various brands of liquor they had on board. He passed the binoculars to his second in command, Bosun Hardy, who knew that calm seas tonight would mean that eager contact boats would soon surround the ships, buying liquor. Wharf Rats were already circle some smaller boats, looking to prey on the money going out to Rum Row or, to seize certain brands of liquor coming back to shore.

"It's going to be a busy night, sir. Six ships. We can expect at least a hundred contact boats." Hardy stayed with the binoculars. "It looks like the *Sweet Revenge* is already at work. Want me to radio for reinforcements?"

Lt. Commander Saunders took the binoculars. "We're closer to Fort Lauderdale than Miami. See what you can rouse from them. Those Wharf Rats are a plague on the Bay. Tonight might be our night." Saunders shifted, following the horizon. "The contact boats are already thick." He recognized a few, the *Marianne* was out there, and *Doubtful Purpose*. Others, too. "I think we've seen enough of those smugglers to lay charges that would stick once we board."

"I'll alert Ft. Lauderdale, sir. Care to listen in?"

Inside the small radio room, Saunders and Hardy hovered over the operator, easily hearing the response from Ft. Lauderdale's station over the crackling of the airwaves. "Aye-aye, sir. We'll dispatch three six-bitters and their pickets to your location."

Returning to the bridge, Saunders and Hardy wait for reinforcements. And they wait. And wait some more. Gun shots echoed across the water.

"Sounds like the pirates on the *Sweet Revenge* are meeting a bit of resistance. Should we send out our own pickets, sir?" Hardy asked.

"Where are Lauderdale's cutters and their patrol pickets? We could pick off a half dozen of the contact boats but we'll have no impact on the majority. There are hundreds out here. And without reinforcements, those Wharf Rats operate unchecked. Radio Lauderdale again."

When Hardy returned to the bridge, he looked grim as he saluted.

"Sir, Fort Lauderdale said they're not going to make it out, sir. Something about mechanical troubles."

"Mechanical troubles? In the whole fleet? What do they think— that ships get measles?" Saunders strode from the bridge, shouting orders as he approaches the radio room. "Put me through to the base commander."

"Frank, John Saunders here from the *Mojave*. What the hell was going on? We have six black ships being swarmed by contact boats. Pirates are out in full force. Where are my reinforcements?"

"John, what can I say? We've had a real run of bad luck here. We're scrapping the hulls of two of our cutters and their pickets are in dry dock. There's another waiting for engine repairs. The remaining fleet is at the far end of the Row, up near Jupiter. Way out of radio range. We won't be able to help you with those pirates tonight."

"You're kidding me. What about our Coast Guard's oath—'*semper paratus*'?"

"I hear you, John, but you know how it is. We're at the far side of payday."

"What's that got to do with it?" John Saunders' grip on the radio microphone had his knuckles white. The *Mojave* crew within hearing distance shuffled nervously.

"A few of those black ships have...ah...made arrangements with some of the men. And before you go Navy on me, you know I don't condone that kind of thing."

"So what you're telling me was that you have no ships and, even if you did, the men are going to look the other way tonight?"

"What I'm saying was that we had an unfortunate concurrence of events that make it impossible for us to assist you. But good hunting, John. Over and out."

There was silence in the radio room. Out in the passageway, Bosun Hardy clenched his teeth. He followed the Lt. Commander as he pushed past to go topside to the bridge.

"Your orders, sir?"

Saunders stood on the bridge, looking out over the sea. "Bad enough these smugglers are hiding in the weeds through a lack of coordination and petty jurisdictional jealousy. The Federal Bureau of Prohibition, the Federal Bureau of Customs, and the Coast Guard, the

Sheriff's office: we're all on the same team for goodness' sakes. But to hear that we can't even rely on our own?"

With a deep sigh that pulled at his gut, he turned to Hardy. "Nothing to be done about it tonight. Let's see what havoc we can cause along Rum Row single-handed. Bring the *Mojave* as close to the line as you can without going over. We'll not be able to do much actual damage, but we can be as annoying as hell."

"You're thinking a good game of keep-away, sir?"

"All we can do. Spread out the pickets and harry the black ships. Patrol slowly and we'll try to intimidate as much of the area as possible. Send the pickets out to buzz and chase, but don't bother with boarding. We don't have the time or resources for that tonight."

* * * *

Reach into that heavy bag marked 'Prohibition'—grab a coin and give it a toss. Good or evil—law enforcer or law breaker—it all depends on that darn coin and your thirst.

CHAPTER 15

Hi Harley. What can I get you?" Edith smiled at the bearded young man standing at the bar.

"A whiskey for me," he said, looking around the barroom and the dozen customers. "And a round for the house." This last comment generated some cheering and back slapping.

"What were we celebrating?"

"I had to make a run for a friend. He'd scuttled some cargo when the Coast Guard was after him and he asked me to help pick it up with him." Harley puffed out his chest. "He took the lot and sold it in Miami. And split a nice tidy profit with me."

"Looked like Billy's just come in. Do you want to include him in the round?"

Harley turned. "Hey, Shaw. Come here and let me tell you about my latest adventure."

"Wouldn't say no. But first, I want you to meet a new fella from the base. This was Ensign Clarence Middleton, but most folks call him Clancy. He's a radio operator."

Harley turned back to Edith. "Better pour something for Clancy." He winked at her. "This place is getting to be a real hangout for guardsmen."

"Here you go Billy, compliments of Harley here. What's new at the base?" Edith said, passing Billy and Clancy their drinks.

"We've set up a radio station to listen into radio conversations among rum runners."

"Ha, you just need to spend time at Goodtimes to do that," Harley roared with laughter, slapping the guardsman on the back. Clancy grinned sheepishly.

"What's heard at Goodtimes, stays at Goodtimes. Understood?" Billy said.

Clancy nodded.

Wiping down the counter, Edith decided to gain a bit of intel herself. It might come in handy for Bill and Darwin. "What's up with the radio station? I thought you had ship to shore already."

"Clancy here specializes in land to air. The Coast Guard's taken a real interest in them Wharf Rats lately. Dinner Key's brought in a couple of planes for better surveillance, which is why they need ol' Clancy here. Lots more chatter over the radio."

Clancy turned his head and belched a bit of beer, then laughed. "Yup. The brass isn't too happy with Saunders' performance on the matter. They figured a few planes would help clean out the rats nest in Coconut Grove."

"That's enough, Ensign. Where do you think that beer you're swilling comes from? Keep it up and you'll be buying your own beer," Billy said, grabbing his bottle and wandering away from the bar to join Harley at a table. Shrugging, Clancy joined him.

There was a good energy in the crowd throughout the evening, making Edith optimistic about the upcoming Grand Opening. Harley left early with a wink and a nod, citing a bit of work he needed to attend to later that night. Billy and Clancy weren't long behind him and, after Edith's said goodnight to the last of her customers, all hands were on deck, cleaning up after another busy night at Goodtimes.

Out of the corner of her eye, she spied Leroy sneaking off to his room. "Hold up there, mister. You head into the tent and give Lucky a hand with those dishes. There's still a ton of work to do."

"Aw, do I have to? I worked hard all night and I'm dog tired, Miz Edith." Leroy said, a whine creeping into his voice.

"Hey champ, we're all tired. You, me, Miz Edith. And Lucky is, too. Which is why we all gotta pitch in," Darwin said, stacking chairs so the floor could be mopped.

Leroy, his arms crossed and bottom lip in full pout, scowled at Edith and Darwin. "I'm just a kid. I don't want to."

Darwin walked over and put an arm around him, steering him toward the back door and kitchen tent. "We all pull our weight around here, Leroy. Sometimes a man must do what a man must do. You want us to stop treating you like a kid, then you gotta stop acting like one. Now, go give Lucky a hand and the job will get done in half the time."

Edith chuckled. *The boy had met his match in Darwin.*

Coming back into the barroom, Darwin resumed his chores. "Business is picking up and the place is finally starting to fill up—at least on the weekends."

"Yes, I'm relieved to see money coming in rather than going out." The construction expenses had seemed to take on a life of their own as she found it hard to deny herself any whim or indulgence. Darwin's efforts at rum running were keeping them from hitting bottom, but a successful Grand Opening was going to be key to getting the bank balance back above the redline.

And that Grand Opening was only a week away; Edith was racing against a fast-running time clock. The visit with Cleo had been great, but it took time away from getting ready. The daily demands of running a popular speakeasy during Prohibition were enough, let alone a million and one marquee event details to attend to, and then there was the thinking, strategizing, and positioning—looking for opportunities and seizing them—the overall business decisions to secure their place in the future with the possibility of expanding their rum running.

Darwin stacks chairs on the tables so Edith could sweep underneath. Out back, Leroy and Lucky were washing dozens of dirty glasses.

"Another good night," Darwin said as he moved a table out of Edith's way.

"You think we're ready for the official Grand Opening?"

"We'd better be, or there's going to be a lot of disappointed people in town. You've had posters up for weeks, Billy's been talking it up at the base. Harley's handed out a brochure with every bottle he's sold through his backdoor bootlegging business. We've got lots of stock laid up, and Lucky's managing miracles in the kitchen tent."

Edith leaned on her broom. "I hope it goes better than last time. Remember 'Gator Joe's when the Wharf Rats told everyone to stay away? That night almost broke my heart."

"I don't think that's going to be a problem this time. You're too well established and too many people are looking forward to it. We'll have a crowd, Edith, don't worry."

"You're right. I should stop fretting about what could go wrong and get excited about what will go right, instead."

Darwin smiled. "That's my girl. Now off to bed with you. The place is as clean as it needs to be tonight."

Edith rescued Leroy from the dish pit and made sure he was tucked in before she went upstairs.

In the comfort of her new suite, Edith was serenaded by frogs and insects—it lulled her, the song of the Everglades. But not for long. Her mind rarely stopped. Tucker Wilson's offer became a crescendo to the night-time music.

"How much should I expand the business?" she muttered into the pillow. "One of the best things about Coconut Grove versus Miami is, if I'm going to fail, I can do it in private." Edith rolled over to face the ceiling and rapped her knuckles on her forehead. "Touch wood, I'm not failing. Goodtimes is going to be bigger and better than 'Gator Joe's ever could be. But a major expansion? Am I ready for that?"

She tossed restlessly. *Its crazy busy as it is. What was that tarot card with the fellow and his sack? I'm exhausted. Getting this place rebuilt has taken everything I've got and then some. Money and energy.*

Edith got out of bed and stepped out onto her balcony. The moon was linked to the shore by a trail of diamonds.

Rum running is a lot like the bootlegging Mickey did so well in Philly. He had supply partners- wholesalers like Cleo.

It's a natural extension of what we're already doing. The places along the Dixie Highway have potential: a bunch of speakeasies and blind-tigers without easy access to Rum Row. Or places along the coast that fear pirates. Although I'll have to be careful not to step on Meyer Lansky's toes.

Expanding the business will definitely expand the risk, but I'm sure I could think of ways to manage it. If I'm going to take advantage of the chance to run liquor for locals, I'll need a steady supply from a trustworthy rum runner. Cleo's the obvious choice. I like her and, more importantly, trust her. What if I strike up a formal partnership with her? If I expand the bootlegging, I'm sure I could get better than wholesale pricing.

The voice of reason broke through her thoughts. "Don't get ahead of yourself. One step at a time. See how it works out with Tucker first," she muttered to the moon.

Edith breathed in the salty night air. Her mind eased away from business thoughts; taking comfort in the nighttime vocals of critters, the music of the waves, and the percussion supplied by the clackety-clack of the palm leaves as they brushed against the railing.

Ah, Goodtimes. I found my piece of heaven when I found you.

CHAPTER 16

Edith may be nestled in her bed, but it was business as usual along Rum Row. Weekends were busy times with lots of small contact boats stocking up for weekend parties.

The Wharf Rat's *Sweet Revenge* roared out of the harbour, the crew on board eager to make some coin.

Everett settled in beside Buford who was at the tiller.

"Calm seas. It's going to be a good night," Buford said as he looked out over the ocean.

"Aye. For us pirates. I feel lucky tonight, Buford." Everett said.

Buford smirked.

Whitey and Jackson were in the boat's stern, scanning the water, hunting.

Buford, hand on the wheel, stared past the glittering black of the night sky. *I've been with the Boss since he was a green sprout. Everything I have is thanks to his brains and the crew he's built. But I don't get why the Duffy dame has him flummoxed. It's not healthy the way he goes on. Something in his brain short-circuited the night of the fire.*

"Hey Buford, you okay at the wheel?" Jackson said.

Buford nodded. "Hopefully we'll be able to nab some top shelf liquor tonight. I know the Boss always likes to keep his liquor cabinet full."

"Think there'll be any trouble tonight?" Everett asked.

Buford looked at him and grinned. "You can count on it. Never ceases to amaze me the stupid decisions folks make. Take that fella last night. Tried to hang on to the money. Whadda we look like? Choir boys?"

Everett caressed the tommy gun in his lap and laughed. The Wharf Rats were hunting. It won't be a fair fight. it never was. The smaller contact boats heading out to Rum Row had two or three people at the most. Many were sole operators. The Wharf Rats carried four to six pirates in their black-hulled boats, a pluming wake from the enormous engines a banner behind them as they raced across the water.

"Ho. Boat at five o'clock," Whitey shouted, pointing to a small craft off the port bow. Buford turned the wheel, adjusting course for an intercept.

* * * *

After leaving Goodtimes, Harley Andrews had gone down to the main pier and headed out to Rum Row in his sea skiff. He had a tidy little business running back and forth between Rum Row and the many hidden coves and inlets along the coastline.

He was a solo entrepreneur: small scale stuff for personal use. He didn't sell to the blind-tigers. Rather, folks around Coconut Grove know they could always knock on his back door if they were looking for a bottle or two. The young fellas he grew up with and their brothers were his best customers. His friendship with Billy Shaw had opened a whole new avenue of business from the Dinner Key Coast Guard station.

Harley had a hot tip on a special shipment of scotch on a ship, the *Victory*, out on Rum Row. He's raided the cookie jar for tonight's run. There's almost a thousand dollars in his pocket so he could pick up a boatload of the stuff. At the going price of fifty dollars a ham, he was going to make a very tidy profit. Harley also hoped to pick up some champagne if he could get it 'cause one of his regulars was getting hitched. Harley figured his little dory was going to be packed to the gunnels on the trip home, but it was a calm night and he knew his boat.

Harley heard his pursuers before he saw them. He knew what that roar meant. His small outboard motor was no match for the powerful engines rumbling up behind him.

Under the brightness of the moon, he could make out dark figures crouched on the approaching boat. One was straddling the cockpit with a tommy gun in his arms, a couple of the pirates bracing his legs so that his aim would be precise.

A hail to stop came over the roar of the three engines, as if there was ever any doubt of their intentions. His boat rolling wildly in their wake, Harley throttled down and put his hands high. In his bulging pocket was the roll of cash.

Over the loudspeaker, Harley was told to pass the cash over quick, the neat aperture of the Cutts Compensator on the tommy gun in an exact line with his chest.

In a final instant of hesitation, Harley glared with a hatred that was blinding. He was going to use tonight's profits to buy a new dragger for his fishing boat. He also had hopes for a four door Nash if his luck was good on the resale price. And, of course, there would be a little something for Nancy. All those things would now be lost.

The barrel of the tommy gun flickered to one side and a barrage of rounds were fired into the water beside him. An eloquent motivation to help with the decision making.

Harley passed his roll to tense hands. The pirate holding the gun kept his stance. "Don't move."

As suddenly as they had appeared, the black-hulled boat was gone, its three motors surging, carving a marble path over the shoulders of the sea, only her exhaust fumes a sign that a minute ago she had been there.

Harley touched the throttle to half speed. Made no sense to head home fast if you were broke.

CHAPTER 17

The morning of the Grand Opening, Edith found a tarot card tucked into the mirror in her bathroom. It showed a man leaning on his hoe, gazing down at his abundant crop. She imagined he had worked long and hard to nurture his tiny seeds into this thriving garden and was taking a break to enjoy the fruits of his labors. *He looks as tired as I feel, but hopefully all my labors will be bearing fruit, as well. Maybe there's something to all this fortune telling nonsense after all.*

Edith turned it this way and that, inviting it to share more of its meaning. "What else are you telling me?"

Downstairs in the barroom, she lifted the telephone to call her friend Mae Capone in Miami. Mae knew the cards. She could also confirm she was still planning on coming out with a carload for the Grand Opening. But there was no dial tone. She banged the receiver cradle several times with growing frustration.

"Argh, another frustration. Two days now, and the lines are still not up from the last storm. This darn telephone is my lifeline to civilization. I need confirmations. The band is supposed to be arriving today."

Leroy was nearby, eating breakfast. "What's the matter, Miz Edith?"

She handed him the tarot card. "Do you know what this means?"

"Sure. It's the Seven of Pentacles. It's telling you success comes from hard work and patience, but don't overdo it or you'll wear yourself out. And you do look worn out, Miz Edith."

Edith perched beside him. "What am I going to do with you, Leroy. Never tell a gal she's looking bad."

Leroy looked confused. "I didn't mean nothing by it, Miz Edith. I think you look great, just tired."

She scruffed his hair. "Okay, hotshot. What else does it mean?"

"Like I said, your hard work will pay off. You rebuilt 'Gator's and now it is even better than before. And there'll be rewards for all that work. That's what you want, right? More rewards?"

"Rewards would be nice. Like a packed house tonight for this band, which hopefully shows up soon."

"Why won't you let me get Aunt Cassie to come read your cards? She's really good—lots better than me."

"I don't think so, Leroy. I don't believe in this fortune telling stuff. Say, did you get that fire pit dug? Lucky's got to get that hog roasting soon."

"You forgot already? We dug the pit yesterday, Miz Edith. And today we got up before the sun to get the fire going. You should go down and see it. It's real neat. There's bricks and rocks in there with all the wood. Darwin said we can't put all our wood on at once 'cause fires have to breathe. Isn't that silly?" Leroy said with a giggle. "Breathing fire, like a dragon."

The screen door opened. Lucky was wiping his hands on a rag. "Hog on, Miz Edith. Salted it this morning first thing."

"It's going to taste amazing. Lucky stuffed it up like a chicken. He put more rocks and bricks inside it and some pieces of banana tree. We don't eat that stuff, though. Just the meat." Leroy was dancing with excitement. "And then we wrapped the whole thing in chicken wire."

Edith had been nodding and smiling, her mind on the missing band. She'd been down that road before. Suddenly, something from Leroy's babble caught her attention. "Banana tree?"

"Moisture very important. Steam pig. Banana tree in pit and in pig. Nice flavor," Lucky said. "We add cabbage. Very moist. And onions."

Leroy rubbed his stomach and smacked his lips.

"And then cover pig with burlap bags soaked in fresh water and big sheet of canvas on top," Lucky said.

Leroy vigorously nodded his head. "That keeps the dirt out." Leroy was puffed up with importance, relaying this exotic news.

"Also very important. Dirt in hog is bad," Lucky said.

Edith grinned. "I can imagine."

"And lots and lots of water gtt poured into the pit. There was steam everywhere," Leroy said and threw his hands in the air to show just how much steam.

"And then we bury it with sand." Lucky wagged his finger at Leroy. "Now Leroy has very special job of watching pit. He needs to plug up holes that let out steam."

"I think you have the right man for the job, Lucky."

Looking between Edith and Lucky, Leroy waited for the joke. Gradually, a smile broke out on his face when he realized the compliment was genuine. "That's swell of you to say, Miz Edith. I won't let you down."

* * * *

A huge crowd of people were milling about on the beach, mouths watering, intrigued with the bar-b-que pit, and ready for a taste of the pork. The tantalizing aroma was all they could talk about.

Up from the waterfront action, Edith was at her station on the veranda to greet guests coming down from the car park. Amongst the crowd were Mae Capone and the carloads she had brought out from Miami, including the infamous gangster Meyer Lansky and his wife Anna.

"Our paths always seem to be crossing, Meyer."

111

"A pig roast on the beach? I wouldn't have missed it."

"Don't you keep kosher?" Edith asked.

Meyer grinned. "I want to see it, not eat it. A pig roast would really catch on at the resorts in Miami. You come up with the best ideas, Edith. You're sure you don't need a partner?"

Edith laughed off his remark, turning to the woman with the pained expression on her face beside him. "Thank you for coming, Anna."

Anna looked around the new Goodtimes with a critical eye. "Mae promised me indoor plumbing. You've got that now, right?"

Edith chuckled. "Yes, all the modern conveniences. Why don't you freshen up and then join us on the beach. Lucky and Darwin are going to be lifting the pig out of the pit any minute."

Edith turned to Mae and gave her a tight hug. "Thanks Mae, for always being there."

Mae returned the affectionate squeeze. "What are family for, doll? Now, where's this pig I keep hearing about? Meyer talked of nothing else the whole drive out."

Edith laughed and sent them down to the beach. Still on official welcome duty on the veranda, she caught sight of Bill and Cleo wandering up from the dock in search of their hostess. Her pulse began to race as she smoothed the skirt of her dress, but she flinched seeing them holding hands.

I've got to get to the bottom of their relationship. Do I have a chance with him or not? And should I even be thinking about it with Cleo being a friend and all?

"Welcome, you two," Edith said. Bill stepped forward, grabbing her by the waist and swinging her off her feet. "Congratulations on the launch, Edith. We wouldn't have missed it. And don't you look fabulous tonight. Doesn't she look fabulous, Cleo?"

"Oh, my, now I'm dizzy," Edith said, smiling coyly up at Bill, her hand resting on his very broad chest.

Cleo offered up a broad smile. "Edith always looks fabulous, Bill. Edith, I was going to get one of the crew to drop me off, but when I told Bill about the pig roast he insisted on coming."

"She said a whole hog cooked underground. On the beach. Is that right?" Bill asked.

Edith batted her eyelashes at Bill. He grinned in return. "It's all that. You won't regret taking the night off."

"I promised leftovers for the crew, if there are any. I won't be able to stay the whole night. I figure it is going to be a slow one out on the Row. From the looks of the crowd, I think I'm right. Everyone and their dog are here."

Cleo stepped close to Edith and she tensed. *Did I overstep? Is she jealous?*

"I thought I'd gave you a hand on the floor. And I'm going to stay and help clean up after. Bill can pick me up tomorrow, if that's okay with you?"

"Are you kidding? Nobody ever offers to help with clean-up." *I've got to calm down. She's not being territorial of Bill, she's offering me help.*

Cleo gave her a wink. "Family eats last and stays to clean up. A rule in my house."

"You're such a great friend, Cleo. Now, let's get down to the beach before they pull the hog. That's the best part. A show in itself." Edith gently pushed them along the veranda and followed them down to the beach.

With growing excitement, the crowd watched as Darwin and Lucky dig the pig out of the pit. "Andrews, you and Billy get over here and gave us a hand. This thing weighs a ton," Darwin said over his shoulder. Captain Bill McCoy stepped in as an extra; they carefully handled and secured the edges of the chicken wire 'basket' the hog had been cooking in.

Accompanied by the crowd's *oohs* and *ah's*, they laid it down on a table covered in canvas. Meat was already felling off the bone. Next to the pork were jars of a vinegar hot sauce, and all kinds of salads and bread. Edith began passing out plates and cutlery. Jasper was first in line. "You managed to get away?" Edith said, passing him a plate.

"Wouldn't miss it, Miz Edith." He winked. "Told the musses I needed to do inventory down at the post office. This will be our little secret if it's okay with you?"

"Mums the word, Jasper. What happens at Goodtimes stays at Goodtimes. Don't forget a splash of that vinegar. It really adds to the taste."

"Does it taste as good as it looks?" Meyer Lansky asked, smacking his lips. "It smells incredible. Spicy, tart, sweet, and salty. I love it even though I can't eat it." He waved his fork at Lucky. "You should come and work for me in Miami. We could do these pig roasts for the tourists. I'll make you rich."

Lucky shook his head. "No, sir. I work for Miz Edith. Always."

When music began to flow through Goodtimes' open French doors, Edith and Cleo hurried ahead to beat the crowd, ready to host the guests inside. Responding, people on the beach, full plates in hand, headed up the path to the barroom.

Serving beer and mixing cocktails, Edith was grinning from ear to ear, remembering a very different Grand Opening at 'Gator Joe's. *My life is finally turning around and the past is behind me.* She tipped a glass of whiskey in Mickey and 'Gator Joe's memory, and to the memory of the woman she had been. A sip and the fiery liquid hit her stomach with a bang. *Whiskey remembers forgotten dreams.* She refilled it and raised the glass again, the second toast to the future.

CHAPTER 18

Goodtimes had the feel of a raucous family wedding. Locals were mixing it up with the Miami crowd, rum runners were trading stories with guardsmen. Well known and liked around town, Harley, Nancy, Billy, and Clancy bounced out of their chairs and to greet newcomers.

"Look who the cat dragged in." "Oh-oh, Miz Edith, them Plett boys just got here. Better add a cup of water to the soup." "Well, howdy. It's been a dog's age since I last seen ya. I figured you'd up and died. Where you been at?"

The evening became more boisterous. "Gracious, look at you, Harley Andrews. Just a tad taller than the last time I saw you. I know your pa from the wharf," said a mild looking man dressed in a Sunday suit and tie. He was holding a plate piled high with food in one hand and a frosty mug of beer in the other.

"Howdy, Mr. Carmichael. Great to see you out tonight."

"Alvin, please. It seems everybody in town is here and then some," Alvin Carmichael said, nodding at the crowded room.

"Please join us. This here's my intended, Nancy."

"So you're finally tying the knot, Harley. That's excellent. Nothing better than married life. My dear wife, Mary, really is my better half." Alvin Carmichael put his plate on the table and sat. "What are you planning on doing after the wedding?"

"I'm sorry, Mr. Carmichael. What do you mean?" Harley asked, head cocked to one side, still smiling.

Mr. Carmichael leaned close. "I know about your backdoor business, Harley. That's no work for an honest man raising a family. You don't want your children to grow up around that, do you? Or heaven forbid, you not around to watch them grow up."

Harley sat back, thinking. He looked to Nancy who was now up dancing with Billy Shaw. "I hadn't thought about it before, Mr.

Carmichael. I doubt that Nancy would be very happy with a bootlegger are the daddy of her children."

Mr. Carmichael slapped Harley on the back. "You think about it and then come see me down at the pier. I can always use an experienced fella like yourself with the boats. Plenty of work; pays nothing like rum running and bootlegging mind you, but you could hold your head high with the kiddies when they come."

Alvin Carmichael settled in with his plate of pork. A cold beer at his side. It wasn't long before he was cleaning the last few bits of food from his plate.

"Can I take your plate, sir?" Leroy said, a stack of dirty dishes in his hands.

"Thanks. It was delicious."

"Ain't this the best? They don't always do up a whole hog on the beach, but the food here is always tasty. You gotta try the opossum stew sometime, sir," Harley said, scraping his plate.

Alvin picked his teeth and took a swig of beer. "You know, I think I might just do that."

Edith was on watch from her station behind the bar. She turned to Darwin who was carrying in more moonshine for the Black Jack's Rootshine specials. "I think we've done it right this time. Everything is going smoothly. The band has almost everyone on the dance floor. Lucky's pig was a huge hit. The beer is cold, and there's lots of gin and whiskey in the shed. What could go wrong?

"Don't tempt fate, Edith."

By the end of the night, even Anna Lansky was impressed. "Goodtimes is such an improvement over that last joint, Edith. I'll come back again. In fact, let's bring Bugsy and Esta Siegel here the next time they're in town. And maybe Reggie and some of the old gang. This place has got real potential."

Captain Bill McCoy was sent off with a pot of leftovers for his crew. Cleo walked him down to the dock, and it was some time before she was back.

The veranda turned out to be both the perfect place to greet guests and to wave goodbye to them. Edith was wrapped in the warmth of success. Behind her, the band tidied up, but left their equipment there. The bunkhouse awaited; they'll be playing again tomorrow night. Judging from the comments of people leaving Goodtimes, it was going to be another sell-out crowd.

The moon rested low on the horizon; the edge of the sky flowed from midnight black to a deep purple before Edith's eyes. It would be dawn soon.

She turned and went back into the barroom. "Off to bed with you, Leroy. We'll finish cleaning up in the morning." She pulled him away from where he was stacking chairs.

It took little convincing for Leroy to scoot to bed, leaving Cleo leaning on the mop like a weary dance partner.

"That was a good night's work. Darwin's running a few folks that shouldn't be driving—or walking for that matter—into town, but I don't feel like calling it a night yet. Still have energy for a drink, Cleo?" Edith asked.

Her friend brightened. "This isn't work, Edith. I've barely started. I'm used to the rum runners' nightshifts. Although I won't say no to putting this mop aside; I've never been fond of swabbing decks. Want to watch the sun come up?"

The silhouettes of palm trees black against the fiery orange and red dawn provided a jaw dropping show for Cleo and Edith as they sat on the veranda, sipping a night cap—or perhaps daycap?

"I must say, I enjoyed meeting your friend Mae. Although I can't imagine her married to a mobster like Al Capone." Cleo sipped her breakfast martini.

"Don't believe everything you read in the papers. Al married Mae when they were just kids, before they were officially old enough. They had to get notes from their parents before the priest would perform the ceremony."

"Childhood sweethearts, eh?"

"It hasn't been easy for her, being married to a mobster like Al. He and Mickey were alike in so many ways, so I speak from bitter personal experience." Edith sighed and poured more martinis from the shaker into the glasses. "How about you, Cleo? How are things going with this mystery man you won't tell me about?"

"It's hardly a secret anymore. It couldn't be on a ship, and I'm sure you've figured it out. Bill McCoy and I are spending time together, but I don't want to make a big deal about it. I made a couple of bad choices early on in my life and they left a few scars. Those fellows said all the right things about my independence and my career while we were courting but, as we got closer to making a commitment, the real truth came out."

"Couldn't handle it?" Edith asked.

"There were one or two like that. They expected I'd gave it all up, everything I worked so hard for, to stay home and be a wife and mother. And they were the good ones. There was one cad who was only after my money. I couldn't work hard enough or long enough for the likes of him."

"That's terrible, Cleo. I can't imagine somebody thinking you were that gullible."

"It's easy to have the wool pulled over your eyes when you're in love."

"What about Bill? He's not like that, surely. He seems proud of your business and is always calling you his lucky charm." Edith gripped the stem of her glass tightly while she watched Cleo mull over her answer. A small splash of her martini spilled on her dress.

"At least with Bill I know what he wants. And he respects me and my career. We suit each other. He's like a business partner with benefits."

Edith released her breath. *A business partner with benefits I can handle.* "Tsk. Cleo, you naughty thing."

Cleo chuckled.

"But is that good enough for you? Don't you want more?" Edith asked. *There might be room for me if it's just casual. Cleo wouldn't stand in my way if he and I wound up with something special. Would she?*

"I'm a realist, Edith. Like many things in life, I'll settle for what I can get rather than chase rainbows. I'm not prepared to give up such an important piece of who I am, and there are precious few men I'd be interested in that would let me be. It would almost be easier to be alone in my old age than with someone like that. One thing about Bill, he's never lied to me. And in my experience that is a rare and wonderful thing."

"Here's to truth and honesty in relationships," Edith said, raising her martini glass. *I'd better come clean with her soon. But maybe I'll wait until I'm surer of where things are between Bill and I. No sense rocking the boat if I don't need to.*

"Your glass was almost empty. Here, let me fill it for you," said Cleo. "Speaking of the men in our lives, Leroy is a great kid. You say he just wandered in one day?"

"He popped up like a bad penny. Ha ha. I'm sure there's more to the story but I don't push. He's an orphan, I think. His mother's passed and there's no father on the scene. You must meet his aunt sometime."

"She's the Fortune Teller, right? That lives out in the everglades? She sounds like a fascinating woman."

It grew brighter and daytime announced herself with the change in tide and a different set of birds.

"You don't have any kids of your own, do you?" Cleo asked.

"Mickey and I never did. I could conceive but couldn't carry them to term. Little angels that God called home. It's too late for me now. I'd have loved to hold a wee bundle in my arms. Sometimes when I see a baby, my arms ache. Or maybe it's my heart."

Leroy. Kids just break your heart. She thought of each cold bundle lying in a new cradle. Reliving the sorrow that overcame her each time. She shivered, her hand trembled, and suddenly her head lowered. "Don't mind me. The night's taken a lot out of me," Edith said, a lump forming in her throat.

Cleo reached over and held Edith's hand. "The walls we build around us to keep out the sadness also keep out the joy, dear heart."

"Men aside, how do you feel about your choices? Seems like you've decided."

"I try not to dwell on it. I've learned to be content with my business and be on my own."

"I hear you. I keep busy with Goodtimes. That's my baby. And it has all the mess and growing pains any kid would."

"And you have Leroy."

Edith chuckled. "Such a scamp."

"He follows you around like a puppy."

"Ah, yes. If only he were house-trained."

They add to the early morning with laugher and clinking glasses. "Another?" Edith asked.

"One more. I don't usually drink martinis for breakfast," Cleo said.

Under a pale blue sky, Edith poured them both a glass, draining the shaker.

Cleo raised her glass. "Here's to a bright future and a successful Grand Opening, Edith."

"Thanks for staying over, Cleo. I'm happy to have someone to share this with. You know, I never had a crowd of friends back in Philly but, here at Goodtimes, my regulars are becoming like family. I never realized how lonely I was until I started 'Gator's—and now Goodtimes. It's nice to have good friends."

"I'm honored to be among that company," Cleo said, her glass raised in salute.

Edith tapped Cleo's glass with the rim of her own. "You are indeed, Cleo. You've been part of this since almost the beginning, and I'm proud of what we've been able to accomplish together. And it hasn't been built on threats or coercion like my late-husband's bootlegging empire. Rather, we've let our reputation as a quality establishment speak for itself."

"That's no small achievement in a man's world and especially when most of the men in this particular world are criminals and lawbreakers," Cleo said.

"It's been an eye-opener for me to find I could be assertive and strong without being dangerous. Like you. You're respected in a man's world."

"And Up until recently, I've had the empty nights to show for it. It's not easy having both. It takes a special kind of man to stand beside a strong woman."

"Here's to strong men," Edith said, draining her glass. "And to the sacrifices we make for success."

"I think I'd better turn in. The sun's up and I need my beauty sleep. Bill will be by to pick me up later this afternoon and I have another long night of work on the *Arethusa* ahead of me." Cleo stood and stretched. "Coming?"

"I don't think so. I need to stay right here. Nourishment for my soul. And thanks again for your help tonight."

"Anytime you need a bartender, I'm your gal. Night-morning, Edith."

* * * *

After a late lie-in, Darwin came up the path from the *Marianne* and found Lucky sitting on a chair outside the kitchen tent.

"That was one tasty hog last night, Lucky. You outdid yourself."

"Thank you, Darwin. Not something I prepare before. A roasted whole pig not common in China."

"Well, that crowd last night sure liked it."

Lucky nodded, intent on removing the remaining skin from the large snake he was holding. "This more delicacy back home."

"Miz Edith shoot another snake?"

"Yes. I put in soup for supper tonight."

Darwin shifted onto his back foot. "Hmm, that might not be the best idea, Lucky. Folks around here haven't acquired a taste for snake. I'm sure it's tasty and you're one heck of a cook but maybe use chicken instead?"

Lucky looked at Darwin, a puzzled frown on his face. "But hot pot restaurants serve snake bone soup all the time. Very popular."

"Really? You eat snakes?"

"Many kinds of snake on menu, from lightweight Uriah Shaw to King Cobra and Agkistrodon. Those are same as copperhead snakes you have here. Like this one." Lucky shook the half-skinned snake. "And snake offer many health benefits. Miz Edith been tired and this help." He looked around slyly and grinned at Darwin. "And snake good for virility."

Darwin laughed. "As tempting as it is, I think it should be chicken soup on the menu tonight. How about you finish that and I'll take the skin and make you a hatband like mine? You could toss the carcass in the creek for the 'gators."

"Fine, no snake soup. I do like your hat, Darwin."

CHAPTER 19

On their walk home after church on Sunday, John Saunders explained to his wife the merits and capabilities of the new sea-planes that were now at the Dinner Key station.

"The wingspan on the Loenings is forty-five feet and the aircraft length is thirty-five feet, while the Voughts are also bi-planes with a thirty-five foot wingspan and are almost thirty feet long."

"Yes, dear. That sounds interesting." *Brother Silas has such power in his voice. He makes me shiver when he speaks of vice and sin.*

At home, Mavis took off her hat and gloves, then tied on her apron to finish up the preparations for roast chicken, their Sunday tradition.

Listen to John go on about those planes. Men are so sure that their world is what's important. I'm content in a much smaller world. Like they say, the hand that rocks the cradle rules the world. And the hand that holds the gavel at the Homemakers' Guild meetings rules Coconut Grove. Mavis chuckled.

"What was that, dear?" John was hanging up his suit jacket.

"Can I get you some lemonade, John?"

"Thank you. That would be lovely, dear."

I don't understand why some women aren't satisfied running a home and raising a family. It's as important a job as John's, although we are certainly unsung heroes. Now, that hussy at the saloon gives all women a bad name. The way she carries on.

"What did you think of Brother Silas' sermon? That saloon sounds like a den of iniquity," Mavis said, pouring her husband a glass.

"I thought it was a bit over the top."

"Why don't you do something about her, John?"

"That would be Deputy Purvis' bailiwick. Our work is on the water."

"But she must be getting her demon rum from rum runners."

"They're a small-time operation, Mavis. We've not had too many run-ins with them and, from what I hear, when our paths do cross, her man is very respectful. You could almost say professional. No, we're after bigger game, like this outfit called the Wharf Rats. Now, they are truly evil."

"Well, I don't think she's so small-time. The ladies of the Homemakers' Guild are worried about the lawlessness out there. Did you know that there's a child working in the saloon? I was thinking that this will be perfect for our next Guild project."

"Mavis. Really. What are you up to?"

"The law protects children from working in unsafe and unsavory conditions. Daddy Fagg said that enforcement of the law is very lax. You work to upheld the law."

"I don't understand why you and your Guild would want to be involved in a private matter like that. The boy's family must be aware of the situation."

"Fine and good for you to sail around on Biscayne Bay fighting corruption and lawlessness, John Saunders. But someone has to look after what's happening here in Coconut Grove." Mavis crossed her arms and tapped one foot.

"My advice to you is to check into the situation before you go charging in. There may be a perfectly reasonable reason why the boy is there."

"Of course we're going to look into it. Brother Silas is going to come with us when we talk to Dade County's Child Protection Office. Miss White from the Children's Home will also be involved. We're pulling together quite the coalition, and our voices will be heard."

John sighed and reaches for his newspaper, shaking it into a screen. Sometimes, trying to stop his wife was like standing in front of a speeding freight train.

CHAPTER 20

Leroy sat on the curb and watched folks make their way home after church. Jay should be showing up shortly. His casual interest in the parade of people was sharpened when he saw a man in a sparkling white uniform, brass buttons, and gold braid on his hat, walking along the street beside his wife.

Say, that's the captain of that Coast Guard ship that saved Miz Edith and me when the Rex *ran out of gas. I never figured he lived here in Coconut Grove. I wonder if Billy knows his name?*

Leroy jumped up, saluted smartly, then plunked himself back down on the curb, giggling. He watched the man and woman walk up to a house with a white fence and go inside. *His ship wasn't as big as Captain McCoy's, but nobody saluted Captain McCoy.*

Leroy reached for a stick and bounced it against the cement, poked it into the ground, tapped out a rhythm on the road. *Maybe Jay forgot that this was the Sunday we were getting together?*

When there were no more churchgoers left in sight, Leroy shuffled impatiently. And then one more figure came into view.

Finally. He stood and waved when he saw Jay. "I figured you forgot."

"The preacher kept going on and on about sin. It made me late. Sorry."

Together they walked back along the road to Goodtimes. It turned from pavement to gravel as they wander through mangrove and cypress. Birds serenaded them as they ambled, the dappled sun lit the way.

When they arrived at Goodtimes, Jay's head swiveled from side to side in the barroom. "Where are the drunks and pirates?" he whispered.

"Dope. They're still sleeping. They don't get here until after dark," Leroy said.

With pride of ownership, Leroy flipped open the top of the cooler and fished out two cold soda pop bottles. They headed outside and followed Snapper Creek into the Everglades. Egrets picked their way along the shore, an alligator slid into the water. A fallen tree had formed a bridge, albeit a slippery one covered with moss. The boys scrambled along it, then draped themselves over, midpoint, trailing their arms below and letting the cool water run over their hands.

"You got any brothers or sisters?" Leroy asked.

"Two older brothers. They're the worst. Always bossing me. You got any brothers?" Jay said.

"Nope. Just me."

"Must be nice. You got your own room then?"

"Yup."

"I have to sleep with my brother. He snores and hogs the bed and the pillows."

"Look, there's a frog. Catch it."

They gave chase, eventually capturing it, staring deep into its bulbous eyes before letting it go.

"What's your pa like?" Leroy asked.

"My pa? I dunno. Loud. When he smacks me, it hurts. He works down on the pier fixing boats and stuff."

"We have two boats. The *Marianne* is fast, and the *Rex* is an old trawler. Darwin sleeps on it."

"Darwin your pa?"

"No. He helps Miz Edith."

"Where's your ma?"

"She died. I used to live with my aunt but now I live with Miz Edith. And Lucky. He's from China."

"No way. Really? All the way from China?"

"Yup. He eats snakes."

Jay rolled his eyes. "That's so gross. You ever eat a snake?"

Leroy shrugged with nonchalance. "Sure. All the time. Lucky cooks 'em up real good.."

"Wow. You're like Huck Finn, living out here."

Leroy smiled. "I guess that would make you Tom Sawyer."

They rolled up their pant legs and waded through the cool water. "What are you doing that old paper route for, anyhow?" Leroy asked.

Jay grabbed at a low branch and plucked a leaf, setting it floating down the creek. "I want to earn money so I can buy a bike. They've got one down at the S&P. It's a Schwinn and has a light on it. And a bell."

"I saw a Schwinn that had a motor on it so you don't have to pedal all the time. If I ever get a bike, I'd get one of those with fat tires 'cause of all the dirt roads out here."

"You saving for anything special?" Jay asked.

"Not really anything special. I get paid to work at Goodtimes."

"You get to work in a saloon?"

"Yup."

"And you don't have to go to school?"

"Nope. It's not man-da-tory. Miz Edith says I don't have to go unless I want to 'cause I'm past ten. I can read and do sums. And I have a library card."

"You have the best life, Leroy. My ma makes me go to school. No skipping, although sometimes I do."

Leroy sat on a rock beside the creek. "You know, Jay, if you want that bike it's going to take you a heck of a long time to earn enough money from that ol' paper route of yours. Too bad you got no way to sweeten the pot."

"You got somethin' else in mind?" Jay threw a stick into the creek, watching it whip around rocks and disappear beneath some hanging moss.

"I might. But, I can't say. It's secret." *This is like fishing. Dangle the lure a little bit to hook him.*

Jay set himself behind Leroy and nudged him with his shoulder. "Tell me. We're friends, ain't we?"

Leroy nudged back. "Nope. It's too good to share." *Jiggle the bait, get him interested.*

Jay jumped up and looked down at Leroy. "Come on... Tell me, please?"

Leroy rose and walked along the bank of the creek. *Keep him hooked but pull away. Tease the line.* "You got folks along your route that would be interested in door-to-door delivery of some quality rum?"

Jay stopped and stared at Leroy's back. He grabbed his arm to turn him around. "Whoa. Illegal hooch? You a rum runner?"

Leroy shrugged and shook his arm loose. He broke off a small twig from a nearby bush and chewed the end of it. "Yeah, I am. See, I knew I shouldn't have told ya. Look, let's get back." *Snap.*

"No, wait Leroy. I got some folks that would find it handy... maybe... having a bottle dropped off to their front door." *Caught. Now reel him in.*

Leroy tossed a few rocks into the creek. He handed one to Jay. "Let me take your wagon and deliver your papers. That would give me a chance to sell them a bottle along the way."

"Why can't I do it? They're my customers. They know me."

"I dunno. Rum running is secret stuff. What if they tell your ma?"

Jay thought about it. "They can't 'cause then I'd say they were buying liquor from me and then they'd be in trouble. Besides, I'd only talk to the fellas. They wouldn't rat me out to my ma."

Leroy kept walking back toward Goodtimes.

"So whaddya say, Leroy. Can I be your partner?"

"How about I give you four bottles you can hide under the newspapers. We can split the profits."

"Only four? I know at least four houses that would buy a bottle. You got more?"

Leroy shrugged and spat. "Let's start with four and see how we go."

"Deal. Spit and shake. Like Huck and Tom did in the graveyard. No blood though, okay?"

"Remember, you can't tell anyone," Leroy said.

Jay nodded solemnly. "I'm no snitch. We're partners. Say, my ma wants you to come back with me for supper so that she can meet you. Wanna come?"

Leroy's heart leaped at the idea. He shrugged and waited a minute before answering. "Sure. I guess. Let's stop by the kitchen tent and I'll tell Lucky I won't be home for supper."

Lucky was happy to meet Jay, and Jay was eager to quiz him about the snake. Shortly, the boys headed back to Coconut Grove, planning and scheming, dreaming of how they'd spend their riches.

Leroy settled round the table in the dining room. Mr. and Mrs. Carmichael and their three boys joined hands. Jay grabbed Leroy's. "For Grace," he whispered.

Leroy reached for Mrs. Carmichael's hand. She gave it a squeeze. During the short grace he took a few quick looks at Mr. Carmichael's bowed head.

"Bless this food, Our Father. And the people who eat it. Amen"

Leroy added an Amen to the chorus.

"Have your folks lived in Coconut Grove long, Leroy?" Mrs. Carmichael asked, passing Leroy a bowl of potatoes.

"No, ma'am. We live out of town."

"Your family farms?"

"Ah, no we fish."

Jay choked.

"My pa has a fishing boat called the *Rex*."

"We don't eat enough fish. It's so good for you. Jay, pass Leroy more chicken."

"I know some of the fishermen down at the pier. What did you say your father's name was, Leroy? You look familiar. Maybe I've seen you at the pier?" Mr. Carmichael asked.

"Don't think so, sir. But lots of folks say I have that kind of face that looks like everybody else's. My pa's name is Bill. Bill McCoy."

"Hmm. Name's not familiar."

"He keeps our boat at our own dock. That's probably why you don't know him."

"And do you go fishing, Leroy?" Mrs. Carmichael asked.

"Oh, yes, ma'am. My pa can't manage without me."

"Good to have a family business. Now, if Jay would apply himself in school, maybe he could work with me at some point," said Mr. Carmichael.

"Aw, Pa."

"Pa nothing. Your teacher says you have potential, boy. You just need to pay attention in class."

"Are you and Jay in the same class at school?" asked Mrs. Carmichael.

"Leroy don't go to school," said Jay.

"Oh?"

"On account of I gotta help my pa on the fishing boat. But I can read and do sums. And I have a library card."

"I never went past the fourth grade myself and look how I turned out. My children will have more advantages than I did. That's why I work so hard," said Mr. Carmichael. "You're sure I don't know your folks, Leroy?"

"Doubtful, sir. Unless you saw them around town sometime."

Leroy was really hoping that Mr. Carmichael wouldn't remember where they'd met... at the pig roast on the beach.

Mr. Carmichael slowly nodded. "That must be it. Or maybe church? Somewhere. Never forget a face. Lovely, dinner, my dear." He pushed back from the table and headed to his newspaper and favorite chair in the living room.

With dinner done, Leroy jumped up to help Mrs. Carmichael clear the table. "My goodness, thank you, Leroy. It's nice to have help, but you're company. You go play with Jay."

"That's okay, Mrs. Carmichael. My ma said if you eat you wash up."

Jay sniggered. "Boys don't wash dishes."

"Your mother sounds like an enlightened woman. I don't see any reason boys shouldn't help out. Jay, you and Leroy wash these up and put them away. It will be good for you," Mrs. Carmichael said.

"This was a dumb idea," Jay grumbled, taking the wet plate from Leroy and giving it a half-hearted wipe with his tea-towel.

"This is nothing. I gotta wash up after closing. On a busy night I gotta fill up the sink with hot water a bunch of times. How come you told your folks I don't go to school?"

"I had a hard time listening to you tell your fishing story. That's my ma you were lying to."

"You're not going to tell them about Goodtimes are you?"

"Hey. I'm no snitch."

"What are you boys whispering about?" Mrs. Carmichael said, coming into the kitchen.

"Nothing." The boys said in unison.

* * * *

"Where's Leroy?" asked Darwin.

"He's met a friend in town and is staying there for supper." Edith was putting chairs around the tables.

134

"A friend? That would be good for him. He's not got anyone his own age to get in trouble with out here," Darwin said, giving her a hand.

"I know. I worry about him spending all his time here. He should have more friends, play baseball, or whatever it is young boys do."

"Play baseball? Knowing our Leroy, it would be more like monkey business than baseball." Darwin chuckled.

"Boys never grow up, do they?"

CHAPTER 21

As part of her daily routine, Edith set up clean glassware in the bar.

"Hey there, Edith. It's a gorgeous day out there. Why are you inside?" From the front door, Captain Bill McCoy's voice was a foghorn. She was smiling before she even turned around.

"Captain McCoy. Someone has to do this. I'm not in command of a grand ship. I had no crew to give orders to."

"Leory might disagree with you, there. Har har. But the glasses can wait, girl. Get your bonnet on and let's go for a boat ride. What you need is some salt air to knock the cobwebs off ya."

She made a great show of brushing down her shoulders and arms. "I'll have you know, sir, I do not have cobwebs."

"Aye, that I can see for sure," he said, giving her a long admiring look.

Edith blushed.

"Seriously, come with me. I've had Cookie pack a picnic lunch. I've got the launch tied up to your dock, or we could take that trawler of yours out instead, if you'd be more comfortable."

His shirt was freshly washed, pants clean, too. His hair had been neatly trimmed. Her heart beat even faster. "Okay, I'll play hooky. Let me go tell Lucky I'm going."

Edith popped into the kitchen tent. "Lucky, do you need me for anything? I'm going to spend the afternoon with Captain McCoy."

"Everything good," Lucky said. "You go to Bill's ship?"

"No, we're going to take the launch out for a picnic on the Bay," Edith said, her eyes shining with excitement. *Oh, I'm telling too much. Am I? Why do I feel dizzy?*

"I wanna come, too. Can I come, Miz Edith?" Leroy was filling up two pots, potatoes in one, peelings in the other.

"You have jobs here, Leroy."

Leroy threw his knife into the pot and crossed his arms. His pouting face made Lucky laugh.

It took only minutes to rush up the stairs to freshen her lipstick. Giggling, Edith grabbed a nice hat; back downstairs before Bill could change his mind.

"And a lovely bonnet it is too, Edith," he said, giving her an admiring glance. Edith's tingling toes skipped her all the way to the dock.

She eyed the skiff, more of a rowboat, despite the small outboard motor hanging off it.

"Let's take the *Rex*. It's been ages since she's been out and she could use a good run."

"Your wish was my command, fair lady." Bill reached into the skiff and hauled out a picnic basket and a bottle of wine.

Bill gave Edith a hand to board the *Rex*. She measured how long they held hands, a bit longer than necessary. *I know Cleo won't mind.*

It was a glorious day with the breezes balancing the sun's warmth. Waves were minimal. Edith was aware Bill was watching her more than he was watching the water. *I know Cleo won't mind.*

She watched the water for him—needed somewhere to train her eyes. "Oh, Bill, look. A dolphin." Edith pointed to the sleek gray shape arching out of the water.

"Watch, there are likely more."

She squealed as two more dolphins surfaced to play.

"Anywhere in particular you want to go?" he asked, comfortable at the wheel.

"It's just lovely to be here." Edith sighed and wrapped her arms around her knees, staring out at the turquoise waters. "I live right next to the ocean, yet rarely spend any time on the water."

"I'm glad I could drag you away from your tasks, at least for today."

Shared smiled sent Edith's tummy into cartwheels.

"I'm heading back to Nassau tomorrow. Tonight will be our last night on the Row for about a week. I wanted to come and say goodbye."

He wanted to come and say goodbye... to me. He must be interested.

"Is Cleo going with you?"

"Oh, aye. She's anxious to get back to her warehouse." He ran a finger along her bare arm. "The two of you are a lot alike that way. Passionate, driven women."

"It must be a lonely life, traveling between the Bahamas and America, parked along Rum Row for weeks at a time. Is it the money thatdrives you to do it?" Edith asked.

"Certainly the money is the reason I got started. I had my eye on a sweet schooner and needed some capital. Since then, I've found that rum running has all the kicks of gambling and the thrill of sport. You're always playing the odds: battling other smugglers, pirates, the weather. It's in my blood now."

"My late husband, Mickey, felt the same way about bootlegging: the big deals, the danger, the adventure."

"Yes, the adventure. But you're like that, too, aren't you? I've seen the way your cheeks flush when you're talking about the smuggling you do. You have a wild side that is very," he paused, looking deep in her eyes, "very appealing."

Edith's hammering heart would not allow her to look away.

"For me, when I'm aboard the *Arethusa*, on the open sea with the boom of the wind against full sails, the dawn coming out of the sea, and nights under the rocking stars… those moments catch and held me most of all."

Edith thrilled at the unfamiliar poetry of his words. *When was the last time someone spoke to me like this… ever? He's so deep. And sensitive. A poetic soul.*

"I feel like that when I'm sitting on the veranda at Goodtimes looking out over the Bay. Behind me there is something solid and thriving I've built. In front of me is the wide-open ocean and a world of possibilities."

Their shared smiles verged on shared dreams. Then, Edith reeled away from the intimacy and scrambled to find safer footing. "I told you we've expanded our bootlegging? I've got half a dozen customers along the South Dixie Highway signed up. Small places; nothing too big yet."

"Make no small plans, girl. They have no magic to stir men's blood."

Edith chuckled and removed her hat, letting the breeze play with her hair. With her face to the sun, eyes closed, she beamed. The sunshine glowing through her eyelids was the same color of peach as Goodtimes.

"You look content."

"At this moment, I'm blissfully happy." She opened her eyes and grinned at Bill. "And hungry as all get out."

Bill cut the motor, and they rocked on the waves. "I have a remedy for that. Cookie's packed us a feast from the weight of the hamper. Why don't you lay out the food and I'll uncork this wine."

Food, wine, and their shared laughter over Bill's tall tales, or at least she hopes they're tall tales, wore away the last of her barriers.

"I'm having the best day, Bill. Thank you for dragging me away." Edith sipped her wine.

Bill leaned over, ready to top it up. He didn't pull back. She put her glass down. Edith could see up close that his eyes were the same blue as the ocean. She held her breath as he moved closer. Ever-so-softly, his lips brushed against hers. Intuitively, she wound her arms around his neck pulling him in for a deeper kiss. As she shifted, her glass tipped over, soaking her dress with a red stain.

"Oh, my goodness," Edith said, breaking away and flustered. She patted at the stain, which was the same color as her cheeks.

Oh, Cleo. Who's worse—Bill or me?

"Such a pretty dress. I hope it's not ruined." Bill leaned in again but Edith pulled back.

"I should be able to get it out." Her laugh was shaky, awkward even. "I guess all good things have to end. Those bar glasses won't put themselves away. Can we head back to Goodtimes?"

Bill sat back against a pile of rope and looked at her with a faux-sad face. "You push yourself too hard, Edith. You should be kinder to yourself."

"Perhaps, but it still won't get the work done. I've always pushed hard." She began to gather up the remains of the picnic lunch while Bill got the engines in the *Rex* rumbling.

"I know we've chatted some before, but never really got to how you wound up running a blind-tiger in Florida," Bill said.

"I've told you a bit about Mickey. I spent a lifetime around bootlegging and speakeasies. When my Mickey passed, I decided I wanted something like that for my own. I like the striving and going to bed tired from hard work. My success won't be because I'm lucky, it'll be because I achieved it on purpose."

"I think that's what I like best about you. Your drive. There's a strength in you I know I could lean against. Rare in a woman."

140

"You'd be surprised, Bill. Times are changing, but slowly. Most women my age never get a chance to discover what they're made of. Or to pursue their dreams like I am. They spend their lives chasing the expectations of others: fathers, husbands, leaders, preachers. It's a privilege to even ask the question, let alone try to search for an answer to 'who do I know myself to be; and what do I want to do in the world, separate from what everyone else wants of me?'"

"It sounds like you're in a good place, Edith Duffy."

"Aye-aye, captain. I am." Edith shifted to stand beside Bill. They faced into the wind as they moved through the water, swaying and balancing with the chop of the hull of the old trawler as it cut through the waves.

Bill's right. I am too hard on myself. And it's not just the rebuilding of Goodtimes. My personal life needs rebuilding as well. I wanted a new life. Stealing Cleo's man isn't a good way to start.

CHAPTER 22

Pouting at being left behind, Leroy watched Edith and Bill pull away from the dock in the *Rex*. *Nobody ever takes me anywhere.* He kicked a stone up the path. "Lucky, I'm going into town to see my friend. I'll be back in time to set up for tonight," he shouted.

Lucky appeared at the tent's entrance, tea-towel in hand. "Make sure you are. I do it last time and I busy cooking supper. What Mr. Darwin tell you about responsibility?" He threw it over his shoulder, muttering away in Cantonese.

As Leroy waited impatiently outside the Carmichael house, the Coast Guard captain appeared further down the street.

"Hey, sir. Captain, sir." Leroy hurried after him.

The officer turned. "Yes, young man?"

"Sir. I never got the chance to thank you for saving me and my ma. We were on the ocean and ran out of gas. We prob-ly woulda died out there if you hadn't saved us."

"I'm pleased we were able to be of service. I'm Lt. Commander Saunders. And who might you be, young man?"

"My names Leroy, sir." Leroy, eyes wide with wonder at talking to the Coast Guard commander, could think of nothing else to say. The brilliant white of the uniform was mesmerizing.

"Was there something else, lad? I'm on my way home and I don't want to keep Mrs. Saunders waiting."

"Um, yes. Yes, there is. Do you need any odd jobs done around your place? I'm a good worker."

John Saunders chuckled. "I think I'm okay for odd jobs, young man. But good on you for asking. It's nice to see character like that in young people these days."

Leroy, head down, was crest fallen. John reached out and put a hand on his shoulder. "Look, if I do need any jobs done, I'll be sure to call on you, all right? What was your name again?"

"Leroy, sir."

"And how do I get a held of you, Leroy?"

"Um, we don't have a telephone. But you could leave a message for me with the Carmichaels down the street. My friend Jay lives there and he'll make sure I get it."

"I'll be sure to do that. You had a nice day now, Leroy."

"You, too, sir. Bye." Leroy saluted.

Chuckling, John returned it.

Leroy watched him go. *Wow. I actually talked to him. He's a real hero. I hope he calls me. I'd better tell Jay and his mom he might leave me a message.*

Leroy returned to the Carmichael's and knocked at the front door, which was opened by Jay's mother.

"Oh, Leroy. Jay's not here at the moment. I sent him to the store to pick me up some eggs. I'm baking a cake for dessert tonight. Can you stay for supper?"

"Sure I can. What kind of cake?"

"Chocolate. With chocolate icing."

"*Mmmm,*" Leroy said, rubbing his tummy. *Miz Edith will probably be gone all day long, having fun on the boat with Captain McCoy. No reason I can't have fun, too.*

"Come in and wait with me in the kitchen until Jay gets back."

Leroy perched on a stool at one end of the counter.

"Does your mother do much baking?"

"No, but Lucky does."

"Who's Lucky?"

"He's from China and does all the cooking."

"Oh my goodness, think of it. China. That's a long way away. Why do you need someone to cook?"

"*Uhm*, we have a café. My pa is always busy 'cause he's a fisherman and... *uhm*... my ma runs the café."

"Is it in town? Which one is it?"

"No, it's out of town."

"That must be why you're so good at doing up the dishes. Is it just open at lunchtime or do you do supper, too?"

"All day every day. Excepting Sundays, of course. Sometimes we have parties there."

"Like weddings and anniversary parties?"

Leroy shrugged. "Something like that."

"Late nights, I bet."

"Sometimes I'm up 'til midnight. Right now the kitchen is in a tent out behind the café. Lucky fills a big tub of water from the stove and I just stand there scrubbing and wiping until I can't scrub nor wipe no more."

"Goodness. A boy like you up to all hours working like that. I can't imagine Jay having that kind of gumption."

"It's not so bad. I get to go fishing and exploring during the day, when Miz Edith doesn't need me to do stuff for her."

"Miss Edith?"

"Oh, *uhm*, my real ma died when I was born. Miz Edith took me in to work in the café a few months ago. Sometimes I call her my ma."

Leroy swallowed a lump in his throat that Mrs. Carmichael's tender look brought on.

"Oh, Leroy, I'm so sorry. That is so sad. But at least you still have your father."

"Yup. He loves me lots. Mrs. Carmichael, is it okay if Commander Saunders from down the street maybe leaves me a message here sometimes? He might need me to do some odd jobs for him and Mrs. Saunders."

"Why, certainly Leroy. But why doesn't he call you at home?"

Leroy was momentarily panicked.

"Oh, you don't have a telephone? Of course we can take a message for you. I'll make sure Jay passes it along."

"What kinds of jobs do you think they might need me to do, Mrs. Carmichael?"

"Well, that's hard to say. Mavis Saunders might appreciate someone to help with her garden, or maybe clean out the garage or something like that. And it would be a great way to earn some pin money, wouldn't it?"

The back door bangs opened and Jay came in with a dozen eggs. "Hiya, Leroy."

Leroy jumped off the stool. "Hiya."

"You boys go play and I'll call you when supper's ready. Now scoot. I've got to get the cake into the oven so it has time to cool before I ice it." Mrs. Carmichael said as she began to crack eggs into the mixing bowl.

* * * *

In bed, next to her husband, her hair pinned for curls, Mrs. Carmichael suspended her reading. "What do you think of that young boy from supper, Alvin? He's wanting to do some odd jobs for the Saunders. It sounds like money might be tight at home."

"Well, good for him to have that kind of enterprise. He's the kind of boy Jay could learn a lot from."

"Jay's spending a lot of time with him. They were playing all afternoon."

"He seems nice enough. Good manners. Sharp," Alvin Carmichael answered.

"His mother died when he was small and his father works for a woman who runs a café. When he's not fishing."

"Oh? Which café?"

"That's what I asked him. It's not in town. It's somewhere on the water, although I guess close enough he can walk into town."

"A café? Outside of town?"

"I thought it strange as well."

"What's the woman's name?"

"Miz Edith something."

"Edith Duffy?"

"Do you know her?"-

"Oh, my dear. She doesn't run a café. She runs a blind-tiger."

"Goodness, no. A boy working at a saloon? What is his father thinking?"

"I don't think there is a father. At least not that I've heard. Edith Duffy runs the place on her own. There was a fire. You remember. At the old 'Gator Joe's place."

"Oh my goodness. That must be the place Mavis Saunders talks about all the time at choir practice. This is terrible, Alvin. The Homemakers' Guild is working with the Children's Home to take the boy out of there. We can't have Jay playing with him. And I'm not sure I want Leroy playing here. What kind of influence was he? Think of all the fibs he's told us. And Jay."

"Lying is a serious accusation, Mary. I'm sure Leroy was just embarrassed about the circumstances. It can't be easy living with that kind of shame. I'll leave it up to you to decide what to do about the boy playing here, my dear. Jay is very impressionable. We don't want him picking up any bad habits."

"You don't think Leroy is drinking, do you? Mavis tells some terrible stories, and Brother Silas is always going on about that place."

Alvin harrumphs. "Brother Silas spends far too much time on the evils of drinking and not nearly enough time on good works."

Mary barely heard. "Or smoking. Lord only knows what goes on out there."

"Leroy doesn't seem like a drinker or a smoker, Mary. He's a nice enough boy, just happens to find himself in difficult circumstances."

"Had you ever been there? Out to this blind-tiger."

Alvin rolled over, his arm tucked under the pillow. "Don't be ridiculous. Why would I be at a blind-tiger? Now, I've got a busy day tomorrow. I'm going to get some sleep."

CHAPTER 23

Edith was startled at the knock at the office door. *"Um*, Miz Edith. Four ladies on path,"* said Lucky.

"A whole group?"

"I see from kitchen tent. I warn you."

Edith moved through the barroom to the front door. "Thanks, Lucky. Can you make some sweet tea and bring it out to the veranda?"

Lucky nodded and disappeared.

Glancing out the French doors, Edith saw two women trailing behind the Saunders woman and her sidekick, Agnes Matheson. *A pair of hyenas.*

She smoothed her dress and stepped outside. "Good morning, ladies. What a lovely surprise. What can I do for you today?"

Startled at her appearance, they hesitated. Mavis Saunders stepped forward.

"Mrs. Duffy, we've come to speak with you about a very serious matter."

"Please come and have a seat. It's so pleasant out here on the veranda." *And away from the evil saloon.* "What can I do for you?" Edith asked, once everyone was settled.

"You know my good friend Agnes, of course. And this is Mrs. Mary Carmichael from our Homemakers' Guild. And this is Miss Mildred White, from the Florida Children's Home Society."

Lucky came out with a pitcher of sweet tea. Leroy carried a tray of empty glasses. "Hiya, Mrs. Carmichael. Is Jay here?"

Mary Carmichael met his sunny smile with sternness. "No, he isn't."

Edith was alert to the strange dynamics. The ladies made a fuss of accepting their glasses. No one looked at her or Leroy. The hair on the back of her neck rose.

"Leroy, honey. Can you help Lucky in the kitchen? I'll come find you after our guests leave."

"Sure, Miz Edith. Bye Mrs. Carmichael."

Mary gave him a thin smile.

Mildred White frowned. "Mrs. Duffy, we are here today on behalf of the good people of Coconut Grove. Perhaps you are unaware of the specifics of Florida's recent child labor law, which outlaws children under twelve years of age from working in saloons and around liquor."

Not to be outdone, Mavis Saunders puffed up and leaned forward. "Yes, Mrs. Duffy. The Homemakers' Guild is also concerned about this grave matter. As the group that sets the moral tone for Coconut Grove, we felt compelled to intervene."

Agnes and Mary watched the drama between Mildred and Mavis, unfold.

Edith turned to meet Mavis's challenging gaze. "Intervene? I see. I wasn't aware of the details. Of course, the sale of liquor is illegal right now in Florida. Goodtimes operates as a café."

Mavis sniffed. "We are not naïve, Mrs. Duffy. We're aware of what goes on out here."

"Really? Please elaborate."

"The drinking and gambling—also illegal. Heavens knows what other debauchery."

"The vice," Agnes hissed. "It's shameful."

Mavis smiled with approval at her friend. "Exactly. Coconut Grove residents are quite concerned. I know I speak for them all when I say this situation cannot continue."

The smugness of the woman. "And this relates to Leroy how?" Edith directed the comment at Mildred White, then moved her eyes to the briefcase resting at her feet.

"I understand that Leroy is not your son, Mrs. Duffy. Do you have proof of legal guardianship of the boy?" Mildred asked.

"Yes, legal guardianship is an important consideration," Mavis said.

"No, not exactly. He was looking for work and I offered it. His legal guardian, his aunt, knows he is here."

"He lives here and not with his aunt?" Mildred looked from Edith to Mavis.

"Yes. She lives in the Everglades and it's too far for him go back and forth. It seemed easier that he stay here, although he often goes to visit her," Edith said.

Mildred turned to Mavis. "Were you aware that his legal guardian knows where he is and what he's doing?"

Mavis huffed. "I only know that an underage boy is living and working here in this evil place."

"Sodom and Gomorrah," hissed Agnes.

Edith raises one arched eyebrow at the outburst. *These two are like those harridans at the Zonta Club in Philadelphia. I was never good enough to sit on the board, but my donation checks always cashed quickly enough.*

"I'm not sure living in a camp out in the Everglades is a proper place for the boy, either. It's difficult, if not impossible, for him to attend school or church. Mrs. Duffy, my son, Jay, was a playmate of Leroy's. Leroy's been in our home. He often mentions... things... about working here."

"What things, Mrs. Carmichael?"

"Well, the hours for one. Goodtimes is open until the early hours of the morning, and then he said he went fishing with his father—"

"His father?" Mildred White and Edith say in unison.

"He said his father was a fisherman. He has a boat called the *Rex*?"

"Ah, he means Darwin McKenzie. He works for me. And yes, they go fishing, although usually in the daylight. Although I've heard pre-dawn can be a very advantageous time to catch fish." Edith's smile didn't quite reach her eyes.

"And he says he has to carry heavy items, and is forced to do all kinds of manual work," Mary said.

"I'm not sure what he's referring to. Leroy helps set up chairs in the café. He helps clean the tables. Like in any restaurant, dirty dishes have to be taken back to the kitchen and washed."

Mildred reached down and pulled a notebook from her briefcase. "And he is responsible for washing those dishes, is he not Mrs. Duffy?" she asked, pen poised.

Edith's eyes narrowed. *I've seen her type before, desperate to be in charge, throwing their weight around.* "I see no harm in a boy washing dishes. I'm sure you'll find similar arrangements in many of the restaurants in town."

The women looked to Miss White. "If we were to do a surprise inspection some evening, Mrs. Duffy, I presume we would not find alcohol for sale on the premises."

"The sale of alcohol is illegal, Miss White."

"And would Leroy's aunt be prepared to testify officially that she has given her permission for Leroy to be here?"

"I'm sure she would agree to that," Edith said through gritted teeth.

"And if a judge were to question Leroy about the hours he keeps, they would be reasonable?"

"Of course."

"And you have pay stubs to support the claim that Leroy is being paid for his labor?"

"I can get them for you now," Edith said, rising. Her body was rigid as she went into Goodtimes.

Fuming, Edith walked into the barroom and out the backdoor into the kitchen tent. Leroy was sitting at the table shelling peas. "Leroy, I want you to go right now to Cassie. Don't take anything, just get there quick. Stay overnight and come back with her tomorrow. Do you understand?"

Leroy stood, his eyes wide. "What's going on Miz Edith. Why is Mrs. Carmichael here?"

"Just go, now." She looked to Lucky. "And you go with him, Lucky. I've got to talk to those ladies some more."

Lucky, gripping his cleaver, nodded. "Come Leroy. I walk with you."

Edith grabbed her payroll journal as she went past the office.

"Here you go, Miss White. I'm sure you will find everything in order," she said, thrusting the journal at Mildred.

The women sit silently as Miss White read through the documentation. "He's been here since February of this year?"

"Yes."

"This documentation appears to be in order," she said. She nodded to the other women and handed the journal back to Edith.

Thank you, Maggie, for insisting I learn how to do this. Edith's friend in Philadelphia was an accountant and a stickler for complete and accurate records.

"Mrs. Duffy, before I go, I would like to look at Leroy's bedroom. And I will need to have a written note of permission from his aunt by the end of the week." Miss White rose, as did the other ladies.

Edith stood as well. "Certainly, Miss White. I'll also need some authorization from someone in authority that you have an official role to play here. While I appreciate the 'community concern' Mrs. Saunders and her cohort are expressing, I think I need to ensure we were dealing with a legitimate situation and not just, pardon me, nosey neighbors."

"Well, I never—" Mavis huffed and puffed her energy throughout the group.

"Certainly, Mrs. Duffy. I will drop them off to you tomorrow. As we're here now, perhaps we could look at Leroy's room?"

Edith listened to the twittering and gasps as they walked through the barroom.

"You have a stage in your café?"

"Yes. We occasionally have music in the evenings."

"And the chalkboard. That is your bill of fair?"

Edith glanced at it. "Yes. We like to add a bit of local color to the menu. Black Jack's Rootshine is rootbeer and named after a local pirate."

"It seems like an expensive bottle of rootbeer."

"My customers haven't complained."

"And the bottles behind the counter?"

"A friend who used to run a bar gave me his leftover stock from before Prohibition. Just waiting for them to repeal the Volstead Act and we can crack them open."

Miss White, walking beside her, was silent.

153

"This was Leroy's room," Edith said, standing beside an open door.

"He has his own room?" Mary Carmichael said, unsure. "He said he sleeps on the boat." Mary looked around the tidy room, a puzzled frown on her face.

"No, he sleeps in that bed."

Mildred looked over the books in Leroy's bookcase, which was next to his desk. On the desk were well used scribblers and notebooks, and a jar of pencils and pens. On the wall behind it was a map of the world with push pins marking Philadelphia, Miami, Canton City, Shanghai, and Venice.

"He has hopes of travel?" Miss White asked Edith.

Edith choked off the retort she wants to give and instead said through gritted teeth, "These are places we have gotten letters from. He collects stamps."

"Oh, like Brother Silas," Mavis said.

Edith's hands clench. "Nothing like Brother Silas's collection."

Startled, the other women stared at her.

"Yes, I am aware of his collection. It's famous in Coconut Grove. Leroy isn't a collector like Brother Silas. He just hangs on to the ones we get in the mail." Edith wanted to spit every time she had to say the preacher's title and name.

The women gawked around at the room. Leroy's clothes were hung up in the closet, a pair of pajamas were folded neatly on his pillow. Mary Carmichael shook her head, a puzzled frown on her face.

Mildred White gave a curt nod. "Thank you so much for your time, Mrs. Duffy. And again, our apologies for intruding unannounced. I'll be back tomorrow with the paperwork."

CHAPTER 24

If Goodtimes had a drawbridge, Edith would have pulled it up. After the hideous delegation left, she went into the barroom and shut the door. Then bolted it. The sound of the lock bolt striking home sent a shiver down her spine. She immediately went to check that Leroy and Lucky had gone, then went into the soon-to-be-kitchen space and locked that door, as well.

Lucky had left with Leroy. Darwin was out on the *Marianne*. She was alone.

Pacing back and forth, she clutched a freshly poured glass of whiskey.

I can't believe it. Coming after me because of Goodtimes I could understand, but to question my fitness to look after Leroy. Who do they think they are?

Edith peered out the window up to the car park to make sure it was empty. Her heart pounded and she shivered in a cold sweat. "Argh," she yells.

Dirty cops I can deal with, and even those biddies from the Guild. But that woman from the Children's Home is going to be trouble. I can see it in her eyes. There won't be any bribing her.

She strode into the office and called Mae.

"I need a lawyer, a good one."

"Who's in trouble, doll?"

"They want to take Leroy."

"What?"

"Those damn women from town. They just left. And they had a woman from the Children's Home. Those meddlesome old biddies in town have it in their head that I'm violating some kind of a child labor law. And the woman from the Children's Home kept asking questions. The took a tour through Leroy's bedroom for goodness' sakes," Edith said. She snarled and spit into the telephone.

"They've called in the people from the Children's Home? Oh, dea. That's not good," Mae said.

"A dried-up old spinster trying to take my Leroy. Said I can't provide a proper environment." Edith took a gulp of breath, and then another, then almost sobbed. "Mae, they're going to take Leroy," she wailed, grasping the telephone as if it was her lifeline.

"Sit tight. I'll have someone call you today. We won't let this happen, Edith. No one is going to take Leroy. Leave it with me."

Mae hung up and Edith clutched the telephone receiver to her heart. *I can't let them have Leroy. He loves me.*

Mickey would have a solution. He'd drive by and unload a few chopper rounds. She held her breath, feasting on the idea of revenge. A silent movie ran in her mind: the barrel of the tommy guns, the puff of smoke as the barrels chatter, Mavis and her posse of harridans spinning from the force of the bullets, the spray of blood. She saw them scream.

Edith took a long, shuddering breath and replaced the receiver. *A lawyer is a better plan. When Mickey had problems with the authorities, he always surrounded himself with lawyers. As far as he was concerned, good lawyers knew the law, great lawyers knew the judge.*

She grabbed the bottle of whiskey. White knuckled as her shaking hand wrapped around the neck, she poured another glass and sat by the telephone, staring at it, willing it to ring.

Another silent movie played out in her mind: Leroy walking up the beach that first day with the huckleberries staining his shirt; the two of them lost at sea, spinning tales of dragons and white knights; Leroy bent over the radio listening to a ball game while she washed dishes; her in her chair, basking in the sun while he was curled up on

156

the dock, nose in a book, reading beside her; the tragic fire, and Leroy's trembling hands untying the ropes to set her free.

Oh, Leroy. No. You can't go. I won't let them take you.

She waited.

Patches of sunlight crawled across the floor toward the office window as the sun rose higher in the sky. She heard the front door in the barroom rattle as someone tried to open it. A shadow passed by the window. The door in the soon-to-be kitchen rattled. A key in the lock. It opened and closed. Footsteps. Edith stared at the telephone.

"Edith. The front and back doors are locked. Where's Lucky?" Darwin, full of normalcy, was standing at her office door.

"Edith? Where is everybody? Why's the door locked? We open in a few hours and Leroy hasn't unstacked the chairs yet. Has that darn kid run off back to town again?"

Edith sat, fixated on the telephone, still willing it to ring. Darwin stepped closer and puts a hand on her shoulder.

"Edith?"

"I'm waiting for a call."

"What's happened? Where are Leroy and Lucky?"

"At Cassie's." she continued to stare at the telephone on her desk.

"Why would Lucky be there? What's happened?" Darwin crouched down in front of her. "Tell me what's happened."

Edith stared at him with blank eyes. "Mavis Saunders was here earlier this morning. She brought backup including a woman from the Florida Children's Home Society," she said in a monotone. A rote recitation of cold facts. "Children under twelve can't work in barrooms or around alcohol. Or in restaurants, apparently. They demanded a note from Cassie giving him permission to be here. We have until the end of the week to save him, or then they'll take him."

"I don't understand," Darwin said, sitting back on his heels.

Edith drew in a breath. She blinked, looking at Darwin for the first time. "That witch is coming to take him away from me."

Darwin stood and took the bottle to pour himself a drink. "Okay. What's the plan?"

Edith shook her head. "I'm waiting for a lawyer to call. Leroy and Cassie will be back here tomorrow, I hope." She looked up at Darwin, eyes wide in fear. "What if they don't come? What if Cassie keeps him hidden in the 'glades? Oh, Darwin, what if I never see him again?" Tears flowed.

Darwin pulled her up and wrapped his arms around her. "We'll figure this out. Don't worry."

The telephone rang and Edith lunged for it. It was Al Capone's attorney, calling from Chicago. Edith filled him in. She could hear him flipping pages and murmuring.

"A mother without support cannot be denied the income from her child. You say you're able to get the mother—"

"Legal guardian."

"The legal guardian to give you a letter to that effect?"

"I will ask. Cassie is a strange one. She kept Leroy hidden for ten years. They might disappear back into the Everglades."

"Then your problem is solved. No boy, no infraction of the Florida child labor law."

Her hands form tight fists. "No," Edith shouted. "That is not the solution."

"It may not be the one you want, but it is a solution." He paused with more page flipping. Edith tried slow, measured breaths. Darwin paced. The lawyer cleared his throat. "You say you're running Goodtimes as a speakeasy?"

"Yes, although we claim it's a café."

"Another option is to bribe the governor. Everything you're dealing with, except the booze, is state jurisdiction."

"I have the funds."

"Everything hinges on the guardian. Call me after you've met with her. In the meantime, maintain your claim that Goodtimes is a café. And don't have the boy on the premises unless you have something in writing from the mother. I mean guardian. I'll get my people here working on a defense strategy. And I'll also reach out to Doyle Carlton. He's your governor down there. We went to school together at University of Chicago. And Meyer Lansky's had some dealings with him around gambling."

"Meyer. Yes, he knows me and Leroy. Thank you. I'll speak with you tomorrow." Edith slowly lowered the receiver.

"What did he say? Can they take Leroy?" Lucky asked. He and Darwin were now crowded into the small office.

Edith looked up, startled. "Lucky, you're back. Is Cassie here?"

"I no see her. Empty camp. The water in the pot over the fire still hot, the fire snuffed out. Look like she hiding."

"Did you wait?"

"For little bit. No sign of her. I left Leroy there. Tell him bring Cassie to Goodtimes tomorrow. And I shouted it to the forest. Said you needed her help." Lucky shrugged. "Then I come back. Need to start the gumbo for tonight."

"What did you tell Leroy?"

"Don't know anything to tell Leroy. But boy is scared."

"So, what's the plan, Edith?" Darwin asked. "Are we closing Goodtimes?"

"No, not yet. We'll call their bluff. It sounds like the governor may be some help. Or Meyer Lansky if that fails. Leroy and Cassie will be here tomorrow and I'll get the permission letter. That's one problem solved. As to the other, we've been operating an illegal establishment since 'Gator Joe's. That's nothing new. We'll scale things back, no special promotions or events, but Goodtimes will stay open."

"Are you sure, Edith? The consequences are different. You'll take that risk?"

"I said no," she said, almost screaming.

Edith stood. "I can't breathe in here." She pushed past Darwin and Lucky and began pacing back and forth in the barroom. "God, I hate when other people have power over me. This is my life now. I've been surviving the sheriff, the Coast Guard, the Wharf Rats, and the weather. A bunch of old women in a tizzy are not going to close me down." She thrust her tight fists into the air to make her points as she strode back and forth, a wild look in her eye.

"You need to think this through, Edith. It's Leroy's future wellbeing at stake," Darwin said.

Edith whirled on him and he took a step back. "What the hell do you think I'm doing, Darwin? You think I'd risk Leroy by keeping Goodtimes open?"

"Isn't that what you're doing?"

Edith sneered. "There's no real threat. Just a bunch of women. Nothing the governor and a bit of cash can't fix." She began pacing again, lashing out and kicking a chair as she passed. "You can't let these kinds of people see you're scared. It just encourages them. Bad enough when they were after *me*, but now they've set their sights on Leroy." Edith spun, pacing again. "Well, it's not going to happen. I won't let it."

"Are you trying to convince me or yourself?"

Edith, lost to her raving, didn't catch the remark. She kicked another chair across the floor.

Lucky looked from Darwin to Edith. "Miz Edith. If we do less blind-tiger, we could build up café so it more convincing disguise."

Edith swirled around, facing him, nodding eagerly. "Now, that's the kind of thinking we need. What are you thinking?"

"Serve lunches. Or say we serve lunches."

Darwin nodded. "Talk it up, get everyone to notice the café and not look too hard at anything else."

"Good. Let's do that. Darwin, can you get some posters up around town?"

"Sure. What about the bootlegging? We've got Tucker and a few other places. Are we going to keep on with the South Dixie Highway runs?"

"Absolutely. Can you and Lucky get the deliveries done tomorrow?"

"I'd rather be here for when Leroy gets back. Lucky and I could take them the day after that. It won't kill anybody to go thirsty for a day."

"But it might kill my reputation. What about doing the deliveries tonight? I can manage Goodtimes on my own," Edith said.

"If you're sure? I'll go with Lucky. You man the fort here. Come hell or high water, we'll be back tomorrow before lunchtime."

"Yes, we will," Lucky said, nodding.

"Then we have a plan, gentlemen." Edith stood and nodded. "For the time being, at least. Now, let's get that barroom set up. We have a blind-tiger to run tonight, and tomorrow we're going to show Coconut Grove a completely different side of Goodtimes."

CHAPTER 25

After a relatively quiet night at Goodtimes, Edith closed early. No one would ever know how much she cried after she went to bed. But this was a new day, and she had a plan, a back-up plan, and a final option after that.

Edith prowled the inside of the barroom, peering out the window at the empty car park. She was patrolling the perimeter of the palisades, on guard. *Who will be the first to arrive, reinforcements or the enemy?*

Alone, she ate a cold breakfast, drank a pot of coffee, and didn't waver from her surveillance.

Where was Leroy? Where was Cassie?

Darwin and Lucky drove into the carpark just before noon. Edith brought more coffee and sandwiches into the barroom.

"Any issues on the deliveries?" she asked, placing the sandwiches in front of the two exhausted men.

"No, everything went smoothly. I picked up more orders; there're a couple of places that want to talk to you personally about setting up an arrangement. Why don't you come with me next time?"

"If I can get away. But with everything going on…" She moved away from the table to stand at the French doors again; a vigilant sentinel.

"I take it there's been no sign of Leroy or Cassie yet?"

Edith shook her head.

"How'd everything go last night? Any issues?" Darwin asked.

"Quiet. Harley and a couple of tables of guardsmen from the station. A few other locals."

162

"Darwin, it's Leroy. He's back. And he's alone" Edith dashed out of Goodtimes, Darwin and Lucky close behind.

Edith grabbed Leroy and hugged him tight. She looked over his shoulder and scanned the path. "Is Cassie with you?"

Surrounded by his Goodtimes family, Leroy shook his head, panting.

"Lucky, bring Leroy some water, please," Edith said.

"Said she won't come. She can't get a reading of any trouble in the cards and she don't know Lucky. Said she won't come see you. Too many people." Leroy gulped from the glass that Lucky handed him.

Edith, wide-eyed, shook her head. "Leroy, she has to come."

"Or you have to go to her," Darwin said. "She probably won't come unless she knows what's going on."

"What's going on?" Leroy asked, looking from one adult to another.

"Don't worry, Leroy. I'd better go to Cassie, then."

"I'll take you there now if you like," Leroy said, handing the empty glass back to Lucky.

"Lucky, one of the ladies from yesterday, a Miss Mildred White from the Children's Home Society, will be here sometime today."

Leroy looked alarmed. "The Kids' Home? Are they going to take me away?"

"Hush, Leroy. I'm looking after it. Nobody is taking you anywhere," Edith said crossly.

She turned back to Lucky. "She has papers for me. If I'm not here, tell her I'm meeting with Leroy's guardian. Can you do that?"

"Yes, Miz Edith."

"Do you want me to come with you, Edith?" Darwin asked.

"No, Cassie doesn't know you well, either. You know how she is, spending all that time alone in the bush. I don't want to spook her. And besides, I need you two to turn Goodtimes into a café. That Mildred White woman was talking about a surprise inspection. Take all the liquor off the shelves and stash it somewhere handy. I hope she was too distracted yesterday to take much in. If she says anything, deny-deny. Let them prove it."

"Stay open or close up tonight?" Lucky asked.

"Close? I don't think we need to panic. We'll stay open. That Miss White," Edith said, looking like she wanted to spit the name into the dirt, "would need the sheriff's office to do anything about closing us down. Roy would let me know if they're coming."

"If you're sure."

Darwin and Lucky share a glance. Leroy watched the three adults. He was close to tears.

"It will be fine. We just need to get Cassie on board. I'll be back after supper. Lucky, do you have any baking I could take her? Something sweet?"

Lucky ducked into the tent kitchen and came back with a huckleberry pie wrapped in a tea-towel.

"Good luck, Miz Edith." Lucky bowed as he hands it to her.

Darwin knelt beside Leroy. "You look after Miz Edith, and both of you come back, okay?"

Leroy threw his arms around Darwin, who squeezed him tight.

As Edith and Leroy walked toward the path and the Everglades beyond, Darwin turned to Lucky. "So, let's do some magic and find a nice, little café in all this sin."

At the car park, Edith and Leroy stopped for one last wave. Darwin waved back and, grim faced, the two went inside.

Leroy led Edith along the path. Only the critters spoke. Leroy constantly checked Edith's worried eyes. She trudged along, lost in her thoughts.

I should have done better by the boy. But I've got my second chance now. I'll try harder. She smiled at Leroy.

"Won't you tell me what's wrong, Miz Edith? Why was Mrs. Carmichael here and who were those other ladies? And what papers do you need from Aunt Cassie?"

"Don't you worry, Leroy. I told you, I'm going to fix everything. Okay?"

"I know you will, Miz Edith. Just tell me what's wrong. Was it something I did? Was it about the comicbook I took?"

"That's long forgotten, Leroy. There's just something I need to talk to your Aunt Cassie about. Maybe I should get my cards read while I'm out here. What do you think about that?"

"Cassie would like that for sure. She's been wanting to read your cards for a while now. Is that why we're going? 'Cause you need to get your cards read?"

"As good an excuse as any. Watch out for that branch."

* * * *

Cassie heard them long before they arrived. The cards hadn't warned her of danger; she'd been sitting in front of them all day.

"Cassie, it's me and I brung Miz Edith with me. And pie."

"I might as well get them to build a road, the number of people walking in and out of this camp," she said, muttering.

Cassie rose to greet her visitors. "Leroy, what brings you here again? I thought I told you that I wasn't going to go talk to Miz Edith." *All this to-ing and fro-ing can't be good news. I know I shoulda gone with Leroy, but every time I tried to take a step my feet carried me back to the camp. Nothing but trouble in the wide world outside.*

Edith stepped forward, holding out her pie. "If you won't come to me, I guess I have to come to you. And I brought dessert, Cassie. A fresh huckleberry pie."

"If you got a pie in one hand, Edith Duffy, it makes me wonder what you got in the other. Koone, you think you can remember how to make coffee on a campfire?"

"Oh, Cassie, I make the best coffee. You always tell me that."

"Well, get to it then. Miz Edith and I are going to sit here and talk. You give us some privacy. When the coffee's ready, you can have some pie."

Edith followed Cassie up the stepped and pulled out a chair to sit.

"Help yourself," Cassie said with a nod.

Leroy fussed with the coffee, glancing over his shoulder often, curious about what was happening under the chickee.

"Cassie, we have a problem. You know that Leroy loves living at Goodtimes with me. And I have to tell you that I love having him there. But those witches in Coconut Grove are trying to take him away from me, from both of us, and put him in a Children's Home."

"You mean, like for orphans? That's crazy. He's got family."

"Exactly. They say that Goodtimes is not a suitable environment to raise a child in and that I am exploiting him."

Cassie snorted. "Have they met Leroy? Him exploiting you more like. The little bit I seen showed me you were wrapped around his finger, Edith."

166

Edith smiled. "A willing victim. They also say that the Everglades is no place for him to grow up, either. I think they're working themselves around to believing that neither one of us is good for Leroy."

Cassie, watching Leroy make coffee, frowned. "That sounds about right. Them town folks have always had it out for my people."

Harsh memories of growlng up Seminole in a small town in Florida flashed in her mind. Cassie's back grew rigid with the generations of abuse that had been heaped upon her shoulders.

"Maybe sending him to you wasn't such a good idea. We were happy here, and he was safe. Nobody knew we were out here, and now look. Half the town is up in arms to take my boy away." She looked hard at Edith. "Keeping that boy safe is all I care about."

Edith gulped. "I know Cassie, and that's all I care about, too."

One eyebrow on Cassie's face shot up and she snorted. "Seems like it was just a few months ago that there was the fire at 'Gator Joe's. And the Wharf Rat devils were threatening you and Leroy. I left him there with you then because I figured you'd know how to deal with all that kind of nastiness. That's your world, not mine. But Edith, it sounds like Leroy's in real danger now. It would kill him and me both if they take him away." Cassie put her hands in her lap. A Fortune Teller's hands were part of the magic of the cards, and hers were trembling.

Edith leaned forward, earnest and pleading. "I understand, Cassie. They're all in a twist to save him. But don't worry. He's perfectly safe at Goodtimes. I've got a lawyer working on it. And pretty soon all this will die down. There'll be another bone for them to chew on and it will go back to the way it was before."

Cassie's head snapped up, her eyes blazing. "You mean to tell me that you got lawyers, the law, and the good ladies of Coconut Grove all in a lather trying to take my boy away?" Cassie stared long and hard at Edith. *This woman don't know nothing if she thinks they'll back off. This whole thing, Cissy dying and us hiding in the 'glades, all*

167

came about because there's nothing they hate worse than other people's sin.

"Edith, you're used to fighting. You understand the lawyers. You have power. I'm a Seminole woman, never been to school. I live in a bush camp in the Everglades. You want to take your chances and ride this out, while everything is telling me to grab Leroy and run. Again." *But maybe I've been living with this fear and anger too long. Maybe it's different now?*

Edith took a deep breath. "Cassie. Leroy's living in my world, and I know how to survive in it. You protect what you love."

"What does Leroy say about all this?"

"I haven't said anything to him. I didn't want him worried."

"You've got him ferrying people back and forth to the camp and you don't think he's worried?"

Edith looked down at her hands.

"Coffee's ready, Cassie," Leroy said from the campfire.

"Bring two cups and three pieces of pie. You can eat up here with us."

A small worry line appeared between Edith's eyebrows.

"He deserves to have a say," Cassie said. "It's his fate we're talking about."

"And mine," Edith said in a whisper.

"Sure enough."

Leroy served coffee and pie.

"Thanks, Koone. Now, sit on the step and listen to what Miz Edith has to say about all this fussing about."

"Leroy, do you enjoy living at Goodtimes with me?" Edith asked.

Leroy looked between Cassie and Edith.

The poor boy doesn't know what the heck is going on. Cassie smiled at him, nodding encouragement. "It's okay, Koone. Just answer."

"You bet, Miz Edith." He gave Edith a giant grin.

Cassie hid a flinch. *Does him being happy have to make me feel bad?*

Leroy chattered on. "I have my own room, Aunt Cassie. And Darwin and I go out on the *Rex* and go fishing. And Lucky is teaching me Chinese words—some of them are cuss words." He giggled. "And the best part is I have a friend. His name is Jay and I eat supper at his house sometimes."

"You remember the ladies that came to visit yesterday," Edith said.

"Yes, Jay's mother was one of them."

"There's a law that said boys under twelve can't work at places like Goodtimes. Because of the drinking."

Leroy shook his head. "The drinking ain't so bad. Nobody pukes or anything. And the only time anybody's taken a swing at somebody was when them Wharf Rats snuck in. But we showed them, didn't we, Miz Edith."

"We sure did, Leroy." Edith smiled at the boy.

Watching her, Cassie could see her love for Leroy. *She may not say the words, to Leroy or to herself, but it's as plain as the nose on her face.*

"Do you want to keep living at Goodtimes, Leroy?" Cassie asked. Her hands were itching to pick up the cards.

169

"Sure, I do. Is this what's going on? You don't think I should be staying there?"

This time, Cassie couldn't hide the flinch. Leroy came over and wrapped his arms around her. "But I get to keep coming here, too. Right, Cassie?"

"That's part of the deal," she said, looking at a nodding Edith.

Leroy gave Cassie another squeeze and then plopped down in front of his pie. He demolished it. One, two, three bites, and it was gone. A purple smear around his mouth was licked clean.

"What about school, Leroy? The ladies might say you have to go to school every day," Edith said.

"No way," Leroy said, shaking his head vigorously. "I don't want to go to school."

"Even if it meant that you couldn't live with me anymore?"

"I don't go to school now, and everything's good. I got my library books and I can do sums."

"That's wonderful. But now that the ladies are involved, we might not have any say in the matter."

"Koone, did you bring your slingshot?" Cassie asked.

Leroy pulled it out of his pocket. "Yup."

"How about you see if you could get me an opossum for the stew pot while you're here."

Leroy grinned and dashed off into the forest that surrounded the camp.

"Is that settled then?" Cassie asked Edith.

"I talked to a lawyer yesterday. He said that Leroy can stay at Goodtimes with me if I have written permission from you. If you say you need his income, he can work for me underage. Not in a barroom, of course. We'll need to call it a café until Prohibition is over."

"It seems like you got two problems, then. Leroy's age and the liquor."

"One I can bribe my way out of. The other is ten months of worry, waiting for Leroy to be old enough."

"I know you don't like the tarot cards, Edith, but they help me see things clearly," Cassie said, gathering up the cards that were spread on the table. "If I had my way, Leroy and I would melt away deeper into the 'glades and no one would be any wiser."

Edith sucked in her breath. "Please, no. Don't do it, Cassie."

"But that wouldn't be good for Leroy. I've lived his whole life doing what's best for the boy. I like the idea of him at school. He's so smart. And friends. A normal kind of life. If he's happy at Goodtimes, and safe at Goodtimes, then I can let him be."

Cassie held up the deck of cards.

Reluctantly, Edith nodded.

Cassie shuffled the cards and fanned them out in front of her. She closed her eyes and drew in all her power. This was a critical question, and she wanted the answer to be clear and true.

Eyes still closed, her hand hovered over the arc. She was barely aware of Edith sitting across from her. A tingle, a pull, and Cassie stopped, reaching down for one card. She turned it face up.

"The Ten of Cups. A good card," she said, giving Edith the first smile of the visit. She handed the card to Edith. "Tell me what you see."

"A loving couple standing together and watching two children play. Their house is on a hill and there's a beautiful rainbow in the sky filled with ten cups."

"Very good, but how does it make you feel?"

171

"These two have everything they could ever wish for—the home, the kids, and most importantly, fulfilling love.

"That's better. The Ten of Cups encourages you to follow your heart and trust your intuition. I think I'll have more coffee. Can I get you some?" Cassie said, relaxed and smiling. She stood and extended her hand for Edith's cup.

Instead, Edith grabbed her hand, holding tight. "Thank you, Cassie. Thank you so much."

Cassie puts down her cup and patted Edith's hand. "Leroy's not my boy to do with as I want. I have a duty to my sister to care for him, to love him as best I can, and to do right by him. And you can give him advantages I can't. You do right by him, Edith, and it will be well between us."

The goodbye hug between Edith and Cassie contained serious undertones. The embrace between the boy and his aunt had a desperation and finality to it that made Edith squirm with guilt. Eventually, Cassie let go and pushed him toward Edith.

"You take care, Leroy, and do what Miz Edith says. She knows what's best." *I have to believe she does. I have to. Otherwise, how can I let my boy go?*

* * * *

The return trip was dark and Edith stumbled several times. The paperwork was safely tucked into her pocket. Leroy guided Edith back to Goodtimes. Through the trees, she could see Goodtimes' lights glowing, the front door wide open, and her heart swelled. Goodtimes was peace and contentment. Goodtimes was safe.

She squeezed Leroy's hand. "I'm glad you decided to stay, Leroy. It must had been hard to not stay with Cassie. She loves you, a lot."

172

"I know that. Hey, I can see the lights on at Goodtimes. Do you think Darwin got the chairs done without me?" He scampered ahead.

"Hey, not so fast. I can't see where I'm going."

As they got closer, Edith saw Darwin and Lucky on the veranda. *If they're outside, who's minding the bar?*

Leroy darted ahead when they got to the car park. Darwin had turned on the path lights for them.

"Darwin, we're home," Leroy called out. "Hi Lucky. I ate all the pie. Sorry."

Edith could hear Lucky laugh as she came up to the veranda. Leroy had one arm around Darwin and one arm around Lucky. A hero's triumphant return.

"How'd it go?" Darwin asked.

Edith could see the worry etched on his face and around his eyes. *This isn't just about me. We're all wrapped up in this mess.*

She pulled out the letter from Cassie. "She agreed. Leroy has her written permission to live here and work in the café."

Darwin untangled himself from Leroy and came over to hug her. "That's wonderful news."

"And what happened here, today? Who's running things inside? Did Mildred White drop off her papers?"

"Yes, I left them on your desk. Lucky was just taking cookies out of the oven when she came. There wasn't a bottle of liquor in sight. We may need to get a few more tea pots to make it convincing, though."

"Well, as long as the saloon customers don't get confused. Speaking of which, who's inside?"

"Usual crowd. All the customers have been served. Lucky and I have been taking turns, watching and waiting for you to get back."

173

Edith relaxed a fraction. "Enough with the waiting. There's been too much of that during the past few days. We're going to be okay." *Taking turns, waiting for me and Leroy. Both of them have my back. It really is going to be okay.*

She herded her little band through the door. "Now, let's get back to work."

Chapter 26

Brother Silas stood and stared out the dining-room window at the children playing in the hardscrabble yard. Once a week, he came to the Florida Children's Home in Coconut Grove to meet with the youngsters. Sometimes it was a quiet chat with a troubled youth. And sometimes, like today, it was a group bible lesson.

Folly was bound up in the heart of a child, but the rod of discipline shall drive it far away. He turned aside and picked up his bible. *The rod never did me any harm when I was growing up.*

"I heard them run outside. Are you done for the day?" Mildred White asked.

"Yes. 'Start children off on the way they should go and they would not turn from it.' I'd keep an eye on Timothy. He seemed restless."

"His teacher at school has talked to me about him. Not paying attention, the usual. I'll see about putting him out to work."

"He must be getting close to aging-out?"

"He'll be twelve next month."

"So not your burden for too much longer."

"It's hard when they turn twelve and have to leave. It would help to arrange some work for him."

"The orange groves are always looking for pickers," Brother Silas said, turning again to the window.

"He will need to earn his keep somewhere."

"I agree. Hunger is a powerful motivator. He's a strong boy. I'm sure he'll find something if he keeps that attitude of his in check."

"Do you had time to stay for a cup of coffee? Cook has just pulled biscuits out of the oven for supper and I could get you one with jam," Mildred said, blushing.

"Thank you, Sister Mildred. That would be lovely."

Brother Silas settled in the dark living room. The walls seemed to echo with the emotions of nervous, prospective parents who had come to meet with children desperate to be adopted. Also hanging in the air were whiffs of Miss White's obsequiousness toward donors, or over Daddy Fagg when he does his monthly rounds. And then there was the hopelessness of abandoned and frightened children that was forever part of the space.

When it wasn't a scene of want or need, the room sat stiff, formal, and unused.

Mildred arrived with a tray she sat down on the coffee table in front of Silas. Brother Silas noted the four biscuits and two plates. *She's a solid woman, I'll gave her that. Feeding her body when she should feed her soul.*

"How are things here at the Home? Did you find someone for night duty?"

"Mr. Bolak, the former caretaker's cousin. He had to give up fishing. His back, I think. He's been coming over."

"That would be a help. I know Walter Bolak. He's a good man. Honest. Never misses a Sunday. And it was his back. He'll not be fishing again anytime soon. And the young lad at Goodtimes—where are you at with that?"

"Not much further than when we last talked. The paperwork was all in order, the saloon appears to be operating as an ordinary café, so Daddy Fagg said to let it be. There are other, more pressing, needs in Coconut Grove."

Interfering old fool. "He is undoubtedly correct. I would never presume to second guess a man with such a strong commitment.

Although my heart goes out to the boy. I was virtually an orphan myself at that age."

"I often think of your early years when I am tending to the children here," Mildred said, her cheeks scarlet.

Brother Silas smiled at her, but then frowned. "I wonder if he lies in his bed, frightened and alone, without a champion. What thoughts go through his head?"

"Brother Silas," Mildred's voice caught. "That's just so sad."

"There is a razor's edge to the woman who employs him. I'm sure you noticed that when you were out there with the Homemakers' Guild. No ample lap to find comfort in when he's afraid. There's no generosity in her spirit that would put a second helping of dinner on his plate. Boys that age are always eating, are they not, Sister Mildred?"

"What? Oh, yes. Grow like weeds, they do. Do you think the boy is hungry, Brother Silas?"

"Would a woman like that care for a growing boy properly? Not like you, Sister Mildred. The Lord had seen the affection and care you give the children here. A real mother to motherless waifs."

"Thank you, Brother Silas. I try, in my own small way, to ease their adversity." Mildred preened under the praise.

"A fine boy like that, tossed away by his own like he was garbage. No longer wanted." Brother Silas, his eyes sorrowful, shook his head. "Shouldn't every child feel wanted, Sister Mildred? You say he grew up in the Everglades? Under primitive conditions?"

"Wanted, yes. I'm sorry, I didn't catch your question, Brother Silas," Mildred said, a faraway look in her eye. She looked at Brother Silas and blushed.

"He was raised in the Everglades?"

"We don't have much information on Leroy. Mrs. Duffy has not been forthcoming. Mrs. Carmichael knows the boy through her son, Jay. She's how we learned of his upbringing."

"A lovely woman, Mrs. Carmichael. Such strong, healthy sons. And an excellent mother. She wouldn't leave the boy alone, hungry and afraid."

"An example to us all, Brother Silas. Even though my brood is much larger and never ending."

"And you are so rarely appreciated. The Lord works in mysterious ways, Sister Mildred."

Brother Silas waited, watching Mildred eat her biscuit. "For example, your work with the Homemakers' Guild is proving useful in the community."

Mildred smiled. "I think I've finally found a project where they can appreciate my skills and experience."

"Alas, to have had this part of your project over so soon. To not be able to completely follow through and shut down such a stain on society. It is such a shame."

Mildred's smile dimmed.

"It's unfortunate Goodtimes has taken on the role of a café. If indeed it has." He leans closer.

Mildred stopped munching.

"Sister Mildred, in your professional opinion, would you trust a woman like that to comply with the law? She never has before. Perhaps the café was not shut down at all." Brother Silas wormed his way into her conviction.

"You see, Sister Mildred, although it was not my place to question Daddy Fagg's actions—oh, certainly not—I feel I am, well, closer to the people of Coconut Grove. I mean, I live here and am part of the community every day. I see more than paperwork. I hear

178

things. And, based on that, it is beyond my understanding why anyone would approve a child be allowed to be in the care and clutches of a woman like Edith Duffy. It may appear to some that she has everything: a beautiful home, security, the admiration of her clientele. And she answers to no one."

Millie twisted the napkin in her lap. "It's not fair, Brother Silas. I've known women like that in the Homemakers' Guild. They have everything but appreciate nothing. While I'm always grateful for their generosity, I don't believe they value their good fortune."

"Good fortune and a good disposition are rarely given to the same person." Brother Silas passed her the plate of biscuits and the jam.

She was thoughtful as she spread the butter and jam. "Oh, Brother Silas. I am sore afraid for the boy. The evil influences he must overcome every day."

"Undoubtedly it is shaping his nature. If only he had someone of your strength of character, Sister. I had always found that true virtue cannot be measured by any means other than performance in the time of need." *Oh, for God's sake, get on with it, woman. How can you be so dense?*

Hands clasped in front, her biscuit apparently forgotten, Millie burst forth. "Brother Silas, we need to save Leroy. I feel it in my heart."

"You have a kind and generous heart. But Sister Mildred, what can we do? You say the paperwork is up to date and the establishment is no longer running as a blind-tiger, outside of the law?"

Nodding, she lowers her head and stared at her hands clasped in her lap.

A flicker of frustration crossed Brother Silas' face and was gone. He closed in. "Are you sure? I've heard things from my parishioners. Goodtimes isn't the café it pretends to be."

Puzzled, she looked to him for more.

"And if that is true, that would mean that Leroy couldn't live there any longer." Brother Silas waited. *Come on. Come on. Do I have to say it?*

Mildred's face flushed, her cheeks were bright pink. "Which would mean that the permission letter was void."

Hallelujah. "We would need proof. Perhaps the sheriff's office should drop in unannounced some evening?" Silas said, smiling, nodding, coaxing her along.

"You mean catch her off-guard?" Mildred asked.

"Exactly."

"I have the authority, nay the duty, to confirm the circumstances of the boy. To protect Leroy. And the Guild would expect nothing less from me."

Brother Silas nodded. "I admire your commitment, Sister Mildred. Involving the sheriff's office is the right thing to do."

"I went once with Deputy Purvis. He didn't seem particularly effective against her charms."

"You might consider contacting the sheriff's office in Miami to bolster the force you need to conquer that den of vice and depravity. Would you like me to make the call?"

"Thank you, Brother Silas. You always provide such wise counsel. I may had been lax in my oversight of that poor lamb."

"Don't be too hard on yourself, Sister Mildred. You have the care of many. Should the concern of one take precedence?"

"Save one child and save the world, Brother Silas."

"Such wisdom you have, Sister Mildred. And such a generous spirit."

Brother Silas smiled. *It would be so much easier if I could just do this myself. Working through others is always an exercise in frustration.*

He lifted his bible, pausing slightly as his hand twitched. "The face of our Lord is in the face of that child, Sister Mildred. Remember the scripture, 'Whoever receives one such child in my name receives me, and whoever receives me, receives not me but him who sent me'."

Brother Silas took her hands in his and a warm glow spread over her face.

"And he needs your protection," he added, giving her hand a gentle squeeze.

He gently removed his hands and stood, twitching again and noting his hay fever symptoms were worsening. "And equally, that Jezebel deserves your wrath. 'But whoever causes one of these little ones who believe in me to sin, it would be better for him to have a great millstone fastened around his neck and to be drowned in the depth of the sea'."

CHAPTER 27

Leroy parked himself across the street from Jay's house. Wrapped in an old shirt were four bottles of gin salvaged from the beach. He waited, watching Jay's mother hanging out the washing. Jay's older brother appeared with his bicycle from around the corner of his house. He swung his leg up and over the seat and took off down the street. *Maybe I should buy a bicycle, too? It would be faster than walking.* Leroy saw Jay coming down the street, a few books wound with a leather strap dangling over his back.

"Hiya, Huck," Jay said as he got closer.

Leroy grinned. *Yeah, a smarter Huck than in the book.* "Hi Tom. Ready for a bit of risky business?"

"You bet. School was so boring today. Math. Math. Math. I just don't get it. Let me dump these in the kitchen and grab my newspapers. You wait here."

Leroy pulled the wagon. Jay on the doorstep. At the first two houses, a woman answered the front door. He handed over the paper and each housewife remarked on the personal service. Usually, Jay left the paper on the step. Many asked to be remembered to his mother. Everything was on the up-and-up, like usual. At the third house, a man answered, his shirt sleeves rolled up.

"Afternoon, sir. I have your Miami Herald here. Mighty warm day, isn't it? Say, I found something you might be interested in."

The man looked from Jay to Leroy at the wagon.

"It's in the wagon, sir," Jay said, stepping aside. Leroy lifted the edge of the newspapers that were stacked there, revealing the bottom of a bottle.

"Whatchya got there, kid?"

"Just something I found. Interested?"

The man walked down the sidewalk carrying his newspaper. He wrapped it around one bottle, slipping Jay a dollar.

One bottle sold, three to go. The next house was again a woman, and they each got a freshly baked cookie. At the next house, Jay threw the newspaper on the porch. "Deputy's house."

They hit it lucky again and unloaded another bottle a couple of houses down. Before they got halfway through the paper route, they had sold all four bottles. When they got out of sight of the last house, they divided the money.

"Here's your cut," Leroy said, giving Jay a third of the money they'd earned.

"Hey, it should be fifty-fifty."

"But it was my booze."

"You found it. It didn't cost you nothing. And these are my customers."

Leroy nodded and handed over more cash. "Seeing as we're partners, I guess that's how I'd want to be treated. Fifty-fifty is fair."

They stood at the end of Jay's sidewalk. "Today was a good trial run. I'll be back in a few days with more bottles. When do you usually collect? Maybe better that way than keep up this in-person greeting with the delivery."

"Every Monday. How many bottles do you think we should sell?"

"How about six? I bet we could have sold six today."

"How long does it take a person to drink the whole bottle? Would those of them that bought one today be ready by next week for another?"

Leroy shrugged. "Sometimes I've seen 'em drink a whole bottle in one night. We could always ask. I'll bring whiskey instead of gin next time. Just in case they haven't finished the bottle yet. They might want something different."

* * * *

Mary Carmichael refilled her guests' coffee cups. Mavis Saunders and Mildred White had dropped by to discuss the Goodtimes 'situation'. "A flimsy excuse for gossip if you ask me," Mary whispered to her coffee pot as she carried it back to the kitchen. She returned with a plate of freshly baked cookies.

"I've seen posters up around town advertising the Goodtimes Café is open for lunch. I guess we were successful at least on one front," Mary said.

"I don't trust those signs. It happened too easily. That woman makes too much money out of running a blind-tiger to just close up shop like that. Brother Silas and I are working with the deputy sheriff on a raid of this so-called café," Mildred said, reaching for a cookie. "We're going to catch them in the act."

"I thought everything was in order with the note from his aunt?" Mary asked. "I'm not sure the Guild should be pursuing the matter further, Mavis."

Mavis declined the plate of cookies passed by Mildred. She took a sip of coffee to clear her throat. "The paperwork is in order. With the note from his legal guardian giving permission for him to work underage, there's nothing we could do about the boy living at the café. However, if Goodtimes is still serving liquor, we must snatch the boy out of there as soon as possible. For his own good." Mildred succumbed to temptation and helped herself to two more cookies from the plate. "These are delicious, Mary."

"I know Leroy. He doesn't seem to be suffering." Mary Carmichael picked up the empty plate, slipped out, and returned with

184

a full one. "And even though Mrs. Duffy's a businesswoman, Leroy always has good things to say about her."

"He just covers it up better than most. That Duffy woman is probably threatening him with the woodshed or no dinner to stay silent. No, ladies. We need to act, and quickly, to save the boy." Mildred's hands were clenched.

"I'm not sure I understand your urgency, Mildred," Mary said. "While I don't know Mrs. Duffy well, it would certainly break my heart to have any one of my own sons taken from me."

"Firstly, the boy is not her son, merely an employee. And more importantly, Mary dear, things may not had changed. Goodtimes is likely still operating as a saloon," Mavis said.

Mildred nodded eagerly. "Mavis is right, Mary. Think about it. Mrs. Duffy has never respected the law before. Why would she turn over a new leaf at this point?"

"She's likely still serving liquor. You wouldn't want your boys growing up in that kind of environment, surely?" Mavis asked.

Mary shook her head. "Of course not."

"And what we want for our own, don't we want for all others?" Mildred asked.

"I suppose I can go along with the idea of a raid so that we could confirm that there's still liquor. But if it is a café, we let the boy be."

Mavis Saunders snorted. "If that's a café, my John is a rum runner. When will the sheriff's department carry out the raid, Mildred?"

"We're working on that now. We'll be thorough, Mavis. I've seen too many lost lambs suffering at the hands of greedy adults."

"Exactly. The Guild has made a commitment to this community and to the child. Remember those hidden pockets of evil. Why, just this past Sunday, Brother Silas was preaching about the very topic."

Mildred dusted cookie crumbs from her ample lap. "I'm very much in support of the Guild's position, which is Brother Silas's as well."

Mildred and Mavis shared a smile and turned to Mary.

"As long as there's cause," she said, red faced at being cornered.

"Working at the Children's Home, I guess I look at things differently than you do, Mary. You have a lovely home and a healthy family. I've seen the other end of things: children without enough to eat, living in deplorable conditions. Often abused, always neglected. And that will be Leroy's situation with that Duffy woman. Those kinds of adults don't deserve to have the care of children, whether they are their own or not. And Brother Silas agrees with me—with us."

"We need to listen to men like Daddy Fagg and Brother Silas, Mary," Mavis said.

"Brother Silas would know. He's had such a tragic past. His parents gone, the death of his grandmother. The poor boy was alone for most of his young life," Mildred said and dabbed a tear from the corner of her eye. "We mustn't let that happen to Leroy. He needs a secure home life, three square meals a day, schooling, and I'm sure there are other things the boy wants, as well."

"Boys like Leroy want to be barefoot and into mischief," Mary said, moving the plate of cookies away from Mildred. "I've three of my own and I can tell you they're no angels. Like the nursery-rhyme said, boys like Jay and Leroy are made of sticks and snails and puppy-dog tails."

Mildred's eyes followed the plate of cookies at it was again passed among the women gathered. "We all have the best interests of the boy at heart, Mary. There is a very legitimate reason to pull him out of Goodtimes. It's a blind-tiger and even if it's dark now, it won't

186

be for long. The legislators in Tallahassee feel strongly enough about the issue to include it in the child labor law. It's not up to us to second guess."

"Precisely," Mavis said. "I'm so pleased that the Homemakers' Guild is able to play such an active role in securing the future of the boy. And good luck on the raid, Mildred," Mavis said, her coffee cup raised in salute.

Mildred, her cheeks pink, raised her own coffee cup in reply. "I am so enjoying working with you and the Guild on this project, Mavis. Would you be so kind to pass the plate of cookies this way? They really are delicious."

CHAPTER 28

Sunlight and birdsong roused Darwin from his bunk on the *Rex*. Standing in the stern, he stretched and yawned. The last few days' double shifts had been exhausting. Long hours at night to pick up the liquor from Rum Row, long hours during the day delivering the liquor and picking up new orders.

He looked nostalgically at the fishing tackle stored in the stern of the boat. *It's been a while. I should take Leroy out. Maybe tomorrow. I'm too darned tired today. I feel like I've got one wheel down and the axle's dragging. It's certainly more than I signed up for when I first got the call from Cousin Henry in Philadelphia asking me to give this gal Edith a hand.* Darwin snorted, picked up a bottle of whiskey and rinsed out his mouth, spitting it into the water. "Coffee, I need coffee."

He found what he was looking for in Lucky's kitchen tent. The first sip of hot, black coffee revived him as he made himself comfortable at the table.

"What are the plans for the kitchen? I've been watching the equipment piling up in the barn," Darwin said.

Lucky poured himself a coffee and joined Darwin at the table.

"It will be real restaurant kitchen. Flat top grill, deep fryer for those hush puppies everyone like, big refrigerator."

"No wonder the space is huge."

"I finish tile work today. Then man from town come and he hook up wires."

"What about counters and cabinets?"

"They building those in Miami. Everything metal. Miz Edith doesn't like rats or bugs."

"Mean shot with a snake though," Darwin said with a wink.

Leroy wandered into the kitchen tent and grabbed two slices of bread and jam for a sandwich. He sat down next to Darwin.

"Darwin. When's the next time you're going out to Rum Row?" he said around a mouthful of sandwich.

Lucky got up and poured him a glass of milk and Leroy thanked him.

"Tomorrow night, probably. The weather looks good and there are those orders to fill we picked up yesterday."

"Can I get you to pick up some stuff for me, too? I got my own money. I could pay," Leroy said.

"What you mean, Leroy?" Lucky asked.

"Don't tell Miz Edith, but I got me a little business in town. My friend and I deliver newspapers and at some of the houses we also drop off bottles of booze. Whiskey is best, then gin. Nobody wanted the brandy."

Darwin laughed. "Where did you get liquor?"

Lucky frowned. "You no take from bar, do you? That stealing, Leroy."

Leroy shook his head vigorously. "No way. I wouldn't steal. I found it washed up on the beach. After we get big storms, Miz Edith asks me to clean up the beach in front of Goodtimes and there're always a few bottles. Sometimes the label's missing and I have to guess. I sell those ones at a discount. And if it looked like seawater got in, I just throw it away."

"What a kid," Darwin said, ruffling his hair. "Why not let Miz Edith know?"

"I'm afraid she'll tell me I can't do it. 'Cause it's illegal."

Darwin nodded, catching Lucky's eye. "She's right, you know. What about if you get caught? Folks in town are just looking for an excuse, Leroy."

"I figure I'm a kid. They'll let me go. Especially if Miz Edith helps like she did last time."

"You mean when you took the comicbook, and she had to pay off the storekeeper?"

Leroy nodded, finishing his sandwich.

"Well, kiddo. If you expect her to bail you out of trouble, you should at least give her a heads up."

"And she good at business, Leroy. She help you," Lucky said.

"True enough. Look at what she did with 'Gator's and now with Goodtimes. Some people just dream about this kind of success. Miz Edith wakes up every morning and makes it happen. You can't go wrong asking her for advice. Smartest dame I ever met," Darwin said.

"What about Miz Cleo? She seems smart. And Miz Mae? Miz Edith is always asking her for advice and stuff," Leroy said.

"Now you've got it. Smart people hang around with other smart people."

"Like I hang around you and Lucky," Leroy said, grinning.

"Exactly. Now, what are you needing me to pick up? Or better yet, if Miz Edith said it's okay, maybe you can come out with me and pick it up yourself."

"Boy, that would be swell. I'll go ask her right now. Thanks, Darwin," Leroy said, dashing into Goodtimes. Lucky and Darwin laugh, hearing him calling 'Miz Edith'.

"Acorns don't fell far from the tree," Darwin said.

Lucky tips his head to one side. "What tree?"

"An American expression. It means that Leroy and Edith are very similar."

Lucky nodded. "Leroy is good boy. And hard worker. He learn a lot from Miz Edith. If he listens."

"True enough. A lot of folks go further than they think they will because somebody believes in them."

Darwin took a second cup of coffee to the dock. The caffeine would help him get through the regular nightly trip he needed to make out to Rum Row. As he prepared the *Marianne* to cast off, he was surprised to hear Edith come storming up.

"What in heaven's name are you thinking?" Her hands were on her hips and there wass fire in her eyes.

"What?"

"Leroy came to ask if I'd let him go out to Rum Row with you."

"I figured it was that."

"Darwin, you having a run in with the Coast Guard or Wharf Rats is bad enough, but to have Leroy on board with you if that happens? With all this extra attention we're dealing with right now? Really?"

"I offered because I figured you'd say no," Darwin said, turning back to untying the lines from the dock cleats.

Edith sputtered, finally stamping her foot. "Why am I always the bad guy? Why can't you tell him no?"

Darwin shrugged and gave her a grin before going back to his lines. "You gotta gave him credit for gumption, Edith. A few years from now and our Dixie runs will have competition."

Edith continued to glower at him.

"Come on, he's a chip off the old block, picking up your business savvy."

"You think so?" Edith smiled despite herself. "What a kid. But I'm not so sure this is a good idea, Darwin. If Miss White finds out, they'll snatch him for sure. And that kid in town he's working with is probably Jay Carmichael. If the Carmichael's find out... It's just too much risk to take on right now."

"Hey, you're the one keeping Goodtimes open. Come on, whaddya say? Leroy worships you, Edith. And wants to be like you. Don't take this away from him."

"And Miss White thinks I was a bad influence before. Whatever you do, don't let her find out about this."

Darwin straightened and checked the horizon. "I gotta get going. Nobody ever said raising kids was easy, Edith." And with that, he hopped into the *Marianne* and the roar of the twin Liberty engines finished the conversation.

He left Edith's commentary in his wake.

Perhaps Darwin had jinxed it when he was talking about the extra runs to the Row drawing attention, or it could had been the law of averages, or maybe it was just plain bad luck; but whatever the reason, the Coast Guard spotted the *Marianne*.

Thank goodness Leroy's not here.

The *Mojave* was equipped with large searchlights: one to sweep the water in search of suspicious vessels, another to light the Coast Guard's pennant displaying the boat's authority. Lights had limited life at sea and could burn for only ninety minutes before the carbon arcs used to generate illumination needed replenishing.

"It figures," he said, glancing behind him at the large cargo of contraband liquor. Deciding to run, he thrust the throttles down and *Marianne's* twin Liberties responded. The boat arched out of the ocean, riding a white plume of water.

The search lights of the *Mojave* caught him, illuminating the bow's deck in front of him. Darwin hoped the odds were in his favor and he threw the throttle forward again, cranking the wheel hard to the left. The *Marianne* was swallowed by the night.

As he cruised along Biscayne Bay's shoreline south of Coconut Grove, Darwin decided to play it safe. *Crazy times we live in when the good guys are the bad guys and I'm a criminal. The Coast Guard's in a tough spot, I'll gave them that; upholding a law nobody agrees with. Billy's a good kid, and that new fella, Clancy, is too. Too bad they all didn't have a let-bygones-be-bygones attitude to the situation.*

At Tahiti Beach, he cut the engines and tied the hams together with strong Manila line attached to semi-submerged buoys.

I'll come back tomorrow while Leroy keeps a lookout. If he's going to get into the rum running business, he might as well lend a hand. There shouldn't be any trouble in broad daylight. Except if Edith finds out. Then the pair of us will be wishing the pirates got us first.

CHAPTER 29

When Edith had laid out her plans for Goodtimes, she had made sure they included an office. She needed a separate space to work, and it was wonderful to have all her ledgers in one place. She didn't have to move them off a table during business hours or try to remember where she'd stuck a receipt or a note to herself.

She was hard at work reconciling accounts when Lucky appeared just outside her office. "Deputy from sheriff's office at kitchen door again, Miz Edith." Like she presumed the deputy would be, Lucky was in uniform: a tea-towel over one shoulder and a white apron tied around his waist.

She looked up from her books. "Roy Purvis? Curious." Edith followed Lucky through the unfinished kitchen to the back door.

"Deputy, please come in," Edith said, holding the screen door open. "Would you like a cup of coffee?"

"Thank you, Miz Edith. But I'd prefer to talk out here, if you don't mind."

"All right. I seem to be seeing a lot of you lately, Deputy." Edith pointed to a spot near the porch where Lucky's wooden table and a couple of chairs had been installed for him to snap beans and shell peas outside in the sunshine.

When seated, Deputy Roy spoke. "I wanted to give you a head's up, Miz Edith. We're going to raid Goodtimes tomorrow night."

"What? A raid? I thought I paid you so I didn't had to worry about that kind of thing."

"True enough. But there's this kid thing, and I got my orders."

"Kid thing?"

"You know. The Kid's Home. I'm surprised that you're still running Goodtimes. I'd had thought you'd shut the place down on account of the kid."

"That's certainly one of the options. What about this raid?"

"What I'm doing is giving you a heads up so you can make arrangements."

"Like what?"

"Well, we're going to be looking to seize your liquor—"

"What?"

"And arrest anyone that's buying liquor."

"Deputy Purvis, I'm a saloon. A blind-tiger. This could put me out of business. I thought we had an understanding, a partnership."

"The Kid's Home wants to prove you're not just a café. They want to nail you for serving booze. You don't have to stay closed for long, ma'am. And maybe with all the extra attention you're getting because of the kid, taking a break ain't such a bad idea."

"Thank you for your concern, deputy. But I'll make the decisions about Leroy and Goodtimes. Will that Mildred White woman be there with you?"

"Not likely tomorrow night, but she's filed a complaint about you with the Miami Sheriff's office, so we gotta play this by the book or there'll be questions asked."

Edith sighed. "When will you be here?"

"We'll be coming around after dark. We'll do a bit of a search on the premises, but we won't be looking elsewhere. Say, down at the dock or nothing."

Edith sat and stewed. "Thank you for the advance notice, deputy." She stood and extended her hand. "I'll see you tomorrow night."

Back in the kitchen space where Lucky was tiling, she asked him to find Leroy and Darwin; a meeting for all in the barroom.

When everyone had arrived, she broke the news.

"It'll be pretty hard to operate discretely when we've got the sheriff's office parked here," Darwin said.

"This is no different from any other raid. I'll slip them a few bucks and everyone will go away happy."

"I don't think so, Edith. It's not just another raid. Miami sheriff is involved. And the Children's Home. They're going to be looking for evidence." Darwin looked at Leroy and then back to Edith.

"Oh, all right. We'll make sure everything's out of sight."

Leroy looked from Edith to Darwin. "Is this about me and Cassie?"

Darwin ruffled his hair. "Just a hiccup, champ. Don't worry."

"Let's get rid of the evidence, if that's what they're looking for. We can move all the liquor onto the *Marianne* and the *Rex*. Just for a few hours."

"Are you sure you can trust him, Edith? What if he's just laying a trap?" Darwin asked. "Maybe he wants us to move all the liquor so they can find it easily."

"Then he stands to lose a generous regular pay-off if we get closed. Roy Purvis and I are on the same side of self-interest. Trusting him is a risk we'll have to take. Unless you have a different idea."

"What about barn?" Lucky said.

Darwin shook his head. "Obvious and accessible. At least we'll be able to anchor the boats in the Bay. Edith, can you run the *Rex* out for me? We'll both take the skiff back."

"Sure, I can manage that. We'll do it tomorrow afternoon. I'm anxious about all that inventory just floating out there. What about pirates?" Edith said.

"After the raid, I'll bring *Marianne* and *Rex* back to the dock. It's a risk we'll have to take."

"All right. But let's also try to think of something permanent. That storage shed isn't that secure either. Normally, we could have built a basement under Goodtimes but we're too close to the beach. Any other ideas about the raid?"

"What about customers, Miz Edith? We close Goodtimes?" Lucky asked.

"We could just close, put up a sign to say we're having a private party or something," Darwin said.

"Except they're coming to search. It'll be suspicious if the place wisas closed. The men with the deputy will know we know something. I don't want them to suspect Roy. Especially after he's given us this heads up."

"Only wrong if they drinking," Lucky said. "We café, right? How about we serve lemonade and strawberry shortcake tomorrow night, at least until after raid? You tell customers; let them know about 'special event'."

"Pretty strange, even for a café, to be serving lemonade and strawberry shortcake at night," Edith said. The plotters sat silent, thinking.

"How about we say it's Leroy's birthday?" Edith said.

"My birthday? I already had my birthday."

"Yes, I remember. But that was the day I bought the refrigerator. I missed out on the party. How'd you like to have another one?" Edith winked at Darwin.

"We could put up a sign on the door saying it's your birthday and we're only serving lemonade and cake," Darwin said. "And I could let Harley know and he'll get the word out so that we have a few 'party guests' in on the scheme."

"It would be great to have another birthday," Leroy said, jumping up to give Edith a hug.

Edith relaxed, then peeled his arms away. "Okay, but let's get the liquor moved first and then, Lucky, you can start baking cake."

"Yay, I'm having another birthday party. And it will be better than last time," Leroy said, jumping around the barroom.

Edith's heart sank. *I gotta do better by that kid.*

"Just a pretend party, kiddo. No presents."

"I think we need presents for it to look authentic," Darwin said. He shot Leroy a wink.

Lucky nodded. "We wrap some things, Leroy."

"But I'll had to gave them back?"

"We don't have time to go shopping for birthday presents," Edith said. "Remember, it's just pretend. I'll telephone Mae and see if she can come help. The more the merrier," Edith said.

"Can I ask Cassie to come, too?" Leroy asked.

"She doesn't have a telephone, Leroy, and I don't think we can spare you to run and get her. How about we make sure she's at the next birthday party?"

"If I get all my work done and let her know about the party, she could come, right?"

"All right. But how—"

"I can't tell you. But she might be here."

Frantic activity ensued; moving liquor to the boats, leaving enough stock on hand to handle the night's business.

Later, Darwin had a quiet word with Harley.

"Private birthday party for Leroy, gotcha," Harley said.

* * * *

That night, after the usual crowd and clean up, Leroy lay in his bed in his new bedroom and squeezed his eyes shut. *Cassie, it's me, Koone. I'm having a pretend-birthday tomorrow.* He imagined the cake and the candles and the presents and the singing. *Please come. Please come. Please come.*

He rolled over and pulled the covers up to his chin. *I wonder what presents I'll get?*

* * * *

The next night at 8:30 sharp, two sheriff's cars pulled into the car park at the top of the hill and the deputies came trooping down the path to Goodtimes. Edith smirked when she saw Deputy Roy wiping his feet on the mat on the veranda before bursting in.

"Raid," he shouted.

The room was filled with birthday party guests—an interesting assortment of customers in the barroom, all regulars. Jasper from the post office had even stopped by for cake and to wish Leroy many happy returns.

Harley, Billy, and Nancy were also there. Billy had a large piece of shortcake slathered in whipped cream half-way to his mouth. He shoved it in and swallowed, then looked unsure of whether he'd get to finish the rest.

Mae Capone had arrived earlier in the day, loaded with party hats, balloons, and presents. Around four o'clock, Cassie had strolled in.

"How on earth?" Edith asked.

"I got the sense that Leroy was having a party. I couldn't miss it," she said, hugging Leroy close.

Draped on the wall was an old tablecloth with 'Happy birthday, Leroy' written on it. In addition to a traditional birthday cake, Lucky had made a longevity noodle that filled an entire bowl. Leroy was supposed to slurp it in one continuous strand. On a plate beside the noodle was another bowl with hard-boiled eggs dyed red.

"For happiness," Lucky said.

The six deputies, who were sporting Miami Sheriff's Department badges on their shirts, checked behind the bar and in the kitchen tent. They also looked in the shed where they found canned goods, other foodstuffs, and some bottles of beer.

"For personal consumption. Buying it was illegal? Thank you for telling me," Edith said.

They sniffed the lemonade suspiciously. Leroy, wearing a party hat, was sitting at the table surrounded by wrapped gifts.

Cassie stood close to Leroy. She didn't take her eyes off the deputies.

The sheriff's deputies seized a dozen half-empty bottles and the beer. "This was a bust, Purvis. You'll have to tell that dame at the Children's Home that there ain't nothing here."

"Can I offer you some cake and lemonade, gentlemen?" Edith asked, all charm and goodwill.

"No ma'am, we'll be going. Sorry to interrupt your birthday party, kid."

Edith walked them to the front screen door, holding it open so the deputies could file out. Roy Purvis stood next to her.

Roy mutters to one of the officers as they leave Goodtimes. "I told you it was just a café. Where'd you get the idea it was a blind-tiger, anyway?"

Edith turned to Roy when the last deputy was gone. "So, we're good here?"

"It appears so. Our end of it anyway. No telling how the Kid's Home will act when they find out that there was nothing going on." Tipping his hat, Roy left.

Once they were alone, Darwin led off a rousing chorus of "Happy birthday". Grinning, Leroy tore into his presents; his favorite was the baseball mitt from Edith.

"I thought you said we didn't had time for shopping." Darwin said quietly to Edith.

"I had to go into town, anyway." She looked over at Leroy, busy slapping his fist into the pocket of the new glove, chattering away with Cassie. With her eyes glowing, Edith smiled. "And I did miss his birthday."

CHAPTER 30

The next morning, Edith wandered out to the kitchen tent in search of coffee. She'd woken up dreaming about Bill McCoy, and the smile was still on her face. She headed to the stove, eyes on the coffee pot, passing Darwin who was at the table wolfing down a plate of bacon and eggs.

"Leroy still sleeping?" she asked, pouring herself a cup.

"Tired from party and presents. You want something to eat, Miz Edith?" Lucky asked.

"No, I'm fine, thanks Lucky. I thought the party went well. And Leroy liked his glove, although I almost didn't get it. I mean, who's he going to play with?"

"I can throw a baseball," Darwin said around a mouthful of egg.

"I'm glad you're both here. I got thinking last night—"

"Oh no, wait for it," Darwin said to Lucky.

"I'm serious. We need a better spot to store liquor than on the boat. And with the Dixie runs, there's a lot of inventory to move."

"I agree. What did you have in mind?" Darwin said, carrying his empty plate over to the sink.

"What about building a root-cellar under the shed? The ground's pretty solid back behind Goodtimes," Edith said.

"A root-cellar? For roots?" Lucky looked puzzled.

"Another American word. People use them to store potatoes and carrots and other root vegetables because it's cool underground. And I suppose there might be roots growing through the walls. They're generally just dug-outs under a house," said Darwin. "But I doubt whether that would be far enough. The high tide would make that a pretty damp spot, which would be hard on the booze and the labels."

"What about near the barn? That's quite a ways from the beach." Edith sat at the table and sipped her coffee. "And a better spot to hide the construction. We'll somehow have to build it in secret so village gossips don't figure it out."

Darwin frowned. "What about the musicians? They'd notice if we're digging in the middle of the night."

"Maybe close to the barn. We could say we're digging a latrine," Edith said. "That should keep people from asking too many questions. I mean, who gets curious about a latrine?"

"We'll just tell the musicians that we're working at night because we were busy during the day," Darwin said nodding. "Besides, they sleep late anyway. They'd probably appreciate a bit of quiet in the mornings."

"How we do that and finish kitchen?" Lucky looked worried.

"We'll get your kitchen finished, don't worry, Lucky. But this takes precedence. We can't operate a saloon if we're worried about the law seizing our liquor."

"How big do you want it?" Darwin said.

"I was thinking the size of a small room. We've got the Dixie runs to think about and probably more raids. Enough for all the Dixie run customers' stock if we had to."

"If we do that, we'll have to keep the booze onboard the boats for at least a couple of weeks."

"Can we manage? We could bring some of it inside Goodtimes. Do you think we could line the cellar with bricks so it's less 'hole-like'? I don't like spiders and creepy crawly things and a big pit would be full of them."

"That makes more work, but I think we can do that. The bricks would keep the stock cool. And we'll put up shelves. What about an entrance?"

"We could put an outhouse on top. With stairs where the seat is. I don't want to be climbing a ladder all the time. And it would need a lightbulb. Although we'd better put a lock on the door, we don't want anyone using it by accident."

Darwin scratched the back of his head. "This is getting pretty complicated, Edith. It'll take more than a few days to dig out a room that big with all the special features you're talking about. Are you sure you want something that elaborate?"

"Aren't you the one that's always saying do it right or don't do it?"

"Point taken. I'll get Leroy and Lucky to help me and we'll get started right away. I'll ask that Harley fella to help, too. I bet he's good at the end of a shovel."

Edith did not exclude herself from the construction team. The crew, plus Harley, worked on the hidden storage room at night after Goodtimes closed. The musicians weren't curious and often the sounds of their music coming from the bar until the wee hours of the morning provide accompaniment to the workers. Darwin stashed some of the liquor in the bar and left the rest aboard the *Rex*. As he slept on the boat, he was somewhat more confident about its security. The *Marianne* remained empty for Rum Row runs.

"Thanks again for helping out, Harley," Darwin said, passing him a cold beer. Dawn was breaking and shovels were down.

"No problem. What are friends for? And besides, Miz Edith said she'll rip up my bar tab. Which ain't no small thing."

"And pleased to do it," said Edith. "We wouldn't be able to get this done as quickly as we are without your help. I'm looking forward to the end of Prohibition and ordering liquor from a wholesaler like other countries do. What will you do when all this is behind us? I don't suppose a back-door business will work then,"

204

"There will always be underage youngsters that want a drink," Darwin said with a smirk. "I remember knocking on a few back-doors myself back in the day."

Harley shook his head. "No way, Darwin. I don't sell to kids." He scratched his head as he sipped his beer. "I expect that after Nancy and I get hitched, I'll turn off the light at the back-door and start working down at the pier. Mr. Carmichael offered me a job and I just might take him up on it."

"Have you two set the date yet?" Edith asked.

"No, not yet. But we're talking about it being soon."

Darwin clinked his beer bottle against Harley's. "Cheers to you. It'll be a heck of a wedding."

"Yes, and you're welcome to have it here," Edith said.

"I don't imagine Nancy's mother would be too keen on that, but thanks for the offer. If it were up to me I'd have Lucky do another pig roast on the beach. Now, that was sumpthin'."

After a long day and longer night of backbreaking work, Edith discovered the Seven of Pentacles underneath the scatter matt beside her bed. "I've seen this darn gardener before. The day of the Grand Opening. Leroy said I've got to stop and smell the roses."

Over breakfast, Leroy explained further. "You're not looking for quick wins, Miz Edith. A project you're working on, could be the root cellar, is getting close to being done. And all the hard work will pay off."

"Well, I'm glad to hear that. I'm not used to shoveling all night."

"Sometimes, however, the Seven of Pentacles can mean you get cranky with slow results. You've been working away at something important, probably the cellar but maybe it's Goodtimes. Anyway, you think all that work will go unrewarded. This card means be patient and appreciate the progress you've made so far."

Edith stomped her foot in frustration. "Does everybody know about these darn cards but me?"

"Didn't you say forewarned was forearmed, Miz Edith?" Leroy asked, an impish grin on his face.

"Shush."

"You really ought a let Aunt Cassie read your cards. They're going to keep turning up anyway."

CHAPTER 31

Most of America admired and perhaps envied the adventurous of the rum runners: heroically battling the elements, pirates, and the Coast Guard; all to bring the coveted forbidden liquor to America's shores.

What they didn't appreciate was the boredom. Smuggler's schooners could be parked along the Row for weeks and months at a time, selling their contraband booze to the small contact boats that made their way alongside each night. During the day, the hours were long. The food became monotonous. There wasn't a radio onboard or a signal that would reach that far, and the men were as sick of each other's stories as they were of the salted meat.

Close quarters, rough seas, bad food, and even nips from bottles in the cargo hold make tempers short. Ships and crews continually contended with limited supplies of gasoline for engines, coal for cook stoves, fresh water, food, and perhaps, most important to the crew, cigarettes.

One afternoon, Bill was surprised to see the *Rex* making its way across Biscayne Bay with Edith at the wheel.

When the *Rex* was close enough for conversation, Bill called out, "Well, aren't you a sight for sore eyes. It's strange enough to see a woman behind the wheel of a car let alone behind the wheel of a trawler."

"I have hidden talents, Captain McCoy."

"Of that I had no doubt, Mrs. Duffy," he said with a grin that made her heart skip a beat.

"I was feeling kind of closed in and needed a change of pace. We've just finished a big project at Goodtimes so the timing was perfect. I thought I'd see if I could make it out here on my own. Permission to come aboard, Captain?" Edith grinned as Bill reaches across to help her over to the *Arethusa*.

He was slow to let it go of her hand, and Edith blushed.

"I've brought out newspapers and magazines, fresh fruit and veggies, and tobacco," Edith said.

"Oh, my darling girl." He picked her up and swung her around, holding her close before setting her down. She couldn't catch her breath, the manly smell of him filling her head.

"Mr. Hardy, send someone to carry those bags." Bill turned to Edith, his hand still around her waist. "The crew will be glad of the break and the treats, they've been sitting sewing new hams from various 'leftovers' created from accidents—repackaging unbroken bottles with loose straw and burlap."

A cheer went out from the crew when Bill and Edith passed out the booty, including newspapers and cartons of cigarettes.

"Do you have to hurry back?" Bill asked, holding her gaze.

Edith swallowed, heat rising to her cheeks.

"No, um, folks aren't expecting me for a couple of hours. As long as I'm back to open up, I'm good."

Taking a bite of an apple, Bill laughed. "Better than good. Come on, let's get Frenchie to bring out his fiddle and make a party out of it."

The crew was happy to oblige. Frenchie picked up the fiddle, someone pulled out a squeezebox accordion, and another sailor grabbed a bottle of gin. Edith laughed along with the rest of the crew at the singing and jigging, and the good-natured jesting back and forth.

Bill watched it all with a tolerant eye. It was good to take a break before they getting down to work later that night. He smiled and threw an arm around Edith. "Tell me, what's new?"

"Well, we finally got that cellar finished; I have a whole new appreciation for pirates and buried treasure. I'm sure Cleo has told you I've expanded the smuggling side of the business. There are plenty of small places that want to avoid the risk of coming out to

Rum Row on their own, and other joints in the interior that don't have the connections to the coast. I figure we're out here on the Row anyway for Goodtimes, we might as well pick up a few more hams for other places."

"I figured something like that had happened. I've been seeing a lot more of Darwin than I used to. You'll do well." The Coast Guard seaplane buzzed by close, watching the festivities.

"That's new," Edith said, her hand shading her eyes as she followed the plane.

"The latest thing. They have great range and radio contact. They can keep an eye on things during the day, although they're blind at night when all the action happens."

Edith peeled an orange, and handed segments to Bill. "I've talked to Cleo about it. This new venture of mine. She's been very helpful with expertise about what kind of liquor I should sell and what deals are out there to increase my profits." She looked at him sideways, waiting to see his reaction to Cleo's name.

Bill slapped his thigh with a meaty hand. "I've just had an idea. Why don't you come back with me to Nassau? You could talk more about it with Cleo, finalize an order, then act as supercargo on way back. You'd love Nassau. The country's beautiful—a tropical paradise. And the people are wonderful."

"Oh, I could never get away."

"Think of it as a business trip. You should understand both sides of the business now you're expanding."

"True. There would be advantages. I like the idea of laying up some inventory. Let me talk to Darwin and Lucky. How long would I be gone for?"

"I can have you back within two weeks."

"Two weeks? I don't know, Bill. It's a long time. And we're just getting our feet under us. And there were some other things going on that don't let me get away easily."

Bill rested his hand on her arm. Her heart was pounding so loudly she's sure he can hear it.

"Please come, Edith. I want to show you my home."

She gulped. *Home—that's a big step.* "I'll think about it. When do you leave?"

"If we stay this busy, we'll be ready for a return trip by next week."

"I'll let you know. Don't go without checking in with me, okay?"

"I'll wait with bated breath for you to decide."

With an eye on the sun as it made its downward decent, Edith prepared to head back to Goodtimes.

Hands on the wheel and a full tank of diesel fuel, she's in control and ready to take on the world.

I'd love to go. It would be a chance to spend more time with Bill. A few hours every week or so just isn't enough time to get to know someone. Could Darwin and Lucky manage?

Although I suppose it was crazy. Miss White from the Children's Home is still sniffing around despite the unsuccessful raid. Maybe I could send Leroy to Cassie while I'm gone. That way he's safe and I get to go to the Bahamas with Bill.

Darwin would need to be responsible for the Dixie Highway runs. Could he do that and run Goodtimes? Maybe its not fair to ask that of him.

And Goodtimes. What about that? The Home and the Guild are just waiting to catch me out. I wouldn't put it past them to plant spies and snitches in the place. Maybe I should put in a secret code to get in at night, like we used to do at the speakeasies in Philly?

But who would look after Goodtimes while I'm gone? Two whole weeks. I wonder if Mae would come stay? She loved working behind the bar at 'Gator Joe's. And Lucky knows what needs to be done. Between the three of them, I'm sure they could manage. I'm only a telegram away if anything serious happens.

Edith, more confident at the wheel, churned through the waves at a steady pace. She naturally adjusted the throttle and corrected the course as she cruised home.

What if I did go? How does Bill feel about me? Cleo seemed to be quite fond of him. And there is something between the two of them. Or is there something between the two of us? There could be if I let it happen, but it would hurt Cleo. She's turning into a good friend; one I would lose if Bill and I get together. Despite all her fine words about it being casual, it's easy to see she's crazy about him. Figuring out how serious I am about him would be another good reason to go to Nassau.

Ha, Bill and I together. I can see it now, me just another one of his girls in every port. Loads of fun and someone interesting to spend time with, but he does have a wandering eye. I've been down that road before. Do I want to go through that again?

"You looked like a real pro coming in," said Darwin. He helped tie off the lines after she docked.

"I'm learning from the best." There was a twinkle in her eye. She took a deep breath. "I've got a proposition for you. How would you feel if I was away for a couple of weeks?"

"You're thinking of closing Goodtimes after all?"

They walked up the path toward the veranda. "No, but on that note, I think we should make people use a secret password to get into the place. We used to do that in the speakeasies up north. That would keep out anyone who didn't belong."

"You're thinking that the Children's Home may send in a spy?"

Edith nodded, frowning. "Or the Homemakers' Guild. I wouldn't put it past either one of them."

"Sounds like it might be a good idea. How about we use 'Philadelphia' as the code?"

Edith smiled at the idea. "But back to doing without me for a couple of weeks. I could ask Mae to come out and help run things at Goodtimes. You'd still look after the Dixie runs. Leroy could go stay with Cassie and away from the clutches of Miss White. I want to go to Nassau and talk to Cleo about the expansion. I'm thinking of bringing her in as a partner so that we can get a break on the retail price. It would increase our profits. The trip would be a mix of business and pleasure. A chance to see where all our booze comes from. Meet a few people. Could the three of you manage without me for two weeks?"

"I don't see why not. Mae's a good pair of hands, and she understands the business the same way you do."

"I'll talk to Leroy about his 'vacation'. You'll keep an eye on his situation?

Darwin held the front door open for Edith. "Don't worry, Edith. I'll watch out for him like he was my own."

Chapter 32

While Edith made arrangements to be away for two weeks, Leroy and Jay worked on their delivery business. The wagon was heavy with bottles hidden under the latest edition of the Herald.

Walking along the sidewalk, the two boys were deep in discussion about which houses had the most potential. They were almost on top of a group of older boys before they realized it.

"Hey, Carmichael. Whatchya doing? Collection day, is it?"

Jay Carmichael backed up. He's had run-ins with these bullies and always wound up on the ground, his pockets lighter.

Leroy stepped between him and the leader. "Get lost."

"Hey, who the heck are you, small fry?"

"No business of yours. Now scram," Leroy said, fists ready. Jay stood off to one side, watching, ready to run.

"Look runt, there's a tax on this sidewalk. Payable to us. Why don't you fork over the dough you have from your little newspaper business and we'll be on our way?"

"Not a chance. These are our papers. And it's our dough."

One of the other boys standing behind the leader sniggered. "Hey, I know who you are. You're that orphan kid outside of town."

"Yeah, what of it?"

"You don't got a pa. Just a runt, all alone. Nobody except scrawny Carmichael got your back."

"That's not true. I work at Goodtimes. I've got plenty of friends there to watch my back."

The boy who sniggered pulled at the leader's arm. "Hey, Stevie. That's a blind-tiger. I've heard stuff about that place. Like mobsters go there. With tommy guns."

"Yeah, that's right. You still want to cause trouble?" Leroy said with a defiant thrust to his chin.

"Nah, not worth it. Just a few pennies from newspapers. Let's let the babies go on their way. Come on, fellas."

Leroy didn't relax until they had crossed the street and turned the corner.

"Hey, that was neat. You're a real tough guy, ain't ya? Those guys always give me trouble."

"Bullies are losers, Jay. They're like them Wharf Rat pirates that give me and Miz Edith all the trouble. You gotta look them in the eye and call their bluff."

"Ah, I don't know, Leroy. They're real jerks," Jay said, his toe trying to dig a hole next to the wagon.

"You have any more problems, you come to me. I've got your back."

Jay threw his arm around Leroy's shoulders. "Thanks, Huck. How about you come back to my house and we'll see if Ma's filled up the cookie jar?"

* * * *

Mary Carmichael watched Jay and Leroy pull an empty wagon along the sidewalk. *There's that boy again. He and Jay are so close. Maybe I should have told Jay that they couldn't play together, but Mrs. Duffy has closed up Goodtimes as a saloon. Even the surprise raid didn't find any liquor. I let him play with the children from other cafes in town. I need to be fair.*

Looks like Jay got his papers done. And those boys look thirsty. When they got close, she shouted through the screen door.

"I've got cookies and lemonade, boys."

That put a spring in their step.

She carried out two glasses of lemonade and a plate of cookies and put them on the step where the boys were sitting. Back inside the kitchen she listen in.

"Them kids have been a problem for a while. They'll be back, you know."

Jay sighs. "I know. I can't always come get you. Whaddya think?"

"When you're dealing with enemies, it's important to know your own weaknesses, and theirs. You're a scrawny kid like me, easy to pick on."

Alarmed at the topic of conversation, Mary moved closer to the door.

"My weakness is there's only one of me and three of them."

What's this? Jay was being bullied again? I'm going to talk to Alvin about this. Poor Jay, always the littlest. Thank goodness Leroy was there. The last time, Jay came home with a split lip and a bleeding nose.

"What you need are allies. Miz Edith had these fellas she knows from Miami that act like muscle for her once in a while."

That doesn't sound like a café. Not at all. Maybe we were fooled?

"Gotcha. Muscle. Sometimes one of my brothers thumps them. But they always come back."

"That's the thing with getting help. It's not always around. Darwin says you gotta know your enemy. That's how he deals with

215

the pirates. Do any of the bullies have a pa on our route, especially one where we make deliveries? The pa wouldn't want us to stop, and he might tell his kid to lay off."

"Yeah, that's an idea. One of the kid's pa has bought a bottle from us. I could talk to him the next delivery."

A bottle? Soda pop? Mary shook her head. *I'd better tell Mavis and the rest of the Guild. If Mrs. Duffy is selling liquor, I can't let Jay be around that. Maybe they could do another raid or something so that I know for sure whether it's all right to let them play together.*

"The bullies just want your dough. What about hiding the newspaper money?"

Ah, newspaper money. They're talking about Jay's collections. That's better, then. So what's this about a bottle? Maybe I misheard.

"Like in my shoe?"

"No, that would be hard to get to and you do a lot of walking. How about we build a secret compartment in the wagon?"

"That would be cool. They wouldn't look there."

"Except they'd expect you to have money. Maybe keep some decoy coins in your pocket so that they get something, just not a lot."

"Good idea."

Mary was fascinated. *Such a clever boy. I wonder where Leroy comes up with these ideas. He did help Jay out with those bullies. I really owe him for that, although I should tell Mavis and Mary White that we need to look into Goodtimes again. Until I know for sure, I don't see any harm in them playing. Jay is so happy. I can't believe Leroy comes from a place like that. He's such a nice boy and seems good for Jay. I don't want it to be true that Goodtimes is open again.*

"Your pa have tools? We'll need a few pieces of wood and some nails. It should be easy to get to, but hidden."

"He keeps his tools in the shed. I know where there's an old crate we could bust up for wood." As Jay jumped up, Mary moved away.

"Ma, do we need that crate in the shed for anything? Leroy and I want to take it." Jay's face was against the screen.

"Help yourself. Just clean up the mess."

CHAPTER 33

Edith's fingers worked the adding machine, entering numbers for the new enterprise. She kept the Dixie run revenue and expenses separate from Goodtimes so she could tell, at a glance, how things were going, which was very well indeed. She glanced at the calendar where she was marking the days until she went to the Bahamas with Bill.

Next Tuesday can't come soon enough.

The last few weeks had been unsettled. The cloud hanging over Leroy had colored everything. Under normal circumstances, Edith would be reveling in the success of Goodtimes and pushing hard for more. A fully operational Edith would be driving the Dixie run forward, looking for more customers and more efficiency. *I don't like being handcuffed. A café indeed. My blind-tiger's declawed. But there's lots of fight in reserve; at least I hadn't lost my stripes. I'm not house cat yet.*

Fortunately—as far as Edith was concerned—the lunch idea hadn't taken off, which meant her days were still relatively free. Without special promotions, the secret password had kept the Goodtimes' crowd manageable. Darwin headed out most nights, and then she or Lucky would jump in the truck with him the next day and deliver the shipments up and down the Dixie Highway. Camouflaged as a fruit or vegetable truck, they buried the liquor under produce. The orange supplier alternated with a cabbage supplier, and Edith had secured contracts to resell their 'harvest disguise' after every second run.

Thanks to the Dixie runs, the bank balance grew. While that was rewarding, the long hours were taking a toll on everyone—and that was from only servicing the highway running along the coastline south of Coconut Grove. Edith itched to see what interest the north leg of the highway could generate.

The ring of the telephone interrupted her empire-building.

"Edith doll, how were you? Have I called at a bad time?"

Edith smiled and stretched out the knots in her shoulders. "Mae, how marvelous to hear from you. I've been up to my neck in accounts and I'd love a break."

"How's everything with Leroy? Is that lawyer helping?"

"I think we've reached a stalemate. I've got a permission letter from Leroy's aunt letting him stay here. And we've dialed back on Goodtimes promotions for the time being. I'm putting as much effort at staying out of sight as I was putting into growing the business. How were things with you? Have you had a chance to find out what I need to know about Florida City and Homestead?"

"Do you ever stop?"

Edith chuckled.

"No, I meant that seriously. Look, sweetie. I'm calling to see if you'd like to go to a house party. You don't head off to Nassau until next week. They're having a party out at the Brickell's on 'Millionaire's Row'. You know where that is?"

"You're kidding me, Mae. Everyone knows where that is. The size of the houses along that stretch of road are impressive. I don't know which house is the Brickell place, though. I haven't been socializing too much since I bought 'Gator Joe's."

"And that's why I'm calling. All work and no play kinda thing. Brickell's is on Brickell Avenue'"

"Of course it is."

"Don't be droll. It's across from Virginia Key. Come. There will be great contacts for you. People you should meet in Miami."

Edith thought of all the work to be done before she went on her trip. "Oh, I really shouldn't. I'm swamped trying to get ready to be away for two weeks. When is it?"

"Sunday afternoon. It'll be lovely. You can fill me in on all the details about looking after Goodtimes while you're away. Dig into the back of your closet and pull out one of those fancy dresses you picked up on that shopping spree we were on after the fire. I bet you've never even had them on."

"True. They still have the tags."

"See. Your business won't fell apart if you take Sunday afternoon off. And Darwin and Leroy probably would like a break as well. When you're there, you just put them to work."

"Darwin has been working non-stop. Fine, I'll come. Shall I meet you there?"

"Heaven's no. Come here and get changed and we'll go together. I have some treats for you: bath salts, bubbles, and I picked up an extra-large jar of olives from the Italian grocer."

"How can I possibly say no to that? See you Sunday morning. Bye, Mae. And thanks."

A party. It's been ages. What will I wear?

* * * *

"I love the way you brunettes could carry off that oyster color," Mae said as they wander through the plantation-style mansion, drink in hand. "And those black accents are perfect."

Edith felt great about how she looked in her tailored business suit with the saucy peplum that drew attention to her curvaceous hips. Professional, tasteful, classy. "Who's here that I should meet?"

"Come, and I'll introduce you to Bill Brickell first. I imagine we'll find him down at his dock, admiring his boat."

Outside on the back lawn, a six-piece band played popular show-tunes. It was a beautiful day and the lawn was crowded with beautiful people. Many knew Mae; most stopped to chat. Edith slipped into her old skin, just like the good old days with Mickey. She basked in the attention, and there were few men who hadn't come over to be introduced. But, in her eyes, none compared to Captain Bill McCoy.

Linking her arm through Mae's, she quivered with excitement. "This is definitely my crowd. Thanks so much for dragging me out, Mae. I've forgotten how much I love a party. Now, how do I get them all to follow me back to Goodtimes?"

Mae laughed. "Just be your charming self, doll, and they'll follow you anywhere."

With numerous interruptions, they made their way toward the Brickell's dock. Edith brought Mae up to date on the smuggling expansion idea. "But I'm being careful not to go head to head with the big boys like Lansky. There're plenty of small-time operators like Tucker Wilson. Places like 'Gator Joe's when I first started. The kind of joints a fella like Lansky wouldn't notice."

"You've got a great business head on your shoulders, doll; growing your business on what you already do well. Anything I can do to help?"

"Keep being my pipeline back to Meyer and Bugsy and the boys. I can't afford a misunderstanding with them over territory. Right now, the route is south along the old Dixie Highway, stopping in whenever I see something that fits the criteria. I don't want to accidently trip over somebody he's already got sewed up."

"Sure thing, doll. I could do that. I do know he's got something cooking in Florida City."

"That would be the furthest south I'd go."

"And north?"

"Small steps. I'll figure out the southern model first and then build on it."

"Well, keep an eye on the politicians and what they're doing up in Washington. I hear lots of chatter and the newspapers are full of 'Repeal' stories. Your Dixie runs only make sense during Prohibition. You need to think about what's coming next."

"All the time. And Goodtimes has staying potential."

"I agree. It's one of the reasons why Meyer has all those casinos. Greed and sin are timeless."

"I appreciate the advice, Mae. We won't get too heavily invested in the Dixie runs, but right now, especially with revenues down at Goodtimes, I need the extra dough. As soon as this thing with Leroy is cleared up, we can throw open Goodtimes' front door and welcome the world again."

"Tell me about this man you're sailing off with. Anything serious?" Mae and Edith worked their way through the lush gardens to the docks.

"There may be. That's one of the reasons I want to go to Nassau. I think you may have met him at the Grand Opening. Bill McCoy? He has a schooner out on Rum Row. A very impressive schooner."

Mae stopped and faced Edith. "Captain McCoy? Isn't that Cleo's fella?"

Edith blushed. "I'm not sure what their relationship is. All I know is that Bill's chasing and I'm debating about whether I want to be caught."

Mae shook her head, frowning. "I don't know about this, Edith. I think it's wrong to poach another gal's man, regardless of the set up."

Edith pulled away, cross. "There are only so many men, like Bill—like Mickey—in a girl's life. I don't want to pass up the chance for that kind of happiness again."

Mae took Edith's hand, forcibly putting it through her arm and turning so that they're walking together again "You and Mickey weren't 'happy' very long. I remember the way your eyes would follow him at parties as he flirted with other women. And I also remember there was a shadow over you, when you first came down here, that I blamed on Mickey. Was I right?"

Edith stood mute. What could she say when confronted with the truth?

Mae reached out to her, but Edith shrugged her off. "Did I ever tell you about my infatuation with Al's brother?" Mae said.

Edith's jaw dropped. "Frank Capone? He's a monster, Mae."

"No, doll, not Frank, who really is the deadliest of the Capone brothers. No, I'm talking about the oldest brother, Vincenzo. Folks call him Jimmy."

Edith shook her head. "I've never heard of a Jimmy Capone. Did he die?"

"He might as well have as far as the Capone family is concerned. He was with Al the night Al got the scar on his face in that dust-up in the joint in New York. Al was about seven years younger than Jimmy. Jimmy got mixed up in it trying to bail his little brother out. A man died, and Jimmy decided to head out of town until things cooled off."

"I know the story of the fight, of course. 'Scarface' Al Capone was famous. Is that when you met Jimmy? In those early years?"

"Those were good years. We'd all hang out together. Go to parties, and out for a drive. Even at that age, Jimmy was different. He didn't have the wildness of Al or the meanness of Frankie. He may have been the only good Capone brother. And I was strongly attracted to him, even though I was dating his younger brother."

223

"So what happened?"

"Believe it or not, he became a Prohibition agent."

"What? Al on one side of the fight and Jimmy on the other? Or was he crooked?"

"No, Jimmy was a straight arrow. He was one of President Calvin Coolidge's security detail when they traveled to the Black Hills. He had a reputation as a sharpshooter and a cool head. When he and Al got together over the years, I always wondered whether I'd married the wrong Capone boy. There's no denying the appeal. And my life would have been a lot simpler married to a calm and steady law man rather than a wild and crazy criminal, especially in the eyes of the church."

"Did anything ever happen between the two of you?"

"That's why I'm telling you this, sweetie. Life is about choices and sticking to them, despite how rosy things may look on the other side of the fence. I married Al and my loyalty is to him. You're working your way into the middle of a relationship between Cleo and Bill. You're going to need to choose because, trust me, you can't have both. And if it were me, I'd choose your friendship and business partnership with Cleo over a man who doesn't understand trust and loyalty. *Capisce*?"

Edith walked silently, deep in thought about Mae's revelation and her own circumstances. *Who would have guessed the matriarch of America's most notorious crime family may have loved a different brother? And what about Cleo and Bill? Mae's right. Those later years with Mickey almost killed me.*

As Mae had predicted, they found their host and his wife at the dock surrounded by a group of men debating the various merits of Chris-Craft boats.

"Edith, I'd like to introduce you to our host, Bill Brickell. Bill, this is that gal I've been telling you about. Edith Duffy."

"So you're the famous lady running a blind-tiger out in the middle of the Everglades."

"Actually, it's only about half an hour from here, just on the other side of Coconut Grove."

Mary Brickell, one hand on her husband's arm, looked her up and down. "I bet you're surrounded by dashing rum runners and pirates."

Thinking of the Wharf Rats, and Buford's big belly, Edith just nodded and smiled.

"I have no idea you were so close by," Bill Brickell said. "Friends of ours were there a few weekends ago. Said it was a marvelous place and loved the music."

With an arch smile, Mary Brickell turned to her husband. "We really must get out of the city more. Darling, the next time we have the boat out, let's go to Edith's place. What did you call it again?"

"Goodtimes. Let the good times roll."

Bill Brickell laughed. "I get it. Sounds like a real adventure."

Edith's smile widened as compliments rolled in. She had always been proud of her success; it pleased her enormously to see it reflected in others' praise for Goodtimes.

From all the kind words being showered on me and Goodtimes at this party, I seem to be more successful at business than love. Maybe I should go with my strengths? Concentrate on what I'm good at and leave this messy love-stuff to others.

"I understand the Brickells were one of the first families to settle in the area," Edith said.

"My grandparents operated a trading post at the base of the Miami River in the 1800s. Miccosukee and Seminole traveled down the river to trade there."

I must remember to mention that to Leroy.

"It gave us the ideal base to be part of Miami's growing prosperity. Luckily, Grandmother Mary timed the expansion of the railroad perfectly. At the turn of the century, she took control of the family's business interests."

"You have some impressive businesswomen in your family," Edith said. She was surprised to hear of a woman from an earlier generation achieve that kind of business success.

"Mary Brickell had a reputation as tough but fair. It was said she never foreclosed on a mortgage," Mae said.

"I love this neighborhood. You've done a beautiful job developing it," Edith said.

"Thank you. We took great care laying it out, especially the broad avenues and landscaped medians. And we've been very fortunate that others have appreciated the sense of design. The grand winter estates help define the character in the neighborhood. Some call it 'Millionaire's Row' or 'the Gold Coast' because of them. Louis Comfort Tiffany, the jeweler, and William Jennings Bryan, who's run for president three times, have recently bought."

"When we were driving here, we passed Vizcaya. The Deering's have a beautiful home," Mae said.

"A friend of mine went to Italy for her honeymoon. Today, I couldn't believe it when we drove past and I saw gondolas tied up in the lagoon," said Edith, still amazed at the sight.

"Doesn't every Italian villa need a gondola or two?" Mrs. Brickell said. "The Deering family will be in residence come November. I'll take you over and introduce you."

"Why thank you. I'd love that," said Edith. *This was exactly the crowd I want at Goodtimes.* She turned to Bill Brickell. "I'm very impressed with your boat. The Chris-Craft people make powerful boats."

Bill's eyes lit up and he rubbed his hands together, eager to talk engine size and speed. "That's quite a compliment from a woman who must know about fast boats."

Edith grinned flirtatiously. "You know Bill, when my mother warned me about being called fast, I don't think she was talking about boats."

CHAPTER 34

Getting ready to go to Nassau didn't just involve get the business ready or the suitcases packed. Arrangements had to be made to keep Leroy safe, as well. And sooner than she'd thought, the fateful day arrived.

Leroy waved goodbye to Darwin and Lucky from the porch off the kitchen and then Edith walked with him up the path to the car park.

"You've got everything you need? And those cookies for Cassie?" Edith fussed with Leroy's hair, brushing it off his face.

Leroy scowled up at her. "I don't want to go. Why can't I stay here?"

"Look, Leroy, we've been through this. It's not safe for you to stay here right now. The Children's Home people are snooping around and the deputy sheriff keeps coming by."

"We're pretending to be a café, so it's okay, right?"

"Normally, yes. But I won't be here, so I'm being extra careful. Besides, I'm worried about you. With this latest business venture of yours, I'm not sure you can keep out of trouble while I'm gone. You've got to promise me to stay at Cassie's and not come back here for two weeks. Promise?"

Leroy scuffed the gravel with his toe. "I told you, I don't want to go. I want to stay and play with Jay."

"And we both know what that means, don't we?" Edith grabbed him by the shoulders. "You're going to Cassie and that's final."

Leroy wrenched away. "I don't understand why it's okay for me to sell liquor when you're here, but not when you're away. What makes you so special?" His jaw thrust out belligerently.

"Because now you're a bootlegger, and that's my world. I know about that kind of thing and could spin a tale for the law if I had to. And I have the cash to apply the grease if necessary. You always have to approach this kind of risky business by thinking of the worst thing that could go wrong. Having you safe at Cassie's means I don't need to worry about all that, and you caught in the middle."

Leroy's bottom lip was in full pout. "Darwin's here. And Lucky, too."

Edith rolled her eyes, remembering Darwin's excuses about Leroy's bootlegging venture. "True, but around here I'm the only person that seems able to say no to you. Let's face it, you and trouble seem to be made for each other, and I don't want to have Darwin or Lucky worrying about you while I'm gone."

"Awww."

"Don't push it, Leroy. Instead of a temporary ban, right now I'm tempted to say you can't sell your bottles at all. Is that what you want?"

Edith arms were crossed, and she glared down at him. Leroy, his arms crossed, glares up at her. A stand-off.

"Well, I'm waiting. Your choice," Edith said, scowling. *This was not how I thought we'd be saying goodbye today.*

Leroy threw his arms up in the air and stomped his foot. "Fine. You're the boss. I'll go to Cassie's stupid camp and stay there until you get back." The pout of his bottom lip cast a long shadow. Edith inwardly flinched. *All I want to do is keep him safe and happy.*

Edith gave a rigid Leroy a tight hug. "You have fun, now. Catch lots of opossums and go for lots of canoe rides."

When he didn't hug her back, she dropped her arms.

"Fine. Have it your way. Now, you'd better get going. Aunt Cassie will be looking for you."

She stood in the car park, watching him head up the road and out of sight. "He's going to be fine, Edith." Darwin, who had come up behind her, rested his hand on her shoulder.

She sighed. "I expect so. But will I? I've gotten used to having the boy around. Keep an eye on things, will you? I've seen that woman from the Children's Home lurking around when I've been in town."

"I will. With Leroy at Cassie's, there's nothing for her to see here."

Edith reached out and rested her hand on Darwin's chest. "We're doing the right thing, aren't we? Keeping him here while Goodtimes is open? It's disguised well enough, isn't it? We don't need to have him stay at Cassie's permanently?"

Darwin's smile and his warm hand covering hers was a comfort. "You know what you're doing. If it gets worse, Leroy can always find a safe place to hide. But there isn't anyone who loves him more than you and Cassie do, Edith. Between the two of you, it would take a mighty force to blow you off course. Come on, let's get your bags downstairs. Bill will be here soon and you'll be off on your adventure."

"Mae will be here later tonight," Edith said.

"I know. Everything's organized. Leroy will be fine. Goodtimes will be fine. Lucky and I will be fine. Now, how many bags do you have? You know you're supposed to pack light when you travel on a ship."

* * * *

Deep in the Everglades and away from the cooling ocean breezes, the thick air carried a taste of decay and rot. Mangrove trees provided some welcome shade for Cassie as she finished her chores for the day. She'd been mending; the humidity and rough living was hard on her clothing. She was planning a trip into Coconut Grove in the next few

230

days and wanted to make sure she looked her best. "I got a pile of customers building up, needing to hear what the cards have to say."

Living on her own, she talked to herself for company. "Leroy should be here soon. Gosh, it will be good to see the boy again. I wonder what he's been up to? I hope he's eating. He's always too skinny. Although, I gotta admit that Miz Edith looks after him good, I'll say that for her. And I want to hear all about where things were at with the Children's Home."

She held up the blouse she'd been fixing, checking her work. She looked front and back and nodded. "This will do. Maybe I'll pick up some fabric from S&P Mercantile when I'm in town and make up some new things."

Cassie put it away in the tent and wandered over to the chickee. Her tarot cards, neatly wrapped in blue silk, waited patiently in the middle of table. Settling in the wooden chair, she leaned back and stretched. "I'm going to sew me a cushion for this chair, too. My old bones need some comfort."

She unwrapped the cards and shuffled. Eyes closed, Cassie focused as the cards slipped through her hands. She sighed, opened her eyes, and split the deck into three. "Has Edith got the situation with the Children's Home wrapped up? Things must be settling down for her to be going away from Leroy and Goodtimes for a spell."

With one hand still resting on the cards, Cassie closed her eyes again. "*Ah-ma-chamee*, you are my champion—and Koone's—and I feel like you're getting worn down. And it's not just because of the Preacher-Man. There's a whole load of woe on your back, Edith. You don't get to set it down just yet, but maybe sometime soon? Someone could help you carry it. Someone bigger than Leroy—he's just a boy. You need broader shoulders. Maybe that nice Darwin fella?"

Cassie's eyes were open when she re-stacked the cards in reverse order. She drew the top card, turned it over, and studied it.

A heart was pierced by three swords. "Hmm," she said, nodding. She addressed the empty chair across from her. "I was expecting something different. Maybe about that romance I saw. When does your king step onstage, *ah-ma-chamee*?"

She frowned as she examined the card again. "Not today, I guess. Instead, we got pain here. Real hurt or heart hurt?" She nodded again, head tilted, listening to the silent words being spoken.

"Betrayal. Always hard to take, especially from one you love, *ah-ma-chamee*."

She put the Three of Swords aside. "Your heart has been pierced by the sharp blades of others' hurtful words and actions. There's a whole lot of sadness here. And pain, too. It cuts deep. I know what you're going through, Edith. The good folks of Coconut Grove aren't any happier to see a fortune telling Indian than they are to see a woman running a blind-tiger."

Cassie cut the cards into three piles and reassembled them. She turned over the top card. "Sorry, Edith. You just can't catch a break today. This is the Death card and it means you are also thinking of someone, your husband maybe? It's time to accept what happened and move forward with your life. But Leroy told you that already. Listen to him. Your focus stays locked on the damage when it should be on the recovery."

She puts the middle card down, shaking her head. "Poor Edith. You've been through a lot. That husband of yours was a real bastard, wasn't he? Will you keep running from love? What you need is a fresh start, or is the past doomed to repeat itself?"

She repeated the cutting into three and re-stacking. Cassie's hand hovered over the top card. "Ah, Strength reversed. Now, what does that mean?" Cassie studied the image of the card, a woman holding a lion, stroking its head and jaw.

"You'll need to tune into that confidence and inner-strength, *ah-ma-chamee*. You're going to have a setback, a powerful setback. And it looks like you'll react with a roar. You got a habit of acting without thinking, and that kind of impulsive behavior is something you could come to regret later. But then again, you know that already, too, don't you?"

Cassie cocked her head to one side, listening. "Koone's coming. I'd better get that gumbo warmed up."

* * * *

Sails unfurled and billowing in the wind, the *Arethusa* rode the waves toward Nassau. Edith leaned against the rail, breathing in the pure, healthy salt-air. "It's incredible, isn't it? Nothing to see for miles and miles except ocean."

"I like that about her. The promise of what's just over the horizon," Bill said. He was close to her and she fought the impulse to lean into him. *Let him wrap his arms around me...*

She caught herself. *Until I figure out how Cleo fits into all this, I've got to keep my distance. But wouldn't it be wonderful to just lean back and let the devil take the consequences.*

"Tell me about what I need to do as supercargo. This is the job Cleo does, right?"

Those strong arms, those lips, a girl would sure feel safe there.

"It's traditional to have a superintendent of cargo to keep an eye on the inventory. We often have Cleo's cargo in the hold, and I enjoy traveling with her. She's much better than a pencil pusher or a gangster."

"Gangster?"

"That's who's buying the liquor, Edith."

"Right," she said, blushing. *I've been so focused on Bill—and Cleo—I've forgotten the reason I'm here.* "Tell me what I need to know about being your supercargo."

"The supercargo's main job is to keep the tally of what liquors we sell from the stock, and to handle the cash. Rum Running is a dangerous business, Edith, so remember rule number one: no buyer is ever permitted in the cabin alone. Rule two; everyone aboard carries a gun or some other weapon. And rule three; I never fill an order until I've got the cash in my hand."

Edith patted the holster she strapped on when she left Goodtimes. The familiar weight of the gun was a comfort. "Right." *He sounds so much like Mickey when he talks like that.* "Does a supercargo have any other duties between Nassau and Rum Row?"

"You're on a ship with a bunch of sailors, Edith. Another job the supercargo has is to maintain balance between the need to keep the crew happy, with the occasional bottle from the cargo, and staying sober enough to sail the ship. You also have to ensure that enough cases survive to make the voyage profitable. And it would be your own liquor in the held, so dole it out wisely."

"You're teasing."

"I wish I were."

* * * *

While the weather stayed balmy, the week's voyage was anything but smooth sailing. it was filled with tension and hidden meanings. The first night, in the privacy of the captain's cabin, Bill was disappointed when she chose to sleep in her own berth—alone. Across the cabin she could hear him breathing. The waves rocked the two of them in their separate bunks. The situation caused confusion, hurt feelings, and wounded pride—both of them were more than a little put out.

Mae was right. The kiss we shared on the Rex *was a mistake. Thank goodness I can use the ship's crew as chaperones.*

As she helped out around the ship during the day, their hands would brush and the current was electric. He'd stop and tuck a loose bit of hair behind her ear and her heart would race. She caught herself letting her eyes wander over his shirtless, muscled body as he hoisted the heavy canvas up and down the mast. And there was that devilish grin that snared her every time.

How long can I keep saying no?

CHAPTER 35

There were several more days at sea before Edith, lying in her berth, heard the welcome news. "Land ho," shouted the boy from the crow's nest. She threw on her clothes and joined Bill on deck. Dawn was just breaking and she could see the far-off outline of land against the horizon.

Nassau was a major port city in the Bahamas, which was Cleo's home base and headquarters for her wholesaling liquor business as well as the port Bill McCoy called home. Close enough to be America's back door, the Bahamas was a clearinghouse within the law. Places like London, Glasgow, and Paris would bring liquor ashore and warehouse it there after payment of duty to the Bahamian government.

Thanks to Prohibition, Nassau was well launched on her third and most prosperous era of activity. When it was dubbed the Spanish Main, pirate ships had lain in her harbors and buccaneers had squandered handfuls of doubloons ashore. During the American Civil War, blockade runners had swaggered along her streets and taken their swift steamers out of her harbor to return wealthy, if they returned at all.

Now the town found herself hostess to a new group of wild ones. The popular press had dubbed them the 'booze buccaneers'. They were a wicked mix of pirate and blockade runner with a troubling dash of violence thrown in for good measure: the rum gang. Todays buccaneers were a harder, tougher, more unscrupulous crowd than Nassau had dealt with in the past: big shots of the underworld who were proceeding to take Nassau apart and remold it closer to their hearts' desire.

The call of big money had summoned them, much like what follows a gold strike, the opening of diamond mines, or the discovery of an oil field. Adventurers, businessmen, soldiers, sailors, loafers, all sought to make their fortunes by keeping America wet.

The *Arethusa's* crew scrambled, starting their docking procedure, furling the sails as they passed through the harbor entrance which was sheltered by Hog Island and New Providence Island. The water was dotted with motor boats and launches, schooners, fishing boats and the small, rough boats the locals used for sponge fishing.

Edith stood wide-eyed at the side of the ship, keeping out of the way and watching all the activity in the harbor and on the pier. Heavy barrels from the docks were being rolled toward the warehouses. Workers were dodging wooden-wheeled horse carts loaded down with precarious stacks of liquor cases moving toward the ships. From what she could see, the motley collection of stables, houses, and shanties near the waterfront had been drafted into service as warehouses. There were mountains of off-loaded goods on the rickety pier, hundreds upon countless hundreds of cases from each boat.

As they pulled closer, they passed several rum running schooners like the *Arethusa*. After months at sea, the ships were crawling with men, many of them hanging off rigging, dangling over the side, getting the boats ship-shape and seaworthy so that they could head back out into the Atlantic. That would soon be *Arethusa's* fate as Bill wanted her ready within the week for the return trip.

Bill guided his schooner expertly in to dock. The crew was all on deck, clamoring for their pay. He waved over a couple of donkey cart drivers. "Take these lads to Grant's Town. They need to recover from a month at sea." This announcement was greeted with hoots and hollers from the men aboard.

Grant's Town was a shanty town 'over the hill' from Nassau proper; plenty of bars, rum was cheap, and there was an abundance of pretty girls and player pianos. "Just make sure you're back by Friday so we can reload and head out again."

The men waved and call out ribald advice as the carts headed off the dock. They were ready to blow off some steam and spend their pay.

"Well, it looks like it's just you and me now. Do you have everything from the cabin?" Bill's manner was polite and stiff. Edith, bright eyed with excitement, and eager to start her adventure, merely nodded.

Bill flagged down a donkey cart and took Edith to the Lucerne Hotel on Frederick Street. Prior to Prohibition, it had been a prim, quiet inn precisely run by an elderly New England woman and her daughter. The chief justice of the colony and others of great respectability had lived there. Most of those departed by one door when the bootleggers and smugglers entered though another. Now it reigned as the 'Bootleggers' Headquarters'.

The Lucerne Hotel was a fifty-odd room, three-story frame structure. From a distance, Edith thought it was two separate buildings surrounded by a high white wall. The front entrance had a winding stairway set in a mass of beautiful tropical plants including royal palms, coconut palms, and croton bushes of brilliant shades and colors. There were wide piazzas on each floor.

While Bill checks in, Edith wandered out to the center garden. Loungers were congregated at small green tables, surrounded by more lush foliage. An old but stately pelican waddled after her looking for tidbits.

"Shoo, you."

Bill, who'd come in search of her, laughed. "That's old Nebuchadnezzar, the hotel pet. Totally harmless unless you have a fish in your pocket."

"He's out of luck today, I'm afraid." Their shared laughter began to melt the ice between them. Edith reaches toward him and held his hand. The hand-holding moment lingered, then Bill moves away.

"I'll wait here while the bellhop shows you to your room," he said, moving toward the mahogany bar next to the patio. "While you're unpacking you can think of what you'd like to do first."

Edith was about to follow the bellhop when a tiny elderly woman, white-haired and withered, with light blue eyes behind gold-rimmed spectacles, arrived. She cradled two Pekingese dogs, one under each arm.

"Captain McCoy. How delightful to see you again. Welcome back," the woman said.

"Mother. How's my favorite gal?"

Mother? Intrigued, Edith stepped forward. "Mrs. McCoy, a pleasure to meet you."

"Mrs. McCoy? Ha, that'll be the day. No, you've got that all wrong, dear. I'm Dorothy Donnelle. No relation to this scoundrel. Everyone here calls me Mother, and you must, too."

Edith left Bill in Mother's care and followed the bellhop and her luggage across the lobby to the staircase and her room on the second floor. With a tip to dismiss the young man, Edith moved over to unlock the floor-to-ceiling windows that opened to the terrace overlooking the lovely walled garden. A refreshing breeze helped with the heat the overhead fan was struggling to contend with. She pushed aside a drape of mosquito netting to sit on the edge of a four-poster bed, bouncing to test the comfort of the mattress.

This isn't too bad. I hope the bathroom down the hall isn't too far away.

After unpacking her bags, Edith hurried downstairs to find Bill.

"Mother looks like she should be among the hollyhocks behind a white picket fence in New England," Edith said, joining Bill at the bar.

Bill chuckled. "Instead, her patrons are riotous hordes of veteran drinkers and lawbreakers, and all the crooks from Hell's Kitchen. Present company excepted, of course. So, what shall we do first? Would you like a tour of the island? Lunch and then nap? We could have dinner here at the hotel. Cleo isn't able to join us, so I'm afraid it will be just you and me under a tropical moon."

Edith's tummy gives a lurch. *There's no crew to act as chaperone now. Is Cleo missing my first night here because she suspects something?* "I think I'd like to go for a short walk and explore Nassau, then lunch, and nap. How does that sound?"

"Perfect." Bill tucked her arm in his and they headed out to the bustling streets of Nassau. They strolled along Bay Street, the chief thoroughfare on the waterfront and principal business street. Bill pointed out the sights, sharing stories and memories of his time in Nassau. They drew together, eventually walking arm in arm.

Edith was breathless from Bill's body in close touch to hers. She was also excited by the sites: exotic looking people, little shops selling liquor, handcrafted goods made from sisal.

But part of their walk was only too familiar. The streets were crowded with narrow-eyed hunch-shouldered strangers, the bluster of Manhattan in their voices and a wary shiftiness in their manner.

Edith leaned in close to Bill who put a protective arm around her, pulling her even closer.

"The faces I've seen in the last ten minutes here on Bay Street would give a cop in Philly nightmares for a week," she said.

"The gangsters and mobsters have full run of the town now. They're like a bunch of sharks, circling dinner. It was a sleepy little place when I first came, but it's not that way anymore."

"I doubt American politicians thought about the consequences of making liquor illegal. It had been a very profitable opportunity for gangsters and the criminal element."

"And for you. Or are you putting yourself in the gangster column?"

"I'm just a businesswoman taking advantage of opportunity." Edith chuckled.

"You seem to love swimming with sharks."

"I love the thrill. And I love making ideas real. I'm less thrilled about the violence—I have a healthy respect for the big sharks."

"Dangerous waters out there, Edith."

"I know. I've got pirates and the Wharf Rats, there are mobsters and gangsters, there's the Children's Home, and Brother Silas—a lot of big, sharp teeth all smiling in my direction. And yet, I keep on. Which tells you how much I love being a business woman with Goodtimes and now the Dixie runs."

"You'd never think about giving it up? Settle down with a good man and a passel of kids?"

"Bill McCoy, Cleo assured me you were one-of-a-kind who didn't mind a strong woman earning her keep. Don't tell me you think some fella is going to sweep me off my feet into a rose-covered cottage?"

"I had no illusions about that, Edith. I can't imagine you settling down or settling period. You're a shark, just like the rest of them. Always moving to survive."

Edith laughed, slapping his arm. "A shark? Me?"

"A pretty one for sure, but the teeth are just as sharp."

The hotel's garden was a welcome respite from the streets of Nassau. The coolest spot to have lunch was under the spreading sandbox tree, its branches almost covering the whole garden.

"I bet this old tree has a tale or two. It looks like the perfect spot for a lovers' rendezvous."

"Or the odd schemer or two, given the clientele these days," Bill said.

A group of local urchins congregated on a large, wooden platform under the large tree. The arrival of the steamers and schooners meant new guests at the hotel, a fresh audience for their performance, and the chance of a healthy tip or two. Bill and Edith enjoyed their performance—local songs and popular jazz-time tunes.

A uniformed waiter delivered two plates of grilled fish, chilled tropical and semi-tropical vegetables, avocados, beans, chiotes, bananas, and pineapples—a refreshing combination in the heat of the day. Mother's speciality completed the meal: homemade lemon pie.

Edith excused herself after the delicious lunch and, having made arrangements to meet again at dinner, it was time to rest. Darkening the room with shutters and drapes, she tossed and turned on the bed.

Cleo, Bill, me. Cleo, Bill, me. Bill. Bill. I've never met anyone like him. All of Mickey's strength and power but none of his wickedness.

In an effort to be more comfortable, she slipped off her dress, returning to bed wearing only a shift. *The other thing they have in common is an easy way with women.*

And then there's Cleo. Cleo who values honesty. What's she doing with a man like Bill. Maybe she's not the right kind of gal for a man like that. Am I?

The afternoon passed with a form of unrest—maybe the temperature, maybe sultry thoughts. Edith felt less conflicted by the time she was getting ready for dinner with him; she dressed with a purpose. The fabric clung to her curves, the tiny straps begged to be slipped off, and the intensity of the red color cried out passion.

That night, under the tropical moon, she swayed through Lucerne's restaurant and felt Bill's eyes on her as she approached the table where he was waiting. It took all her willpower not to run into his arms. *Cleo be damned.*

He reached for her hand. "I'm glad you decided to come to Nassau with me, Edith."

Edith purred and coyly pulled her hand away. "So am I. It's been such an eye-opener for me. I've already picked up quite a few pointers that will be helpful when I get home." A knowing look, and then eyes cast down to the floor.

Bill threw back his head. "That's what I love about you, Edith. You are so damned unpredictable."

"A girl should always have a few surprises up her sleeve."

"I prefer the arms bare." He ran his hand along her bare arm.

Edith's heart hammered. Her skin tingled where he touched her. Concentrating on Bill, the evening slipped by unnoticed. She ate her meal, drank her wine, and swallowed him whole. Tension mounted between them with the unspoken promise. A small, delicious shiver ran over her.

"You know, it might be a bit chilly. Maybe I should go get my wrap."

Bill leaned in closer. "Why don't I come upstairs with you and help you look for it?"

Her lips part to answer him and she shivered again.

Now or never. Cleo? Friendship?

Edith closed her eyes and saw her friend sitting on the terrace under the moon at Goodtimes. She felt a warm wave of friendship. Perhaps not as electric, but it was just as fulfilling as this flirtation she was having with Bill.

A friendship that would stand the test of time.

"No, I think I'll maybe turn in for the night. It was a perfect day, but suddenly I'm quite exhausted."

A friendship that would stand the test of time. I'll just keep saying that.

Bill pulled back, his smile frozen in place. "Of course. I'll see you after breakfast and I'll take you on a bit of a sightseeing tour."

"I'm looking forward to it, Bill. And thank you for a lovely evening."

* * * *

The next morning, awake and refreshed, Edith and Bill toured the island. They drove past the site of a three hundred room hotel that was under construction, the famous esplanade along the waterfront, and historic Fort Charlotte They passed beautiful white beaches and stopped when they arrived at Jane Gail's cave where she had acted in the silent film Twenty Thousand Leagues under the Sea. At low tide it was a mere cave, but at high tide it was filled with transparent waters, which allowed the film's cameramen to use lights and mirrors to shoot the underwater scenes.

After stretching their legs at the cave, Edith and Bill got back in the car, driving past scrub palm trees, sisal, and a few houses. When they arrived back in Nassau, they stopped and visited the Queen's Stairway, where Edith climbed all sixty-five steps hewn out of natural rock by the island's former slaves.

After the day's excursions, Edith was looking forward to daiquiri cocktails and dinner. And was delighted to find that Cleo was at the bar and would be joining them for dinner in the garden.

Thank goodness I made the right decision last night or seeing Cleo again would have been unbearable.

Edith watched Bill and Cleo together. They had so many stories in common, finishing each other's sentences. He ordered her favorite drink without asking. They were a good fit.

I wish I had that. What woman wouldn't? I must be as vile as the women in Coconut Grove say I am. I've seen how Cleo feels about him and yet there is something about him I just can't say no to. What kind of person does that make me?

244

"They're having a fire-dance tonight in Grant's Town. Do you want to go?" Cleo asked Edith. "You'll not see anything like it back home."

"I don't think that's a good idea, Cleo. Things can get out of hand there pretty quick," Bill said, frowning.

"Oh, come, Edith. We'll just sneak in and watch. We won't actually be dancing."

"As long as you promise to be careful. I can't have my two favorite gals getting into any trouble now, can I?" Bill said, still frowning.

The gals overruled him. Not long after, the adventure began.

Her heart now racing, Edith gripped Cleo's hand as they scurried through the dark streets of Nassau and out to the countryside. The moonlight picked a path for them to follow along a dirt road that ran along the edge of a pineapple plantation. Over the waist high plants, lights from workers' huts twinkled in the distance.

They could hear the drums before they could see Grant's Town. Cleo had spied on the fire-dance before and knew where they could watch from the shelter of a grove of trees. A huge fire was blazing in a clearing on the edge of the shanty town.

There was a barbaric quality to the night. A drummer was pounding away on a drum made from a keg with cow hide stretched on top, the rhythmic beat reverberating inside Edith's chest. Orange firelight flickered on the glistening skin of the semi-naked dancers. They were a mix of locals and gangsters; some she recognized from the hotel. Cases of gin were open and stacked for self-service.

Edith and Cleo remained hidden, spying on the dancers. The gin and bonfire worked their magic; remaining clothing was thrown away. When the couples tired of dancing they disappeared into the darkness and the bush surrounding the clearing. Soon, rhythmic moaning accompanied the pounding of the drums.

"You won't see this in Coconut Grove," Edith said, whispering. Her pulse was racing.

Cleo smothered her laughter with her hand. "No, that's for sure."

The night wrapped its magic and mystery around the two women. Cleo took a deep breath and then took Edith's arm, pulling her away from the bonfire scene. "If you're ready to go, I think I'll stop by Bill's after I drop you at your hotel." Cleo gave a low chuckle that twisted in Edith's belly. "Just to let him know that we made it back safely."

CHAPTER 36

"Bill isn't with you this morning?" Edith asked Cleo at breakfast the morning after the fire-dance.

Cleo giggled and gave Edith a wink. "He got a late start this morning and wanted to go directly to the harbor to check on the *Arethusa* to see some of the repair work they're doing while she's in port. He thinks everything will be shipshape by the day after tomorrow and you can head back out to sea."

"Is it time to go home, already? It feels like we just got here." *And just tin time. I keep backsliding about Bill and me. Mae's right, I have to choose between the woman sitting in front of me whose respect and friendship I value, or deceive that woman and share the man standing between us.*

"Rum runners don't make any money sitting in the harbor, Edith. They're loading the *Arethusa* right now. I've brought my order book so we can put together your Dixie run cargo. I'll have it delivered to the ship this afternoon and they can get it loaded. Have you thought about a warehouse yet? I don't think it everything will fit in the hidey-hole under the outhouse."

"Oh, I hadn't. A warehouse is a good idea. We've always done order-on-demand. I've never pre-purchased before. I suppose we could use the barn. Although it would cost me a bigger contribution at the sheriff's office."

Two heads bent together over Cleo's order book and it was quickly filled.

"I want to thank you for all the help and advice you've given me on this Dixie run venture, Cleo. It's nice to be working so closely with you."

"I feel the same way, ducks. There are too few women in our line of work."

"How would you feel about making it more formal?"

"What, the working together?"

"Yes. You could be my exclusive supplier for the Dixie orders. Rather than pay retail from a bunch of different wholesalers and take my chances on inventory availability, you sell liquor to me at wholesale prices in exchange for all the Dixie business. The south highway volume is growing, and there are huge opportunities if we turn our attention north."

"Exclusive supplier, eh? What about Goodtimes?"

Edith laughed. "You're so ambitious, Cleo. It's one of the things I admire about you. No, Goodtimes is mine. Darwin will be out on Rum Row buying from whoever has the stock we need. Although, of course, you and Bill are always our preferred suppliers."

"I see the potential. It would be nice to have a steady and reliable stream of revenue rather than peaks and valleys. I'm always having to scramble to fill my order book. Tell me more about these Dixie runs."

Edith grinned. "Business is booming. The smaller places are happy to pass the risk of running out to Rum Row along to us in exchange for a commission."

"So that's the business you currently have on the books, but what about new business?"

"That's the exciting part. While I love working with you now, what I'm really proposing is what's coming next. I've got a profitable situation with the south end of the Dixie Highway. But we have the Tamiami Road across the state and the north end of the Highway from Miami all the way up to north of Jacksonville. No one is doing what we're doing in a coordinated fashion. That's the opportunity I'm laying out for you this morning."

"Now that is definitely something I would want to be part of."

Edith sat back, a huge smile on her face. *If Cleo's in, it means she thinks I can get it done.*

Cleo flipped to a new page in her order book. "Tell me what you're thinking of for the second phase of your expansion."

"I'm focused on the smaller operations which means the more affordable brands seem to be the most popular. Using your connections to source deals on bar stock would really give us an advantage."

"I'll start working with my suppliers and see what I can do. I'm honored that you've come to me with this opportunity, Edith. What do you think about a sliding scale of commissions? Given the uncertainty and the potential of future growth, we could use a sliding scale: the more you buy the cheaper it gets. I'll give you a good price right now, but the real business advantage for us both comes from the bootlegging, rum running empire you're proposing."

"I like the flexibility. Why don't you put together a scale based on tomorrow's cargo? That's our minimum. It will only get bigger," Edith said.

"Deal. And when I'm aboard, working as supercargo, I'll also keep an ear open for independents that are struggling to get inventory or find it difficult to make it out to Rum Row. Maybe I can find you some new customers. For a finder's fee, of course."

"You drive a hard bargain, Cleo. We can keep in touch through telegram or talk in person the next time you're supercargo for Bill." Edith's eyes were shining. "I'd love to work with you, Cleo. We think alike on so many things, and you know this business inside and out. With your expertise on the supply side and mine on the deliveries, we can make a great deal of money."

"I do like the sounds of that. Let's do it. Shake?"

Edith laughed. "Are you sure you don't want to run the numbers first? Or check my references? I've never pegged you for impulsive."

Cleo grabbed her outstretched hand.

"Not impulsive, just quick to figure out the benefits. Unless there's other information you're not sharing, I'm good to go right now."

"Now? Do I get my special wholesale price on this cargo?"

"Edith, always pressing an advantage. Let's go with the normal prices and gave me time to find specific stock for our arrangement. You're still making a healthy profit on what I'm selling you today."

"True enough." Edith went up to the bar and brought back a bottle of champagne. "Let's toast to this new arrangement."

Tucking away the order book, Cleo raised her glass. "Here's to a lucrative partnership between good friends."

"I've had such a lovely visit. It's nice to see where you and Bill live," Edith said.

"It has been fun. You've not talked much about home. What's new?"

"It's not good." Edith grasped Cleo's hand. "I'm having some trouble and I'm not sure that I'm handling it the right way."

"Ha. That doesn't sound like you. You're always full steam ahead and no second thoughts. What's going on?"

"The ladies in Coconut Grove have a bee in their bonnet about Leroy. They've always disapproved of me, and now they are saying that I'm violating child labor laws."

"What?"

"Really. Children under twelve can't work, especially in an establishment that sells liquor. And Leroy's eleven. Although, It's got more to do with getting back at me than any special concern for Leroy. And it's an added complication in my already complicated life."

"What are you doing about it?"

"I've got a high-priced lawyer talking to the governor. And we're keeping a low profile until all this blows over."

"You've closed Goodtimes?"

"That's the part I'm not sure of. Officially, we're a café. But we're still operating as a blind-tiger. We've always been illegal, so really it's nothing new. We've always taken precautions, and just recently we've started asking for a password to get in. I'm worried that the sheriff's office or the biddies in town will send in a spy. Like I said, business as usual."

"Unless they take Leroy away."

"Yes. Unless they take Leroy away."

Cleo sat back, studying Edith.

"What are the chances?"

"I think it depends on how motivated they are. Right now, the Homemakers' Guild has sent the Florida Children's Home and the sheriff's office around. They've found nothing. I'm counting on them to get bored with this cause of theirs and move on to something else. The lawyer assures me Prohibition is in its dying days, and Leroy turns twelve next year. If I play my cards right, everything should work out."

"But you're anxious. Why?"

"Because I've never been particularly lucky with cards."

Cleo gave her hand a squeeze. "I don't see you doing anything that would jeopardize Leroy. So carry on until circumstances indicate otherwise."

"I'm glad to hear you say that. I don't had too many other friends to talk to about this. Who understands how much I love Goodtimes, and how much I love Leroy. I'm proud of what I've built and I don't want to gave it up."

"It shouldn't be a case of 'what do you love more?'. It will work out, ducks," Cleo said.

"My head says it will, but my heart thinks otherwise."

"You wouldn't consider giving it up for a bit?"

"I can't. Maybe because that's one of the things I love about business. As strange as it sounds, I thrive on the responsibility. Everything rides on my shoulders. The fate of the business is in my hands."

Cleo nodded. "I feel the same way. It's the control. Making my own decisions, calling the shots, being in charge of my own destiny."

Edith took a breath, the sigh coming from deep within her. "I knew you'd understand. Succeeding at business is my destiny."

"Destiny?"

"It's a big word, isn't it? For me it's not a matter of chance, it's a matter of choice; not a thing to be waited for but a thing to be achieved."

Cleo's eyes shone. "Exactly. The only person you are destined to become is the person you decide to be. A long time ago, I decided to rule the world. Or at least my little part of it."

"Ah, the person you decide to be. That's a tall order, isn't it? I thought I had it all figured out, and now with this threat to Leroy..." Edith paused, and then leaned forward, her eyes filling with tears. "I'm afraid to risk Leroy. I'll risk Goodtimes and myself, but I won't put that kid in harm's way."

Cleo grabbed Edith's hands and held them tight. "Listen, sweetheart. It will be okay. Sometimes when it feels like things are felling apart, they're actually falling into place. You'll know what to do. You always do."

Cleo's empathy and wisdom sealed the deal for Edith. "Before I leave Nassau, I want to say how happy you and Bill look together. He's a one-in-a-million catch, Cleo. I wish you both all the happiness."

Cleo leaned back in her chair, her head cocked to one side. She studied Edith. "Why ducks, thank you so much. I know Bill and I are an odd pair, but we're a pair that fits together. I used to worry about being alone as I got older, and then I met Bill. He's the perfect man for me. I get my independence and time to focus on my business and, when his ship's in port, I'm the luckiest girl in the world." By the time she finished speaking, Cleo was blushing and her eyes were shining.

"Maybe someday I'll have someone that fits me that well. But, until then, I'm going to put all that energy into keeping Leroy safe and growing my business."

"Those are no small tasks, either one of them," Cleo said with a chuckle.

Edith grinned. "Yes, I'm not sure which is going to cause me more sleepless nights. It'll be a race to see which makes me go gray first."

With hugs and promises to be at the dock to wave them off, Cleo went to work. Edith spent the rest of the day wandering Nassau, picking up souvenirs for Lucky, Leroy, and Darwin.

After a day under the sun wandering the shops, Edith grew thirsty and returned to the hotel. The garden was full of diners enjoying the cool shade of the sandbox tree. At the bar, a crowd of broad-shouldered, wide-lapelled guests gathered, suspicious bulges under their arms. Bill wandered in and joined her for a pre-dinner cocktail.

Watching the gangsters' shenanigans, Bill's lip curled in distaste. "I can't believe you were married to fellas like this. Gangsters. Forever scheming against each other, fighting for liquor, plotting for ships, tricking and battling. A bunch of murderers, thieves, hijackers, and thugs."

Edith just smiled. *I could never explain about Mickey. He was life itself. Until he wasn't.*

"It's amazing. I think the only person who has any control over these gangsters is Mother," Edith said.

253

Bill laughed. "Once I saw Big Harry and another rum runner, both drunk, collide, draw off reeling, and attempt to pump lead at each other. Each fired an entire clip but, thanks to the alcohol inside of them, neither was hurt. Later, I found them standing shoulder to shoulder in the bar here, buying each other drinks and the best pals in all the world."

As Bill was telling the story, Edith kept an eye on some shoving that was happening at the bar between a pair of gangsters arguing over stolen goods. It quickly grew heated. They were two stray street dogs, fighting over a bone.

As she watched, Mother calmly waded into the fray, beaming short-sightedly at the pair of them whose criminal records would have made a jail warden shudder. She gently chided the killers as if she was merely correcting the bad manners of two gentlemen—gentlemen no man would be mad enough to cross.

"Now, boys, is this how you were raised? If you aren't going to behave yourselves you'll have to get out of my barroom. Right away, understand?"

"Yes, Mother." "I didn't mean to, Mother." "I'm sorry, Mother."

Mother wandered over to Edith's table to see how her visit was going.

Edith regarded her hostess with new eyes. "I saw what happened at the bar. I run a blind-tiger in Florida and I don't think I would have the nerve to get between those two. They are armed, you know."

"It's sad to think, but most of them are. I never give it much thought. They're just a bit wild, but they're still good boys at heart."

Chapter 37

It was smooth sailing home, at least on the water. Those aboard the *Arethusa* trod lightly. The captain and his special guest kept their distance, which was tough to do even on a one hundred-thirty foot schooner. Edith would have preferred a blow up.

It was the way Mickey always handled things, but Bill just squares his shoulders and keeps that strong jaw of his clamped shut.

It's probably as good an indication as any that Bill and I are oil and water. I like a sudden storm that clears the air. This heavy silence is exhausting. It will be good to get home, where I can captain my own crew. I hope Leroy enjoyed his visit with Cassie—but not too much. And Darwin and Mae managed to keep Goodtimes humming—but not too well. And I've got to tell Lucky about the food—maybe he'll work up a few Bahamian recipes. I'm sure Cleo can help with that.

Edith returned to Goodtimes, full of stories of her adventures. She'd timed it perfectly to arrive on a Sunday so that she had the day to regroup.

That night, with a martini in her hand and a cold beer in his, she and Darwin headed down to the dock. "Anything interesting happen while I was gone?" she asked.

"Actually, there was. Your password saved us. I was standing on the veranda checking people when a couple of fellas I didn't recognize came up. I got a bad feeling about them. You know the way a couple of fellas walk into a new saloon? They shoulda been laughing or talking, getting ready for some action."

Edith nodded as Harley Andrews and Billy Shaw came to mind.

"Well, they just marched up. They wore their clothes like a uniform. I asked them for the password and they made out like they didn't hear me. Just tried to push past. I could see them trying to look into the windows. Harley came up right then and helped me strong-arm them up to the parking lot. I don't know whether they were the sheriff's people or from the Children's Home, but they sure were looking for more than a glass of whiskey."

"I was hoping they had backed off by now. Thank goodness Leroy was at Cassie's, although I was hoping he'd be here when I arrived. Any sense of how much longer he's staying?"

"I imagine he'll show up tomorrow or the next day. We weren't sure exactly when you were going to be back and didn't want to take the chance that he was here before you were. Just as well, as it turned out."

The silence between them hummed. Finally, Darwin broke the ice. "You're home earlier than I expected. Good trip?"

Edith squared her shoulders. "It was perfect. I picked up lots of tips and Cleo and I got the first Dixie order squared away. It was great to get away, and it is awfully good to be home."

Darwin took a long look at her, and then his gaze fixed on the ocean.

Another strong, silent type. I seem to be surrounded by them. Thank goodness for Leroy. At least I always know what he's thinking.

The news of the strangers trying to get into Goodtimes left Edith feeling unsettled; she got back into routine, but it was an uneasy one. Bill was tucked away into a secret part of her heart; it was the idea of Bill she missed more than the man himself.

Pinned to her wall was a map of the entire Dixie Highway spanning the northern border all down the length of Florida to the Keys. It came in handy when she sent a few coded wires to Cleo for liquor orders for Goodtimes and the Dixie run customers.

The map, an expanding business, and Leroy bursting back on the scene at Goodtimes, drove aside thoughts of Nassau and any twinges of regret. Leroy was as full of tales of his adventures in the 'glades as Edith was about her trip to the Bahamas. And the ritual of tucking him into bed at night was a salve that healed her wounds— her memories of Bill and Nassau taking on the rosy tinge of nostalgia.

It's curious. I cheated on my husband, but I wasn't prepared to cheat on Cleo. I couldn't betray her like that. She trusts me and I trust her. I'm not going to let her down. And that Bill—what a rat—the way he was prepared to sneak around on a great gal like Cleo. What did I ever see in him, anyway?

Edith stared at the ledger she'd been working on and realized that she had entered the same information three times. Exasperated, she ripped out the sheet of paper and crumpled it. She almost threw it in the trash, but reconsidered, smoothing it out again.

Trust is like a fresh piece of paper you crumple: you can smooth it out but it's never the same as it was before.

I won't hurt Cleo. There can never be anything between Bill and me. Right now, my first priority is Leroy, and then getting Goodtimes running at full capacity again.

She leaned back in the office chair, staring out the window, but was oblivious to the lush mangrove forest and the creek with the cranes feeding along its banks.

One day slowly folded into another. With the thought of lurking spies, Edith took to carrying her pistol in either her pocket or her handbag. She'd be ready for any attack or threat.

During the evening, her sentimental memories were forced aside as she scanned the faces of the customers, seeing a spy or saboteur in everyone. Folks pick upped on the suspicion and began to drift home earlier. The business got quieter. Folks found a friendlier place to drink.

Amidst all of this, when she was in town with Leroy, she watched over her shoulder and around corners for Mildred White. At Goodtimes, she kept watch from the veranda.

Since his return from Cassie's, Edith's noticed a cloud over Leroy's usually sunny face. Answers were shorter, he spent more time in his room alone, and while he didn't shirk his work at Goodtimes, the excited helpfulness was gone. Darwin was at a loss to explain it.

On a fishing trip together on the *Rex*, all that Leroy would say was that he was bored a lot at Cassie's.

A few days into it, and Edith decided to confront him head on. "Come on, Leroy. I've got to go into town and I need your help." As she drove, he stared mutely out the window of the truck.

"So, if you're going to be a bootlegger, there're certain things you have to know," she said, hands on the wheel and eyes on the road.

Out of the corner of her eye, she could see Leroy turn and look at her. After a few minutes, he asked, "Like what?"

"Never trust your business partners. Mickey taught me that. Everybody's in it for the money."

"But Jay's a good guy."

"I didn't say he wasn't. Just remember, information is power and dangerous if used against you. The only one you can trust is yourself. Know why you're in the game and how far you want to go."

"What's the next thing?"

"Always let the customer buy. Never sell."

"I don't get it."

"You're doing the customer a favor. He's not doing you one. You've got an illegal product that he wants. Make sure he owes you the favor for selling it to him."

"Is that related to the first thing? About trust?"

Edith grinned at him. "You catch on quick. Customers are gold but also your biggest weakness, because they know who you are and what you're doing. And that's the third thing."

Leroy nodded and gave her a small grin. The ghost of old Leroy flickered there, warming Edith's heart.

"Is there more?"

"A lifetime of things to learn. About the liquor. About the law. But partners and customers are good enough for today."

Leroy squirmed over closer to her on the bench seat of the truck. Edith kept her eyes forward. "I didn't have a good time at Cassie's."

"Oh?"

"There wasn't anything fun to do. I went out hunting a couple of times. And we went for a canoe ride through the 'glades, but I missed Goodtimes."

"I missed you."

Leroy leaned against her. "Sometimes it's hard trying to be in two places at once. Cassie wants me to be with her and you want me to be at Goodtimes. I don't want to make anyone sad."

"Cassie and I only want you to be happy, kiddo, whatever that means about where you live or what you do. And we want to keep you safe because there's some wicked people out there that want to do you, me, and Cassie harm."

"I know. Darwin said that 'a man must do', and right now I think that means being here with you at Goodtimes. But it hurts to see Cassie lonely, off by herself at the camp."

"She's always welcome here, Leroy. She knows that."

"Being around people is hard on her. And she worries about Brother Silas. If I were bigger, I could look after her better. And look after you, too, Miz Edith." The last part of the sentence came out shyly.

"You know, you'll always be my little Leroy and, even when you're taller than Darwin, I'll still be worried about you."

"What are we going to do when we get to town?"

"I think we need an ice cream float from Stella's Café. Then I want to buy you a Panama hat like Darwin's."

Leroy sat straight. "Wow. A hat. Like Darwin's?"

"Yup. A bootlegger has got to look the part. You're a good enough hunter to get your own hat band, but I want to be the one that puts the hat on your head."

"I love you, Miz Edith."

A lump formed in Edith's throat and she blinked back tears. "You're a great kid, Leroy, and I admit I'm mighty fond of you, too." She pulled the truck into a parking spot on the street in front of S&P Mercantile. She looked at him and gave his bare knee a squeeze. "Come on. Let's go see what the well-dressed bootlegger is wearing this year."

* * * *

Leroy, bounced back to his old self; the Panama hat helped. it was not many days before there was a snakeskin band to show off. Everyone at Goodtimes was relieved to be back to normal, except Edith. The strain of having the Children's Home situation unresolved was etched on her face. Sleepless nights had left their mark. A worry-frown on her brow had made a permanent home. She refused to change routine or admit that the risk was having an impact, but that didn't mean she was ignoring it.

The threats to the things that Edith held dear left her wary as she traveled the now familiar streets of Coconut Grove. In town to gather her post and run a few errands, she looked into every face, attempting to discern friend or foe. Her shoulders were rigid as she strode down the street, ready for attack. Edith's hands were fists gripping her handbag. *Damn it. I want an enemy I can fight.*

She yanked open the door of the post office. "Afternoon, Jasper. Do I have any mail?" Her words came out as a bark and she regreted it. Jasper was a good soul and one of her allies in town. *At least he always has a smile for me.*

"Afternoon, Miz Edith. You have some bills from Miami contractors. How's the new kitchen coming along?"

"Almost done. The cupboards are in and we've started hooking up the appliances. It'll have everything a professional chef would dream of."

"I'm sure it will be classy. Everything you've done out there has been. You still bringing in the bands from the city?"

"We're taking a break from the entertainment for a while. Goodtimes is open, but on the QT. We're pulling back on the special events and promotions."

"Oh, I heard about your troubles. It's a shame, a nice gal like you. Why, I was just saying to Mary Carmichael the other day when she was in that—"

"Oh, my goodness," Edith stared at the bulletin board to the side of the counter.

Someone had scrawled 'HUSSY' over the front of an old Miami Music events poster.

"Not again? Sorry about that, Miz Edith. It's out of date, anyway. Here, gave it to me and I'll throw it away with the others. When you start up again, give me the poster and I'll hang it behind the counter so foul folks can't get to it."

"I'll do that."

"There're some folks that don't do Coconut Grove proud, picking on a gal like you and a little boy. I don't think it's right. Keep your chin up, Miz Edith, I'm sure it will all work out."

Edith tucked her mail into her handbag and returned to the truck. *I've got to go to Miami to pay these and pick up what I need for the kitchen. I'm not going to gave that fool at the hardware store here in town the benefit of my business.*

Tucked under her wiper blade was a crudely lettered note, "Whore of Babylon." She ripped it off and crumpled it up. Glaring, she looked around, expecting to see a mob of sniggering townsfolk.

This is Brother Silas's handiwork. I bet he's been preaching about me again. If Leroy weren't involved, this would be so much easier. I owe it to him to try to get Brother Silas to see reason.

With the crumpled note still clutched in her hand, Edith marched down the street. Her anger built the closer she got to the church. All the slights and slurs from the past six months, the resentment, the cold shoulders, the snubs and insults, the worry about Leroy—they piled up, one slight atop another, until she was in a smoldering rage. She was beside herself as she went up the steps and tried the front door. She gave it a mighty yank, but it was locked.

That's the last straw. "Brother Silas. Open this door right now." She didn't care if she was yelling. Let people talk.

She pounded her fist on it. She yelled louder. She kicked it. No one came to answer.

Edith remembered the door behind the altar which meant there might be a back door to the church. She walked around toward the back and saw the preacher's car parked near a barn, along with several other cars and trucks.

Without breaking stride, she changed direction and walked over to the old, gray weathered barn, long grass growing up around it.

Something about the look of it made Edith hesitate. The hair on her arms and the back of her neck stood up, and she shivered.

I should turn around.

She approached with caution. As she got close to the open door, Edith could hear the murmur of men's voices. There was a coarse jocularity she recognized from Mickey's world and the bar in the hotel in Nassau. That checked her stepped even further until she was standing just behind the door.

She caught the name 'Goodtimes'. The surrounding laughter was ugly, but pulled her closer. She listens intently, trying to figure out what was happening in the barn. The sun went behind the cloud and she shivered, her breath coming in small gulps. Inside, they said a few coarse things about Mildred White, and Roy Purvis's name came up. She picked up that 'they' hadn't been able to get the goods on Goodtimes for the Boss. More oily snickers made her skin crawl.

Another man spoke. *Wait.* She recognized his voice. it was...

Brother Silas. Why would he be here with these men?

She dare not go past the open door, but went around to the side, looking for a window to see inside. The long grass caught at her legs. She crept quietly and carefully so as not to trip on abandoned farm tools and wooden boards.

Someone talked of hassles with the Coast Guard, bragging they gave as good as they got. More laughter as they talked about Harley Andrews limping back to port.

Edith carefully stepped around a stack of loose boards to reach a broken window. She looked but didn't touch the frame out of fear of being cut. She stretched to look inside.

Brother Silas was sitting in a room full of men. *Those are the men that came to 'Gator Joe's the night of the fire.*

Edith ducked down out of sight. She's trembling, remembering the smoke, the heat, the destruction. Her breath came in rapid gasps.

Why is Brother Silas talking about this? Someone said boss. *Boss?* She heard Brother Silas give orders about an expected shipment of immigrants. *Human smugglers?*

Sitting on her heels with her back resting against the barn wall, the pieces fall into place. *These are Wharf Rats and Brother Silas is the Boss!*

Fear and rage. Fight or flight?

She carefully crouched below the window, desperate to see inside and learn more. As she took a small step, she knocked against a pile of boards. They clattered against the side of the barn. Edith held her breath.

"Who's that? Check it out, Whitey."

Panicked, Edith made a beeline toward the trees. Her racing heart stopped when she heard the screech of the barn door's rusty hinges. She ducked deeper behind some bushes. Peeking through the branches, her face scratched, she watched a man with a shock of white hair walk around the barn.

I've seen him before: down at the pier when we put all the smuggled liquor on board the Wharf Rats boats. And he was there the night 'Gator's burned down, and the night they hit Leroy. Shivering, Edith forced herself to be still lest her trembling gave her away.

Whitey stopped at the spot where Edith had watched. He looked around and yelled into the window. "Nothing here anymore, Boss."

Edith's legs barely carried her back to the truck. She climbed in and locked the door.

CHAPTER 38

Safely back in Goodtimes' car park, Edith sat and stared blankly. She didn't remember driving home.

This explains so much. Hiding in plain sight. This changes how I deal with this Leroy situation. The old biddies may give up, but not Brother Silas and the Wharf Rats.

Edith walked down the path and past the veranda, feeling the need to have the ocean around her. She stood on the deck, looking at the vast expanse, the endless horizon. *This is too much. How can I possibly cope with this? Brother Silas and the Wharf Rats?*

Leroy ran out onto the dock, his bare feet pounding along the wood boards. "Miz Edith. Miz Edith. I got an opossum today for Lucky. He's going to make gumbo with it. And Darwin and me are going fishing tomorrow. Maybe I'll catch a whopper. Did you bring me back a comicbook? Is it Orphan Annie or Buck Rogers?" Leroy stoops, shooting his pretend ray gun. "Zap. Zap."

"What? No, sorry kiddo. No comicbook today. Can you gave me a minute or two? Then I'll come and we can...." Edith words drifted off as she looked back out over the water.

"Can what, Miz Edith?" Leroy waited for her to answer. "Miz Edith. Are you okay?" He took a step toward her, his smile dying as his brow furrowed.

"What? Sorry, Leroy, I've got a lot on my mind. You scoot. I'm thinking."

"Okay, then. I just wanted to tell you what happened to me today." Leroy, head hung low, dragged his feet off the dock and back up the path.

Darn, now I've hurt his feelings again. I'll make it up to him later.

Edith faced the ocean while the wind played with her hair. The rhythmic sound of the waves lulled the confusion and panic she was feeling. *Maybe I should call Mae. She might have some ideas. A mobster approach. Or should I call Henry in Philly? He's a long way away to be much good here. If I tell Darwin, will he just go off half-cocked? That's all I'd need right now. Cleo's dealt with this sort before. Some of her stories...* The waves roll onto the shore, ceaseless, inevitable.

Brother Silas has got the law in his pocket. Whatever I do will have to be outside of that.

Edith's hands were fists. *And in cahoots with Mildred White and the Children's Home, too. How am I going to protect Leroy from the Wharf Rats?*

She shivered, remembering the night of the fire and being tied to the tree. *It was only luck that Leroy was smart enough to hide and wait to rescue me until they were gone. Would he know enough to hide again?*

Information is power they say. Brother Silas doesn't know I know. Is everyone in town in on it? If Darwin knew, surely he would have said something.

The knot between her shoulder blades was like a knife, twisting. *I need a plan. Leroy's not safe. We were lucky with the fire, but I don't want to take that chance and go through something like that again.*

Edith's jaw clenched and her hands were still fists at her side.

Okay, Silas, I'll gave you this round. You want Goodtimes closed? Fine, I'll do it. Whatever it takes to get you to back off for a while until I can pull a plan together. Even when that means putting the dreams on hold. I've got to keep Leroy safe. You've got him like a knife at my throat.

Edith turned and walked up the path to the veranda. Darwin was waiting for her, his face a frown of concern.

"What's up?" Darwin asked.

266

"When you talked to the Wharf Rats, did you talk to the top guy?"

"I talked to Buford. He's in charge as far as I know."

"Does he seem smart enough to be pulling all this stuff off?"

Darwin shrugged. "What do you mean?"

Edith turned and stared out at the ocean again. "I think I'm going to have a bath. A bubble bath."

Darwin looked confused. "A bath? Right now?"

"I need some thinking time and, if I'm down here, there would be constant interruptions."

"Okay. Anything I can help with?"

"Everything okay around here?"

"Sure. Why wouldn't it be? Say, what's wrong?"

"We'll talk as soon as I'm out of the tub. Has Lucky turned on the flat-top you fellas just put in?"

"Grilled cheese sandwiches for lunch, if you're hungry."

"Gave me an hour of soaking and thinking, then I'll be good to go."

Darwin checked his watch. "A late lunch then. I'll let Lucky know."

"And give something to Leroy to snack on to tide him over. See you in an hour." Edith waves and headed upstairs.

She opened the French doors that connected her bedroom to the balcony outside. This room was her private indulgence. The sunny yellow quilt that had delighted her so much at 'Gator Joe's was lost in the fire, as was the blue bed. She replaced it with a big four-poster. A chenille bedspread in shades of blue and green was as close to sleeping underwater as she could get. In the corner, next to the French doors, was a chaise lounge with a throw in the same colors as the bedspread draped across the foot. She could lie there and watch the sun rise or set and feel all was well with her world. Those days were gone.

Turning on the taps, hot steaming water filling the tub. She added a generous helping of the bath bubbles Mae had given her. The steamy air was filled with the scent of jasmine. She slipped beneath the bubbles and sighed as the knots between her shoulders eased.

A bath at mid-day. How indulgent. Like the old days. Edith smiled. *I know how Mickey would play this. The only choice would be whether to do it quick on a drive-by or up close and personal with a double-tap to the head.* Edith slipped lower into the bubbles, savoring the idea of both.

The scent, the steam, and the warm water, calm her thoughts. *What to do. Talk to Mae? Talk to Meyer Lansky up in New York for some muscle? Talk to Cleo? Do I want a confrontation? One way or another, he has the whole town in his pocket. Folks like Mavis follow the preacher, others follow the Boss. Maybe a bit of cooperation and try to cut a deal? Something along the lines of a Nucky Thompson-Atlantic City approach. It brought peace for the East Coast mobsters.*

Edith frowned. *Could I make a deal with someone like Brother Silas? Would I even want to? You can't make a deal with someone you don't trust.*

Edith piled little mountains of bubbles. *Whatever his problem is, it's personal. Otherwise, he'd have had his boys shake us down for protection money, like the other blind-tigers.*

What would you sacrifice to save what you love? 'Gator Joe's and now Goodtimes has been a sacrifice of time and money because I had a dream I loved. But could I sacrifice that dream to protect Leroy? And Darwin? Brother Silas and the Wharf Rats won't care who they hurt as long as I'm caught in the crossfire.

Closing her eyes, she slid under the water. *He torched 'Gator's. He's behind this Leroy thing. That makes it personal for me, too. I may not know how to handle a preacher, but I sure know how to deal with a mob boss. I've killed before. Can I kill again?*

CHAPTER 39

Skin smelling of jasmine, hair damp from the bath, Edith strode down the stairs and into the barroom She knew what she had to do.

She paused at the doorway. *The Boss—Brother Silas—won't be happy until he takes away something I love. I either sacrifice Goodtimes, or Leroy. Everything that's happened shows me that. It's not even a choice.*

Darwin and Leroy were already at the table and Lucky was coming down the hall behind her with a mountain of grilled cheese sandwiches.

"Flat top works great, Miz Edith. Nice and crispy. No mess. Will be fast for dinner orders," Lucky said.

Lucky put the plate in the middle of table. Darwin and Leroy, in their matching Panama hats, reached in and both grabbed a sandwich at the same time.

"Like a pack of hungry wolves," Edith said with a chuckle. "Sorry about delaying lunch, but I have news."

Everyone stopped eating.

"We're going to close Goodtimes—"

"What?" "How come?" "What's happened?"

Edith held up her hand for quiet. "We're going to close Goodtimes for a couple of weeks. Nothing drastic. There're some folks in town that are upset about Goodtimes and they're causing some of the trouble with this tug of war with Leroy."

"Is this my fault? I didn't do anything wrong, did I? Am I in trouble?"

Edith reached over and covered Leroy's hand with hers. "No, you didn't do anything wrong, kiddo. There're just some people who are grumpy with me, not you. Nothing we can't handle. I just need to buy us some time."

Her eyes met Darwin's over Leroy's head.

"Do I need to go back to Cassie's?" Leroy asked in a small voice.

"No. I don't think so. I think if we close Goodtimes, for real—no pretending this time—folks will back off. We have the note from Aunt Cassie to say you can stay here. It will be okay." Edith gave his hand a squeeze.

"Money will be tight. We'll have to live off the South Dixie earnings." She looked to Lucky. "And we'll finish the kitchen. It's almost ready and you've been in that tent long enough, Lucky."

"I make do, Miz Edith. You no need to finish kitchen right now."

"Thanks, Lucky, but there are no more big expenses in there. Just some elbow grease. And Leroy will be able to help with that. Right, kiddo?"

"You bet." He flexed his skinny arms like a muscleman. The laughter broke the tension.

"We'll put up posters. I want everyone in town to know that the café is closed until further notice."

"No lunches or suppers?" Lucky asked, turning to look back at the hallway to the kitchen.

"Just for now. Goodtimes is going dark. We will reopen. I promise. I just don't know when."

Lucky and Leroy gathered up the plates and glasses from lunch and headed back to the kitchen tent. "We get the sink hooked up in next couple of days and no more washtub. That good, eh Leroy?"

Edith can't hear Leroy's answer but makes a mental note to call the plumber right away. *That will keep Leroy distracted, and it's a problem I can actually fix.*

"Okay, so what's going on? What happened in town?" Darwin asked.

"Brother Silas is the head of the Wharf Rats." She let the information lie in the middle of the table. Darwin sat back, a look of surprise on his face.

"You're kidding me. The preacher? Running a gang of smugglers and pirates?"

Edith nodded. "And he's the big push behind this thing with Leroy. Preaching about sin from the pulpit, getting Mavis and the Guild ladies all riled up. It all comes back to him."

"But why? What's he got against you?"

"I don't know. I wish I did. This would make figuring things out easier. It might be greed. And the first day I met him I injured his pride a tad when I knocked him on his keister. Who could have imagined it would come to this."

Darwin was still shaking his head, trying to come to gripped with the revelation. "You think he might try and hurt Leroy?"

"If he thinks that would hurt me. And don't forget, he's a pillar of respect because of his preacher's collar; he's been working with the Homemakers' Guild, and Mildred White from the Children's Home. This situation with Leroy is a lot more dangerous than we thought."

"Should we send Leroy to Cassie? He'd be safe there."

"I'm giving up a lot to keep that boy, Darwin. I can keep him safe. We can keep him safe. We've got to let Brother Silas and all the other plotters involved in this scheme believe they've won. That will buy us time."

"Okay. That's the plan for the short term. What's the long-term plan? You can't be thinking of shutting Goodtimes forever."

"I need time. I need to make a decision or two, none of them good. And I'm not prepared to do it right now. I don't think it's just Leroy he'd hurt. You be careful out there, too."

"I don't go looking for trouble, Edith, but I don't run from it either. If they try and come at you through me, they'll be inviting a whole world of trouble. More than they expect."

"I know, Darwin. Just be careful."

"And what about the Dixie runs? Won't he want us to shut that down, too?"

Edith's hands that had been resting on the table, clench. "How much will it take? He can't have everything."

"None of the customers except Tucker Carlson are anywhere near Coconut Grove. I can't imagine his territory extends to far outside of town."

"Then we'll have to talk to Tucker and tell him that he'll have to make alternate arrangements. I don't want any threat to Silas. No competition. If we cut out Tucker, do you think it will be alright if we keep going?" Edith asked.

Darwin shrugged. "We'll know soon enough. Nothing about this has been rational, so who knows."

"It won't come as any surprise that cash is going to be real tight."

"I figured as much. Maybe this is the time we look at expanding the route? Bring in more smuggling money to make up for the shortfall from Goodtimes?"

Edith looked at him, her eyes overflowing. She knew what it cost him to suggest expanding.

"Edith, honey. It will be okay."

273

She wiped the tears away. "I know. I don't know why I'm crying like this. I wanted to have somebody to fight and now I do."

He gathered her up in his arms and for a brief instant she thought of Bill and then put the idea aside. "Thanks Darwin. It feels good knowing I can always trust you."

"I'll always had your back. You know that. Whatever it takes, Edith. We're in this together."

CHAPTER 40

On Sunday, Brother Silas approached the pulpit. Given their recent conversations together, Mavis Saunders was eager to hear what he'll say.

"Today, my brothers and sisters, I wish to share with you the wisdom of Revelations 17:1-18: 'Then one of the seven angels who had the seven bowls came and said to me: Come, I would show you the judgment of the great prostitute who was seated on many waters, with whom the kings of the earth had committed sexual immorality, and with the wine of whose sexual immorality the dwellers on earth have become drunk. And he carried me away in the Spirit into a wilderness, and I saw a woman sitting on a scarlet beast that was full of blasphemous names, and it had seven heads and ten horns. The woman was arrayed in purple and scarlet, and adorned with gold and jewels and pearls, holding in her hand a golden cup full of abominations and the impurities of her sexual immorality. And on her forehead was written a name of mystery: Babylon the great, mother of prostitutes and of earth's abominations.'"

Several members of the congregation squirmed. One young family at the back of the church used a squealing baby as an excuse to leave.

Mavis, rapt in his words, nodded and whispers, 'Whore of Babylon'.

Her husband, John, looked askance. "Mavis. Your language."

Harley Andrews was in the pew behind her. He'd been bored, but now was sitting up paying attention to the sermon. He leaned over to Nancy and whispered. "Is he talking about Miz Edith down at Goodtimes?" Nancy slapped his leg, glancing at her parents frowning with disapproval. "Hush. And yes."

"Well, that's just wrong. We've been there and she isn't like that."

Mavis Saunders turned around and glared at Harley before turning to face the pulpit again.

Nancy jabbed his ribs. "Shush, you. People are looking."

After the service, Harley and Nancy said their goodbyes to her parents and headed toward Harley's truck. They've planned a picnic in the park.

"I don't care what people say, I like Miz Edith. And I like Goodtimes. Even if it is closed right now," Harley said.

"Closed?"

"There are posters all over town. You liked going there, didn't you?" Harley asked Nancy.

"Of course I did. It's just you can't go rubbing people's noses in it."

"In what?" Harley looked at her, puzzled.

"You know. A woman running a saloon. Especially an attractive one. Makes folks get ideas in their head."

"I don't think Miz Edith's as pretty as you. And you definitely put ideas in my head."

"Harley Andrews," Nancy said, playfully slapping his arm. "You behave yourself. My parents can still see us."

Harley turned around. Sure enough, they were looking. He waved and pulled Nancy closer.

"And what about that preacher? He seems to really have an ax to grind about Miz Edith. All that talk about prostitutes and whores—"

"Harley!"

"Well, it's kinda creepy. He's a man of the cloth after all. Shouldn't he be more understanding and forgiving?"

"Creepy is right. There was some strangeness between him and his housekeeper about ten years ago according to gossip. Not that I listen or take much stock in it. But they say she got pregnant."

"The minister's housekeeper? And he said stuff like that about Miz Edith?"

Nancy shrugged. "Different rules for men than women, I guess. Even if you are a preacher."

As they passed a knot of women standing around Brother Silas, Harley and Nacy nodded politely.

"Why didn't they get married?" Harlen asked in a low voice once they were out of ear shot.

"I think she died. I'll have to ask Dorothy and see if she knows. Dot's mother is one of the biggest gossips in town—she's that woman who's standing next to Brother Silas."

"Not Mrs. Saunders? That's Dorothy's mother?"

"No, the other one, silly. Mrs. Matheson. She knows everything going on in town. Did you bring a blanket for the picnic?"

* * * *

Mavis watched the Andrew's boy and his girlfriend walk past. She turned back to catch something that Agnes Matheson was saying to Brother Silas about choir practice.

"Excuse me for interrupting, Agnes, but Brother Silas will be interested that Lt. Commander Saunders got another letter from his brother and I saved the envelope," she said, handing it to him.

Out in the bright sunshine, Brother Silas blinked rapidly, his eyes watering. "Where is the commander's good brother these days?" Brother Silas said, licking his lips and reaching for the envelope.

277

She looked over at her husband who was chatting with one of the other men on the front lawn of the church. *I'm going to need to head home and get that chicken in the oven for John's supper.* "That's a question that Commander Saunders is better equipped to answer. I'm not sure where Indochina is, except that it's a beautiful stamp."

Brother Silas beamed at the envelope. "French Indochina. Excellent. I don't have this one and I've been trying to complete all the French colonies and protectorates. I've got stamps from Togoland, Cameroon, and Inini. You don't suppose he'll be going anywhere close to Madagascar?"

"We never know where he'll be. I'll let him know what you're looking for. Excellent sermon by the way, Brother Silas. I'm glad to see someone is concerned about what's happening down there at that horrible blind-tiger."

"We do what we can, Sister Mavis. We are merely vessels of God's Will."

Mavis nodded, a look of sympathetic concern on her face as she took in his red, watering eyes. "I have some lovely local honey that I've always found very effective for hay fever, Brother Silas," Mavis said. "I mix it with a bit of ginger and take it several times a day." The ladies in the circle coo concern for his health, offering their own 'special' recipes with garlic and apple cider vinegar.

Brother Silas nodded, and dabbed at his eyes with a handkerchief pulled from his pocket. "Thank you, good Sisters. I shall try them all."

A screech from one of the children playing on the lawn outside the church drew their attention. Mavis frowned and looked for Mildred White. "Can't she keep them in order? What they need is a firm hand."

"Sister Mildred is doing the best she can. The Bible would approve. 'She got up while it was still night, she provided food for her family, and portions for her female servants. She set about her work vigorously. Her arms were strong for her tasks.' You must have more tolerance, Sister Mavis."

Mavis swallowed a retort. "You know we at the Guild have been quite concerned about the boy that lives out at Goodtimes."

"Even with it closed, a leopard can't change its spots. She's a woman of loose morals and evil ways. Always has and always will be," Agnes said.

Brother Silas nodded encouragement. "Amen, Sister Agnes."

"Were you aware of the good work that Mildred White is trying to do to rescue the poor lamb?" Agnes asked.

"Yes, Sister Mildred made me aware of the situation. She, too, is a helpful servant of the Lord. I know she has deep concerns about a young child like that being exposed to vice and depravity. She has mentioned that the boy has a note from a guardian giving him permission to work at Goodtimes when it was a café. It's unfortunate that the café is now closed." Brother Silas put on his most authentic act of concern for all.

"Why? I would had thought you'd be pleased that it's no longer operating," Mavis said.

"Ah, Sister Mavis. In the end, regardless of why the café is not operating, the Lord finds ways to have transgressors punished," Brother Silas said with a gentle smile. "Otherwise, how would those that are tempted learn any lessons?"

"Now that it's closed permanently, will the Homemakers' Guild be moving on to other projects? Perhaps that fundraising drive for the migrant workers?" Agnes asked Mavis.

"Don't be hasty. If that den of iniquity is closed, then the reason for the boy being there is gone, isn't it?" Brother Silas appeared to stand taller. "I presume he's not being employed, which means he won't be sending money back to his guardian, which is the purpose of the arrangement."

"You must excuse me, Brother Silas, Agnes. I've got to get home and get a chicken in the oven to roast for John's dinner," Mavis said, looking at her husband who was tapping his foot impatiently.

"Of course, dear. You run along. Mustn't keep the commander waiting. Although, we should investigate this matter further. For the good of the boy. I'm going to make sure Miss White is aware of the new circumstances," Agnes said, her eyes gleaming. "Imagine the trauma the poor boy had to deal with."

* * * *

Leroy's supposed traumatic life is nowhere to be found at Goodtimes, where Edith is reclining on a chaise lounge on the veranda. A novel lies open on her lap, a glass of sweet tea beside her.

I love the tranquility of Sundays.

Instead of reading, she's watching Lucky, Darwin, and Leroy down at the dock. Lucky had his hat over his face and was snoozing on the *Rex*. Darwin was bent over Leroy, explaining the finer points of some fly they've attached to Leroy's rod. Optimistically, there was a pail ready should they catch anything.

Edith chuckled. *It looks like the fish are safe today. Maybe I should put a chicken in the oven for supper.*

CHAPTER 41

Living near and working on the ocean necessitates awareness of currents. Those tidal forces swirl unseen and could easily pull the strongest vessel off course—much like life itself. Across town, a conversation in a churchyard can create eddies that might swell into something strong enough to rock a steady, little boat—a small event can form a breeze that filled your sails.

Mavis Saunders hung clothes on the line in her backyard, a basket of damp sheets at her feet. She pinned them quickly and went inside for another load. She was surprised to find her husband, John, standing in the middle of the kitchen, surrounded by laundry in various stages of completion.

"John, I didn't realize you'd be home for lunch. Here, let me put these aside and I'll make you a sandwich." Mavis reorganized the piles, clearing a chair next to the table.

"I have Coast Guard business in Coconut Grove and thought I'd come by. I guess itis an inconvenient time. Don't you do laundry on Monday, Mavis?"

"It was storming that day, remember?"

"Ah yes, so it was. The Florida weather always seems to knock aside routine. Say, a young fellow approached me on the street the other day looking to earn some pocket money. Do we have any odd jobs that need tending?"

With the late morning sun streaming into the kitchen window, Mavis Saunders began to pull out the bread and meat. "Odd jobs? I don't think so. Do we know the boy?"

"A friend of one of the Carmichael brothers."

"Oh, I suppose that's all right, then. There are so many strangers passing through town these days. It seems everyone is looking for work." She put the sandwich down in front of him. "This should hold you until supper."

"Thank you my dear and, again, my apologies for interrupting you."

Mavis sat across from her husband. "Nonsense, I'm delighted you're here. Gives me a chance to chat. You know, Agnes and I went to Miami for a day of shopping the other day. We both want new hats for church. You wouldn't believe the number of people rubbernecking. There are more tourists coming all the time. The restaurants and hotels must be happy to have paying customers and the big conventions, and not just the tin-can families in those horrible tents who bring their own food."

"It's a mixed blessing. Tourism revenue is one of the reasons the authorities are not anxious to interfere with the flow of liquor. Which makes our job in the Coast Guard harder."

"The crosses you have to bear, John."

"Those scofflaws are getting brazen, Mavis. The mayor of Hollywood and the President of the Shriners approached the Ft. Lauderdale Coast Guard—"

"Fort Liquor-dale? They have a terrible reputation for wickedness and corruption at that base. I've heard the most outrageous stories about them."

"And they're probably all true. As I was saying, the Shriners are going to be having a big national convention, bringing in Shriners and their families from all over the country. The mayor personally went to the base commander to see that they would be properly supplied with the necessary amount of liquor to handle their needs."

"You mean they are asking the Coast Guard to bootleg the liquor?"

"Essentially. I guess they figured, with all the seizures, we'd have product to move. While he said no to that, at the end of the day he agreed not to interfere. Looking the other way while people break the law is just as bad as supplying, as far as I'm concerned."

"*Tsk-tsk.* We're a long way from when you first joined up. Speaking of recruits, I forgot to ask you about the recruitment parade you had. How did it go?"

"You'd be hard pressed to find a guardsman in the bunch. With Prohibition, the new job we're being asked to do is attracting a new kind of recruit, one more interested in what they can get out of it rather than serving with any sense of duty."

"Brother Silas would say that neither thieves nor the greedy nor drunkards nor slanderers nor swindlers will inherit the kingdom of God."

* * * *

Under a full moon, a picket crewed by new recruits, and a few seasoned guardsmen, were on patrol. While they'd seized the cargo of a contact boat, they've let the boat and the smugglers off with a warning.

"Okay you boots, listen up. That search and seizure went well."

One of the new boots raised his hand. "But skipper, we only got a dozen hams, and we let the smugglers off. Why are we concerned with the small fry?"

"Paperwork, son. The bigger the seizure, the more paperwork to do. And the more the smugglers squawk. A dozen hams are the perfect haul for us." As he's speaking, the skipper was tying a glass jug to a line. He then attached each ham to the line. He shoved a rock and a shining flashlight into the jug and sealed it. "Toss 'em overboard."

The recruits gave each other a puzzled look. "Aye, skipper." They started throwing the line of hams overboard. "I don't get it, skipper. What's with the flashlight?"

"I'll come back at the end of shift and haul 'em out. Makes it easier to find in the dark," the skipper said with a wink.

"And what's our take, skipper?"

"The usual cut and all the training I'm giving you."

"What about old man Saunders?"

"Forget about him. Remember how little you're getting paid by the government. Picking off a few hams now and then is just a work bonus to supplement the peanuts they're giving us."

CHAPTER 42

Brother Silas pulled the car into the dark parking area above Goodtimes. His hands were clenched on the wheel. He could smell the sweat on Deputy Purvis sitting next to him, and grimaced.

"Are you ready, Sister Mildred? You understand the new situation?"

Mildred White leaned forward from the back seat. "Yes, Brother Silas. With Goodtimes closed, there's no reason for the boy to be there. The letter from his aunt doesn't apply. I'll make sure we take him to a safe place away from her evil influences."

"And deputy, I presume there won't be any trouble."

"No, sir."

Mildred and Roy got out of the car and walked toward Goodtimes. Brother Silas watched them in the cone of light from the headlights. There was a determined step in Mildred White that he respected. Deputy Roy, on the other hand, was a weak link. *Greed is such an interesting motivator. Unlike true missionary zeal, it was so easily corrupted.*

* * * *

Darwin and Edith had a map of south Florida spread out on the table in the empty barroom. Edith ran her finger down the South Dixie Highway as they discussed potential customers. If the Dixie runs were now their sole source of revenue, they were going to have to make sure they had enough business.

They turned as they heard a car on the gravel of the car park. The glare from the headlights hid whoever was getting out of the vehicle.

"Customers?"

Darwin shrugged. "A few came by earlier and I told them we were closed until further notice."

A car door slammed. And then another. Footsteps sounded on gravel.

Darwin and Edith peered out the window, squinting against the bright light as two figures made their way down the path.

"It's the deputy, again. And Mildred White. They must be here for another surprise inspection," Darwin said.

Edith's laugh was bitter. "I seem to be the most popular gal in town these days. Well, they won't find anything. Except an empty barroom." She patted her pocket, taking comfort in the weight of the gun hidden there.

Edith answered the knock at the front screen door. "Deputy Purvis, Miss White. What a pleasant surprise. Please come in." Edith took a deep breath, her fury hidden behind a smile as she held the door open wide. "Darwin, can you go ask Lucky to put the kettle on?"

Darwin was already moving toward the back door and the kitchen tent where Lucky and Leroy were.

"That won't be necessary, Miz Edith. Thank you, though. We just thought we'd come by for a visit to check out the place," Deputy Roy said, hitching his belt around so it sat more comfortably around his ample waist.

"So what seems to be the problem that brings the two of you around this time of night," Edith said.

"I've seen the posters that claim Goodtimes was closed. Let's just say we want to confirm that for ourselves," Mildred White said.

"I have nothing to hide. Come see for yourselves," Edith said. She led them on a tour of Goodtimes. The liquor shelves were empty.

"As you could see, we aren't even open as a café at the moment." They moved into the kitchen. The construction was almost done.

"This is a very large kitchen not to be used," Mildred said, glancing at the commercial stove and flat top, the large commercial refrigerator, the stainless-steel counters.

"An idea ahead of its time. We had plans to expand the lunchtime and supper menu when we were operating as a café, but we've put those aside. Now, all I have is a large kitchen and an excellent cook—for personal use."

"The closure of this establishment is the reason we were here, Mrs. Duffy. With Goodtimes closed, you won't have a need to employ Leroy any longer," Mildred said.

Edith took stock of Mildred's expression: raised chin and narrowed eyes. There was a glint in those eyes that made her uneasy. "I'm not sure what you mean, Miss White."

"The letter of permission you have from his guardian is for him to live here while he's working. And now he's not working, he needs to go back to his guardian. Except we don't believe living in the Everglades in a camp is a suitable environment for a boy, do we Deputy Purvis?" Mildred had her shoulders thrown back and was ready for battle.

Edith, looking out the screen door, could see the silhouettes of Darwin, Lucky and Leroy in the kitchen tent.

"Perhaps we should finish this discussion in the other room?" Edith said, leaving the kitchen.

Deputy Roy, Mildred, and Edith sat around the table in the barroom.

"You were correct in the details of Cassie's permission letter. However, Leroy is still in my employ."

"Doing what? You're closed," Mildred was almost screeching in frustration. Edith smiled seeing her flushed cheeks.

"Yes. Now that we were essentially a private residence, I want to work on some of the exterior landscaping: enlarge the path to the dock; put in a cabana on the beach."

"You see, Miss White, the boy still works here for Miz Edith. It's all in order." He stood. "We should be on our way."

Mildred remained seated. She glared at Edith. "I don't believe you are a fit woman to be raising this boy."

Edith gripped the edge of the table. "I beg your pardon?"

Mildred leaned forward. "You heard me. Brother Silas had told me what went on out here. You are a pathetic excuse as a substitute mother for the boy."

Edith's eyes flashed. She stood, leaning over the table, both of her hands planted in front of Mildred. "You are a dried-up old spinster who acts as a parasite, sucking the joy and innocence out of other people's children. If there is any judgement here on the suitability of who should be caring for Leroy, it would be you, you old witch, who would be lacking. Now. Get. Out." Edith spat out her final words.

Deputy Roy tugged at Mildred's chair. "Let's go, Miss White. I can see we had come at a bad time."

Mildred stayed planted, glaring at Edith. "At least I'm not a criminal. At least I have the respect of the good people of Coconut Grove. What have you got, Mrs. Duffy?"

At that, Roy yanked the chair away from the table and pulled Mildred up. "We're going now, Mrs. Duffy. Sorry to intrude."

Edith stalked around the table, her eyes never leaving Mildred's face. She barely noticed Roy's pale panicked face. Only Mildred's hatred. Coming within an inch of Mildred's face, she sneered. "I have the genuine love of a little boy. My good looks. And the respect of my bankers, Miss White."

Mildred tried to lunge at Edith, but Roy held her back, spinning her toward the door.

Edith stood triumphant in the middle of the barroom. "Regardless of your opinion, I have authority to employ him and I am. Your judgement on my moral character is irrelevant." She looked at Roy. "Isn't that so, Deputy Purvis?"

"Please, Miz Edith. We're on our way out."

"Which was why I want a clear understanding on the matter. I won't tolerate any further misunderstandings on Miss White's part."

Roy, caught in Edith's glare, nodded. "I don't see any evidence of impropriety that would indicate you should take the boy, Miss White."

Edith flashed Mildred a triumphant grin. "And now I'll ask you to leave. Good night, Miss White, deputy."

Deputy Roy pulled Mildred by the arm. "Everything looks fine, Miz Edith. We'll be on our way now. Come on, Miz White. Let's let Miz Edith be."

As Roy reached for the door, Edith heard Leroy barreling down the hallway. "Lucky said tea would be ready in two minutes, Miz Edith." He skidded to a stop when he saw the Deputy Sheriff and the woman from the Children's Home.

Mildred gave Edith a smirk of her own and pulled her arm away from the deputy. "Leroy, how nice to see you. We hadn't met yet. My name is Miss White and I work at a wonderful place full of happy children. I hear you've been to visit your aunt?"

Leroy came and stood close to Edith. She wrapped her arm around his shoulders. He nodded.

"These people are just leaving, Leroy. Say goodbye."

Mildred walked over to a table and pulled out a chair. "Why don't you come sit for a minute? Your employer, Mrs. Duffy, has said such nice things about you. Deputy Purvis, I think we should take this opportunity to get to know Leroy better. Heaven forbid I have to submit a report that says Mrs. Duffy refused to let me interview the boy. That would make it difficult to close the case. And isn't that what we all want, Mrs. Duffy?"

"It is."

"But, what about..." Deputy Roy looked from Mildred to the window where the car park can be seen.

"Our driver will wait." She looked at Edith with a challenge in her eyes.

Leroy looked up at Edith and then, when she nodded, he went over and sat down.

"Do you enjoy living here, Leroy?"

"Yes, ma'am," he said in a quiet voice.

"And do you get enough to eat?"

"Miz Edith says I'm a bottomless pit. That she can't fill me up," he laughed and then stopped. His glance darted between Edith and Mildred. He looked down at his feet.

"I think that's enough, Miss White. It's late and getting past Leroy's bedtime," Edith said, standing behind Leroy's chair. She glared at Roy.

Now that Goodtimes is closed, am I going to have to pay him protection money to keep Leroy safe?

"Oh, I won't be but a few more minutes. Please, Mrs. Duffy? I want to submit a complete report to the authorities." Mildred's smile could slice bread. She turned back to Leroy. "I saw your room. Do you like to read?"

Leroy nodded without looking up.

"What's your favorite book?"

His head snapped up and he smiled at her. "That's easy. I've read all the Huck Finn and Tom Sawyer adventures. They have a raft and once everybody thought they died. But they weren't dead."

Mildred smiled and nodded. "I remember. I like that book, too." She reaches over and patted Leroy on the hand.

He quickly pulled it away and put it in his lap.

"And that's enough for tonight. Thank you for coming by, Miss White. Deputy?" Edith pulled Leroy's chair out from the table.

Roy Purvis cleared his throat. "I think we should go, Miss White. You've got enough for your report and the boy needs to go to bed."

"I'm not quite done yet. There are just a few more questions to clear up my report. Leroy, do you help Miss Edith here at Goodtimes?"

Edith held her breath. She heard Darwin standing behind her in the hallway.

Leroy looked from her to Mildred White. "That's okay, Leroy. Just tell the truth," Edith said.

He nodded.

"Can you tell me what kind of things you do?"

"I help wash dishes," he said looking at Edith. She nodded and smiled.

"What else. A big boy like you. Do you help carry things?"

"Sometimes."

"Like what?"

"Stuff for Lucky in the kitchen, and for Mr. Darwin."

"What do you help Mr. Darwin with?"

"He's a fisherman. Sometimes I help him carry fish." Leroy looked past Edith and smiled at Darwin who smiled back. "And sometimes he lets me go fishing. But not at night."

"Does Darwin go fishing at night a lot?"

Leroy looked from Darwin to Edith to Mildred. He shrugged.

"Leroy wouldn't know. He would be in bed sleeping," Edith said. "Which is where he should be now."

"Yeah. I'm sleeping then. I dunno what Mr. Darwin does after I go to bed."

"I think that's all I need for my report. Thank you for your patience, Leroy." Mildred stood and smiled at Leroy. She pulled the deputy off to one side and asked him a question that no one else could hear. He looked at Edith, then whispers something back to Mildred.

"I think we're all done for tonight, Leroy," Mildred said. "Thank you for answering my questions. We'll have to talk about Tom Sawyer some time."

Leroy jumps up and scampers over close beside Edith and Darwin.

"Oh, one other question. Do you know Harley Andrews, Leroy?"

"Sure. He came to Goodtimes all the time. Sometimes he gives me a dime as a tip."

"Can you tell me what he looks like?'

"He's big like a bear," Leroy said, puffing out his chest and lowering his voice to a growl. "And has a big, bushy beard. And he likes to laugh." Leroy giggled and Mildred chuckled.

"And what's his favorite drink?" she asked.

Through his giggles, Leroy said, "He likes the Black Jack's Rootshines that Miz Edith makes. It makes him act silly."

The silence in the room was deafening. Mildred was smiling. Leroy, hand over his mouth, looked up at Edith. His eyes were wide with panic.

She patted his shoulder. "It's all right, Leroy. Everything's fine."

Edith pushed Leroy toward Darwin. "Little boys and their imagination. You never know what they'll come up with. Of course, you can't rely on a tall story, now can you, Deputy?"

Deputy Roy looked from Mildred to Edith and blinked. "True enough, Miz Edith. Don't matter what the boy says, we need to see evidence for ourselves."

"But deputy..." Mildred said.

"There's nothing here, Miss White," Edith said. "Just a small boy's story. Maybe Harley was here for lunch when we were open as a café and had a rootbeer soda." Edith smiled and shrugged. "I've had a long day, Miss White. Unless there's something else, I'd like to turn in soon."

"Certainly, Miz Edith. Good night to you." Deputy Roy tipped his hat and tugged at Mildred.

Edith shut the door and bolted it as she watched them go up the path to the car park where car headlights were shining.

The car started as they were halfway up the path.

"That's the car Brother Silas drives." Her hands clenched. "I told you he'd be involved in this somehow. I hope you didn't put the whiskey too far away. I need a drink."

"There's a bottle in your bottom drawer." Darwin reached for two teacups. "This will have to do for now."

Edith handed him the bottle and he filled the cups to the brim. Leroy looked from one to the other, eyes wide. Edith tried to smile.

Brother Silas.

Mavis Saunders.

Mildred White.

Her knuckles were white as she raised the cup to her lips. Her hand shook and the whiskey spilled. *"Argh,"* She threw the teacup at the front door, smashing it. Shards of broken porcelain littered the floor. The sticky, brown whiskey dripped down the door, flooding the room with its sour, sharp perfume.

* * * *

Silas's hands gripped the wheel of the car. He turned and snarled at Mildred as she got in the front seat. "Where is the boy?"

Deputy Purvis, in the back seat, cleared his throat.

"Well?" Silas said. "Don't tell me you didn't take him?"

"There was nothing to be done, Brother Silas," Deputy Roy said. "She still employs him. If I took him without cause it would be kidnapping."

Mildred twisted to face Roy in the back seat. "This lummox did nothing to help, Brother Silas. The boy admitted that they serve liquor there. I tried to take him, but he and the Duffy woman are in cahoots."

Brother Silas turned, an eyebrow raised, waiting.

Roy, his face pale, looked from one attacker to the other. "I couldn't do nothing, Brother Silas. It wouldn't stand up in court."

Brother Silas gripped the wheel of the car. Those in the car could feel the air crackle with his rage. "You pair are useless to me," he snarled. The car rocked with the force of the blow he delivered to the steering wheel.

Mildred gasped. Roy sat frozen in the back seat.

"Oh please, Brother Silas, gave me one more chance. For Leroy's sake. I know we have the evidence now, from the boy's own lips. I'll get Daddy Fagg to intervene personally. He'll listen to me."

"A second chance doesn't mean anything if you don't learn from your first mistake, Sister Mildred."

"Oh, I've learned, Brother Silas, I've learned."

CHAPTER 43

Cassie sat in her chair by the campfire. The dark Everglades close around her, giving her a sense of safety. The frogs were in full-throated chorus tonight. And the mosquitos were especially aggressive from recent rains.

It's amazing the things you collect over the years to add to your comfort. A chair here, a blanket there. From her trips into town, she rarely came back empty-handed. Besides food supplies, there was always some treasure waiting to be found at a rummage sale or tossed away in an alley.

"I hope I've done the right thing by Leroy." She looked around the camp, at the main sleeping tent, at the canvas lean-to she'd fashioned tied to a tree, at her chickee. "Could I give all this up and start again, literally from nothing? Take only what Leroy and I can carry? I doubt it. I'm too old."

She stirred the fire with a stick, sending sparks flying up into the night.

"What if I'm wrong? What if that lady from the Children's Home takes Leroy? I'd have to go to court and then that whole mess with the Preacher-Man and my sister, Cissy, would come out. And who'd take the word of a crazy fortune-teller over a preacher? Then I'd lose Leroy for sure. I can't let that evil man get his hooks into my sweet boy."

She closed her eyes, remembering Cissy and her smile. "I'm sorry Cissy. I thought I was doing the right thing by Leroy, but I don't know. Mr. Preacher-Man's come close a couple of times. I shoulda gone further. Maybe to our family along the Tamiami Trail. But I couldn't leave you. You being buried in that graveyard, all alone. I ain't done right by the boy and I ain't done right by you."

Cassie rolled her shoulders, trying to work out the sudden knot between them. "What I wouldn't give for a long soak in a hot tub." She eyed the galvanized wash tub propped against the washboard. "I'd never fit."

It felt like lead weights were attached to her feet as she walked over to the chickee. A lantern cast a soft glow up into the undersides of the palm leaves that formed its roof.

She picked up the deck of cards. They were still wrapped in their blue silk; the whole package was made for her hands. There was bitterness in her deep sigh as she held tightly to the pack of cards.

You've asked a lot from me. Because of you I'm an outcast from my community, living hidden in this swamp. And I have a boy I'm afraid to raise as my own. There are days like these when I feel like I's too hard to keep going.

Under the chickee the flame of the lantern flickered, casting shadows in the night's darkness. She slowed her breathing, let her shoulders relax. Cassie unwrapped the cards.

She shuffled and dealt out eighteen cards face down. The nineteenth card she turned up on top of the pile. Setting aside the remaining cards in the deck, she picked up the Ace of Swords. It showed a gleaming hand appearing from a white cloud, holding an upright sword. Resting on its tip was a crown with a laurel wreath resting on its tip. Like all cards, there was a cautionary note in an otherwise triumphant card. The jagged mountains in the background suggested the road ahead would be challenging.

"Well, at least one of us has got something to look forward to. Exciting times ahead, *ah-ma-chamee*. The Ace of Swords shows you could be on the verge of a significant breakthrough or a new way of thinking that allows you to view the world with clear eyes. Or, you may figure out an issue that has been troubling you and can see the path ahead of you. Is this Goodtimes, or the smuggling for the other blind-tigers you're doing? Is it personal? Where are things at with Captain McCoy? Or perhaps it's Leroy? Has something changed on that front?"

Cassie stared hard at the card, trying to see clearly what it was trying to tell her. Resigned that nothing more would come, she wrapped the deck in silk and placed it in the center of the table.

"You got too many things on the go, *ah-ma-chamee*. I can't get a fix on you tonight. Whatever that Ace is telling us, just remember that the road ahead may be bumpy, and you should expect challenges. That sword has a double-edged blade, Edith. It can create and destroy."

Taking a deep breath, Cassie blew out the lantern's flame.

CHAPTER 44

The next evening, Edith and Leroy walked Darwin down to the dock. They all looked out over the water checking the weather and the mood of the water. The clouds had been gathering since lunchtime and were dark and unyielding, smothering the last few rays of sun.

Edith pulled her sweater tighter as the wind buffeted them. "I wish you weren't going out, Darwin. Not with everything that's going on. I don't think we've seen the last of Miss White."

"It can't be helped."

Leroy piped up. "Yeah, Miz Edith, sometimes a man's gotta do stuff he don't want to 'cause it's his responsibly. Right, Darwin?"

Darwin laid a hand on Leroy's shoulder. "Right, sport. You know the drill. A man must do—"

Leroy nodded, finishing the now familiar phrase with Darwin. "What a man must do."

Darwin clapped him on the shoulder. "Good lad. You remember that around here while I'm gone." He turned to Edith. "Our Dixie run customers are counting on fresh inventory. I've been through worse storms. The *Marianne* is a sturdy boat and I know what I'm doing. Smooth seas never made for skillful sailors, Edith."

Edith tried to smile and failed. "Well, you be careful out there. Don't take any chances."

Darwin leaned down and patted Leroy on the shoulder. "Batten down the hatches around here, Leroy. Looks like we got some dirty weather coming in." He straightened and turned to Edith. "You'll get Lucky to help you with the storm shutters?"

She gave a brave nod and they watched as Darwin fired up *Marianne*'s powerful Liberty engines and cast off.

She slipped an arm around Leroy, as much for her comfort as his. "Come on, kiddo. Let's get the furniture off the veranda and those shutters closed. We'd better check the water supply and the generator, as well."

"You think it's going to be a bad storm?" Leroy wore a worried frown as he looked at the disappearing *Marianne,* and then up at Edith.

Edith looked up at the sky. "Best to be prepared."

The wind continued to pick up over the course of the day. By nightfall, Edith was tucked into bed and listening to the storm shutters rattle. The room shook as a crash outside as a tree branch hit the roof.

There was a knock at her door.

"Come in."

Leroy's head peeked around the corner. "I heard something smashing."

Edith held out her arms and he scrambled up beside her in the bed. She tucked the blanket around him. "It sounded like a tree branch hit the roof. Nothing to worry about. We're safe and snug in the house."

"Darwin's not back yet?"

"I know, Leroy. I know. But he knows the water. If he can't make it home, he'll find a safe harbor to ride out the storm."

The two lay in the dark, silent with worry as the wind continued to howl.

* * * *

Loaded from his trip to Rum Row, Darwin tried to head into shore but the wind was too strong, even for the pair of powerful Liberty engines at the back of the boat. The storm pushed hard against the *Marianne*. The air was thick with salt, carried by the gale.

Battling the waves, Darwin considered his options. The storm promised nothing but hardship. A huge wave surged over the bow, swamping the boat. A crack of thunder and the heavens opened and torrents of rain pound down.

That decided it and he turned the *Marianne* toward Bimini which, while further out to sea, was closer than home.

It was a rough trip, crashing through the waves, the rain so heavy he could barely make out what was in front of him in the pitch-black dark.

In the flashes of lightening, Darwin was relieved to see coastline; wharf lights blinking through the rain. He threw the fenders over the side to protect the boat and tied the *Marianne* to the dock at Bimini. He battled against the storm on the slippery dock to a building he could see at the end of the pier. The wind tried to rip the door from his hands as he was thrust inside.

Darwin looked around as he rubbed the salt from his face. It was a dank, dark, seedy bar commonly found in many seaports. Stranded sailors were huddled around tables, clutching their drink and hoping for better weather. Standing next to the bar were a trio of rough-looking men who turned as he came in.

Darwin's hands clenched as he recognizes Buford, Everett, and a third man from the Wharf Rats. He shifted his legs apart slightly, preparing for trouble.

"Well lookie what the storm blew in, gentlemen. How *for-to-it-us*. Didn't the Boss say we should deal with him?" Buford said with a sneer.

Everett grinned and glanced at Buford who hadn't taken his eyes off Darwin.

Darwin pulled himself up tall as he returned Buford's glare.

Next to Buford and Everett was a man Darwin had seen before with the Wharf Rats, a squat thick man with a cauliflower ear. He could see from the way he carried himself that this wouldn't be his first fight.

"I don't want any trouble, boys. Just a spot to ride out the storm." Darwin put his back to the door and kept his arms loose at his side. He looked around to see if he'd get any help if there was a fight, but the other customers were either wrapped around their drinks or enjoying the show.

Buford stepped away from the bar. "This works out. I got a score to settle with you, and the Boss wants to make an example of ya. He don't want you working for no dame. And here you are, dropped right into our lap."

"Look fellas, why don't we park ourselves in separate corners and wait out the storm?" Darwin said. The three at the bar laughed. Buford spit on the floor.

Darwin eyed up the odds. Three against one. Buford he knew. A big fella. If he landed a punch, you'd feel it. Everett was a hothead and would be unpredictable. The last one of the three looked to have spent time in the boxing ring.

Might as well get this party started. "Your boss has a real thing for my boss. What's up with that?" he said and stepped to one side behind a table, to give himself some protection. "I'll say this for Edith Duffy: she's got a set of stones on her. Maybe that's what's got your boss in a twist. A bit of envy, eh?"

Buford yelled and, head down, arms out, fists ready to pound, charged Darwin. The other two held back to gave Buford the chance to flatten him. Glory to the leader.

Darwin shoved a chair in front of Buford, tripping him up as he went around it. Darwin grabbed Buford's arm and swung him around, headfirst against the bar. He groaned and sank to the floor.

The other two lunged forward. Darwin tried to keep Everett between him and the fighter.

"Get 'em, Jackson. Knock his block off," Buford yelled as he clutched the edge of the bar in an effort to stand.

Everett took a swing. Darwin ducked and counter punched. As Everett wound up to land another blow, his arm knocked the other Wharf Rat behind him. He swung around to see who was there, expecting a barroom brawl. As he turned, Darwin gave him an uppercut to the jaw, sending him sprawling into Jackson.

Darwin made a dash for the door, but a pair of strong hands grabbed him. "Not so fast, buck-o." Jackson took him and rammed him headfirst into the wall.

Dazed, Darwin struggles to stand. A fist landed on his gut, doubling him over.

Darwin got a swing off, his fist connecting with the fighter's chin. Jackson grunted and staggered and then came in swinging. Buford was now on his feet again. Three against one, and they're quickly outside on the wooden dock.

Darwin was kicked and pummeled and left in a heap. The rain was coming down in sheets, pounding away at his battered body and washing away the blood.

* * * *

It was close to dawn, and the storm had finally blown itself out. Wrapped in her dressing gown, Edith picked her way through debris and fallen branches to the dock. After the wildness of last night, the sun's first rays made the sky blush a bronzy gold, the remaining clouds painted with light from beneath.

The ocean was no longer an abyss of black, nor did it appear blue. Instead it resembled metallic gray, glistening as the occasional spear of light pierced through the clouds and danced over the surface. Waves, full of the last of the storm, pound against the beach. Edith strained her eyes to see a tiny black spot that might be the *Marianne* coming home. But the horizon stayed empty.

Edith waited a few more minutes, hopeful, then turned back to Goodtimes.

* * * *

The first gentle rays of dawn tickled Darwin's swollen eyelids. He opened them as far as he could and groaned as he moved to sit up. He held his head as and struggled to get to his knees and then stand. It was a slow and painful process. His face was a pulpy mess of bruises and cuts. One eye was swollen shut. Tasting copper, he coughed and spat blood onto the wooden dock. With the cough came a red-hot knifing pain in his ribs.

Darwin's first thought was the *Marianne,* and he breathed a sigh of relief to see her sitting there, secure to the dock and undamaged from the storm.

He looked back at the bar and spat again as he remembered the brawl. *Beating, more like. Three against one is too much, even for me.*

Looking to cast off and be out of there before the Wharf Rats wake up from whatever hangover was beating at their brain, he groaned and limped over to the *Marianne*. Every muscle screamed in protest at being forced to move. His vision swam and there was a persistent ringing in his ears.

They better be suffering.

As Darwin got closer to his boat, warning bells began to go off in his head. He shook it, trying to clear it, sure that his eyesight was damaged. The bulky tarp that should be covering his cargo was flapping in the breeze. The cargo was gone.

Darwin began to curse and then was struck silent as he climbed aboard. The boat had been ransacked. The stern was smashed, looking like someone had taken a mallet or ax to his Liberty engines. The console had also been damaged, with the wheel lying broken on the floor. Ropes, line, and gear were dangling into the water, clumsily thrown overboard in some kind of frenzy of destruction. Darwin collapsed, the deck of the *Marianne* littered with debris and scraps of splintered wood and metal.

The world spun and Darwin staggered to the edge of the boat where he hung on, vomiting into the water. He groaned. *Bastards did the same thing to the* Marianne *as they did to me. How will I ever make it home?*

Looking around the marina, he spied the *Sweet Revenge* moored at the next dock. *Bastards.*

With thoughts of revenge driving him, Darwin climbed back onto the dock and snuck close. No sign of anyone. Darwin waited, alert beside the boat. Doubtful the Wharf Rats slept on board because of the storm, but there may be a guard on the boat. He's careful not to rock the *Sweet Revenge* too much as he climbed aboard, his senses wired. *Once beaten, twice shy.*

Darwin looked around for something heavy to beat the Wharf Rat's engines. He picked up a crowbar with shaking hands and then drops it. *I'm as weak as a kitten.* Reaching down, he removes the gas-line from the motor, wrenching it clear and tossing it in the water. To add insult to injury, he took off the fuel cap and urinated into the diesel tank, splashing the deck of the boat.

My aim's off this morning. This won't slow you down much, but it sure is satisfying.

Shaking himself off, he zipped up and discovering a bottle of whiskey lying on a coil of rope, emptied it into the diesel tank, as well.

There, that's better, but not good enough. What else?

He leaned down under the dash. Taking a fistful of wires, he yanked down, pulling them out.

Breathing hard, his head spun. *Not 100% by a long shot. I should get out of here.*

Before he stood, Darwin peered over the gunnels, looking up and down the dock. The sun had cleared the horizon, the wooden docks and boats painted with a rosy glow. He's alone.

Darwin made his way along the marina to the harbor master's office. He slumped against the side of the building and pulled a tarp around himself as a bit of camouflage. Someone would be by soon. Beaten, battered, exhausted, and marooned, he closed his eyes, gave in to despair, and slept.

Chapter 45

Leroy was still sleeping when she returned to her room. She went out onto her balcony. Not a boat in sight. The dock looked lonely without the *Marianne.*

He'll have put in at a safe port somewhere and will be home soon.

She returned to the bed. "Come on, sleepyhead. We've got work to do. Let's try to get things squared away before Mr. Darwin gets home."

The overnight storm had inflicted some minor damage on Goodtimes, and major damage on the kitchen tent. It had come loose from the pegs and lines that secured it. The canvas had blown against the barn. As it ripped loose, it had knocked over the shelves. Foodstuffs and debris were scattered about the yard.

After a pull-together breakfast, Edith grabbed her hat and her handbag with its customary new weight. With Darwin not around, she's taking no chances.

Leaving Lucky with the clean-up, she and Leroy climbed into the truck to head into town to try to buy materials to repair the damage— if the town wasn't hit, if the townsfolk would sell to her.

The kitchen tent has served its purpose, but it was meant to be a temporary solution. And last night's storm showed how temporary it is.

And hopefully the Marianne *will be back when we get home.*

Driving down the Main Highway, Edith noticed the storm damage had been hit and miss. In town, it was clear there was no major damage. She spied Mildred White. *Where was she coming from? The church? The sheriff's office? It gets to me the way she's always there, lurking, watching.*

"Miss Edith, do you need me to help, or could I go find Jay?" Leroy asked as Edith parked.

"I don't think that's a good idea, Leroy. Mrs. Carmichael's not too happy with either of us these days."

"Please? I'll be back at the truck before you're finished your errands."

"Well, okay, but be careful. And don't be long. And keep an eye out for that woman from the Children's Home. If you see her, you high-tail it back to the truck and lock the doors."

With Leroy out of the truck, Edith gave in to her worry over Darwin. Her stomach churned as she ran through the worst. Stranded out on the water. Smashed on the rocks. Drowned. She took a breath and shook her head to clear it.

It's only been a few hours. He'll be fine.

Edith's first stop was the grocery store to replace the bread, eggs, and other foods that perished in the temporary kitchen. When she got to the counter, the shopkeeper hissed 'Whore of Babylon' and turned his back.

Edith stiffend. "What did you say?"

When he ignored her, she slapped her hand on the counter. "I asked you something," she said through gritted teeth.

He turned to face her. "Brother Silas said you're the Whore of Babylon and must be driven out."

Leaving her items on the counter, she turned abruptly and marched out of the store.

Stupid, small-minded people.

There was a similar reaction at the lumberyard and the hardware store. Backs were turned, slurs cast. Brother Silas had done his work.

She marched back to the truck, her back rigid and her face scowling. Dark thoughts of Darwin's fate and the hostility of the town roared over each other, grating against her nerves, causing her to clench her teeth.

"Here we go again," she said, wrenching open the truck door. She settled, arms crossed, to wait for Leroy.

* * * *

Leroy headed over to Jay's house. Along the way, he met Lt. Commander Saunders coming home from the Coast Guard Station.

"Hiya, sir," Leroy said, snapping a salute.

Gray with exhaustion from a night spent rescuing mariners from the storm, he peered at Leroy. "Ah, Leroy. No odd jobs today, I'm afraid."

"Sir, you do rescues, right? Like you did that day with me and Miz—my ma. My pa was out on the Bay last night and hasn't made it home. Do you know if Darwin McKenzie is okay, sir?"

"McKenzie. McKenzie. No, the name doesn't ring any bells."

Commander Saunders watched Leroy deflate. "Have your mother get in touch with the Coast Guard in Miami, and the hospitals." He took in Leroy's worried face. "I'm sure he's fine. It's too soon to start worrying yet."

Leroy gulped. "Thank you, sir. I'll tell my ma to call."

Hands stuffed deep into his pockets, he trudged along the sidewalk to the Carmichael house. Jay was in the backyard.

"Jay," Leroy whispered loudly. "Jay. Over here." He waved his arms.

Jay looked up and spotted him. He glanced at the house to check that his mother wasn't watching from the window, walked over to Leroy and dragged him behind a hedge out of sight.

"Whatchya doing here, Leroy? My ma said I can't play with you no more."

"What?"

"She said I can't see you or talk to you."

"How come?"

"On account of that lady you work for was a horse in Babylonia, or something like that."

"What does that mean?"

"I haven't a hot clue," Jay said shrugging. "But I know I'll get whupped if she sees me talking to you. She's mad because it was a big, fat lie that you were working at a café.

"But we're closed now. What about our door-to-door delivery?"

"You're gonna have to do it on your own. If she catches me doing that, I'll get grounded for sure."

"Can you sneak off and come to Goodtimes?"

"I don't want to go over there anymore. It's nasty."

"But Jay—"

Jay pushed Leroy into the bushes. "Get lost, would ya. You're just going to get me in trouble."

Leroy watched Jay go inside the house. His lip trembled and his shoulders hunched against further calamity as he walked back to the truck.

"Why do people think you're a horse, and where is Babylonia?" Leroy asked when he was in the truck with Edith.

Edith froze. "Where did you hear that?"

"Jay said that's what you are. And he can't play with me nomore on account of the horse thing." Leroy kicked the dashboard. "Heck, he can't even talk to me. Oh, Captain Saunders said to call the Coast Guard just in case Darwin's dead."

Edith gasped. "Leroy. Why would you say that?"

"Jay won't be my friend anymore. Darwin's still not home. And it's all your fault." Leroy, red faced, was yelling at her.

Something in Edith snapped. "Why is this my fault?" she said, yelling back.

"You made Darwin go out last night. You and your stupid Dixie run. And Jay's mother won't let me talk to him because... because you're just bad. They're right. You are a horse in Babylonia."

"Don't say that. They're vile words meant to hurt my feelings."

"So, are you?"

"Leroy. Apologize."

"I'm not gonna. Maybe Darwin's dead. Maybe you are one."

"Stop it!" Edith raised her hand to strike him and he jerked away, stunned.

Tears ran down his face. "Why can't I play with Jay? Where's Darwin? This is all your fault."

"Leroy." Edith reached for him.

"You are nasty. Them folks are right."

Leroy got out of the truck, slamming the door. He headed down the street that led toward home.

Edith jumped out, hanging onto the open door. "Leroy. I'm sorry. Come here. Leroy?"

He kept walking.

"Now what have I done?" Edith got back behind the wheel. Instead of driving after Leroy, she turned toward the church. "This is all Brother Silas's fault. It's time he and I had a little talk. And boss of the Wharf Rats or Man of God, he'd better listen to me."

She parked the truck half on the church lawn and leaped down from the cab, slamming the door behind her.

The church was unlocked and Edith barged in. 'Brother Silas. I need to talk to you," she hollered into the space.

The door behind the altar opened and Brother Silas stepped out. He looked her up and down and sneered. "Mrs. Duffy. You are not welcome here."

The sight of him got her blood pounding. Images flashed in a red tinge of rage: the fire at 'Gator Joe's, the attack on Leroy, all the petty moments of harassment. There was a ringing in her ears and she shook her head to clear them. Taking two steps forward, her eyes focused on Brother Silas. Edith's hand slipped into her handbag and around the grip of the handgun.

"I have a score to settle with you. I know about—" Edith bit her tongue. *He mustn't find out I know about the Wharf Rats. That's my weapon to use, but not now.* She took her hand out of her purse and choked back the words she was going to hurl at him.

"I know what you've been saying about me. The ugly names you've been calling me behind my back."

Brother Silas eyes narrowed. "Job 19:29 Be afraid of the sword, for wrath brings the punishment of the sword, that you may know there is a judgment."

"It's you who would be judged, Silas. You are evil. Masquerading as a man of God, you and your pirate friends terrorize the Bay."

Silas stepped back as if slapped. "What?" he hissed.

Losing all reason, Edith advanced until she was face to face. "I know your little scheme. And you won't get away with it." She jabbed him in the chest with her finger. "I'll call the governor and get you, not me—you, run out of town. You'll be the one that people loath and revile."

Suddenly, Agnes Matheson came through the front door of the church. "Brother Silas? Someone's parked a truck on the front lawn. They must be drunk." Agnes saw Edith. "Oh, it's you. I should have guessed," she said with a sniff as she walked past Edith. "Sorry to interrupt Mrs. Duffy, but the ladies are starting to arrive for choir practice."

"This isn't the last you've heard from me, Brother Silas. No one treats me this way and gets away with it. And leave Leroy alone." She whirled around and marched down the aisle to the front door. Mavis Saunders was just coming up the walkway.

She smirked when she saw Edith. Behind her, Agnes hissed: "Whore of Babylon."

Edith's hands were clenched as she walked out of the church, past Mavis on the walkway, her back rigid and her head high. She kept her eyes focused on the truck, counting the steps, knowing that if she lost control, she'd kill the witch. She climbed in, backed off the lawn, and drove home.

When she got back to Goodtimes, Lucky was raising the tent. "Is Leroy back yet? We had some trouble in town."

Lucky nodded, pointing toward Goodtimes. "He in his room. Door closed."

"Any sign of Darwin yet?"

Lucky shook his head, a grim look on his face. "What happen in town?"

"Nothing I can't handle. Let's go look at the kitchen and see how fast we could get it ready. If Brother Silas felt threatened by me before, he hasn't seen nothing yet."

CHAPTER 46

"Thanks for letting us come, Mae. We needed to get away for a while," Edith said, letting her friend wrap her strong arms around her. Behind her, on the step, Leroy waited with a straw carryall full of swimwear.

Edith had woken at first light and checked the dock at Goodtimes. Still no Darwin. It had been two days and she was worried. More than worried. She was frightened. The façade of confidence she maintained around Leroy was beginning to crack, and she had fled to the only place she knew that would provide a safe harbor—Mae Capone's.

It had been a long few days of waiting, with dread creeping in. She was a woman in definite need of a hug and some mothering and Mae was just the friend to give it.

"I presume no news from Darwin?" Mae searched Edith's face.

"Nothing yet. I called the Coast Guard and the hospitals and no one knows anything."

Mae hugged her again. "But that's good news, right? They would know something by now if something bad had happened." Mae looked past Edith to Leroy, standing worried and forlorn on her sidewalk. "Look, come in you two. I've got lunch ready and we can eat by the pool. Leroy, you go get changed into your swim trunks."

Edith and Mae began to ferry food outside to the pool. "Have you thought of searching?" Mae asked.

A small sob escaped from Edith. "Where? The ocean's a pretty big space. I called Harley and he said he'll keep an eye out. I have to trust Darwin's skill and instincts. He's put in somewhere and we just have to wait." Edith put her tray down on the table and then collapsed on a nearby lawn chair.

Mae gathered her up. "And that's a good attitude, doll. The man was born on water. I'm sure everything will be fine."

"Oh, Mae. What if it isn't? What if he's hurt… or worse? I don't know if he's alive or dead." A small sob escaped.

"Don't go there. Darwin's too stubborn to give up, and neither should you." Mae stood, her face brightening. "And look, here's. Come and grab a plate. Let's try and fill you up."

"Give me a sec to change into my swimsuit. Back in a jiffy," Edith said as she dashed away tears and put a smile on her face. For Leroy's sake.

The pool, sandwiches, and endless ice-cold lemonade soothe frazzled nerves. Mae went to the cabana and hauled out pool toys, an old pair of goggles, and a snorkel.

While Leroy played half-heartedly in the water, Mae and Edith sat under umbrellas, the shade from the sun creating the perfect atmosphere for their dark conversation.

"Fill me in on all the goings on. We haven't had a chance to really catch up since you got back from your trip."

"And thanks again for looking after Goodtimes."

"I was happy to do it and I had a ton of help. So… Nassau? Sandy beaches? Tropical moonlight?"

"I took your advice and made my choice about Bill. When I left Nassau, he and Cleo were very happy together."

Mae reached over and patted her arm. "It's for the best, doll. The right choice is rarely easy."

"I feel bad that I'm always coming to you with my problems."

"What are friends for? Things still bad in town?"

"More of the same, only worse. I've now been labelled the Whore of Babylon. The town shuns me. Brother Silas is out to get me.

And then there're the Wharf Rats. I can feel them lurking in the weeds."

"Sounds like just another day in Coconut Grove."

Edith's lip trembled. "Oh Mae, you have no idea."

"Edith honey, you'll eventually come to some kind of understanding with the people in Coconut Grove. You all have to live together, despite what Brother Silas says. He's crazy and there's no reasoning with someone like that. But the Wharf Rats are a whole other kettle of fish. However you decide to deal with them, remember the only thing they understand is brute force," Mae said.

"I just don't understand what they want from me. Why are they doing this?" Edith watched Leroy splash around, his heart only half in it. She knew they're both pretending that the world was normal and not turned on its head.

"Why didn't you just shoot him?" Mae asked, rubbing suntan oil on her arms.

"Someone came in and there would have been a witness," Edith answered grimly. "And I probably would have regretted it in the long run."

"It sure would have made things simpler."

"Maybe in the short term, but strange things happen when you act with your heart rather than your head. The last time I went off half-cocked I wound up in Florida."

"See, it always works out for the best."

"Seriously, Mae, you of all people should understand. I'm smarter than Mickey and should be able to figure a way out of this. I should have learned something with his death."

While Edith had been talking, Mae was watching Leroy. "Leroy. Come here, sweetie." When he was dripping in front of her, she said, "Go into the kitchen and get a popsicle out of the icebox. There's grape and banana."

With a whoop, Leroy dashed into the house.

"What's with you two? He's acting like a dog that's been kicked," Mae said.

Edith shook her head. "I lost it the other day in town, and I almost took it out on Leroy. We're walking on eggshells around each other now, and I don't know what to do about it."

"Had you tried saying sorry?"

Edith blinked at Mae. "It's not so simple."

"But it's a place to start."

"Cannonball!" Leroy screamed, running and throwing himself into the swimming pool in a tight ball. The splash swept up over the edge of the pool, soaking the area in front of the gals' chairs. He swam to the side, a crooked grin on his face. "Oh, did you get wet?"

"Good thing we moved the chairs back," Edith said, looking at Mae over her sunglasses.

"Boys and swimming pools. Its only a matter of time," Mae said, smiling. "I remember when Sonny was this age. What a scamp he was. Al let him get away with anything. I wish he, Diana, and the girls would come visit more often. Between New York and Chicago, they're hardly ever here."

Leroy, his arms rigid and extended in front of him, sweeps the water, sending it cascading to the gals again.

"Leroy. Stop that," Edith said, scowling.

He tilted his head, looking right at her and then splashed them again.

"All right. Out of the pool. Now," Edith said, standing at the side of the pool, hands on her hips.

"Make me," Leroy said, a challenge in the thrust of his jaw.

Edith looked back at a smiling Mae.

"Cannonball!" Edith screamed, plunging in right next to Leroy. When she came up for air, he was gasping, hanging onto the side of the pool. He glared at her and she giggled. "You got soaked."

He stops. Slowly, a smile crept onto his face.

"Gotcha." Edith laughed.

Leroy laughed with her.

"Come on, slow-poke. I'll race you to the other side of the pool." Edith took off, making sure Leroy passed her in the water.

"Whoa, you're fast. Faster than I remember."

"I've been practicing," Leroy said, proudly.

"You can tell. I'm going to go back and visit with Mae, but how about on our way home we stop and grab a couple of burgers and shakes?"

"Can I have chocolate?"

Edith grinned. "Double chocolate. With a cherry."

"Swell," Leroy said, and swam with her to the other side of the pool. "I'm going to get a double chocolate milkshake with a cherry on top," he announced to Mae with a grin. Mae grinned back and waved, tossing Edith her towel.

"Smart. No matter the size of the man, the way to his heart is always through his stomach," Mae said.

"It's a start," Edith answers.

Settling back in her chair, Edith admired the natural way Mae had with Leroy. "I'm sure Sonny's busy with work, but why doesn't Diana just pack them up and come down for a couple of weeks?"

"She got in the habit of avoiding us when Al was around. Said he and his business were a bad influence on the girls. Even with Al in prison, she still can't be bothered to make time. And I hate the judgemental hypocrisy; it's Al's business that gives her the life she leads."

"She and the biddies in Coconut Grove have a lot in common. How can this be a bad influence?" Edith said, her hand taking in Leroy splashing in the pool.

Leroy waved back. "Hey, Miz Edith. Look at me. See how high I can jump off the diving board."

Mae shook her head. "I don't know. Maybe Diana has a point. Even Al agreed that we needed to keep Sonny away from the rough stuff. It's tough on kids when the cops are the bad guys who want to hurt their pops. It's not great for a child when the consequences of talking to strangers—rival gangsters—can be a bullet or a kidnapping. Raising kids in this life, it has its moments."

"Baker's kids, pastor's kids, teacher's kids. Every kid gets saddled with their parents' crap. Leroy's got a lot on his shoulders because of me and Goodtimes, and he's not even my kid," Edith said.

"I thought you had shut things down at Goodtimes. Surely those witches have no reason to keep pursuing this?"

"It's not just the Guild. There's this woman, Mildred White, from the Children's Home. She's totally obsessed with Leroy. She thinks she's saving him from damnation. And Brother Silas is in on it. His sermons are fuel to the fire."

Edith debating more about the preacher's role in all this but just couldn't bring herself to dump more on Mae's shoulders.

If only Darwin was here...

Leroy dashed over and grabbed a glass of lemonade from the table. Grinning, his eyes were bright red from the chlorine. He ran and leaped back into the pool, purposely splashing water over the edge.

"Leroy." Edith warned. She turned to Mae. "This visit was just what we needed: a bit of sunshine for dreary times."

"Edith, why are they being so difficult? With all the destitute families because of the depression, you'd think there would be legitimate cases of children needing care."

"There's more to Brother Silas than church-going people think." Edith checked that Leroy was at the far end of the pool. "I found out he's the leader of that group of thugs that's been giving me all the trouble. The Wharf Rats."

Mae gasped. "Not the ones that burned down 'Gator Joe's?"

Edith nodded. "And he's been driving this frenzy about Leroy."

Mae also looked over at Leroy who was dropping a stone into the pool and diving to retrieve it.

"I should have figured it out the first day we saw him with Leroy's aunt. Real pastors don't raise their hand to a woman. What are you going to do? Want me to make a few phone calls? Offing a preacher might make some squeamish, but the head of the Wharf Rats is fair game."

"No, not yet anyway. I want to see if he backs off now that Goodtimes is closed."

"Oh, Edith, how long are you going to wait?"

"I'm not naïve, Mae. I know what lies ahead if he doesn't back off. And now with Darwin still gone, I don't feel strong enough to take that all on. I figure I'll try moderation one last time before I bring that craziness back into my life."

Mae peered at Edith over her sunglasses. "Moderation? Gave me a break. It's Leroy we're talking about. I've never seen you back away from a fight."

Edith watched Leroy. "I wish it were that simple. It's not just Silas. This Mildred woman from the Children's Home is relentless. Even if Silas were out of the picture, she wouldn't give up. It would probably just motivate her more. She's a woman with a mission and the law's on her side."

"Don't wait too long. Let the lawyers deal with the Children's Home. It's what we pay them for. To keep the law at bay. And if you do want to deal with this Wharf Rat boss, you let me know. I know people. You know people." Mae gave Edith a long look before settling back in her lounge chair. "Women like us who live in the mob world understand that family is everything. And you're like family to me, Edith. And that means Leroy is, too."

Edith arched one eyebrow.

"You know what I mean. We go to the funerals and the weddings, comfort the wives, worry about each other's children, celebrate the successes, and close ranks against the threats. In the mob family, you always know who's got your back," Mae said.

"Miz Edith. Watch how long I could hold my breath." Leroy pinched his nose and put his face in the water. One, two, three, four, and he came up gasping for air, shaking the water from his head.

"Good job. That was four. Keep at it and I bet you can do six."

"The thing with Diana is that she only sees the tough part of being Al Capone's daughter-in-law. She doesn't understand that there are good points, too. Like loyalty. As you know, loyalty is everything when you're in the 'family'. It's not something you pick up and put down for convenience. It's a matter of life and death."

"Maybe that's what scares Diana—the intensity," Edith said. This was all so familiar, the sentiment buried deep in her bones from her years with Mickey.

"When 'family' calls, you step up," Mae said. "And it's a two-way street; you have to be able to give as well as benefit from it. If you ask me, that's what she's trying to avoid. She's always too concerned about what the neighbors will think."

321

"That give and take has got me out of a lot of jams over the years. I was the den mother to Mickey's crew and their families. And I still call on them for help when I need it."

"Those kinds of friends are my two-in-the-morning family, because I could count on them and they could count on me, any time of the day or night. I wish I had some advice to gave you that would make it better, doll. Those women in Coconut Grove are making their judgement based on what they think they know about you and Goodtimes. Some of it is fear—you're a very independent woman Edith Duffy. And let's be real, some of it is jealousy. They're protecting their family by attacking yours. A small part may even be genuine concern for Leroy."

"Would it help If they got to know me better? What if I got involved in the work that the Homemakers' Guild is doing? They'd get to see the real me and that I'm not some Jezebel or horse in Babylonia."

"Horse? Babylonia?"

"Long story. What do you think of the idea?"

"I don't know... It's a real long shot, Edith. Maybe, if you had reached out to them sooner, it wouldn't seem like you have an ulterior motive."

"Of course I have an ulterior motive. They might have some influence over Miss White."

Mae shook her head. "Exactly. Theyll see right through you."

"Well, I gotta do something, Mae. The Dixie runs are doing well enough, but it's all on Darwin's shoulders. I want to get Goodtimes back up and running, build my business, and see it thrive. I'm prepared to sacrifice it short term for Leroy, heck, who wouldn't, but there has to be a way I can have both."

"Time will look after that, sweetie. Leroy will be twelve next year and able to work, you have the note from Cassie in the meantime, and if those politicians haven't repealed Prohibition by then, there will be riots in the streets. Let alone empty tax coffers in Washington."

"If I could be sure it was only a few months, I could manage. I wouldn't like it, but I could do it. What I'm worried about is that the working is just an excuse. What they really want to do is hurt me. And that won't go away anytime soon."

On the drive home, Edith listened to Leroy's chatter with half an ear. She was relieved the visit with Mae had cheered him up. It had certainly done her a world of good. But, alas, when they arrived home, the *Rex* was the only boat tied up at the dock. Even it looked worried and lonely.

That night, martini in hand, Edith sat on the dock staring out at the black water. In the heavens stars twinkled and the ghost of a moon drifted above. A new worry had begun to creep in around the edges of her concern for Darwin.

I need to be realistic. It will be three days tomorrow. And still no news. The only bright spot has been no sighting of wreckage. But that leaves me without Darwin, the Marianne, *and a rum runner. My Dixie highway customers are getting thirsty. No booze to sell, no money to be earned. And I really need their money.*

Moonlight bathed the water in silver. The waves lapped gently against the dock. Edith was comforted by the soft night and drawn to the moon's eternal solitude.

But every shining moon has a darker side.

I could replace the Rex—*it won't be easy, but I'll find the cash somewhere. But Darwin? He's irreplaceable.*

I should let Henry know that his cousin is missing. And he'll know how to contact Darwin's folks. They should know, too. Telephone lines are still down, but a telegram should be able to get through. Or at least a letter by train.

Edith's chest tightened. *Oh, what can I say to his mother? How can I tell her he's gone?*

Slow breaths helped steady her. It was the sitting that was getting to her. She needed to be doing something... anything.

There's no way Darwin's gone. I have to stop thinking that way. I need a distraction. First, the threat to Leroy, and now this. It's too much. I need something to take my mind off everything. I need to be strong for Leroy's sake.

The waves rolled onto shore, their rhythm soothing. A small breeze played with her hair. Edith's mind shed the clamour of worry and she began to plan.

Sitting around doesn't solve anything. Tomorrow, if there's still no sign of Darwin, I'll go check with the Coast Guard and Harley again. And then I'm going to pay a visit to my good friends at the Homemakers' Guild.

* * * *

Edith took a deep breath to settle her nerves. She'd been in plenty of dangerous situations that hadn't scared her as much as walking up to the front door of Mavis Saunders's house. She'd bought a simple summer frock to wear to the meeting, something demure and non-threatening. Her face was fresh-scrubbed, not even lipstick. She was trying her best to blend in, when her natural inclination had always been to stand out. But for Leroy she'd adopt the 'Plain Jane' persona and try to win the good ladies of Coconut Grove over.

The expression on Mavis' face as she opened the door to find Edith on her doorstep was priceless.

"Mrs. Duffy?"

"Good afternoon, Mrs. Saunders. I heard that the Homemakers' Guild was meeting here this afternoon and was hoping to help out."

"Help out?"

"Why yes. We all love Coconut Grove. And I've long admired the good work of the Homemakers' Guild. I was hoping I could help out in some small way."

"Mavis, dear, who's at the door?" Agnes asked as she moved to the door, then stepped in front of Mavis.

"Oh. Mrs. Duffy," Agnes said in a cold voice. They both heard the Whore of Babylon silently echoing. The welcome mat was not rolled out.

"She wants to help," Mavis said, her eyes narrowed.

"May I come in?" Edith said, a sweet smile on her face, and she brushed past Mavis and stepped inside.

* * * *

"So what did you think? I can't believe Mavis actually let her in."

Mary Carmichael and Agnes Matheson were standing in Mavis's kitchen washing the teacups and luncheon plates following the meeting.

"She wasn't exactly invited in. What a pushy woman," Agnes said.

"From the sounds of it, she has plenty of experience with the women's clubs in Philadelphia. And I thought she made some excellent points about fund raising. That's an area we always struggle with," said Mary.

"If she expects to waltz in here with her check book and buy her way in… " said Agnes.

"Like we'd say no to her money? Don't be silly. But it's the money she knows in Miami that interests me. Imagine rubbing elbows with the Brickell's. Maybe she could ask them if we could do a fundraiser at their home. They live on Millionaire's Row. I'd love to expand the library project we've got going, and that'll take real money."

"Well," said Agnes, "I, for one, hope we don't see her again. It's hard enough to convince my Robert that what we're doing is appropriate for ladies."

"Robert doesn't approve?"

"You know what I mean. I'm sure Alvin thinks the same way. The letter writing and meeting with politicians. Robert said it's entirely too forward, and involves matters better left to the men. The last thing I need is for him to find out that the hussy from the blind-tiger is part of the Guild. He'd not let me come again."

"Let you come? Oh, really Agnes. That's just not right. What about all the good work that's been done at the school and the hospital? And along the waterfront. None of those projects would have been accomplished if we hadn't gotten involved."

"If I had to choose between the Guild and my marriage, well, there's no choice. There's no way I'm going to let that woman become involved. I love what we do and working with all you ladies. I will not give it up. Not for the likes of her."

Mary watched Agnes stalk out of the kitchen. *It's so unfortunate Mrs. Duffy has to carry the burden of Agnes's husband's narrow-mindedness. They're not even giving her a chance. Leroy is a lovely boy and has obviously been brought up well. He stood up for Jay when he was in a corner; maybe I should return the favor?*

Mary stacked the last of the teacups on the kitchen table for Mavis to put away, and folded her towel over the rack.

I shouldn't judge Agnes. I'm just as bad telling Jay not to play with Leroy. Why should an innocent boy like Leroy suffer just because the adults are arguing? And I've never liked Mildred White. There's something about her that makes me want to scoop up my boys and lock the door.

Mary walked back to her house. *Leroy was a huge help to Jay. He was so clever to come up with the hiding space idea for the wagon. I never would have figured it out. And I've never seen Jay so confident. I owe it to Jay to gave Leroy a second chance. And maybe even Mrs. Duffy deserves one, too. Her influence can't be all bad.*

CHAPTER 47

Edith was standing behind the bar, polishing glassware. Leroy came around the corner and then skidded to a stop when he saw her.

"Whatchya doing, Miz Edith?"

"Just polishing these glasses."

"Why? We ain't got no customers."

Edith shrugged. "I know. It's habit, I guess. And it makes me feel better, knowing that we'll reopen some day."

Leroy shook his head, a puzzled frown on his face. "That's pretty weird. You could be fishing, or baking pies, or sitting on the dock, or anything you want, and you're polishing glasses."

"Work keeps me happy. I—"

She's interrupted by someone knocking at Goodtimes' front door. Leroy rushed to answer it.

"Captain Saunders, sir. Whatchya doing here?"

"Leroy. Manners." Edith arrived behind him. Her heart clenched as only one thought flooded her mind.

Darwin!

A tall Coast Guard officer was standing there. He removed his hat. Her face paled and a small moan escaped. Alarmed, Leroy looked from Edith to John Saunders.

"Everything is fine, Mrs. Duffy. I'm Lt. Commander John Saunders and I had good news about Darwin McKenzie."

"Thank God. I saw you and thought you were here to tell me—" A relieved laugh bubbled forth. "Please, come in."

"Perhaps we can talk outside?"

"Of course. Leroy, see if Lucky had any lemonade in the refrigerator. Or sweet tea."

As Leroy scooted to get the refreshments, Edith and John settled on chairs on the veranda.

"He's fine. It turns out your man has been stranded on Bimini. I have a note for you from him." John reached into his pocket and pulled out a folded piece of paper, handing it to Edith.

With shaking hands, she unfolded it.

'Edith- Sorry for the worry. The Marianne *and I got into a bit of trouble during the storm. We're both fine, but Nuta is bringing me parts for repair and I'll be a few days. Can you stop by his warehouse and settle up with him? It will be expensive. Cheers, Darwin'*

"He's fine?" she asked, after reading the letter several times.

"Yes. One of our members put into Bimini and he asked that we take a note to Mr. Nuta listing the parts he needs, and deliver this to you. I didn't realize you were Leroy's mother. He's a fine lad."

"Leroy's my ward, not my son. But I agree, he was one in a million all right."

"Mrs. Duffy, you'll forgave me for being frank, but it's obvious the business that you and Mr. McKenzie are involved in. I'm sure you appreciate it's illegalities. I am committed to the safety of mariners at sea and upholding the laws of America. I've strayed far outside the boundaries I'm comfortable with to deliver both the parts list and this note to you."

"And I appreciate it. Leroy and I have been terribly worried about Mr. McKenzie. I recognize you now. You were on the Coast Guard ship that rescued Leroy and I when we ran out of gas in the Bay."

Leroy came out with a tray of four glasses of sweet tea. "Here you go, sir. This will wet your whistle."

"Thank you, son." John took a long drink.

"So Darwin's all right?" Leroy asked Edith.

"He's stuck on Bimini for a few days making repairs to the *Marianne*. But otherwise, he's fine." She looked questioningly at John who nodded and smiled. "See, nothing to worry about." Edith wrapped her arm around Leroy and gave him a quick hug.

Leroy wiggled free and stood in front of John. "Did you want to come down to the dock and see the *Rex*? That's the boat Miz Edith and I were on when we ran out of gas. You remember. We use it for fishing. It's a great fishing boat. You can catch redfish off the dock. Big ones, too."

John Saunders put down his empty glass and stood. "Thank you, Leroy. Maybe another time. Now that my duty is done, I think I'll be heading back to the station. It was a pleasure running into you again, son, and meeting you, Mrs. Duffy. "

Edith stood and shook his hand. "Thank you for delivering the note, Commander. I'm grateful."

He smiled and put on his hat, returning Leroy's salute. "And I'll keep you in mind for when it's time to clean out the garage, Leroy. Perhaps you can gave me a hand with that? Now that I know where to find you."

"You bet, Captain, sir."

* * * *

"Thanks for telephoning me, doll. I've been so worried," Mae Capone said as she wrapped Edith in a big hug. Edith relaxed into her. There were times when everyone needed someone to mother them.

"You were the first person I called after I got the note. And I'm so glad you could come for the big ribbon-cutting today. We were going to wait until Darwin's home, but that could be a few days yet and I think we need to celebrate."

"Oh, my, this was positively charming," Mae said, taking in the checkered cloths on the table and the collection of tea pots on the shelf in the barroom. "All you need were a few doilies on the tables and bud vases for flowers."

"Our own little café. Empty like a stage set, but you're right, it was charming."

"How were you managing? Darwin's been gone a week and Goodtimes is closed."

"I won't deny it. Money's tight. I've been working on the expansion for our Dixie runs, which is keeping a roof over our heads. But if I don't get out to Rum Row soon, I'm going to lose the customers I've got. Thank goodness they've been understanding. When Darwin gets back, we're going to have to double down on that part of the business—gotta rebuild the bank account. Two new Liberty engines aren't exactly in my budget this month."

"What about bringing down a charter of the baseball players who are in Miami for Spring Training?"

"Is that the Grapefruit League?"

"Exactly. The teams are all from up north. Make a day of it for them. Get them out of the city and show them a different view of Florida."

"How would that square with the eagle eye of the Children's Home. I feel them lurking, waiting for me to make a mistake."

"Spring training isn't until February. Four months from now. Surely things will be resolved by then? It'll take some organization and connections to set it up. And it's something to keep your mind occupied on something other than losing Leroy."

"You're right. Seeing if I can pull off this baseball idea of yours might be the perfect thing, although the price of those two new

Liberty engines have provided me with plenty of distraction." Edith gave a wry grin. "I had to dip into my bribe-the-governor fund."

Mae took Edith's hands in hers. "You know, I have a bit of money tucked away, and I know people who know people. You'll let me know if I can help?"

"Thanks, Mae. Although it's your shoulder I seem to need most, not your money. Things aren't good right now. Remember I told you that Leroy got teased in town? The mother of his only friend said they couldn't play together."

"Have you done something about it?"

"My first reaction was to stomp over there and give her a piece of my mind."

"A regular mother-tiger," said Mae.

Edith chuckled. "But then I thought about what Leroy would think, and whether it would actually solve anything." Edith sighed, looking around the empty, cavernous space of the barroom. "Maybe I should back off trying to build up the business if they're going to take it out on Leroy."

Mae wrapped her arms around Edith again. "Sweetie. It never gets easier. But things will sort themselves out. They always do. These are crazy times with Leroy, but Prohibition is just temporary. It'll be easier when liquor is legal again. And then you'll have your Dixie run locked down and Goodtimes bursting with customers tossing back legal booze."

Edith looked at her friend with a wry grin. "Do you think people will ever accept a woman running a saloon as good mother material? Come on, enough doom and gloom. Come see our latest addition."

Edith led Mae through the barroom to the newly finished kitchen. "So, what do you think?" Edith spun like a top, a wide grin on her face.

"It's gorgeous. I can see why you are so excited. I'd love to have a kitchen like this. But are you sure this was the best use of your time and energy these past weeks?" Mae asked. It's newness gleamed, and Leroy and Lucky were stocking shelves with dishes, pots and pans, and canned goods.

"Not doing the kitchen would have been giving up on my dream, and giving up was failure. I'll not let these people have power over me," Edith said.

"But—"

"I'm not stupid, Mae. A commercial kitchen is also great cover. It's restaurant quality and, if anyone asks, that's what I'll tell them. Lucky already has a plan for lunch and supper menus which have some potential. I can't stop pushing forward Mae, even with Goodtimes closed. I've not come this far—to only come this far."

"I don't know, Edith. I see how much is on your plate right now."

"The kitchen had to get done, Mae. It got bumped on the priority list a few times. First with the barroom, then with the hidey-hole for the liquor. And then the storm took out the tent. It's like Henry Ford said, you can't build a reputation on what you are going to do, only on what actually gets done. I promised Lucky. We'll need it when we reopen, so we might as well be ready."

"I'm happy it's done. The wash tub, the old cook stove. No fun. I cook good food for you now." Lucky came back in carrying a tall stack of plates.

"I don't know how you've tolerated it for as long as you have, Lucky," Mae said. "I would have gone mad after a week at that wash tub doing dishes."

"Hey, that wash tub was me. I did all the dishes and washing up." Leroy was right behind Lucky with a box of cups and saucers.

Edith laughed and ruffled Leroy's hair. "You're right, kiddo. My hero. Come on, Mae," Edith said, linking her arm through her friend's and leading her into the barroom. "I'll fix you a martini."

CHAPTER 48

Standing in his bathroom, looking in the mirror, Silas straightened his clerical collar. "The father of my flock," he said and, with a final tug, headed into the kitchen at the manse to get the coffee started. Dawn was just breaking, and the birds were a riotous tumult outside the open kitchen window. Buford would be here shortly with the account of the night's work.

He was just measuring the grounds into the coffee pot when there was a soft tap at the back door. "It's open," Silas said.

"Morning, Boss," Buford said, coming in. He dropped his hat on a peg by the kitchen door and took a seat at the table.

Silas, his back to Buford, continued to prepare the coffee. With the pot on the stove, he took out two mugs from the cupboard. "Can you grab the milk from the fridge, please?" Silas said over his shoulder.

"Sure, Boss."

"Do you want anything to eat? I could scramble you some eggs," Silas said, bringing two cups of coffee to the table.

"Nah, I'm beat. I'm going to head home as soon as we're done here. Margie will fix me something."

"How's your hand?" Silas said, nodding to the white bandage around Buford's hand.

Buford stretched the fingers in and out. "Still stiff. That McKenzie bugger sure has a hard head."

"You should get Jackson to show you how to punch. There's an art to it, you know, so you don't break any bones."

Buford shrugged. "I'll do that. Or better yet, I'll leave the slugging to him. I'm too old for this kind of crap, Boss."

Silas chuckled. "You and me both. Are the repairs done on the *Sweet Revenge*?"

"Yup. Nothing compared to the damage we did to his boat. It looked like we'd set off a bomb on board. And them Liberty engines, I doubt even Nuta himself could get them running."

Silas nodded, satisfied. "So how did we do last night?"

"It was a great night," Buford said, reaching into his pockets and putting handfuls of money on the kitchen table. "Plenty of cash. Ain't counted it yet, but I'll be ready for report at the barn later."

"Did you manage to acquire any interesting stock?"

"Some Chivas, if you want it. We were picking off boats before they got to the black ships, rather than on the way home. Which gave us the dough rather than cargo."

"Fair enough. Bring a bottle with you tonight. How's everything else?"

"Everett has got himself into a bit of a mess."

"Oh?"

"Got his girlfriend knocked up."

"That's the girl from Cutler? Lizzie? Elizabeth? Betty?"

"Lizzie. Nice enough dame. He could do worse."

"He's going to do right by her, I hope."

"He's at the complaining stage, but I imagine he will."

"Make sure of it. He can't be leaving a trail of babes behind him, or destitute mothers in need. Can you make a note somewhere so that we don't lose track of this. I want to make sure she gets a share of the family allowance cut after the baby's born."

Buford nodded, sipping his coffee. The night's haul was always split evenly. Silas got a third, Buford got a little less, and the men shared the rest equally. One portion was set aside, and the Wharf Rats refer to it as the Family Allowance. Single fellas didn't get it. It went directly to the women and children of the Rats. Silas learned early there was too much temptation for his Rats to drink and gamble their share of the profits and he wouldn't be having the families of the men go hungry. Delivering the packets at the end of the month was one of Buford's extra jobs, and the women were grateful.

Silas poured a shot of whiskey into Buford's mug. "For medicinal purposes."

Buford smiled. "Thanks, Boss."

"What else happened tonight?"

"I heard that the Duffy gal's been in Nassau with McCoy."

"Oh? The harlot seeking a richer bed. When was that?"

"A few weeks ago, I guess. Before she closed up Goodtimes for good. I just learned about it."

"Why didn't I know sooner?" Silas asked, his face clouding.

Buford scrambled to find an excuse. "There's been lots going on, Boss."

Silas whirled on Buford, throwing the whiskey bottle against the wall. "Damnation, Buford. I should have known." He stood panting in the middle of the kitchen.

Buford sat motionless, waiting. Silas slowly recovered, tossing a cloth to Buford. "Clean that up." While Buford mopped up the spill, Silas sat down. "So, beyond the obvious, why was she in Nassau?"

Buford shrugged as he shook the pieces of glass into a bin. "Didn't ask for details. I hear that he's bringing back a big cargo for the smuggling enterprise they got cooked up over there at Goodtimes."

Silas clenched his coffee mug. "I've heard about that. Going south along the Dixie Highway is a brilliant idea."

"How come we never did nothing like that?" Buford asked.

"We didn't have the right manpower. Nor the trucks for delivery," Silas said, still with gritted teeth. "It was definitely an oversight."

"Missed out on making a lot of money. Any chance we can do it now?"

"Only if we take men off the boats," Silas said. He glared at a place just over Buford's shoulder, still damp from the smashed bottle. "It makes me gag. The money she's making that should be ours."

"I know what you mean, Boss. I hate it when someone gets a leg up on us. Especially a dame."

"They're supposed to be the weaker sex with no head for business. Where the heck did she learn about business?"

"Her husband was Mickey Duffy up in Philly. Had a heck of a reputation. For business and for trouble. She probably picked up a few tricks from him," Buford said.

"She is undeserving of the success. It's unnatural and against the laws of God. 'But I would have you know that the head of every man is Christ, the head of the woman is the man, and the head of Christ is God'."

Buford nodded and finished his coffee. "We had the chance to get a taste of her action, Boss. You're the one that decided that a payoff wasn't good enough. You wanted it all. Or nothing, which was what we're getting."

Silas slammed his hand down on the table, half rising from his chair. "You forget yourself, Buford."

Buford ducked his head down between his shoulders, remaining silent.

The two men sat with their thoughts at the kitchen table. From the living room, the ticking clock was heard.

"How are things, Boss?" Buford ventured to ask. "Still not sleeping so good?"

Silas rubbed his forehead wearily. "It's fine. Better than it was."

"Maybe the collar helps keep things under control?"

"Could be," Silas said, nodding. "No matter. Jezebel and Goodtimes will not continue to prosper. I have been tasked with patience as I must work within the ways of the Lord. But that patience will be rewarded. He will show me a way to bring her down."

"Things seem to have gotten better since you started just focusing on the job and left off some of that craziness with the Duffy dame."

Silas stared at his coffee. The answer might be in its murky depths.

"Just saying, Silas."

"I thought that the boy was our ticket to breaking her, but we're not making any headway there, either. Neither the woman from the Children's Home nor our deputy seem to be able to get at him." Silas slowly stirred his coffee. "This liquor smuggling business she's started worries me. We've got to stop her quickly, before she gets even stronger. I feel this is a test from our Lord, Buford, but I am a weak vessel unable to discern the path forward."

Buford shook his head sadly. "Gave it up, Silas. I know you had a rough go of it when you were a young'un, but not all women are like your grandma. Look at my Margie, for instance. Hardworking, doing a great job raisin' our kids, puts up with me, and that takes some doin'. I've told you plenty of times, you should leave off the Duffy woman.

What is it you preachers say, 'turn the other cheek'? We got other fish to fry."

Silas got up and stood with both hands on the counter, his back to Buford. "A good woman submits to her husband as to the Lord. Meekness and piety are desirable virtues. Harlotry is to be cleansed, Buford. I cannot set aside my calling."

"Speaking of meekness, I'd better shove off. If I'm not home soon, Margie was going to put her meek foot on my backside."

"She's a good woman, your Margie. Please tell her hello for me. I'll try to drop round and visit with her mother today. I have an errand to do first, but should be there after lunch."

"She'd appreciate it. Margie tries to help out, but it's hard with the kiddies and all."

"Not to worry, Buford. I'll look in on her. And make sure you talk to Everett."

CHAPTER 49

Mildred White caresses Harry Carey's face. "You were wonderful in *Trader Horn*. The first time I saw it I couldn't look when you swung over the river of crocodiles. You were so brave. And the way you wear your hat, *mmmm*. It doesn't matter if you're a cowboy or an African explorer, I bet you sleep in that hat." She gently turned him face down and slathered the back of the picture with glue.

Mildred had a whole album of Harry Carey. Like her, he was a reliable character actor. He might be too old now for leading men's roles but Mildred would see every movie he was in, spending hours in the dark with his gravelly baritone voice and rugged good looks.

Her kitchen table was piled with the latest movie magazines. Mr. Peacock from downstairs always put the new issues aside for her. It was one of the few perks of living above S&P Mercantile. She didn't get the front apartment with the wide balcony that overlooked the hustle and bustle of Main Highway, marked as Ingraham on the maps. That was for the store manager. Her small bed-sit was at the back of the building where the trucks made their deliveries. She was a sound sleeper and they never woke her, although the exhaust could be a bit smelly at times.

She had albums for all her favorite movie stars: Ramón Navarro with his Latin good looks and smoldering eyes. So much like Rudy Valentino, God rest him; Lionel Barrymore: he might be a bit too old for her but he did win an Academy Award last year for *A Free Soul*. Ah, she loved that movie. She wasn't so fond of his latest flick *Mata Hari*. Greta Garbo hogged all the best scenes. And then there was Clark Gable; he has had his own album since she saw his first film where he had a walk-on role. She always knew he'd do well. He was in *A Free Soul* along with Lionel. Always the villain. Shoving Norma Shearer like that, even if he was a gangster, was electric. His latest film with Joan Crawford just burned up the screen. Yes, Mildred had an eye for talent.

Too bad he's married to his agent. What an old battle-ax she is. And seventeen years older than Clark. What does he see in her?

Mildred raised her head as she heard someone climbing the stairs outside her apartment. "It can't be Mr. Saunders for the rent. I've paid that already." She got up to answer the knock at her door.

"Brother Silas, oh my," Mildred said, breathless. She glanced behind her to the table with her clippings and pot of glue.

"Sister Mildred, my apologies for intruding. I hope I haven't caught you at a bad time," he said, his eyes warm and brown, just like Ramón Navarro. "I would have waited to talk with you until you arrived at the Children's Home, but it is urgent, and perhaps a subject that should be discussed privately."

Mildred looked out over his shoulder, scanning the back lane to see if anyone was around. Flustered, she patted her hair, giving a little laugh. "No, I was just working on a project for the children. Please, come in." She held the door wide to let him enter. Brother Silas was actually standing in her apartment.

It's not a dream, he's really here. She glanced to the narrow single bed in the corner of the room and blushed.

"I have news that you might find distressing, and I wanted to tell you personally, rather than you hearing it at church. May I sit down?"

"Oh, yes. Of course. Bad news?"

He settled in an armchair with worn upholstery, the doilies on the back and arms attempting to disguise hard use. Mildred's suite had come furnished, and she'd done the best she could with what she had.

"Would you like something cold to drink? I have sweet tea in the refrigerator."

"No, but thank you. Please sit and I'll tell you my news," Brother Silas said, glancing around for another seat.

With Brother Silas ensconced in the only armchair in her tiny apartment, Mildred pulled over a wooden chair from the table. She perched on the edge, twisting her hands together.

"Sister Mildred, I recently learned that we've missed a golden opportunity to save the motherless boy at Goodtimes."

"Brother Silas, I'm not sure what you mean."

"That harlot Jezebel went to the Bahamas with her paramour, abandoning the wee lad. It would have been an ideal time to pluck him from that den of vice and place him in your protective custody."

"She went with her paramour? I didn't know she had one. Oh, dear."

Brother Silas gave a deep sigh. "I suspected the news would catch you unaware, and I'm very disappointed that you didn't know this. Sister Mildred, I had personally given you the task of watching Mrs. Duffy. You've let me down for the third time. First, when Goodtimes was pretending to be a café and you did the initial inspection, again that night with Deputy Purvis—"

"That wasn't my fault, Brother Silas. I tried. It was the deputy that wouldn't take the boy."

"And now, this third time by missing out on an opportunity right under your nose that was obviously a gift of God. You've let me down, Mildred. And more tragically, you have let young Leroy down as well. We were counting on you, and, well...." Brother Silas shook his head and gazed down at his hands in his lap.

"Brother Silas, I am so sorry. I had no idea. This is all my fault. You're right, I should have known about her man. And the trip. This would have been the ideal time to save Leroy. Oh, I am sorry." Mildred got up and began to gather up the movie star clippings spread out over the kitchen table, her hands seeking something to do.

"Be at peace, Sister. I have a portion of the blame to shoulder as well. It may have been my own error of judgement in selecting you for this very weighty duty. I had initially thought of asking Sister Mary

Carmichael to take on your responsibilities. She seems to have established a rapport with the boy. Or perhaps Sister Mavis Saunders. She is relentless in her pursuit of a goal. Truly admirable. And of course, for a truly devout effort, no one can surpass Sister Agnes."

Those others. Always ahead of me. I must do better. Brother Silas trusts me to complete this task.

"Please, come sit." Brother Silas nodded toward the wooden chair and Mildred was pulled back.

"Three times you have failed me and our Lord, Sister Mildred. Like Peter denying Christ. I shouldn't have asked you to take on such an important role. Not with all your obligations at the Children's Home. So much responsibility. Too much, I guess."

"No, Brother Silas. Please. I will try harder. It's not too much. I'm honored to be helping you. Please, gave me another chance. I'll find another opportunity. I won't let you down again."

"Sister Mildred." He paused and looked at her searchingly. "May I call you Milly?"

Mildred blushed a deep scarlet. Her secret fantasy was to have Brother Silas call her Milly. She managed a garbled, choking noise and nodded her head.

Does he realize how much I care for him? It must be the reason why he entrusts me with this sacred duty. I must not fail him again.

"Sister Milly, I don't often share this with others, but I feel that you will hold this in confidence." Brother Silas leaned forward in his armchair and took one of Mildred's hands in his own.

Mildred, still speechless, nodded again. Her eyes were wide and full of wonder at what was happening in her own little place. A heavy truck rumbled down the back lane with deliveries for the mercantile below her apartment. Lost in the miracle of Brother Silas in her home and his trust in her, the sound was an unwelcome intrusion of reality. She glanced at the open window over the kitchen sink.

Seeing her distraction, Brother Silas gently squeezed her hands to pull her focus back to him.

"Much like Leroy, I was abandoned by my selfish parents. Placed into the cruel clutches of a woman who cared naught for me. It took all my strength, and the strength of the Lord, to be able to survive her cruelty. I fear for Leroy. Our circumstances were so similar." Brother Silas held her hand tighter. "Sister Milly, for my sake, would you please watch over the boy? And dare I ask...?"

Mildred nodded, mouth agape.

"I need your best effort. That woman is evil and it will take you and I working together to be able to save the boy. Can you do that? For me?"

Mildred moistened her lips and took a deep breath, squaring her shoulders. "Brother Silas, I won't let you down. You can trust me. I'll find a way."

Brother Silas let go of her hand, patting it. He rose and looked down at her. "I know I can trust you, Sister Milly. You won't let me down again. I'm counting on you, now. As is the boy, Leroy."

Mildred stood, blushing and nodding. "Yes, Brother Silas. And thank you, Brother Silas."

"My apologies for having to leave so quickly. I have to call on the mother of one of my parishioners who is ailing. I would have enjoyed spending more time with you... Milly."

Mildred makes another garbled noise in her throat. Brother Silas moves to the door with Mildred trailing behind him.

"God bless you, Sister," he said, laying his hand on her bowed head. Brother Silas opened the door and was gone. Mildred leaned against the door, sighing, eyes closed. "He called me Milly."

* * * *

Brother Silas descended the stairs, wiping his hands on a handkerchief he'd pulled from his pocket. *At least that is done. We won't have any more mistakes. The Lord isn't the only fisher of men, or women. Although, over the years, I've discovered that sometimes, when you want to catch the biggest fish; you have to use tasty bait, while other times you need a very sharp hook.*

At the bottom of the stairs, Brother Silas paused and looked to the heavens. *I am doing your work, and together we will make that woman pay for her sins, for I have taken up the cause of the fatherless in your name, Lord.*

CHAPTER 50

The sounds of singing birds woke Edith just before dawn. She smiled and stretched. Last night they'd 'cut-the-ribbon' on the new kitchen. It was a symbolic ribbon and cutting—Lucky had untied an apron strung across the doorway; it was the thought that counted.

Edith loved the room. All sleek and new, shiny metal counter tops, professional appliances, a double sink, clean white subway tile. It was modern, efficient, and spoke of potential. It symbolized something positive in her future she could lean on in troubled times.

Walking into the kitchen, desperate for a cup of the coffee she'd been smelling, Edith found Lucky with two strangers—Chinese men. Spying her, Lucky shouted at them in Cantonese, and they both bow deeply toward her. He came over, wringing his hands.

"Miz Edith. Please excuse me, but I was going to tell you. With everything going on, and then travel plans change—"

"Lucky, who are these gentlemen and why were they in my kitchen?"

"Cooks, Miz Edith. My cousins, Bo and Cheng. They come from China like me. The same way I did. Been working in Savannah. Not good for them there. I buy train tickets. We need more help. They family, work cheap. They sleep in the barn in Leroy's old room."

"Hey Lucky, did your brothers from China come for a visit?" Leroy appears at the door holding a line full of freshly caught fish.

"No brothers. These my cousins." Lucky turned and explained something in a flood of Cantonese. The two cousins bow to Leroy who giggled and bowed back.

"You say we open again soon," he said, waving his arms around, "We need cooks for supper and lunches and maybe big parties."

"Are we opening again, Miz Edith?" Leroy asked.

347

"And we have big kitchen. We need to use it."

Edith looked at the two men huddled together, looking from her to Lucky.

"Do they speak English?"

"No, Miz Edith. But they learn fast. I teach them." Lucky half turned and said something in Cantonese. Bo and Cheng nodded and smiled, bowing again.

"And they'll be in the barn? And they can cook?"

"Very good cooks. We can get one to be baker. Do fancy deserts for ladies at lunchtime. Miz Mae bring friends out from Miami."

"It was a trip like that which got me started at 'Gator Joes, Lucky. Did I ever tell you about the time Miz Mae and some friends and I drove up to Cap's Place outside of Fort Lauderdale?"

"No, Miz Edith."

"Cap's was very popular. I suppose we could do something like that," she said. "How about this? They can help Darwin on the delivery runs until we get reopened. He's been saying he needs help."

Taking her coffee into the office, Edith settled into her chair at the desk. While the day that started out with a surprise, it gently evolved into a day with the luxuries of normal rhythms. In times of change and chaos, routine had become a precious thing.

Inspired by Mae's idea, she worked on sketching out a baseball-themed event, and made a list of casinos and resorts in Miami that might be interested in offering day tours.

Lunch was a successful trial-run of Lucky's family members who were now in the kitchen.

Discovering that Cheng had some carpentry skills, Edith set him to work repairing a chair and some shelves that had been damaged in the recent storm. They'd been set to one side with all the other priorities.

Sitting in her office, Edith was absorbed in working on her projects Lucky cleared his throat and, when she didn't turn or answer, he tapped on the door.

"Miz Edith, you busy? Can I talk to you?"

Turning, Edith put down her pen and smiled. "Certainly, Lucky. What is it?"

Lucky gave her a deep bow, his hands pressed together. "Thank you, Miz Edith, for allowing my cousins to stay. I am grateful."

"By all means, Lucky. We are friends. You and they must be close for you to pay for their travel and to bring them here."

"No. I never meet Cheng, and only saw Bo as little boy. Their family live in countryside where my family live. I live in Canton City for many years."

"Then it's a wonderful thing you're doing."

"Family is very important in China. Confucius say it is most important duty. The father of my father would expect me to provide for them."

"Family is important here, too."

"Not the same, Miz Edith. I owe my family everything. My father's father, my father, my brother who was Number One son. They are the leaders in my family and I owe great duty to them."

"And yet you are here?"

"Times are difficult in China right now. My duty as Number Two son is to come to America and earn money to send home. I am proud that I have been able to do this. Now my cousins come here with same responsibility to their parents."

Edith smiled. "Number Two son is a good son. Your parents must be proud of you."

Lucky gave another short bow. "There is saying in China, 'falling leaves returning to the root of the tree that sired them'. I live for the day I can return to China and see them and the graves of my ancestors again."

"I am honored to help your cousins, Lucky. Here at Goodtimes, your family is my family."

Lucky gave another deep bow.

Family isn't the most important thing, it is the only thing. And I guess our Goodtimes' family just got a bit bigger.

The last orange rays floated in the sky before twilight beckoned the stars. Edith turned on the light as she kept working on her accounts. Occasionally, she paused, looking at the map on the wall.

Edith reflected on where she was right now: the expanded liquor distribution, the kitchen finally done, more staff to help Darwin with the Dixie runs when he got back.

Things are looking good. There's been no sign of Wharf Rat trouble since I closed Goodtimes for real. That part of the strategy seems to be working. Of course, Mildred White continues to stalk Leroy like he is big game, but that's just annoying rather than dangerous.

She remembered Bill McCoy's words "In time, I learned to dread the periods when everything looked rosiest. Experience taught me it would be then when something would blow up in my face."

"Miz Edith," Leroy yelled from outside.

Edith's head snapped up.

Right on cue.

She ran across the barroom and flung open the front door on the veranda. Her heart was in her mouth, watching him race toward her, waving his hands in the air.

Edith's heart leaped to her throat. *Wharf Rats? Mildred White? Silas himself?*

"Miz Edith. Lucky. Come quick. It's Darwin and the *Marianne*. They're home."

Edith ran down to the dock, Lucky right behind her. Darwin was tying the lines and straightened up at her shout.

Seconds later, she was in his arms, laughing, crying. Leroy wrapped his arms around them both. Lucky pounded on his back. "Welcome home, Darwin."

"A hero's welcome. I'm going to have to go away more often."

Edith pulled back, seeing the yellowed bruises, the swollen eye, the cuts now scabbed over, and laughed. "Not a chance, buster. Not until you give us the lowdown on what happened to you."

"And you need to meet Lucky's cousins. They're from China, too," Leroy said, tugging his arm toward Goodtimes.

Darwin, being pulled along by Leroy, shot a questioning look at Edith.

"For the Dixie runs. You said you needed help."

Darwin shook his head, laughing.

"And we finished the kitchen. It very fine. I have food for you. Come. come," Lucky said.

Darwin laughed, tucking Edith under his arm as he walked off the dock. "Sheesh, I go away for a couple of days and look at all the changes."

Lucky, coming up behind him said, "At high tide, fish eat ants. At low tide, ants eat fish."

Darwin looked at Edith and smiled. "Another Chinese proverb that makes no sense. Now I know I'm home."

* * * *

Buford watched the reunion from his hiding spot near the car park.

McKenzie's back, looking none the worse for wear. And those sounded like new Liberty engines. The Boss ain't going to like this. Doesn't seem to matter much what we do, that dame and the rest always bounce back.

CHAPTER 51

Edith was back at her desk making a list of baseball team managers. Voices drifted in from the veranda.

"I know those voices," she said with a grin, getting up to greet her guests.

The wide shoulders of Bill McCoy filled the doorway. Right behind him was Cleo.

Everyone got wrapped in hugs and kisses. "What a surprise. I didn't know you were back on the Row already."

"We arrived yesterday. I expected to see Darwin last night, what with the Dixie runs you are doing."

"He didn't get in until early this morning. Yesterday was delivery day for the Dixie customers. He's sleeping right now. I'm surprised he didn't wake up when you pulled into the dock and follow you up. But he'll be out tonight with the new orders."

"If you give me a list of what you want before I leave, I'll have everything ready for him," Cleo said.

The three settled around a table in the barroom. Edith had dug out the bottle of whiskey for Bill and made a couple of her famous martinis for Cleo and herself. There was a lot to catch up on.

"That's terrible about you and Leroy," Cleo said, a comforting hand on Edith's arm.

"The lawyer is talking to the governor. I should hear back in a few days what the verdict is. Until we get Mildred White and the Children's Home issue dealt with, Goodtimes stays dark."

"That must be cutting into your bank balance, Edith. How are you managing?"

"Having all this time on our hands means we are building up a sizeable bit of business along the South Dixie Highway, so it's not totally disastrous." Edith gave her friends a wry grin. "And if Goodtimes stays closed, then I guess I got myself a pretty nice house to live in."

"You make sure to let me know if there's anything I can do to help. If you and the boy want to disappear and sail away to the Bahamas, I can make that happen," Bill said.

"Thanks, Bill. I'm not ready to run—yet, but it's good to know there's an escape hatch if I need it."

Bill's answering smile warmed her heart.

"I can sympathize with your predicament. Unfortunately, I'm in a bit of legal trouble myself and would like things to cool off for a bit. I'm getting out of the rum running racket. I'm thinking I'll go explore the South Seas or even start up a little business on the side," he said.

Cleo shot a 'not now we'll talk later' look to Edith.

"That sounds like more than a bit of trouble."

"Oh, it's not just that. I've been mulling this over for quite a while. Rum Row isn't what it used to be. Back when I first started it was lots of adventure and easy profit. Now it's full of gangsters, pirates, and the damn Coast Guard. You saw it first hand in Nassau." Bill leaned back in his chair, his hand wrapped around his whiskey glass.

"I can't believe you're getting out of the rum running business. What will you do instead?"

"I'm going to organize the British Transportation and Trading Company to buy and sell ships."

"Really? Well, you sure know your way around a boat. And you've got a reputation for being a square dealer," Edith said.

Bill broke out in an expansive salesman's grin. "You know, you gals should let me be your agent and buy a couple of ships for you. You could have your own fleet, Edith. Really get into the supply-side of the business. Take out the middleman."

"Ha. Ha. A friend of mine in Miami suggested I do that instead of buy 'Gator Joe's. He had the *Washington*. You've supercargo'd with Reggie, haven't you Cleo?"

"I was on the *Washington* when we first met. There could be some promise to the idea, Edith. At Christmas, I knew of one rum runner who landed 96,000 bottles of liquor near NYC, and repackaged them on shore into nearly 750,000 bottles of bootleg booze. Figure out the profit on that!"

"I like the money well enough, and it works well with the Dixie run side of the business. But I'm no sailor. My strength is on land. I don't know enough about it even to find a captain and crew."

Cleo leaned forward, her cheeks flushed. "That's one of the reasons we're here. When Bill told me he was going to stop rum running, I got thinking about who else might be our transport between Bahamas and Rum Row. There are a lot of ships, but none that I trust more with our cargo than Bill."

"Why, thank you, Cleo. That does a body good to hear that."

"Don't let your head get too swollen. I've already thought of your replacement."

"Ouch, that hurts," Bill said, clutching his chest as if he's been shot.

"Oh, you." Cleo laughed and turned to Edith. "I have a friend you need to meet. You may had heard of her? Spanish Marie? She has a fleet out of Havana."

Bill laughed. "Another dame to the mix? What was it about you gals?"

Cleo slapped his arm, but only half in jest. "Sometimes it's easier to work with women. And it's always good to support another woman in business."

Edith nodded. "My friend Mae says that. She has a wonderful network of businesswomen. Tell me more about Spanish Marie."

"She's a little firebrand. Hot Latin blood," Bill said, a faraway look in his eye.

"Besides that," Edith said, frowning at Bill. She turned to Cleo. "Is she solid?"

"Marie's superb at what she does, which is smuggling illegal liquor. I'm not sure solid is the right term, but I work with her whenever I can," Cleo said.

"I thought I heard you folks," Darwin said, coming in and sitting down.

"Sorry to wake you, Darwin. Whoa, what's that expression you Americans use? 'Rode hard and put away wet'?"

Darwin chuckled, rubbing his unshaven face still marked with yellow bruises and half-healed cuts. "It's been a long few days."

"Edith said you were up all night on the Dixie run. And you'll be out tonight on Rum Row," Cleo said.

"Yes. The *Arethusa* will be my first stop."

Bill laughed and slaped Darwin on the back. "She'll be your only stop, mate. We have everything you might need and more. And fair prices."

"Gave me your list, Darwin, and I'll make sure that everything is ready for you. If there's something we don't have, I'll send one of the crew to another ship to pick it up and add it to your order. It will save you some time and trouble and we can travel behind the twelve-mile limit more easily than you do in front."

"Thanks, Cleo. I'll go get it now." Darwin turned to head back to the *Rex.*

"How much do you have left from the Nassau order you brought back?" Cleo asked Edith.

"We're going through it quickly. When we do our deliveries I've been taking a listing with me of what we have on stock. I find that the customers are ordering more with temptation in front of them than when I was waiting for them to think of what stock they may need."

The two discussed brands and quality.

"You must have signed up new customers as well?"

"Edith is very persuasive," Darwin said, returning with his list in hand. "She's been taking cocktail recipes with her. Everybody wants the latest." He handed Cleo the list of liquor they needed. "These are bottles we don't have in inventory. Nothing too special, although we'll need to be careful on what brands. A lot of our Dixie customers are not too particular what they drink as long as it's cheap."

"Why don't you give the list to Bill? I'm hoping Cleo might stay overnight?" Edith was dying of curiosity to hear more about Bill's announcement. "It's been ages since I've seen you, and I'd love to just spend some girl-time on the veranda."

Cleo patted her hand and then turned to Bill. "What about it, Bill? Can you do without me for one night?"

"We just arrived, Cleo. There's lots of merchandise to move, and this will probably be our last run together with you as supercargo." He looked from one gal to the other. "But sure, we can make do one night. As long as you trust me to keep the accounts organized."

"I'm sure you'll do fine. And Darwin can run me out tomorrow before dark."

After supper and Bill's departure, Cleo and Edith settled on the veranda to watch the sun set.

"This is a different view than I thought I'd be seeing when I woke up this morning," Cleo said.

"I'm glad you could stay. Bill sure had shocking news. Can an old sea dog learn new tricks?"

"The Feds have it in for him, Edith. They seized two of his boats up near New York for smuggling. It's only a matter of time before they nab him, too."

"I can see how he'd like a change of scenery. Will it last?"

"I think between the authorities and the inevitable end of Prohibition, he sees the writing on the wall."

"What does that mean for the two of you?" Edith asked. *A month ago this would had been good news, now it just makes me sad for Cleo.*

"Probably not much will change. I'll still be Bill's girl when he's in port, and I'll still be the boss of my wholesaling business and living the life I've fought hard to achieve."

"I hope it works out for you both. And for the two of us, as well. With Bill's departure, that leaves us short a ship for the Dixie runs."

"Spanish Marie is perfect for us. I've known and worked with her for years. What do you think about making another exclusive arrangement? Are you busy enough?"

"I think I could build up the business to justify it. We'd need to start exploring the north half of the coast. Mae Capone has great intel about how to avoid stepping on Lanksy's toes."

"Great. Then I think you and Marie and I need to talk. The Bootleggers' Ball is coming up in a few months in Nassau. Timing would be perfect."

"That would give me time to get some exploratory work done north of Miami. Not that I wish any ill on Bill, but this couldn't have come at a better time, Cleo. This whole Leroy thing has me rattled."

"It sounds grim. And it must be hard on you to have Goodtimes closed, although it sounds like you're trying to get things fixed. How's Cassie about all this?"

"She seems okay. I was worried she might pack Leroy up and the two of them disappear deeper into the 'glades. But she's prepared to let me try and work things out, which I'm grateful for. She and I are reaching an understanding. I didn't realize how important Leroy was to me until someone threatened to take him away."

"He must be for you to close up Goodtimes."

"I think of everything that Cassie gave up and Goodtimes doesn't seem to be such a big sacrifice. Besides, there are a couple of issues all rolled up in this. The blind-tiger illegal liquor is only a small part of it, and one I know how to deal with. The child labor law is another, which the governor can help me with. The big problem is the Children's Home and whether I'm providing a good environment for Leroy to grow up in."

"Well, that's just nonsense. Anyone can see that the boy is crazy about you. And you seem crazy about him, too. That's the most important part of all this."

"But that's the thing, Cleo. I'm not like Mary Carmichael, his friend Jay's mother. She stays home all day, baking and sewing, doing good works in the community, active in the church. If that's what I'm measured against, there's no way I can meet that."

"Oh, pooh, Edith. That's just silly."

"No, I'm serious. I've been thinking about this a lot. Maybe his life would be better with people like Mary Carmichael. I met her at a Homemakers' Guild meeting and she seems very nice."

"You went to a Guild meeting? Oh, my. Tell me what happened," Cleo said, laughing. "Oh, to have been a fly on the wall."

359

"Well, I tried my best, but I'm not sure the good ladies of Coconut Grove are ready for Edith Duffy yet," Edith said, chuckling. "If it weren't so important to try and be more of a normal mother-model, it would be funny."

"What's normal?"

"You know... school, baseball, a mother who bakes him cookies. Cassie and I weren't really the baking types."

"Look Edith, I'm the wrong person to be talking to about this. I've no kids of my own, nor likely to have any. If Bill and I ever hook up for good, he's not the settling down type."

"Do you regret not having children or a family?"

"No sense crying over something that can't be changed. I like my life and can't see myself giving up being in charge and traveling the world, to sit at home and raise children, or let my husband run things."

"It doesn't have to be like that, Cleo."

"Who are you trying to convince? And you're right. In this day and age, there are options, although maybe not for me. I've worked too hard to get where I am. And I'm too stubborn and set in my ways to live happily with someone else for any amount of time."

"If it weren't for Leroy, that would be my story."

"Leroy, and the cast of characters you've gathered around you. Family isn't always about blood. It's the people in your life that want you in theirs. The ones who accept you for who you are. The ones who stand by you, no matter what. And it's got nothing to do with baking cookies."

"If that's your definition, then I consider you part of this family."

"You are a treasure, Edith. And I'm honored. I'll be the cranky eccentric spinster aunt who shows up for visits with bags of sweeties," Cleo said, laughing.

Edith clinked her glass to Cleo's to toast the occasion. A companionable silence blanketed them, letting each woman get lost in her own thoughts.

Cleo poured more martinis from the shaker. "Darwin looked exhausted. Are you pushing him too hard?"

"Since we closed down, he's taken on most of the Dixie run responsibilities. Which means some days are double ended, spending the night on Rum Row and the day on the highway."

"It's a lot to ask, Edith."

"He could say no."

"Yes, but would he? He wants you to succeed. He wants Goodtimes to succeed. If you ask him to do something, he'll get the job done. Even if it's the last thing he does."

"You make it sound ominous. It's just long days."

"Smuggling is a dangerous game, Edith. The weather, pirates, Coast Guard, mechanical malfunctions. You need to be at the top of your game when you're out on the water. Not half asleep."

"All right. All right. I'll talk to him about cutting back. Bo or Cheng will be giving him a hand with the deliveries. That should help. A bit." There was a pause in the conversation. "Besides, it's all just temporary. Things will get back to normal once we get the Leroy issue settled and Goodtimes open again."

Cleo sat on the edge of her chair, her hand on Edith's knee. "About Leroy. Don't sell yourself short, sweetie. You give him something different than the cookie-baking brigade—independence. You don't molly-coddle him, but instead you expect him to use his brain, to be a good problem solver. He sees women making decisions, earning money—imagine how he'll treat his own wife and raise his own daughters."

"Maybe you're right," Edith said, sipping her drink.

Cleo leaned over and took her hand, squeezing it tight. "I know I'm right. Strong, independent women raise strong, independent children. Never doubt that Leroy loves you for who you are."

CHAPTER 52

A foul wind blew along the coastline of Biscayne Bay that evening. Fog rolled in bringing with it the smell of rotting seaweed. It smothered sound and light, rendering the moon a small, white dot through the swirling mists.

Inside the barn, the men shuffled restlessly, anxious to be gone about their business and home safe before the weather worsened.

Buford stood and report began. "Whaddya got, Everett?"

It's a profitable evening. The closure of Goodtimes has had a definite impact on the remaining blind-tigers, and the Wharf Rats have reaped their share of the rewards. In addition to the cash that filled the metal box on the table, Jackson carried a wrapped ham of liquor to the front of the room. "Thought you'd enjoy this, Boss. A bit of last night's haul."

"Well done, gentlemen. We deserve to celebrate." The Boss nodded at Buford who unwrapped six bottles of Chivas Regal, tossing one to the Boss and one back to Jackson. "Open them up, gentlemen. You're heroes tonight."

Amidst the drinking and bragging, proceeds from the regular roll call overflowed the strong box next to the Boss. Buford nodded toward it. "Having Goodtimes shut down is good for business, Boss."

"It's only temporary. An evil man brings evil things. Those who plow evil and sow trouble reap it."

"Ah, sure Boss."

"I hear from our friend in Cutler that her smuggling business is expanding. We need to stop this."

Buford scratched his head. "If going after that man that's with her isn't enough, what else can we do?"

A chorus of suggestions were raised, each one grislier and more graphic than the last.

"What about another raid with the deputy?" Buford said.

Silas waved the idea away. "Another raid would be as ineffective as the others. No, forget about the money." He leaned forward, his eyes narrowed and scheming. "I have something more valuable than money. I have leverage."

Silas stood before the Wharf Rats. Staring back at him were scarred faces and scarred men. He bowed his head and the room quieted.

"But you, oh Father, do see trouble and grief. You consider it to take it in hand… You are the helper of the fatherless. And I am but your servant."

Looking up, he saw frowning faces and shaking heads.

"That Goodtimes whore may think she has us licked, but she is wrong. Cornered in an alley, a street dog will bare its fangs and growl. It doesn't cower. It knows it must fight to survive." He gestures to the overflowing cashbox. "We can see the results of having her gone. We cannot allow her to reopen. We must make Goodtimes go dark—permanently. Where are our fangs, gentlemen?"

The men in front of him, several clutching half-drunk bottles of Chivas, mutter and shuffle their feet. A few shrug and take another drink.

"There is a soft underbelly just waiting to be ripped out. Can you feel it?"

A few begin to nod, punching their fists into open palms; murmurings for action grow loud.

Silas wiped his face with his handkerchief. "She will fear us." He dabbed again, milking the pause for more effect. "That Jezebel will fear our fangs that rip and tear. She and her cohort will be the ones that cower. Wharf Rats are vicious."

The men yell.

"Wharf Rats are victorious." The men howl.

"Let us go and make weak men tremble. Sow destruction and chaos."

The crowd roared its approval, stomping feet on the dirt floor, pounding chests. The Boss glared out at them, challenging them to be invincible.

"We will take action." The Boss stood, eyes crazed, his fist thrust in the air.

"We are invincible." He strode into the center of the room.

"Goodtimes and the Duffy woman are weak." He sneered his contempt.

"Let us show her that our fangs are sharp. We will make her suffer. We will hit her where she is weakest." He drove his fist into his open palm.

"Mr. Buford," he yelled over the tumult.

"Aye, Boss," Buford yelled back.

"None of this eye for an eye business. Soon, we will take both eyes. We will blind her with grief, Mr. Buford."

* * * *

The men stormed out for a night of mayhem on Biscayne Bay, fortified by strong words and strong drink. Lagging behind, Buford warily approached the Boss. He was unsure of the zeal he saw flashing in Silas's eyes.

"Boss. It sounds like you have a plan. Care to let me in on it?"

Silas, crouched on his chair, stared at the open doorway where his men have just left. Through it he could see the silhouette of the church in the sickly fog-shrouded moonlight. "They are my sharp hooks ready to pierce soft flesh," Silas muttered under his breath. He rubbed at his red-rimmed moist eyes.

"What was that, Boss?" Buford asked, his face creased with concern.

"My leverage, Mr. Buford. Women cannot be wounded through intellect; we must rip out her heart. Miss Mildred White and I are going to be making a call on Goodtimes. She and that man of hers will soon be on the road for one of their Dixie runs, and the boy will be alone. Alone and vulnerable. We made a mistake when we missed a similar opportunity and, unlike some, I learn from my mistakes."

"So, you're going to make another go at the boy? Is the deputy going to be in on it, too?"

Silas regarded Buford through puffy-lidded eyes. "Not this time. This time the servant of the Lord shall be the one bearing the flaming sword."

CHAPTER 53

The church door quietly opened and Mildred White slipped in. The chairs were set up for choir practice and the music was laid out. She would have waited until later that afternoon but her news was too exciting to delay sharing.

Brother Silas was sitting in the front pew, head down.

Oh, I've disturbed him at prayer. A true servant of the Lord. And to have found the Lord after such a horrible childhood, well I's an inspiration to us all, especially the children at the Home.

She waited quietly at the back of the church. *He looks lonely. I should invite him to dinner.* She saw him raise his head and took a step forward and then another. She can see he's not praying, but rather studying a sheaf of papers, a metal box at his side. *Church collections? He's always working. Such a good man.*

"Good morning, Brother Silas. Am I interrupting?"

Startled, Brother Silas shoved the papers in his pocket and pushed the box to one side. "No, Sister Mildred, not at all. Please come in. You have news?"

"It's what we've been waiting for. I was watching Goodtimes, as you asked. They are loading the truck with smuggled liquor. I imagine they're going to drop it off to the other saloons in the area."

Brother Silas stood and took her hands in his. "You have done well, Sister Mildred."

She blushed and ducked her head. "You can call me Milly again if you like."

Holding onto his hands, she felt Silas tremble. *He must feel so passionately.*

"It would presume too much, Sister. Did you see evidence to indicate that she was traveling with Mr. McKenzie and not one of the other minions?

Mildred nodded. "She carried her bag up to the truck herself. I heard them talking about setting off at first light."

"So the Jezebel is about to head off. This is our chance to rescue the boy from her evil clutches."

Mildred shook her head. "Poor Leroy. Tethered to her like a dog."

"And the Lord has given us this opportunity to slip off his leash and bring him home."

* * * *

Darwin was sitting on the veranda, a cold bottle of beer on the table beside him. His hat was pushed back from his forehead and he stared out at the wide, blue sea.

Edith sank into the chair next to him, tossing an order book on the table between them. "Let's hope we can fill this up on the trip. The well is dry and the bankers are anxious."

Darwin, his eyes red with fatigue, looked up at her. "Not to worry. We'll get it done."

Edith gazed out over the water and the rising moon. "I'm thinking of selling one of the neighboring parcels of land I bought. It would give us a bit of a cushion."

Darwin turned. "That's not necessary, is it? I thought you liked the seclusion."

Edith sighed. "It's a luxury we may not be able to afford much longer." She turned to look at him. "Are you sure you're up for this trip tomorrow? I could take one of the cousins to help with the unloading. You're burning the candle at both ends, doing the deliveries and making the runs out to Rum Row." Edith gave him a rueful smile. "Besides, Cleo said I work you too hard."

"I'm fine. You gave me the responsibility and I'll get it done."

"That's what I told her. I was thinking we could drive south along the South Dixie Highway. I marked a couple of small blind-tigers in Gould, Princeton, and Naranja on the map." Edith passed over the map from her wall, folded up. "There are a few places in Homestead that look promising, but I'll wait to hear from Mae about what Lansky's interests are there. I don't want to butt heads with him. We could turn round at Florida City and head home."

"That's quite the trip. A six hour drive each way."

"We leave at sunrise and I'm sure we can make good time on the new highway. Leroy was pretty excited when I told him about an alligator farm along the way. He's in the kitchen now, talking to Lucky to see if he'll put it on the menu when we reopen."

Darwin grinned. "You know, it might be part of the blind-tiger adventure scheme of yours that pull people from Miami."

Edith nodded at the map. "I also got thinking about your truck. We could paint the side of it with McKenzie Farms to help with the disguise when the liquor is buried under fruit or vegetables."

"That's an idea. I'll look after it. You're okay with us both being away at the same time? I could drive and take Lucky with me instead."

"I'm so restless just sitting here, Darwin. I know we have to keep Goodtimes dark for the time being, but I'm itching to start building the Dixie run and see how big we can make it."

Darwin smiled at her. "You are one of the most ambitious women I know, Edith Duffy."

"Someone once compared me to a pretty shark: always moving, always feeding."

Darwin shuddered. "Not exactly the description I'd use, but the sentiment fits."

"I've been seeing Mildred White around town a lot. Thinking of she and Brother Silas in cahoots makes me uneasy. Although the Wharf Rats have been pretty quiet. Toward us at least."

"Well, let's hope this peace holds out. When I was on the road during the last run, most of the places I stopped in at had heard of Goodtimes. The other customers we have along the route are happy with our business and, apparently, you're notorious."

"I guess being a lady running a saloon has some advantages. There are a few more businesses that I'm sure would be interested if I am the one to stop by and make the sales pitch. Do you think we'll had any trouble securing the orders?"

"Nah, you're a natural. Who could say no to you?" His easy grin fades and he yawned. "I'm going out to the Row tonight. Although, given the size of our cargo held, I'll have to go out again as soon as we get back. With those new Liberty engines, the *Marianne's* fast, but with these extra trips, we're just looking for trouble."

"Bill has a machine gun mounted on the deck of his ship."

Darwin frowned. "I'm hoping to avoid that. Like I said before, I'm not a shooter."

"Self-defense is a powerful argument, Darwin."

"Let's see how it goes."

Edith stood. "I'm going to turn in. We leave at dawn and at least one of us should be well rested. If you like, I can take the first shift driving. The truck's loaded and we're ready to go as soon as you're up and ready. I'm sure Lucky will have a thermos of coffee for us."

Darwin leaned back in the chair, eyes closed and his hat pulled low. "Night, Edith. I'll see you tomorrow."

* * * *

As soon as it was dark, Darwin fired up the new engines and took the *Marianne* out to Rum Row. He tuned the radio to a special frequency Harley Andrews had told him about.

Spanish music flowed out. In retaliation to the Coast Guard's ship-to-shore radio messages, a rum runner based out of Havana and known as Spanish Marie, had set up her own tower on the Florida coast for contact boats. She was broadcasting the Coast Guard movements in code. Whenever the announcer said 'Madre Dios' and talked about attendance at the bullfight the night before, the numbers were the headings where the Coast Guard's been spotted.

I don't know whether I'm going to be able to keep up this pace. Maybe I should give my own cousins a call, like Lucky did. Bo and Cheng are good workers, but what I need is help on the pickup end, not on deliveries. A few extra pair of hands to manage Rum Row and our new customers would be great. We'd need to get them another boat or two, with the engines to go with them. Now maybe isn't the best time for new expenses like that, but the Dixie run seems to be our only source of income these days. And the way Edith is priming the pump, it's only going to get bigger.

CHAPTER 54

Following an early breakfast, Edith and Darwin poured a couple of thermoses of coffee and headed up to the car park. Leroy, his eyes still blurry from sleep, carried the basket with the order book, map, and sandwiches.

"Okay, we're going to be gone for two days and one night. You'll be okay on your own?"

Leroy nodded and handed her the basket.

"And make sure to listen to Lucky. He's in charge."

"When can I be in charge?" he asked, grinning up at her.

"Ha, not for a few years yet."

"Aw."

"How about we make you second-in-command until I get back?"

Leroy grinned at her and saluted.

She reached for him. "Come here and gave me a hug goodbye."

Edith pulled him close, relishing the sleepy boy smell. *It will be okay. We'll fill up the bank account, Prohibition will end, and life can get back to the way it's supposed to be.*

"And keep an eye out for the woman from the Children's Home. If you see her, you find Lucky. He'll know what to do."

Leroy went to release her and she pulled him back for another hug. "And, if you can't get to Lucky, you go hide like you did at the fire." She cupped his face in her hands, searching his face. "Understand?"

"Aye, aye, captain," Leroy said with another salute.

Darwin leaned out the truck window. "Time to go, Edith."

The truck doors slammed and Leroy waved goodbye. Edith and Darwin were on another Dixie run.

"Did you bring the map?" Edith asked him as they head toward the South Dixie Highway.

He tapped the basket. Edith dug it out and poured them both a cup of coffee from one of the thermoses.

"Lucky's packed sandwiches. Let me know when you get hungry." She unfolded the map across her lap and started marking towns with a red circle. Their plan was to hit up the current customers and do a bit of schmoozing and fact-finding, and check in on potential new customers. The overall goal was adding at least five new names to the order book.

"Have you thought about another boat and driver?" Darwin asked, eyes on the road.

"Now's really not a good time, Darwin. Things are stretched thin. How about we look at it another time? You're managing okay on your own, aren't you?"

"Sure."

Edith lowered the sun visor against the dawn light. She took a good look at Darwin: shadows under his eyes; weariness in his shoulders.

The silence between them stretched tight as the miles role by. "You have anyone in particular in mind?" Edith asked.

"I was thinking about two people. I'd train them up on the Dixie run we got now and then base one in Key Largo and one somewhere around Port. St. Lucie or Vero Beach. They could help coordinate the north part of the state."

"You've thought this through. Do you have anyone specific in mind?"

"I thought I'd pull a Lucky and bring down a couple of cousins of mine."

"I don't get this whole family thing you and Lucky have going. My folks died when I was young, and my fiancé didn't make it back from the Great War. I was on my own until I met Mickey, and well, I won't get into it except to say that after ten plus years of marriage, I was still on my own. I've never had this network you and Lucky have, family to call on when you need them. It seems like anytime we need something, you have a cousin or a nephew or a brother-in-law or somebody's cousin twice removed that can help us out."

"That's what family's for. And it's a two-way street, remember. Helping out cousin Henry was what got me down here working with you."

"Something I'm eternally grateful for," Edith said, smiling in the dark. "Look, if we could get more sales, we should be able to carry the additional expense, although I may not be able to outfit them with two Liberty engines each."

"We could check out the Coast Guard auction that's coming up. They may have something."

"Think they'll have decent motors?"

"Doubtful. Anything faster than the current Coast Guard inventory and Billy Shaw will have it stripped off, re-serviced, and remounted onto official watercraft. They'll not pass up a chance to do a bit of under-the-table upgrading. No, it's the seized boats we want to look at, already modified for smuggling with extra cargo space. And with modifications in place to drop in new Liberty engines." He looked at her. "Eventually."

"Not more engines. What, do they grow on trees?" Edith grinned to take out any possible sting in her words. She was trying to be mindful of Darwin—nothing like almost losing him to make her appreciate him more. "So tell me about these cousins of yours."

"They're sorta local kids, from up toward Daytona Beach. Familiar with the coast and have a lot of experience on the water."

"Smugglers?"

"Not quite. Former Coast Guard."

"That's not what I was expecting."

"They signed up for search and rescue and didn't take kindly to hauling in fellas they knew doing something they didn't think was wrong. A couple of run-ins with the brass and they were politely asked to leave."

"You have the most amazing network of family, Darwin. What do you think of the baseball idea?"

"I like it. They'll be down around February, right?"

"Yes. I talked to a couple of the general managers and they seem interested. You said you had a friend with a ketch that could bring them over from Miami?"

"Sure." He grinned at Edith. "Brother-in-law, actually. My sister Rosie's husband. I could call him and see how much he'd charge."

Chuckling, Darwin caught sight of a road sign. "Do you want to stop at Tucker Wilson's? Cutler is just up ahead. We can check and see how busy he is and how many faces we recognize."

"We should fly the flag. He's always a good source for leads. Although don't forget that anything we say will probably wind up in Silas's ear."

Tucker was glad to see them. "Business has been steady. We're too far south for the Dinner Key station boys to head this way. They're probably going into Miami on their days off. But yeah, some of the locals have remembered where to find us. Is this closed-thing at Goodtimes going to be permanent?"

"Hard to say, Tucker. Definitely we'll stay dark until circumstances change and we can slip beneath the radar again."

"That's too bad. I actually do a better business when you're open than when you're closed. Folks make plans and then don't get in to Goodtimes so come this way with money burning a hole in their pocket. Any chance you could put me on your Dixie run again, Miz Edith? It was sure convenient having Darwin pick up my Rum Row supply, rather than going out myself," Tucker asked as they stood at the door shaking hands goodbye.

Edith shook her head sadly. "Sorry Tucker, but we're out of the local neighborhood bootleg business. It was getting some folks riled up that I'd rather see settled and quiet." She paused. "If you know what I mean." Edith hung onto his hand, making sure he's got the message and trusted it would wind up in Silas's ear. "Our Dixie runs are a long ways down the highway and of no threat to anybody local."

Tucker nodded. "Shame though, all the same. I liked it better the way it was before."

"Same here, Tucker," Edith said with a wry chuckle. "But this new deal seems to be working out for all concerned. And that's the important thing."

"Okay, where to next, boss?" Darwin asked, once again behind the wheel of the truck.

"Don't call me that." Edith shivered. "I'm still not sure what we're going to do about this Brother Silas situation."

"Things are pretty quiet. Maybe, with us being closed, he's going to back off and leave us alone?"

"Not likely. He's too vested in this little vendetta he's got going. Gould was just up ahead. We could swing past Charlie's and see how he's doing, and then check out that new cabaret that just opened," Edith said.

"You wouldn't think that a place the size of Gould could support showgirls."

"It's something different, and I guess it depends on the quality of the show." Edith winked.

At Charlie's, Edith laughed and brushed a bright pink feather off Darwin's shoulder. The showgirls were impressive. Edith came away with the first new name in the order book.

"What about something like that once a month at Goodtimes? We could get Meyer to send us some crap tables and some card dealers. Get us some showgirls and a band."

"Let's try to not rely on Lansky. He makes me anxious, Edith. But I like the idea of a chorus line. It would really be different from anything else around," Darwin said.

"He's got the casino market pretty much to himself." Edith shrugged. "I'm not sure who else to ask."

"What about subcontracting with one of the Miami casinos for an off-night? We could do it on a Monday, when they're slower."

"Good idea. It would put them between us and Lansky. Always nice to have a buffer. Anything in Princeton?" Edith asked, checking her map.

"There's a Mexican restaurant that has a back room. I drove past it on the last run, but didn't have time to stop. Want to check it out?"

"Sure. How Mexican is Mexican? My Spanish is *nada*."

"The place is owned by a retired cop from the Bronx that loves hot chilis but whose Spanish is also nada. We should be fine."

At the restaurant, while Darwin made a pit stop, Edith tried to confirm an order.

"A beautiful dame like yourself, what would you know about business?"

Edith fluttered her eyelashes. "Oh, you'd be surprised."

"Are we talking monkey business?" Al asked with a leer.

She wanted his order. Edith gave him a wink.

He smiled and took a swig of the flask in his pocket.

What am I doing? I'm a successful business owner offering him a quality product on good terms. I should be getting respect, not a come on. I don't care if he's a potential customer; I's just not worth it to do business with someone like that.

"You know, Al, I think I'm going to take a pass on your business. No hard feelings, but my order book is full and I wouldn't want to create an expectation I can't fill."

"Doll, you come by anytime. Maybe next time there'll be an empty line or two in that order book of yours."

Climbing back into the truck, Darwin asked, "Everything okay back there? I thought we had a sure sale. The place looked crowded; we could make some money here."

"Sometimes there were things more important than money. I don't chase people anymore. I've earned my stripes and I'm not going to run after people to prove that I matter. My terms or no terms."

"Sounds good to me. Where next?"

"We've got two regulars in Naranja. After that, it's Modello."

"There's a couple of places along the way that could be worthwhile. How were we doing for time?"

"It's not midnight yet. Still lots of time. Two quick stops just to touch base with our existing customers, and then let's see what new business we can find."

The order book filled up. "What shall we do about Homestead? Lansky's there," Darwin said.

"Let sleeping dogs lie. How about we turn north and start working our way home along 997? Redland's there and the Tamiami

Trail crosses it. We could follow it along toward Tampa and see what business we could drum up," Edith said.

"The last time I was on the Tamiami Trail I almost hit an alligator. Maybe we could do that one in daylight."

"Imagine what Leroy would say if we brought home a 'gator," Edith said and chuckled. She peered out the window into the darkness. The headlights from the truck cast cones of light only a short way in front of them.

"Did you want to go as far as Aladdin City? It's going to be late when we get there. But it might be worth the drive," Darwin said. "There are no plans for tomorrow are there?"

Edith looked at Darwin in the dark and smiled. "My dance card is empty."

"Then Aladdin City it is."

CHAPTER 55

Leroy, Lucky, and his two cousins, Bo and Cheng, were sitting at the kitchen table. Lucky was trying to teach Leroy to play mah-jong—a tile-based matching game involving skill, strategy, and a degree of luck. Leroy was focused on his tiles, and on the tiles of the other players. He shook and tossed the dice into the center well formed by the wall of tiles.

"Now what?" He looked to Lucky for help.

"You have pong. See?" Lucky said, placing one of his tiles in front of Leroy. They match.

Ping-pong, this game is hard. Leroy drew an eight of bamboo. Across from him, Cheng hisses.

A knock at the back door interrupted the game.

Lucky looked to Leroy who shrugged and continued to study his tiles.

Lucky reluctantly rose to answer the knock.

Mildred White was framed by the doorway. The light from the kitchen washed out her already pale features. She checked over her shoulder, and licked her lips. "I tried the front door, but no one heard me."

Lucky shook his head, putting himself between Leroy and the woman from the Children's Home who had caused such upset at Goodtimes. "We closed. Come back tomorrow." He tried to shut the door, but a hand reached out from behind Mildred and pushed it further open.

Brother Silas stepped into the kitchen. "Good evening, Leroy."

Leroy looked up at the two intruders. He tensed.

The preacher man who makes Cassie so scared and that Miz Edith is afraid of.

Eyes wide, he looked to Lucky, ready to run. As Leroy pushed back from the table he accidently knocked over the wall of tiles, scattering them on the floor. Heart pounding, he jerks back, alarmed at the clatter.

Bo and Cheng went and stood beside the boy, watching Lucky.

"Here, let me help you pick these up," Mildred said, bending down, setting her handbag down on the floor beside her.

Lucky grabbed her arm and pulled her up. "No. No. We closed. You come back tomorrow." He tried to push her toward the door.

Brother Silas loomed over Lucky. "Unhand her, heathen." He pulled Lucky's hand off Mildred's arm.

"I'd like to speak to Mrs. Duffy, please," Mildred said, her lips pressed into a thin line.

Lucky stepped back, holding the door open. "No. We closed. You go now."

"Is Mrs. Duffy here?" Brother Silas asked Leroy, sneering.

Leroy held his breath, staring back at Silas. *He grabbed Cassie and was hurting her that time in the café. He's real crazy.*

Bo and Cheng frantically speak in Cantonese. Lucky whirled around to them, spitting out a response only they can understand. The two fall silent.

"Mrs. Duffy isn't here, then?" Mildred's hand was on her hip and there's a belligerent thrust to her chin.

Lucky looked at Leroy who was pale and wide-eyed. The boy was shaking in terror. "You go. We closed."

"So you said. Is Mr. McKenzie here, Leroy?" Brother Silas asked.

Lucky tried again to push Mildred back through the door. Brother Silas slid over and stood beside Leroy.

Lucky will save me. Lucky will save me. Lucky will save me.

"Leroy, are you here alone?" Brother Silas asked in a dry whisper. The others froze at his tone.

What would Miz Edith do? She shoved him on his butt that time. I wish she was here now.

Leroy sat straight, shrugging off the hand that Brother Silas kept trying to lay on his shoulder. "Lucky is here. And Bo and Cheng."

Mildred stepped forward. Leroy was surrounded. "I can't believe she abandoned you like this. Does Miss Edith do this often?"

"I'm not abandoned. Lucky is here. And his cousins." Leroy struggled to get up. The preacher's iron grip pushed him back down and stayed clenched on his shoulder.

Leroy's eyes fix on Lucky's hand as it glides over to a cleaver on the counter.

Brother Silas didn't turn, continuing to stare at Leroy. "Don't do that, Chinaman. It will go badly for you and the boy. Move against the wall."

Lucky grabbed the cleaver, advancing on Brother Silas.

Bo and Chen moved toward the preacher.

Mildred screamed, clutching her purse as a shield.

Leroy yelled and tried to duck out from under his tormentor's bony grasp. Instantly, Silas pulled a gun and pointed it at Leroy. The click of the hammer being drawn back ricocheted around the room.

Leroy held his breath. All he saw was the monstrous gun— pointed right at him.

Mildred gasped and glanced wildly from Brother Silas to the gun. She clutched her handbag to her chest. What little color she had drained from her face. "You're just like Clark Gable in *A Free Soul*."

Silas glanced quickly at her and she stepped away.

"You three. Stand against that wall," Brother Silas said. "Leave the cleaver on the counter, Chinaman."

The clang of the blade hitting the metal counter rang through the kitchen as Lucky, Bo, and Cheng shuffled to the wall.

Hatred flashed in Lucky's eyes as he glared at Brother Silas.

Leroy's pounding heart attempted to leap from his chest. *Miz Edith and Darwin wouldn't just sit here.*

"The weapon is purely for your protection, Sister Mildred. And to ensure that the boy comes with us." Brother Silas' voice had the power of the pulpit in it. "Do what you need to do, Sister Mildred, and we'll be on our way."

Mildred White glanced once again at Brother Silas; a small smile trembling on her lips.

"Of course, Brother Silas. The Chinamen aren't proper supervision." Her voice, which had been shaky, gathered strength. "And what is this?" She points to the mah-jong tiles. "Some kind of heathen gambling? This is much worse than we thought, Brother Silas."

"The boy's things, please, Sister." Mildred gave Lucky and his cousins a wide berth as she scuttled from the room.

Still watching Lucky and the other men, Brother Silas pulled Leroy off the chair. "You will be coming with us, young man."

"I'm not going nowheres. And you can't make me." Leroy's defiance blazed. "When Miz Edith and Darwin get home they're going to get you and fix you real good."

A slow smile crept across Brother Silas' face, although he didn't take his eyes off the three men against the wall. "You're wrong about that, boy."

"Am not. Miz Edith's not afraid of you. She knocked you down before and she'll do it again."

"Silence." Brother Silas whirled on Leroy, striking him with the back of his hand. Leroy's head slammed against the metal edge of the counter, cutting deep. He cries out as blood started to pour.

He slides to the floor—dazed, holding tight to his wound and glaring at Brother Silas. "Miz Edith is going to whip you good for that. And Darwin's bigger than you. He's going to punch your lights out." Images of Darwin, fists flying like the Shadow battling bad guys, flashed through Leroy's mind.

With Silas distracted, Lucky leaped forward, cursing in Cantonese. Silas yanked Leroy off the floor, pulling him close.

Silas jerked Leroy even closer and jammed the gun against Leroy's head.

Lucky froze.

Menace filled the room, making it hard for Leroy to breathe.

Lucky stepped back gingerly. "Please, sir. We have letter from boy's aunt. Miz Edith want you go away now."

Pressing the gun hard into Leroy's head, Brother Silas' smile snaked its way across the room to Lucky. "You had no idea how little I care what Miz Edith wants."

"Ow, ow, ow." Leroy whimpered.

"No hurt Leroy." Lucky's back was to the wall.

"Behave and the boy will be fine."

"I had everything," Mildred said. She's returned to the room every bit the church lady—handbag dangling from her arm and carrying a pillowcase with whatever she's deemed Leroy would need. She took in Leroy's bleeding head. "What's going on, Brother Silas? What's happened?"

"Nothing to be concerned about. Leroy needed some convincing."

Mildred's presence with the bag holding a few of Leroy's possessions confirmed the message that Leroy would be going; Silas eased off with the gun.

Immediately, Leroy twisted, trying to escape the iron grip around his arm. "I'm not going and you can't make me."

Brother Silas rattled him back and forth. "I said be silent, boy."

Leroy, chest heaving, felt the blood wet on his face. He held himself in check, trapped.

"Much better," Brother Silas said and gave a curt nod. "It's time for us to leave. The apprehension was necessary. Do your duty, Sister Mildred."

Mildred stepped forward, pulling documents out of her handbag. She laid them on the table. "I can make you come with us because these documents give me the authority to remove you from these premises due to unsafe conditions. Your employer and guardian, Mrs. Edith Duffy, has failed to provide the care required, putting you at risk. Do you want me to come back with the sheriff and arrest Miss Edith? She'll go to jail because of you. And I bet these Chinamen wouldn't want to see inside a jail cell, either. They'd get sent back to China and it would be your fault."

"You can't put them in jail. You're not the police." Leroy scowled at Mildred White, one hand clenched, the other pushing on his wound. He could feel the preacher's boney claw dig deeper as the grip on his shoulder tightened and the gun barrel tapped against his head.

Mildred's eyes narrowed at Leroy. "No, but Deputy Purvis can lock her up and he'll do it if I tell him to."

Mildred and Leroy stared at each other. Huffing, Leroy was the first to look away.

Brother Silas leaned close to Leroy's ear and hissed. "Jail may be the nicest thing. Don't doubt what I can do, boy." Leroy winced, the pain from his head sharp.

Mildred took another breath and tried to soften her approach. Her voice was soothing and calm. "Leroy, there's a reason why saloons are run by men and not women, and certainly not mothers. They're not a good place for children. With you here, Miss Edith has broken some laws. And maybe these Chinamen shouldn't even be here. I really don't want to have to call the deputy, but I can't leave you here alone."

Leroy's eyes darted around the room, looking for escape. *I don't know what to do. What should I do?*

"We're going to take you to a safe place, Leroy. When Miss Edith returns from her smuggling run, she can find you there."

"Where? Where were we going?"

"It's all in these papers," she said, nodding to the pile of documents on the table. "The state is assuming legal custodial guardianship for your own protection and you will live at the Children's Home. Unless there's somewhere else I can take you. What about your aunt? Can we take you to her?"

Leroy shook his head, his lips pressed tight. The hand on his shoulder dug in and he winced. *I won't rat out Cassie.*

From the sack she's holding, Mildred pulled out a book. Tom Sawyer.

"Hey, that's mine. Gave it back." Leroy tried to lunge at Mildred but Brother Silas held him firmly.

Mildred White smiled and tucked it back inside. "You see, we only want what's best. We mean you no harm. I know you like to read." She rummaged around inside it again, pulling out the baseball glove. "We'll take this as well. You can play catch with the boys at the Children's Home."

Brother Silas guided Leroy roughly to the door, the barrel of the gun resting on his head. "We will be going now, Miss White. You can finish the sales pitch in the car."

Leroy pretended to stumble, shoving himself against Brother Silas. The preacher's arm whipped around Leroy's neck, pulling the child tight against him. "Easy, boy. Don't be stupid."

Lucky tried to pass Leroy a dishcloth to put against his wound. Silas snarled, but Mildred grabbed it.

Choking and sputtering, Leroy was dragged sideways up the hill to the car park, yelling for Edith. Darwin. Lucky. He choked as Brother Silas's arm wrapped tighter around his neck. Mildred scurried around to the back of the car and climbed in. Leroy was shoved in beside her. She put an arm around him, holding him tight, pressing the cloth to his head. Leroy jerked his head away and snatched the dishcloth from her, holding it to the gash himself.

Tears streamed down his face. "I don't want to go. Miz Edith will find me. And Darwin's going to get you." He looked back at Lucky, once again holding the cleaver, standing on the kitchen porch. Bo and Chen were behind him.

Mildred tried to soothe. "This will be better for you. I know that Goodtimes is a blind-tiger, an evil place. Miss Edith was pretending it isn't but she can't fool me. This place is rotten with vice and wickedness, Leroy."

Brother Silas pulled out of the car park.

"I want to go home," Leroy said through his tears.

"And tonight we find you gambling in the kitchen with Chinamen. No proper adequate supervision. More depravity. It's only right that you to come with us," said Mildred.

Leroy whimpered, choking back his tears.

Mildred looked at him as she glanced behind her. "It will be better for Miss Edith, too. Remember, you're keeping her out of jail."

As Silas changed gear as he joined the highway, he turned his head and snarled. "Remember what might happen to your precious Miss Edith, boy. And it would be all your fault."

Leroy gulped and then stared out the car window, the passing scenery a reminder that Goodtimes was disappearing behind them.

He screwed his eyes shut, his face wet with tears and blood. *Cassie. Help me. Cassie. Help me.*

CHAPTER 56

Darwin and Edith pulled into the parking lot just as the sun was rising. They stood side by side, tired from the trip but pleased with the results.

"Oh, Darwin, just look at that beautiful sunrise," Edith said, point to the fiery globe rising out of the water, the sky a deep magenta streaked with gold.

Darwin pushed back his hat and smiled at Edith. "The sun loved the moon so much he died every night to let her breathe."

"You're such a poet, Mr. McKenzie."

"A Seminole folk tale you should get Leroy's aunt to tell you."

"I'll be sure to ask her. And you should get some rest."

Darwin headed down to the *Rex* to catch up on some sleep before the Rum Row run later that night, and Edith went into her office.

Lucky rushed toward her. Bo and Cheng hovered in the hallway to the kitchen.

"Miz Edith, Leroy gone. That lady take him to Children's Home. And a preacher here, too. He had gun," Lucky said, grabbing her arm.

"What. A gun? Where's Leroy?"

"Leroy gone." Lucky explained what had happened while she and Darwin had been gone. He handed her the papers that Mildred White had left behind. She scanned them and then flung them on the desk. Edith clutched the edge of the door, her knuckles white.

"Go to the *Rex* and bring Darwin here. I have to make some telephone calls."

Edith's first call was to the lawyer. The telephone at the other end rang and rang without answer. Edith looked through the window at the dawn breaking over the water and threw the telephone across the room.

Darwin burst through the front door.

"Silas has Leroy." Edith could barely breathe.

"Lucky came down and told me. What do we need to do?" Darwin said.

"I'm going to the Children's Home to get him back."

"I'll drive."

The truck tore out of the driveway and barreled through the empty streets of Coconut Grove. They jerked to a stop in front of a large clapboard house and Edith flung open the truck door and hurried up the path. Crossing the veranda, she banged on the door, yelling for Mildred White.

When the door opened, Mildred was smiling like the cat that got the canary. "Back so soon from your little criminal jaunt? I wasn't expecting you until much later in the day, Mrs. Duffy."

"Where is Leroy?"

"He's sleeping upstairs. Safe. Unharmed."

Edith tried to push past, Darwin behind her. A large man came up from behind Mildred and started to close the door on them. Darwin forced his foot over the threshold, preventing the door from closing.

"I want my boy back. You stole him from me," Edith screamed at Mildred.

Darwin forced the door open a little more.

"No. I have the authority to take the boy. You neglected him, abandoning him to the care of those Chinamen. Probably here illegally. He was at risk," said Mildred.

"No, he wasn't." Edith lunged at Mildred, her hands wrapped around the woman's throat.

Mildred gasped then gurgled, tugging at Edith's hands.

Darwin tried to pull Edith away.

The man behind Mildred yanked Edith's hands away and pushed her back onto the veranda.

"You take your missus home, mister. I called the sheriff's office when your woman was banging on the door. They'll be here soon."

Darwin pulled at Edith who was grasping and struggling to get back to Mildred. "You stole Leroy. Leroy! Leroy!"

Mildred quickly slammed the front door shut and locked it.

Edith broke free of Darwin, banging on the door again and yelling for Leroy.

"Edith. This isn't going to work. We need to go back to Goodtimes."

Collapsing against Darwin, she wailed into his chest. "They took Leroy."

"We'll get him back," he said, guiding her to the truck.

* * * *

A plan was hatched on the drive back to Goodtimes. Lucky met them at the door, his eyes searching for Leroy and then looking to Darwin for answers.

"What time is it? Is it too soon to call the lawyer?" Edith glanced at the clock in the kitchen. "I'll call Mae first."

"Miz Edith. Aunt Cassie here in your office."

"Cassie is here? How did she know?"

"Leroy needed me. What had happened? Where's Leroy? Lucky said you'd gone into town to get him," Cassie said, standing in the doorway to the kitchen.

Edith began to tremble. Panic over Leroy was a cork in her throat. She tried to clear it.

Darwin stepped forward. "Silas has stolen Leroy on some bogus charge of abandonment and neglect. The woman from the Children's Home was involved and there's a whole pile of legal paperwork on Edith's desk."

Cassie nodded. "I saw the papers. Explain them to me." The two women head off to the office, shutting the door.

As Edith closed the door, Cassie wheeled on her. "First the fire and now this. You were supposed to keep my boy safe."

Edith glared at Cassie, and then the defiance flickered and was gone, replaced by a woman who loved Leroy.

She collapsed into herself and said in a hoarse whisper. "It was Silas. I thought they had backed off now that Goodtimes was closed. Oh, Cassie, I am so sorry. What have I done?" The anguish in her eyes was deep.

"You were foolish. Mr. Preacher-Man doesn't want Goodtimes. He doesn't even want you. He wants Leroy. I thought you understood that." Cassie continued to shake her head. "This is not good, *ah-ma-chamee*. I told you to keep Leroy safe and away from the Preacher-Man."

"I don't understand. Why would he want Leroy so much?"

"Because Leroy is his son."

Edith gasps. "Oh my God, no. That's not possible." Edith's eyes blazed. "Cassie, Silas is the leader of the Wharf Rats."

Now, Cassie is the one in shock. "He is one of the pirates?"

Edith glowered. "The Boss."

Cassie collapsed into the chair, a blank look on her face. "How did I not see that?"

Edith sank to the edge of the desk, also confused. "How he could be Leroy's father?"

Cassie shivered then took a deep breath. "This has been with me for ten years. Few know, fewer still remember. It doesn't go beyond this room. Understand?"

Pale, Edith nodded.

"My people are from the Everglades. I had a sister, Cissy. We grew up there, paddling the streams and creeks, hunting and fishing in the channels. We also grew up in Coconut Grove. The wrong side of the tracks for sure, but we lived in a house and slept in a bed. I worked cleaning fish at the fish market and reading the cards.

"Cissy worked as the housekeeper for the church's pastor. The one before Brother Silas. He was a crotchety old man and I don't think anyone was sad to see him retire. If only we had known what was coming next. Better the Devil you know than the one you don't as the saying goes.

"Brother Silas took over and moved into the manse and Cissy was smitten. She was young, like a deer with big brown eyes and a gentle soul. From the first day, I knew Silas was trouble. She hung on his every word, any kindness. And at first, he was kind. But the further she fell under his spell, the meaner he got. She stopped smiling. He made sure anything she did was wrong or not good enough. He was always finding fault, picking away at her like an old crow.

"She tried to make him happy, but he twisted everything. She grew small and her shine dimmed. When I saw her in town, she'd flinch and walk away. She stopped coming by the house. He cut her off from everyone in town. Cissy was like a prisoner—of fear. And then the inevitable happened. He got her pregnant. She didn't even tell us. For months she told no one, letting out her dresses, growing thinner, until she could disguise it no more.

"One day, he physically kicked her out. I found her bleeding, crawling toward our home by the docks. In a rage, he had beaten her, called her unclean, wanton, a harlot. She didn't even know what that word meant. The baby, Leroy, was born that night, and Cissy died the next morning."

"Oh my goodness." Edith sat there, shocked by the tale. "Brother Silas is Leroy's father."

"Leroy has no idea. Brother Silas railed at the funeral service, calling her all kinds of words that were nasty and vile. He asked me about the baby and I said the baby had died. He called sweet little Leroy 'a witch's spawn'. Was glad to hear he died. That night, I went to Cissy's grave with Leroy. We said goodbye and together we disappeared into the Everglades."

"And now Brother Silas has Leroy."

"Leroy is in terrible danger if Silas has figured it out. There is a deep wickedness in Silas. Something died inside him a long time ago, and it has rotted and festered."

"And now the Children's Home is in league with that monster."

"Not unusual for them to be aligned with a local pastor. God's lambs." Cassie snorted. "To the slaughter, more like."

"I've heard Brother Silas use those same words he called your sister when he talks about me. And the Wharf Rats have been singularly focused on running me out of town. You know they torched 'Gator Joe's."

"They are truly evil men," said Cassie.

"At every turn I've been blocked. And they attacked Darwin. It took me awhile to tie the Wharf Rat harassment to Brother Silas's abuse. We have to rescue Leroy from Brother Silas before he realizes who he is."

"I agree. I cannot be seen by the Children's Home, or Mr. Preacher-Man would know for sure who he is. But somehow, I will talk to Leroy. And you must speak with those in charge. Leroy is not alone, an orphan. He is Seminole, and his family want him home."

"We'll get him home. We need to deal with this on several different levels. First, straight up and legal. I'll call the lawyer and get this custody order overturned. Leroy was kidnapped, pure and simple."

"That will deal with the Children's Home and Miss White," said Cassie.

"Second, we need to deal with Silas. The church gives him a great deal of power in Coconut Grove. It'll be difficult."

"What about going after him as the Boss of the Wharf Rats?" Cassie asked.

"That's what I'm thinking. I'll call Mae Capone. She is a good person to have on our side, and brings her own kind of power to the situation."

They emerged about an hour later, and Darwin handed them both a cup of coffee.

Edith accepted hers gratefully, holding his eyes with her own. Fear. Rage. Despair. Revenge. All-out war on her face.

"The lawyer is going to call back. Mae is on her way."

Lucky approached, wringing his hands, his head bowed. "I sorry, Miz Edith. I did not know what to do. They had gun. She say she call sheriff and you go to jail. I figure you know what to do. So sorry."

Edith laid a hand on his shoulder, giving it a pat. "Lucky, it was going to happen. I should never have left him alone. We need to fight this, and together we'll find a way to bring Leroy home."

Darwin, Lucky, Edith, and Cassie huddled around a table in the barroom.

Cassie sipped her coffee. "While we wait for Mrs. Capone to arrive and the lawyer to call back, I'm going to talk to Leroy and get him away from them."

"I tried and they wouldn't let me in."

Cassie looked grim. "You tried to go through the front door, *ah-ma-chamee*. Seminole know different ways. And if all else fails..." Cassie tapped her forehead. "He got me here. When I have him, I will take him back to the camp. You can find us there."

"That would be best. The first place they'll look, once they realize he's missing, will be Goodtimes," said Edith.

Cassie put down her coffee and wrapped her arms around Edith. "You keep banging on the front door with your lawyers. In the meantime, I will see what I can do. Together, we would make sure Silas cannot hurt Leroy."

CHAPTER 57

Under the afternoon sun, at the car park at the top of the hill at Goodtimes, Cassie paused only a few moments to hug Edith goodbye before she turned toward Coconut Grove. She refused Edith's offer of a lift, preferring to head to town unseen, then watch the Children's Home from a distance.

The Children's Home was unfamiliar territory; a sense of their routine was needed before she could safely spirit Leroy away. There was no detailed plan, just a powerful yearning to snatch and hide him—much like the night she left Coconut Grove, Leroy swaddled in her arms as she said goodbye to Cissy in the graveyard.

"I swore no harm would ever come to you. I won't go back on my word to her."

Cassie settled herself behind a hedge near the Children's Home. The large, four-square frame building with a wrap-around veranda had plenty of windows. The ones on the second floor were probably the bedrooms. A line of washing flapped in the backyard. A lone car was parked on the street. A rusty swing on a tree branch swayed in the breeze. Not a child in sight.

Where would that boy be at? School? Inside?

About thirty minutes into her surveillance, a pair of girls in pigtails dawdled down the street toward the Home. They chatter back and forth, swinging a strap-load of books. Turning, they headed up the sidewalk to the veranda, and into the house.

School's out, I guess. Not that I'd know much about that. I never went, not even for a day. I wonder if Leroy is in school? And how he got on?

Shortly, a few boys came down the road: a couple of small ones, a big boy, and Leroy lagging behind. *He looks thinner and-and-and so all alone.*

397

Her hungry eyes feasted on the sight of him, her body leaned forward, ready to spring. *I could stand up right now and call to him. But the other boys would see. And tell. What happened to his head? He looks like he's been scrapping.* She retreated as they troop into the house.

As dusk falls, lights inside the house went on. None of the children have left the house. Smells of supper drifted over. Cassie waited and watched.

The bigger boy and Leroy came out the back door and wandered close to where she was hiding. They looked around and crouched behind a tree. Hidden from the main house, the boy pulled out a crumpled package of cigarettes and lit one. He took a long drag, coughed, and passed it to Leroy.

Cassie stared at Leroy, then closed her eyes, channeling all her sight toward the boy. Leroy talked and joked, taking a puff of the cigarette.

She tried again, failing each time. Red in the face from the exertion, she felt around for a small pebble and tossed it toward Leroy. It rolled near his feet, but he didn't notice; his attention was on his friend. The next one she tossed struck his shoe. He glanced down and around. Shrugging, he took another puff from the cigarette.

Those shoes must have cut off circulation to your brain, Koone. A third stone struck his shoe again; Leroy looked to the hedge. Cassie jiggled a branch.

Passing the cigarette back, Leroy said something to the boy and then sauntered along the road, picking up a stick and dragging it in the dirt behind him. The older boy finished his cigarette and went back inside the house.

At the slam of the door, Leroy headed to the hedge.

"Cassie. Cassie," he whispered. He threw himself onto her crouching body.

398

"Hush, Koone," she crooned, holding him tight in her arms, kissing the top of his head. She touched the scab on his forehead, still ugly and raw. "You okay?"

He pulled away. "It's nuthin'. Just something that happened." He looked away.

"Leroy. What happened?"

"I went to school today."

"I figured. What was that like?"

"I had to wear these," he wiggled his feet in the shoes.

"Ouch. They look heavy."

"They say we're supposed to wear them all the time." He unlaced them and slid his feet out. "Ahh, that's better."

"Do you need anything inside, or can we go?"

Leroy looked at Cassie, something flying across his face. He gently touched the scabbed cut.

"I have to stay." His voice was small. "Brother Silas said so."

Cassie grabbed his hand and locked her eyes with his. "Brother Silas is the reason we got to git. We'll be safe out in the 'glades. He can't find us there."

Leroy dropped his eyes, shaking his head. "I can't. I have to stay here. And they have papers."

"Those papers are false, Leroy. They lied in those papers. Miz Edith is getting a lawyer to have a judge throw them away."

Leroy had tears in his eyes. "It don't matter, Aunt Cassie. I have to stay." He pulled in a shuddering breath.

Cassie's arm tightened. "That's crazy, Koone. They kidnapped you. I'm here to take you back to the camp where you'll be safe."

Leroy sat silent, nestled in her lap. He was shaking.

"Leroy, honey, let's go. We'll be away before they know you're gone."

Leroy's trembling body leaned into her. "I gotta stay, Aunt Cassie." He gulped. "They say the sheriff will put Miz Edith in jail. And Brother Silas kept asking about where you were at. He's mean, I don't like him. He said you'll go to jail, too. I can't bear you to be locked up. It'd be my fault."

Cassie held him close. "Silas is bad, and I'll keep you safe. I always have He's just a man, not one of those monsters in your comicbooks. And Miz Edith has fancy lawyers to make sure she don't go to jail."

Leroy pulled away, shoving his feet back into his shoes. He yanked on the laces, tying them tight. "I don't want to go to the camp. Brother Silas will find you. And... and... and there's a baseball game at school tomorrow. I get to play, so I'm going to stay put."

Cassie pushed him to arm's length, so she could look him in the face. "Leroy, you're lying to me. You don't want to stay."

Leroy stared up at her, his eyes filled with tears. "Darwin said sometimes you gotta do stuff you don't want to do. Darwin's always looks out for Miz Edith. Now it's my job to look out for her, too. And I need to protect you. A man must do what a man must do."

A car approached then stopped in front of the house. Deputy Roy got out of the Sheriff's car, hitching his belt and heading up the sidewalk.

Leroy twisted away. "That's the law, Cassie. He's here to talk to me. He mustn't find you here. I gotta go."

"Leroy? I don't understand."

Leroy hugged her tight. "He's the law. He can put you and Miz Edith in jail."

Cassie hugged him back. "They'll never find us, Koone. We'll be safe."

"They said they'd use dogs."

Cassie snorted. "That's just silly, Leroy. There's too much water out there. Dogs wouldn't be able to find us."

Leroy shook his head. "They got guns, Cassie. They can hurt a person." He worried his scab, still sticky and smarting.

Cassie squeezed him tight, refusing to let go. "Come on, time's a wastin'."

Leroy pulled away. "You don't understand. You're not listening. Nobody ever listens to me. They find you and Miz Edith and hurt you or even worse. Lucky and his cousins will have to go back to China. Too man folks are going to get hurt if I don't stay. And it's not so bad. If I go to the camp, I'll have to stay hid. I'll have to stay in the 'glades forever. I'll never get to come out to town again, Cassie."

"But—"

Leroy jumped up and ran to the house. At the bottom of the steps he turned. Slowly his hand came up and then he dropped it. He turned and went inside.

CHAPTER 58

The next few days passed in a blur as Edith marshaled her troops. Not a moment passed when she didn't feel the weight of what Leroy was dealing with; Cassie had told her about the jail threat and Leroy's unwillingness to put anyone at risk by leaving the Home.

Edith took Mae's advice to use the lawyer to fight the authorities. The call with the governor went well. He assured her he could fix it so that the sheriff's department continued to buy into the cover story that Goodtimes was a café. That would solve the problem about the illegal liquor.

"And what about the kidnapping charges?"

"I won't accuse Daddy Fagg and the Children's Home of kidnapping, Edith. And certainly not Brother Silas. I won't open up that can of worms, even for Mae Capone," the governor said.

"But I have a note from his guardian that said he can live at Goodtimes."

"That's fine and good for the child labor law. No one would deprive a single mother of a source of livelihood. But she's going to have to come forward and assert her guardianship rights."

Edith reigned in her frustration, trying to explain. "I told you, the aunt is an odd duck. To prove guardianship in court, she'd have to publicly disclose who Leroy's mother was, and she's afraid of the father and what he might do, or the claim he could have on Leroy."

"It's a dilemma, for sure Mrs. Duffy. As I said, the child labor and liquor issues are wrapped up. Regarding the custody issue, you're on your own. The boy's out of the system in less than a year, anyway. And they will look after him. I hear very good things about that Children's Home."

"Surely you can talk to the man that runs it, Mr. Fagg? Tell him to let Leroy go."

"Daddy Fagg has been working closely with the state to pull together an aggressive program to deal with the crisis with abandoned children. This depression has caused a lot of grief for families. I can't alienate such a well-connected advocate for the sake of one small boy. The public love him."

"I'm not suggesting that you get rid of the man, just talk to him."

"I'll see what I can do, but I won't make any promises."

"Look, Governor. I made a very generous donation to your election campaign because you were going to get Leroy back, and I'm rethinking that decision. Leroy's not here and that was the deal."

Edith slammed the telephone receiver down. Fuming, she headed to the dock for a talk with Darwin. She found Lucky there with him.

"I can try talking to Cassie again. Maybe some kind of court document would help with the Children's Home. Or maybe I could talk to Mildred White?"

"What would that accomplish?"

"She crazy lady, Miz Edith. No right in the head." Muttering under his breath in Cantonese, Lucky headed back up the path to Goodtimes.

Darwin sat down on the edge of the dock. He slipped off his shoes and, with bare feet dangling in the water, patted the spot beside him. "Join me?"

Edith plunked down beside him, wrapping her arms around her legs and resting her chin on her knees, staring out to sea. "I agree it's a long shot. From what I've seen of her, she's not interested in bending rules, especially for the likes of us here at Goodtimes."

Darwin heaved a sigh and faced her. "Everything we could do, we've done, Edith. Sometimes, you have to stop pushing."

403

"Stop pushing? You mean gave up on Leroy?"

"No, I'm not saying that. But it sounds like he's made his choice. Maybe it's time for you to make a different choice, too."

Dazed, Edith turned to really look at Darwin. Her eyes began to clear. "You can't possibly mean…"

"Yes. As hard as it was to hear. He'll be in school. He'll have boys his own age to play with. It's only a year. And with Leroy settled at the Children's Home we'd have a chance to go back to our old ways and reopen Goodtimes. Interested in at least thinking about getting your club open again?" Darwin asked.

Edith sucked in her breath, shocked. "That would be foolish. It reinforces what the folks at the Children's Home think. It won't matter what story the governor has cooked up with the sheriff's department, everyone in town would know that we've reopened a blind-tiger."

Darwin put his arm around her. "I'm not saying give up on Leroy. I'm only suggesting that we can wait. The lawyers take time. Getting Cassie to come forward will take time. Let's go on with our lives. Like you said, he's going to be back home in less than a year."

She looked at him with hurt in her eyes. "I can't give up on trying to bring Leroy home."

"You need to put your energy into moving forward, Edith. It's time to move on. I know it hurts to let go, but sometimes it hurts more to hang on."

She pulled away, flushed and frowning, and got to her feet. "I don't like to hear that kind of talk, Darwin. Leroy's coming home and that's all there is to it. Even if I have to drag Cassie out of the swamp myself. Nobody steals from me, and that's what they've done. Snuck in and stole him away."

Darwin gave her a long look and reached for his shoes as he stood beside her. "I've got to go into town. We may not be open, but we've still got to feed ourselves. Lucky said he's running short. Why don't you think about it some more and we can talk tonight, before I head out on the *Marianne*?"

"I'll go into town. Gave me the list. I need to get out of here for a while."

By late afternoon, Edith was driving toward Coconut Grove. *What's got into Darwin? Thinking I should put my energies into moving on?* The mangrove trees flashing by along the side of the road might as well have been invisible. Edith was consumed with thoughts of Leroy.

Everything keeps circling back to Brother Silas. He can't act against me as the boss of the Wharf Rats, but on this matter, he has all the power as a pastor of the church. He'll poison their ears with lies about me and about Goodtimes. I've got to get Cassie to come forward. I just can't see any other way.

A stop for mail and a community update from Jasper at the post office, filling the truck with gas, loading groceries into the back of the truck, and her errands were complete.

I'm going to stop by the mercantile. Maybe I'll pick up a few comicbooks and drop them off at the Children's Home, just in case they let me talk to Leroy.

Inside the store was cool and dark compared to being outside in the midday sun. It took a few moments for her eyes to adjust.

Edith scanned the shelves, picking up the items that Lucky needed. Suddenly, her heart skipped a beat. Jay and Leroy were checking out comics. She stepped behind a display of canned goods, wanting to prolong her opportunity to simply watch him.

He does look happy. And he's with Jay. Mrs. Carmichael must have had a change of heart and is letting them play together again... now that he's away from my supposed evil influence.

Jay puts the comicbook back and threw his arm around Leroy. "Come on. Ma will be waiting with supper if we don't get a move on.

We'll pick it up next week after collections day. I'll have some money then."

Supper? Could Leroy have moved from the Children's Home already? To the Carmichael's? Look at those shoes. And a school bag. I guess they convinced him a classroom isn't such a bad thing.

Leroy's fingers lingered on the comicbook he'd been reading, then he followed Jay out of the store. Edith's eyes never left him and she moved to the window to watch him walk down the street.

She quickly plunked down the money for the comic he'd put back, and hurried out of the store. "Leroy," she called. The boys were at the end of the next street. She started to run. "Leroy."

* * * *

Leroy turned and his face broke open in a wide, happy smile. "Miz Edith!" He ran into her arms and buried his face in her shoulder.

Edith touched his hair, smelling his good boy smells. "Oh, I have missed you."

"Me, too. Miz Edith. And Darwin and Lucky and the *Rex*. I miss everything." He stepped back, looking around. "Is it okay for you to be in town? I mean, is it safe? Shouldn't Darwin be with you or something?"

"Don't be silly. Here, I bought this for you," she said, handing him the comic.

"Gee, thanks. This is swell."

I won't let them put you in jail, Miz Edith. I'll do everything I can to keep you and Aunt Cassie safe. He gave her another tight squeeze.

"Oh my goodness, your forehead—Lucky told me—it's so big. Oh, Leroy, I'm so sorry. We're working on it all. Brother Silas is to blame for all this trouble and we'll get you out of it."

"It's scabbing over now. Just a little cut from me being clumsy and felling against the counter."

"That's not how Lucky tells it."

"Lucky sometimes gets confused," said Leroy, fingers crossed behind his back.

"Fine. But how are you? Really?"

Leroy rubbed gently at the fresh scab on his head, thinking about Brother Silas's gun. And his threats.

"I'm okay." *I wish I could come home.*

"And school?" Edith asked, tugging on the strap of the schoolbag.

Leroy shrugged. "I guess sitting in straight rows isn't as bad as I thought."

Edith laughed and smoothed his hair.

Leroy scuffed the toe of his shoe against the sidewalk.

"And look at you, wearing shoes. How's that feel?"

"It's okay. Sometimes they pinch, but I gotta keep wearing them."

"Are they looking after you at the Children's Home?"

"They got too many kids at the Home. We was stacked like cord wood, Mrs. Carmichael said. She said I could live with them on account of Jay and me being friends and all. I get to sleep on the porch upstairs. It's got screens so the bugs don't get in." *See, that made you smile.*

407

Edith looked over at Jay, waiting at the corner. Her breath caught. "Everything has happened so fast, Leroy. But I'm glad Mrs. Carmichael is caring for you. It's very generous of them to open their home to you."

"It's kinda neat. I got a pretend-mother and a father and brothers. My first real family. No dog or sister though." *I wish I could go home.*

Edith bowed her head.

"I didn't mean it that way," Leroy said. *Oh, oh. I've hurt her feelings.* "She told me she thinks you got moxie. What does that mean? Is that like the Babylonian horse?"

Edith kissed his forehead next to the healing cut. "No, sweetie. It means she likes me."

"Leroy, we gotta get going. We're going to be late for supper and you know what Ma's like." Jay hopped from one foot to the other.

Leroy looked past Jay, seeing the church spire looming above roofs of nearby buildings. He gulpped. "I gotta go. And so do you."

His little smile was a salve for her broken heart. Her own smile was tremulous, too. "You scoot, then. And enjoy your comicbook. I'll come by the Carmichael's to visit you."

Leroy hugged her again. "Tell Aunt Cassie about me living with Jay? And let Darwin know that I'm growing up, okay? That I'm doing what a man must do, just like he taught me."

"I will, sweetie. He misses you. And so does Lucky."

"You'll be able to open up Goodtimes again now that I'm not there. Right?" *It was all my fault it had to close. I wish I could go home. Which home? I used to have two and now I got none.*

"Oh, Leroy, you're worth more to me than Goodtimes. I know you're scared. I know you're worried about us, but you don't need to be. You're a child. The grownups around you have to be responsible, and we are. We're doing everything to make sure you can come home. We're working on it, but it's taking longer than I thought."

Leroy pulled away, shaking his head.

"Don't you want to come home, Leroy?" Edith looked hurt and confused.

Oh, I do. But I gotta keep you and Aunt Cassie safe. "I'm okay, Miz Edith. I'm in school and get to live with Jay and play baseball and stuff. Really, I'm okay." *Why won't she listen? I don't want her to go to jail. I don't want her to have to keep Goodtimes closed. I can't let them ship Lucky off back to China.*

Leroy pushed her away. "I gotta go now, Miz Edith." His lip trembled. "Say hi to Darwin and Lucky for me, okay?"

Edith pulled him back for one last hug. "All right. If that's what you want. We all miss you, but I'm glad you're happy. And Leroy?" He stopped squirming to get away.

"Yeah, Miz Edith?"

"I love you, Leroy."

Leroy tightens his arms around her. "I love you, too, Miz Edith. And I gotta keep you safe."

With a sob, Leroy unwraps himself and headed in Jay's direction. After he crossed the street he turned to wave, but her back was to him. Her truck was blurry due to his tears, but he could see her shoulders shaking.

Is she crying? Naw, Miz Edith never cries.

CHAPTER 59

Low, rolling thunder woke Edith. At first, she was unsure of whether she was awake or still caught in troubled sleep. Another stormy rumble pulled her wider awake. She lay in bed, snuggled warm and cozy beneath her covers, and listened to the rainstorm. The rain pelted down on the balcony outside the open French doors.

Leroy seemed happy. It's hard to fight against something when it doesn't appear to be a threat any longer. Am I being shellfish insisting Leory be here with me? The Carmichael's are nice people. They'll look after him.

Tears escaped from her closed eyes.

Why does doing right by the boy have to hurt so much? Cassie and I should stop fighting this. For sure, Leory doesn't need any more conflict in his life. And I never could get him to go to school, so that's a good thing.

The rumbling moved further inland.

Maybe I'll just stay here a bit longer. Sun will be up soon, dragging me into a new day that I do not want to start.

Edith flipped the pillow over to the fresh side and burrowed in. She pulled the bleak sorrow up to her chin, and soon she was asleep again.

A tapping at her door woke her. The room was filled with sunshine.

Goodness. Look at the light. What time is it?

"Miz Edith?" A louder knock. Lucky's voice.

She sat up in bed, pulling the covers close. "Yes, what is it?"

The door opened a crack, but Lucky didn't even poke his head around the corner. "Lady downstairs. Leroy's aunt. Wants to see you."

410

"Tell her I'll be right down. Pour her some coffee, please."

Edith found Cassie sitting on the veranda with a cup of coffee and a muffin just out of the oven.

"I could get used to this. It'd be like living in a fancy hotel," Cassie said, greeting Edith with a smile. Her pale face and the dark circles under her eyes told a different story.

"Good morning, Cassie. Has something else happened?" Edith pulled a wicker chair close to Cassie.

"Coffee, Miz Edith?" Lucky asked.

"Yes, please. And one of those muffins too, please."

"The cards say we need to talk, and I figured I'd save you the walk through the 'glades to my place." She lifted her coffee cup in salute. "And no muffins there."

Edith relaxed into her chair and noticed the quality of the day for the first time. There was a sparkling freshness from the overnight rain. "You must have walked through the rain last night to get here," Edith said, taking her coffee from Lucky.

"It was a bit damp, for sure. But when the cards tell you to move, you gotta move."

A silence settled between the two women. So much to say and so difficult to hear.

"So, what did the cards say?" Edith asked.

Cassie sighed deeply. "Nothing that I could understand, so I'm hoping, if we put our heads together, I can figure it out. There were only happy cards for Leroy. I went and found him. Talked to him outside of that place he's living in. Didn't want to come with me. Said he wanted to play baseball, instead." She looked to Edith, her eyes full of unshed tears. "He doesn't really think baseball is more important than me, does he? Is it wrong to feel bad that he seems happy?"

Hearing the echo of her own earlier thoughts, Edith got up and wrapped her arms around Cassie's shoulders. She felt Cassie begin to cry. All the sorrow of seeing Leroy yesterday bubbled up and out of Edith and she also wept.

"I know. I saw him, too. It felt like we were saying goodbye. You know that he's not at the Children's Home anymore? The Carmichael's have taken him in. He told me straight out that he wanted to stay with them."

The two women held each other close, joined by the circle of Edith's arms and their shared grief.

Eventually, Cassie pulled away and used the edge of her long skirt to wipe at her face. Edith returned to her chair, wiping her eyes with a handkerchief.

"Who are they?"

"Nice people. I know the mother a little. Their boy, Jay, is Leroy's best friend. He seems happy there. He calls them his pretend family."

Cassie tried to smile through the tears still wet on her face. "That boy was always hungry for family. I tried to do my best, but I guess it wasn't good enough."

"Don't say that, Cassie. You are Leroy's family and he adores you. He talks about you all the time. He's just making the best of a bad situation."

Cassie nodded. "Maybe like we should be doing, too?" She grabbed Edith's hand and squeezed. "You think maybe Leroy not having his own mama raise him, and then spending that time with you, means that the idea of family isn't as important to him as it is for you and me? You think those happy cards mean we should let Leroy be?"

Edith patted Cassie's hand before pulling her own away. "He's happy. He's in school. He has friends to play with. He's getting a chance to be a regular kid."

"These last few years he was always yapping about living in town. He started to get antsy and bored out in the 'glades. It was the reason I let him stay with you. And it was even worse when he came to stay while you were in Nassau. Nothing would do. He was cranky and moody; I was almost glad to see him high-tail it back to you. Maybe If I'd done a better job, or been stronger and stood up to Mr. Preacher-Man, things would had been different. Maybe I shoulda taken him away from here."

Cassie stared into her coffee, brooding over what ifs and could have beens.

"Sometimes love makes us blind, Cassie. I made lots of mistakes with Leroy, too. I should have told him I loved him. And I should have never left him behind that night. I didn't keep him safe."

"Regret is bitter, ain't it? It's always about the things we didn't do instead of the things we did. Maybe we should learn from him? Leroy is content. He's finding his place," Cassie said.

"A place without us? He gave us up so easily, Cassie." Edith choked back a sob. "What do you think we should do?"

"What we've been doing. Trying to do the right thing by the boy. The tug of war between us and the powers that be must have been hard on him." Cassie stared out at the water. "And he was wearing shoes."

"It's good that he's in school," Edith said, following her gaze. Gulls were circling, small moving bits of gray against the white puffy clouds in an azure blue sky.

"He'll be twelve on his next birthday. Then he can decide on his own what he wants to do," Cassie said.

"If he wants to keep living in town and going to school, we could work something out. I could get a little place there." Edith sipped her coffee.

"We could live together. You could run Goodtimes and I could stay with him." Cassie said, nodding.

"What a strange family we would be. We could go to baseball games and watch him play." Edith smiled at the thought.

"And school. We could meet with the teachers at the end of the year. Sign report cards and notes about school trips. That's what you do, isn't it?"

"I haven't the foggiest." Edith chuckled. "I guess I'll keep on with the Homemakers' Guild. Like the other mothers."

Cassie turned to Edith with a shaky grin. "Better you than me."

Edith gripped Cassie's hand, searching her face. "I guess it's decided then? That we'll respect Leroy's wishes and let him stay with the Carmichael's. At least until he's twelve?"

Cassie raised her shoulders in a shrug. "If that's what he wants."

"It's going to hurt," Edith said, her voice quiet.

"It already does." Cassie gripped her hand. "You know, a while back I read about you having a breakthrough. Didn't really understand it at the time, thought maybe it had something to do with Goodtimes."

"A breakthrough? I don't understand, either."

"This is the first time I ever saw you willing to gave something up, *ah-ma-chamee*. To put someone else's happiness ahead of your own."

"I always put other people ahead of myself, Cassie. I'm a very kind and generous person."

Cassie merely smiled.

"What?"

"I imagine it will be a relief to get Goodtimes back open," Cassie said with a knowing look.

Edith bristled. "I would never put this place ahead of Leroy."

"All is good, *ah-ma-chamee*. I know that's not the reason why you were agreeing to let Leroy be. This war between us and Coconut Grove is too hard on the boy. You've made the wise decision."

"As long as you know that I would have kept on fighting to bring him home if I had had any encouragement from Leroy."

"I know, *ah-ma-chamee*. But there's no standing still. Time moves forward and so must we."

"What about Brother Silas?" Edith asked.

A grim silence settled. Lucky came out with more coffee.

"Of course. Silas! I've been blind. Silas is the issue," said Cassie. "Just listen to us. Sulking about how Leroy's given us up. He hasn't. He's afraid. He didn't want you in jail or me locked up either. He doesn't want to play baseball; he wants to come home. But he knows we're all playing with fire. He's being strong trying to protect us."

"Home. Which home? And which home is the safest? Most likely the Carmichael's at this point. Oh, Cassie, Silas won't give up trying to tear me down, to hurt me. He's behind everything evil."

"At some point, we'll have to deal with him," Cassie said. "To keep Leroy safe."

"And as a bit of payback. For all the trouble he's caused. And all the hurt."

Cassie nodded.

"My late husband, Mickey, would say that if we hit him it needs to be hard enough so he won't get up."

Cassie nodded again. "I could hit him that hard."

Edith nodded grimly. "So could I."

415

Cassie raised her coffee mug in a toast, and Edith tapped it with her own. "I can see it working out. Leroy gets a new life and we get revenge."

CHAPTER 60

On Sunday, the children were scrubbed and their shoes shined. "Get a move on, boys. We don't want to be late for church," Mary Carmichael said, a stern inspector.

Leroy was excited and nervous about church. He'd never been, and neither Edith nor Cassie ever had much good to say about it. But he did like being included in the family outing. He was now one of the 'boys' that needed to get a move on.

The Carmichaels and Leroy walked to church along the shady streets of Coconut Grove, Mr. and Mrs. Carmichael in the lead, their augmented brood trailing behind.

Mary glanced behind her and saw Jay and Leroy's heads close together. She took her husband's arm and leaned close. "I'm worried about Leroy, Alvin. He's not been himself these past few days."

"It's early days. He's hardly been here five minutes. I'm sure it's nothing. It must be difficult, settling into a new routine, getting used to new people. Give him time."

"I suppose so. But he was fine when he first came. A joy, really. No, something's on his mind."

Alvin patted his wife's hand. "Mary, you're making too much of it. Let the boy be. If you're worried, talk to Jay. He'll know if there's anything bothering Leroy."

* * * *

"What's it like? This church thing? What'll I have to do?" Leroy whispered to Jay.

"Stand up and sit down. Just watch me. No laughing. No talking. No napping. No squirming. You sit quiet and pay attention. At least that's what you're supposed to do. If Brother Silas catches you napping you're done for."

"I don't like Brother Silas. He's creepy."

"Nobody does. Sometimes we make spitballs from the pages in the hymnal and flick them. Although Gerald got caught once and there was holy hell to pay. So if you do that, be careful."

"He has a gun. I saw it." Leroy whispered, casting a nervous glance at the Carmichael parents.

Jay was wide-eyed. "No way. He's the preacher. You're lying."

"Nope. He pulled it on me the night they took me away." Leroy's bravado covers the chill the memory brings.

"Wow. Does my mother know?"

Leroy looked alarmed. "No, nobody but you knows. And you can't tell." Leroy squeezed his eyes shut, trying to block out the memory of Lucky backed up against the wall, the feel of the gun barrel, the taste of blood running down his face from the gash, the glint in Brother Silas's eye when he was threatening Cassie and Miz Edith. He took a breath, shaking his head to clear it. "Don't say nuthin to nobody. They'll do something bad to Miz Edith if anybody finds out."

Jay's face had confusion written all over it. "I don't get it. You mean the deputy? My ma said what's she's doing out there at the blind-tiger is illegal. But she's closed, right? Why would Deputy Purvis do something to Mrs. Duffy? Brother Silas is the one with the gun."

Leroy shrugged. "It ain't the law that's the problem. Bad stuff happens when Brother Silas is around. And the law don't seem to mean much where he's concerned."

The boys walked along, taking turns kicking a round, black stone down the sidewalk.

"If you didn't have to go to church, what did you do on Sundays?" Jay asked.

"Sundays were the best. With Cassie, we'd go out in the canoe, paddle along creeks and marshes, watch the birds. Sometimes I'd go hunting. And at Miz Edith's, chances were me and Darwin would be fishing or, if Darwin were sleeping, I camp out on the dock with a good book until he woke up. Sundays were lazy days."

"That sounds swell. Sure beats sitting in church," Jay said.

Mary Carmichael turned and gestures for the boys to hurry up. "Jay. Leroy. You're dawdling. Walk faster, please. We don't want to be late."

Leroy looked around the unfamiliar building as they filed in and found a place to sit. The stained glass, the hard pews, all the people. So many people. First school. Then church. He sat, his legs swinging so that his shoes knocked the pew in front.

"Stop that, Leroy," Mrs. Carmichael said, laying her hand on his knee. She handed him a hymnal. "You'll need this for the service. The numbers of the hymns are printed on the board over there."

The arrival of Brother Silas was the moment Leroy'd been dreading. Face to face with the Devil himself. *He's got this whole town fooled, but he can't fool me.* He sucked in his breath, prepared to flee, but was shocked when Brother Silas ignored him.

As Brother Silas preached, Leroy imagined the revenge he'd have on the way the Preacher-Man treated his Aunt Cassie and Miz Edith. Sometimes he pulled a gun like a cowboy, and sometimes it was a ray gun like Buck Rodgers. Sometimes he tied him up and left him for alligators to eat. The words from the pulpit droned on.

Something in Brother Silas's sermon caught Leroy's ear. "Be strong enough to stand alone."

Yup, I can do this. I ain't no chicken.

"Be yourself enough to stand apart."

Sheesh, what the heck does that mean? Preacher's talk, I guess.

"But be wise enough to stand together when the time comes."

The flash of brilliance that lights Leroy could have been sunlight through the stained-glass. *When the time comes.*

Leroy squirmed, thoughts of revenge making his heart pound. *When the time comes.* He stood when everyone else stood, tried to sing but didn't know the tune, sat, knelt, and forced clenched fists to open in prayer.

Freedom at last as they all filed out; captivity made it so much sweeter. Leroy leaped off the church step and dashed after the other children as Mary Carmichael joined a clutch of older women on the grass outside.

* * * *

"You've done wonders, Mary. He's like all the other children," Agnes said.

Mary gave her an arched look. "Leroy has beautiful manners. And has quite a sharp mind. He's been pestering Alvin to show him how to fix motors, something none of the other boys seem to care about."

"You are an angel for taking him in. I don't know too many others who would have had a boy from that background living with them," Mavis Saunders said, giving Agnes a knowing look.

"And thank goodness the Carmichael's offer came in when it did. The Children's Home was overflowing with so many children abandoned while their parents look for work. This depression is so hard on families," Mildred White said.

"We were glad to do it. As soon as I heard Leroy was at the Home, I rushed over. I felt we should stand by him. He deserves to have a secure home life. No disrespect, Mildred. He's a fine boy and besides, when you've got the brood I do, one more at the table takes no extra effort," Mary said, giving Mildred a grateful smile for her support.

"It's fortunate that Brother Silas has taken such an interest in the boy," Mavis Saunders said, her frown following Leroy's laughing, darting body.

"They share a very similar upbringing. Brother Silas knows what it's like to be a little boy left in another's charge," Mildred White said. "He's often involved in our cases; the Lord's teachings are often a comfort for the children."

"Such a good man. Close to God," Agnes said.

Mildred gave a little shudder. "Brother Silas has been under a great deal of strain, not acting like himself at all."

"Really? I hadn't noticed," Mavis said. Her thin lips were held tightly in disapproval as the boys whooped and hollered playing some game on the front lawn of the church. "Too much noise."

"I feel like we've saved Leroy's soul," Agnes said. "He'll be grateful we rescued him when he's older and can understand the circumstances. Thank goodness for Brother Silas's help. And here he comes."

"Morning, Sisters."

"Good morning, Brother Silas." Mavis, Mary, and Agnes parrot in unison.

"How are your charges this morning, Sister Mildred?"

Mildred tried to hide a flinch. "Full of energy, as you can see, Brother Silas. I'm sorry if they caused a problem in church this morning."

"And you, Sister Mary? Leroy seems to be fitting in nicely."

Mary smiled at her boys' energy.

Brother Silas turned back to Mildred. "Have you managed to locate his family?"

"No. Senior officials at our head office are looking for his guardian. An aunt signed the original paperwork that let him stay at Goodtimes. She's a Seminole by the name of Cassandra Osceola. But they're not having much luck. She's a recluse and lives in the Everglades."

Startled, Brother Silas gawked at Mildred. "Osceola, you say? We must find this aunt. This Cassandra woman."

His intensity pushed Mildred back a step. "We're trying, Brother Silas, but it's proving difficult. It's like she's disappeared."

"Like a phantom." He took another step toward her. "His natural mother is deceased?"

Concerned, Mary stepped between Mildred and Brother Silas. "Yes, in childbirth, poor thing. Leroy said he never knew her."

"And his father?" He choked out the words.

"Why, Brother Silas," said Mildred. "You look as if you've just seen a ghost."

"Brother Silas, are you well?" Mary asked, laying a tentative hand on his arm. He shook her off.

"He looks about ten. When is his birthday?" Brother Silas clutched Mary's arm.

Alarmed, she tried to pull away. "Just turned eleven. In July."

"Impossible." Brother Silas dropped Mary's arm, turning to watch Leroy tag a boy and then run off, being chased by another. "Born in July 1921 to a Seminole mother who died." There's a faraway look in his eye.

"I don't know if the mother was Native American, but the aunt is," Mildred said, peering at him closely.

Mary's mother's intuition makes her turn to watch Jay, Leroy and the other children play. "Leroy said his mother died and his father ran off. So sad, really. He's such a bright boy."

Brother Silas's eyes devour Leroy as he scampered about with the other children. He nodded solemnly. "I imagine he is. Blood does tell out in the end."

CHAPTER 61

Leroy was curled at one end of the couch and Jay at the other, each with a nose buried in a comicbook. The rain was keeping them inside, or maybe it was the delicious smells coming from the kitchen.

Mary Carmichael came through the living room to answer the knock at the door, wiping her hands on her apron.

"Brother Silas. What a lovely surprise. Won't you come in?"

Brother Silas smiled at Mary and looked past her to Leroy who had put down his comicbook and looked ready to dash away. "Good afternoon, Leroy. I wanted to stop by and see how you were settling in."

Leroy's eyes were wide with panic as they fixed on Mary. He inched closer to Jay.

"It's all right, Leroy. Jay, honey, why don't you go upstairs and finish your book there? Brother Silas is just here for a visit with Leroy."

Jay looked between the adults and Leroy.

"Scoot now," Mary said firmly.

Once past Brother Silas, Jay shot Leroy one more look and trudged upstairs.

"Why don't I go get some lemonade and let you two chat."

"I'll get it for you," Leroy said, leaping up.

"No, I can manage. I think Brother Silas wants to talk to you, Leroy." The kitchen door swings shut behind her.

"Shall we sit?" Brother Silas said, perching on the couch and patting the seat beside him. Leroy chose the chair furthest from the couch.

"How are you settling in with the Carmichaels, Leroy?"

Leroy glared at Brother Silas. "You were mean to me at Goodtimes. You had a gun. And I remember you were nasty to Aunt Cassie. And nasty to Miz Edith, too. I don't think I like you very much. And... And... Your eyes. I've seen frogs with nicer."

Brother Silas leaned back, giving Leroy a long look. "You are a very rude boy. Not surprising I guess. I shouldn't expect much, given your upbringing in the wilderness by a Seminole woman."

Leroy crossed his arms over his chest and focused on something outside the window.

"As to my eyes... The Lord says not to judge by looks—I have a touch of hay fever."

"Aunt Cassie taught me manners. I just don't need to use them on people like you."

Silas raises an eyebrow, but otherwise there was no reaction.

Leroy refused to look at Brother Silas.

"You must had learned this disrespect from Edith Duffy. She has quite an attitude and I see you've picked it up."

"Stop talking about Miz Edith like that." Leroy jumped up, fists raised.

"Or what, scamp? You'll push me down?" Brother Silas said with a sneer.

"See, you do remember that day. And maybe I will. If Miz Edith could do it, so could I."

"Your Miz Edith is a wicked woman, Leroy. I see we got you away from her in the nick of time. I only hope it's not too late."

"She's not wicked. She's swell. You're the wicked one."

425

Silas leaned forward, eyes narrow, and hissed. "Sit down, boy. Before I have to come over there and teach you some manners."

Leroy gave him an angry stare. "Mrs. Carmichael is coming back and I'll tell on you."

"And who would she believe? Her pastor or a pathetic little foster runt like you?"

The clock ticks as the two combatants lock glares, Leroy ready to fight, fists tight against him.

When Mary entered with a heavily laden tray, Leroy jumped to help.

"Thank you, Leroy. And how are you getting along in here?"

"We're just getting to know each other a little," Brother Silas said, a gentle smile at Leroy. "And how is school? Not too far behind the other children in terms of studies?" Brother Silas asked Mary.

"He's very strong in math and reading comprehension. Some of the other subjects like science and geography he's struggling to catch up with. Did Brother Silas tell you he collects stamps?" she said to Leroy. "Leroy has some stamps, too. They help him with world geography."

"Really? What an admirable hobby. What stamps are you collecting?"

Leroy sipped his lemonade.

"Leroy? Brother Silas asked you a question," Mary said.

"China," Leroy mumbled, pulling a chair close to where Mary was sitting.

"You're lucky. I only have a few stamps from China. How do you get yours?"

With a nudge from Mary Carmichael, he muttered "Lucky gets letters from home."

"Lucky is Mrs. Duffy's cook," Mary said.

"Ah, indeed. Would you like to see my stamps some time, Leroy? I have them from all over the world and some of them are very old."

Leroy gave Silas a hard look, the chin back out. "No."

"Leroy," Mary said, aghast. "My apologies, Brother Silas. I don't know what's got into him."

Brother Silas leaned forward, smiling his church smile. "That's all right, Sister Mary, I think I do. I know how difficult a time this is for Leroy." He turned to face Leroy who immediately looked away. "Did Mrs. Carmichael tell you that my mother and father left me with my grandmother when I was a small boy? I grew up without them."

Leroy shrugged, back to staring out the window.

"Yes, it was hard. Learning to live without them. I was very lonely growing up. And my grandmother wasn't as nice as Mrs. Carmichael. I missed my mother and father a lot."

Leroy continued to stare out the window. The ticking clock emphasized the awkward silences.

"Mrs. Carmichael tells me you like to read, Leroy. Do you have a favorite book?"

Leroy shrugged.

"Come, Leroy. Brother Silas asked you a question." Mary patted him on the knee.

"Comicbooks. I like comicbooks."

"I have a book of Bible stories you might like. I'll bring it with me the next time I come. Would you like that?"

Leroy shrugged.

"That's very kind, Brother Silas," Mary said.

"Mrs. Carmichael, can I go outside with Jay now and play? Please?" Leroy looked at her, pleading.

"Leroy, I don't think—"

"That's all right, Sister Mary. Let the boy go play. I must be off as well," Brother Silas said, checking his watch. "I'll come round again in a few days with that book. And maybe I'll bring one of my stamp albums."

"Thank you, Mrs. Carmichael," Leroy said, dashing up the stairs to get Jay.

"Leroy, come back downstairs and say goodbye to Brother Silas."

Leroy shouted down the stairs. "No. I won't and he can't make me."

CHAPTER 62

It was Saturday night at Goodtimes and the place was rocking. The musicians out of Miami, who've been on a break, come back onstage and launch into a crowd favorite.

Darwin glanced at the long lineup at the bar. *Edith's always thumbing her nose at fate.* He stifled a yawn. *I'd better switch to coffee or I'll never make it out to the Row.*

Billy Shaw and Clancy Middleton were off on another story about something to do with engineering. Darwin's eyes grew heavy and his head nodded.

"Hey, we're not boring you, are we?" Billy said, giving him a friendly shove.

"What? I must had nodded off. Sorry. I'm going to go and grab a coffee. Can I get you anything while I'm up?"

"Nah, we're good. Say, Clancy, what do you think of the Packard 1A-2500. Do you think it beats the Liberty?"

Darwin moved off, shaking his head and chuckling. *Gee, I hope I don't sound like that when I'm talking about boats.*

"Hey, McKenzie. Come 'ere and I'll buy you a beer." Harley Andrews was waving at him. Weaving would be a better description. He almost fell off his chair.

"Hey sport, maybe you've had enough beer tonight?"

Harley stood, his chair crashing backwards and threw his arm around Darwin. "Opps," he said, looking behind him. "Sorry. Whad did you say?" He said, squinting at Darwin.

"I think you've had enough."

"'Nuff beer? Never. I could drink this place dry single-handed. Miz Edith, a couple of beers for me and my buddy."

Darwin caught Edith's eye as she stood behind the bar and gave his head a small shake.

"You bet, Harley. I'll be right there," she said, giving Darwin a wink.

"You heard the lady, have a seat and she'll bring them over," Darwin said, unwrapping the arm from around his neck. He picked up Harley's chair from the floor and slid him into it.

"So, what are we celebrating?"

"Nope. Not celebrating. Drowning my sorrows. Nancy, dear sweet Nancy—the love of my life, ya know?" Harley turned around to look at Darwin and almost slipped off the chair again.

"Whoa there, fella. What's up with Nancy? Women troubles?"

"Aren't they all just trouble? She wants to get hitched at Christmas and I want to wait. Don't make sense to get hitched at Christmas. But no, I'm wrong. Says I don't love her. And now she's called the whole thing off." Harley focused on Darwin's face. "She's called it off."

"That's rough. I'm sure she'll come round. What's wrong with a December wedding?"

"Storms. Gonna jinx it. Gotta get married in June." Harley nodded wisely and tapped his forehead. "Married in the month of roses June, Life will be one long honeymoon," he recited in a singsong way.

"I haven't heard that one."

"What's her big hurry anyway? Say, where's my beer?" Harley puts both hands on the table and struggled to rise. Darwin pushed him back down.

"Let me go and check. I'll be right back." Darwin patted Harley on the back and headed over to the bar.

"Great crowd," he said, shouting to Edith to be heard above the music.

She smiled and nodded. "They're lined up out the door tonight. Same as last night. What's up with Harley?"

"Women troubles." Darwin looked back and saw that Harley's head was in his arms and he was fast asleep. "I could use some of that," he said, yawning.

Edith looked at him with concern. "You're heading out tonight? It looks like a storm may be blowing in."

"No way around it. We built up the business so much while we were closed, and now we have a raft of customers to keep happy. Can you spare Lucky or one of the cousins tomorrow to come with me on deliveries?"

"Of course. Whatever you need."

"I'll probably just leave it on the boat overnight, rather than put it in the cellar and then haul it out again in the morning."

"You should get some help, Darwin."

Darwin yawned again. "I know. I know. But right now the help I need is to get some coffee."

The conversation was interrupted when a couple of new customers came up to the bar. The Black Jack's Rootshines were a popular choice this evening.

"Do you need me to bring up more root beer or moonshine?" Darwin asked.

Edith waved him off, then started mixing the drinks.

Darwin headed down the hall to the kitchen.

Coffee cup in hand, he stood leaning against the wall of the barroom watching Edith work. There was a feverishness to her that he didn't like.

She's trying to fill that hole Leroy left with hard work, but she's going to drive us all into the ground. I can barely keep up this pace, let alone a wee slip like her.

A man bumped into him, spilling a bit of his coffee.

"Sorry, pal," the man said.

"No harm done. Missed me and hit the floor."

"Can I get you another cup?"

"It's okay."

The two stand and watch the room.

"Great band, eh? Love that high-lonesome sound."

Darwin nodded, still watching Edith. The strangers eyes followed to where he was looking.

"She's something. I heard that she's got brains as well as looks."

"Really?"

"Yup. Friend of mine runs a speakeasy down near Homestead and she supplies all his booze. Said she drives a hard bargain but would never cheat ya. And once, he had trouble paying the bill, on account of some family troubles up north, and she actually loaned him the cash to go home. Amazing, eh?"

"She is indeed."

"Well, I gotta see a man about a horse."

"Down the hall on the right."

"Thanks, pal."

Edith never told me about that. She's got a soft spot for family, all right. This is going to be one long year, waiting for Leroy to come home. I hope she makes it through.

* * * *

Edith finally kicked the last customer out around three—every customer but one. With Darwin already having left for Rum Row, Lucky and Bo helped her to close up. Harley had been left sleeping at the table, a blanket around his shoulders. Bo said that he'd let him out when he woke up—the cousins would be up; there was going to be another all-night mah-jong game in the kitchen.

On her way to bed, Edith put her head in the kitchen to say good night to her three cooks and wish them good fortune at their game, then stopped at Leroy's door to say goodnight and check on him.

Her hand gripped the doorknob. *I forgot. Just for that moment it was like he was asleep behind the door.*

She rested her other hand on the closed wooden door. *Good night, Leroy. Sweet dreams.*

CHAPTER 63

Clouds gathered in the dark sky. "We should be done with that, this time of year. December's no time for rain," Cassie said, glancing at the sky as she sat down at her table under the chickee.

It had taken a few weeks, but the sharp pain from when Leroy was cut out of her life was now only a dull ache. She pulled the Wheel of Fortune from the cards fanned out in front of her. Animals, ancient Egyptian gods, and the other figures were arrayed around the wheel. Cassie nodded, pleased.

"It's been an eventful nine months since the fire, Edith," she said to the empty chair in front of her. "It's been a period of change, and you've had to adapt. We both have. The wheel is good luck. Some folks call it karma: 'what goes around comes around'. And it's not over yet, *ah-ma-chamee*. The Wheel of Fortune reminds you that the wheel is always turning and life is in a state of constant change."

Cassie sighed, dropping her chin into her hands, elbows on the table.

I hate change. It wasn't so bad before. From time to time, Leroy would at least visit when he was with Edith. I don't see him so much anymore. Too busy with new friends and baseball, I guess. No time for me in a run-down camp buried in the Everglades. I guess I should have known this would happen, if not now, then at some point. Leroy's future is with town folks, not with me.

She looked over the campsite and the silent emptiness made her heart ache.

"Ah well. That darn wheel is always rolling." She looked at the card again, picking it up and shaking it at the empty chair. "What goes around comes around. Be a kind and loving person to others, and they'll be kind and loving to you. Be nasty and mean, and you would get nasty and mean turning back your way. Hear that, Brother Silas? Maybe this card's for you, too."

Despite everything, it don't look like the Preacher-Man has figured out who Leroy is—which is a blessing. Edith and the Carmichael woman are the ones to keep him safe now, although I'm not sure they're up for the job. But what can I do? I don't want to draw any attention to the boy.

Cassie cleared her throat trying to spit out the heartache as she swept up the cards and began to shuffle. "While things are looking better than they were, *ah-ma-chamee*, I hate to tell you that there will be a shock to the system coming. And one of the challenging aspects of the Wheel of Fortune is that no matter which way the Wheel turns, it's impossible to try to change it. You need to accept what is going to happen and adapt. Go with the flow, Edith. And I know how good you are at that. Ha—not. Always trying to have your own way, instead."

Cassie pushed back her chair and stared out over her camp.

Less than a year and then things will get back to normal. I can wait that long. Leroy won't forget about me, surely.

The tent with two cots, one empty and waiting for Leroy, the campfire with the pot of coffee she made on her own this morning, the chickee she's sitting in with one empty chair.

Maybe I'll go visit with Edith more. She's lonely for Leroy, too. We can wait together.

She gave a little shake to focus herself. A deep cleansing breath and Cassie was ready to continue, addressing the empty chair across from her. "The Wheel of Fortune shows a critical turning point, Edith. You should see this as an invitation to turn things around and take an entirely new direction in your life."

I wish this was my reading. A new direction does sound inviting. Ten months of being alone, waiting for Leroy's birthday. A significant and positive change coming for Edith. Always Edith with the good fortune.

Cassie rolled her shoulders and picked up her cards.

435

I don't know what's wrong with me today. My mind keeps wandering, pulling me off track. I'm going to bed, and I'll finish this reading in the morning.

"You get off lucky tonight, Mr. Preacher-Man."

Thunder rolled as she pulled back the woolen blanket.

Heaven's got an attitude tonight. Probably as ticked off as I am about Silas. You shed your skin like the snake you are. No preacher. No man of God. Just a brutal gangster. Should have figured that out myself.

She slipped between the covers, shaping the pillow to fit her head.

The Preacher-Man's got Leroy so scared and wrapped up into thinking he's protecting me and keeping the camp hidden. That's not a boy's job. He should be playing, having fun, and enjoying himself. Taking on Silas is a job for adults, not little boys.

Unable to find a comfortable spot, Cassie tossed and turned, her muttering drowned out by the approaching storm "I can't let you get too close to him. Maybe it's time to get into the picture myself somehow. And not just for the readings."

Outside her tent, the wind picked up and rattled the branches in the trees overhead. "That Wheel is turning for you Silas and, if there's any justice, you're going to get crushed by it. Leroy's safe enough for now and that gives us time. Edith has plans for you, and I need to be there when you finally meet your maker. And for sure it ain't God that will be waiting to greet you, Mr. Preacher-Man."

A flash of lightning split the air. Outside, it was as bright as day and then plunged back into darkness. Cassie was snug in her tent, the chorus of frogs and insects, and the night bird calls a lullaby. She cackled in amusement: the image of Silas meeting his maker, the flames of Hell around him.

* * * *

The storm rumbled and moved away, leaving a full moon shining brightly, painting everything with a silvery glow. Coconut Grove was sleeping; the townsfolk snuggled into their beds. Edith was dreaming in her special room, the French doors open to the sounds of the sea.

In the bar, Harley's slurred words were only in his dreams as he was folded in a chair, head on a table, blanket draped over him.

Back from Rum Row, a bone-weary Darwin was being rocked on the *Rex*, gentle waves lapping the sides of the boat.

In Coconut Grove, Leroy lay on his cot in the screened-in porch on the second floor above the kitchen, restless and fidgety. He was anxious to get going. Downstairs, Mr. Carmichael had fallen asleep in his chair in the living room. To Leroy, the man's snores were a faint copy of the earlier storm's thunder.

Thoughts of Brother Silas and his threats against the two real mothers in his life wind around Leroy tightly, leaving him tangled in the sheets.

Be wise enough to stand together when the time comes. The words had been a bell tolling in Leroy's mind since church.

It's time. He sat up, his legs dangling over the side of the cot.

He stripped the pillowcase and reached underneath the cot to grab some clothes, his baseball mitt, and the Tom Sawyer book. He tied his shoes and a used pair of baseball cleats the Carmichaels had given him and hung them around his neck. He crept into the bedroom Jay shared with his brother; checking to make sure they were both still sound asleep.

At the desk, Leroy wrote a note to Jay.

'Town life ain't for me, Tom. I'm off to find myself a raft and more adventure. Thank your ma for me. Don't come looking. Your pal, Huck"

He folded it and tucked it in Jay's shoe, careful not to make a sound.

A soft breeze rattled the palm fronds and whispered through the leaves on the banyan tree just outside a second-floor window. The rusty swing, tied to the large, low branch, squeaked as it rocked back and forth in the light wind.

Next to the banyan tree, the window slid up. A bit of light curtain fluttered outside before a hand reached out and dragged it back inside. One skinny leg emerged, then dangled. A bare foot stretched to find a tree branch. A cloth bag dropped to the ground. The body, halfway out the window, froze at the soft sound as it landed.

Carefully, quietly, the boy descended, swinging from the branch until his bare feet hit the dirt. Bag in hand, he began to jog along the road, following the moon.

Leroy was going home.

The End

But wait...Don't go!

Are you interested in what happens to Edith and the crew next?

Turn the page for a sneak peek at Book 3- *Eye of the Storm*

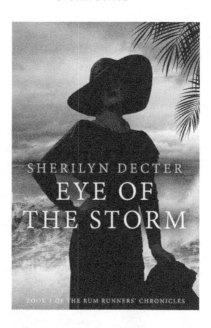

Her illicit empire was growing. But it isn't the police this rum mistress fears most...

Florida Coast, 1933- Edith Duffy was determined to fortify her business to protect those she loves. And a liquor partnership with powerful women was exactly what she needs for trade domination. But she couldn't had prepared for the white-hot rage still boiling in the local preacher's heart.

With Prohibition's days numbered, Edith was desperate to secure above-board revenue for the family she's built. But one misstep could see her religion-wielding adversary's animosity turn deadly.

Would Edith survive a bitter man's seething hatred and reinvent herself on the right side of the law?

Eye of the Storm was the thrilling conclusion to The Rum Runners' Chronicles, a fast-paced historical women's fiction trilogy. If you like female empowerment, heartrending conflict, and vivid Depression-era settings, then you'll love Sherilyn Decter's grand-slam finale.

... and if you'd love to get an exclusive copy of when Edith met Mickey, sign up to be part of the Bootleggers' Readers Group newsletter by sending me an email at sherilyn@sherilyndecter.com and you can start reading today!

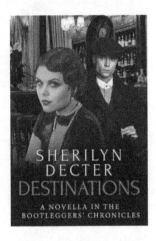

And please take time to read the Author's Note for *Storm Surge*, which was on the next page....

AUTHOR'S NOTE FOR STORM SURGE

I hope you enjoyed the second book in the Rum Runners' Chronicles. Writing the middle book of a trilogy is a challenge- the first book is all about introductions, and the third book is the grand finale. But what should happen in the middle book.

At the heart of Edith's story is her relationship with Leroy. In *Storm Surge*, I built on that, adding in some conflict and a few new villains. And of course, her arch nemesis, Brother Silas, really starts to lose it.

Writing historical fiction, especially when you're as enamoured by real history as I am, is a challenge. Historians are vital for those who want to understand our present and get a sense of what the future may hold. They sift through the detritus of people's lives, pulling out facts and patterns and then reweaving them into a whole to provide us mere mortals with a path forward.

As appealing as that is, I am not an historian. I am a story teller. I take those same facts and attempt to reshape them into something that I hope you will find entertaining. My fictional characters get to live with factual characters.

These books are works of fiction and should never be considered anything but. While I've tried to stay true to the grand arch of history, occasionally I've moved an event that happened in one month into another so that it has a better flow through the story.

The Rum Runners' Chronicles series is based in Coconut Grove in 1932. It is set during the time of Prohibition, an era that reshaped America. Many of the characters found between the pages of the Rum Runners' Chronicles were actual people, walking the streets and living their lives in Miami during this time. I have been inspired by their individual stories, but have reshaped them to fit the plot of my books. Sometimes things happened in real life in a similar fashion to what I have laid out, and sometimes it is a complete fabrication.

If you get the chance, dig deeper into the information about Gertrude "Cleo" Lythgoe and Spanish Marie Waite. These two people were central to the Prohibition legacy and lived and breathed legendary lives. I have blog posts that go into a bit more detail about their lives and legacies on my website https://sherilydecter.com, however they only scratch the surface.

I have taken liberties with the character of Mae Capone. Al Capone: Stories My Grandmother Told Me, a biography of a wonderfully complex woman and written by her granddaughter Diane Patricia Capone, helped shape her character. I have, however, taken liberties with the age of her son, Sonny. In real life, Sonny would have been 14 during this period.

Cassie and the tarot deck are central to Edith's story. The references to Cassie's deck are based on the Rider Waite deck, originally published in 1910. They remain a popular deck, especially for amateurs like myself because of their symbolic images and archetypal images.

The Florida coastline and the community of Coconut Grove of the 1920s are based on extensive research.

The Children's Home Society of Florida is still in existence, with a national reputation for the role they play in helping children realize their full potential. In 1910 – Marcus "Daddy" Fagg joined and worked tirelessly to share the Home's mission and garner support. Not only did he lead CHS' efforts in philanthropy, but he also put the organization at the forefront in helping to create, pass and reform child labor and welfare laws still in effect today.

Another organization mentioned throughout the series, but playing a central role in *Storm Surge* is the Homemakers' Guild. In 1891, five years before Miami became a city, Flora McFarlane and the women of Coconut Grove formed the Housekeeper's Club, now called the Woman's Club of Coconut Grove.

As a woman homesteader and teacher, Flora McFarlane was keenly aware of the isolation and loneliness of the pioneer women. She invited women in the community to take part in weekly gatherings. Her goal was "to bring together the housekeepers of our little settlement by spending two hours a week in companionship and study." By working together their pioneering spirit built a community. Their motto was "lend a hand."

It seemed a natural outlet for Mavis Saunders and other women in my fictional Coconut Grove to showcase their leadership talents.

Now, 130 years later, the spirit of the early pioneer women remain. The Woman's Club of Coconut Grove is a place where women come together, build relationships, and create community through their civic service activities

Finally, on a personal note—

There is the romantic image of a writer, toiling alone in a garret, suffering for her muse. Of course, nothing could be further from the truth. I write all my books with a couple of bad dogs curled up at my feet in the comfort of my home in Canada.

I have a great team of people working with me to make the Rum Runners' Chronicles the best books they can be. They include my developmental editor Joe Walters from Independent Book Review, as well as my primary editor Marie Beswick-Arthur and her trusty partner in crime, Richard. I've also been lucky enough to work with a great cover designer, Jane Dixon-Smith. She reached into my imagination to bring the idea of a beautiful gangster widow at the crossroads of her life in tropical 1920s Florida to life.

I also had a great team of beta readers for Storm Surge: Jessica Decter, Kim Mitchell, Jeanne Millis, Lori Cumming, Linda Forward, Johann Laesecke, Denise Birt, Sam Millis, Betty Brit Strange, and Boni Wagner-Stafford. They were the first 'readers' to dig into this second installment of Edith's story and were invaluable at letting me know what parts of the story were working and what parts needed polishing.

Finally, where would I be without my husband Derry. He listened to the subtle difference of phrasing many, many times, provided his medical expertise for several key scenes, and kept me going when I was ready to give up.

I hope you enjoyed Gathering Storm. And there are two more books in the Edith Duffy story, as well as an exclusive novella that tells the tale of when Edith met Mickey.

If you're interested in learning more, please visit my website https://sherilyndecter.com to connect with me on social media, sign up for my newsletter, or check out what's coming next.

Thank you, one and all.

Sherilyn Decter

April, 2020

Made in United States
Orlando, FL
04 March 2024